T0005656

SECTION 8

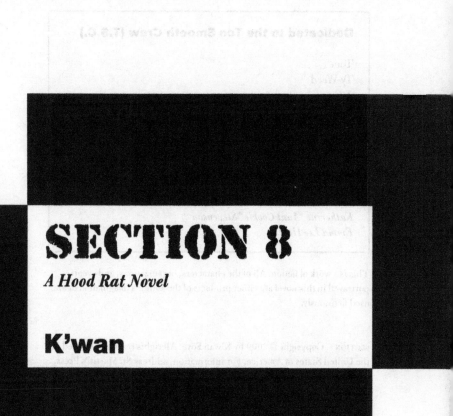

SECTION 8

A Hood Rat Novel

K'wan

St. Martin's Griffin
New York

Dedicated to the Too Smooth Crew (T.S.C.)

Tone
Ty-Weed
A.C.
E.Z.
Mikey
I'm still on it!

RIP
Frankie "Crumb Louie" Foye
Katherine "Aunt Cookie" Stevenson
Emma Lee Holder

This is a work of fiction. All of the characters, organizations, and events portrayed in this novel are either products of the author's imagination or are used fictitiously.

SECTION 8. Copyright © 2009 by K'wan Foye. All rights reserved. Printed in the United States of America. For information, address St. Martin's Press, 175 Fifth Avenue, New York, N.Y. 10010.

www.stmartins.com

Library of Congress Cataloging-in-Publication Data

K'wan.
   Section 8 : a hood rat novel / K'wan. — 1st ed.
       p. cm.
   ISBN 978-0-312-53696-1
   1. African Americans—Fiction.   2. African American neighborhoods—
Fiction.   3. Brooklyn (New York, N.Y.)—Fiction.   4. Street life—Fiction.
I. Title.   II. Title: Section eight.
   PS3606.O96S43 2009
   813'.6—dc22

                                                            2009012530

D 21

K'WAN KEEPS THE STREET FICTION GAME ON LOCKDOWN

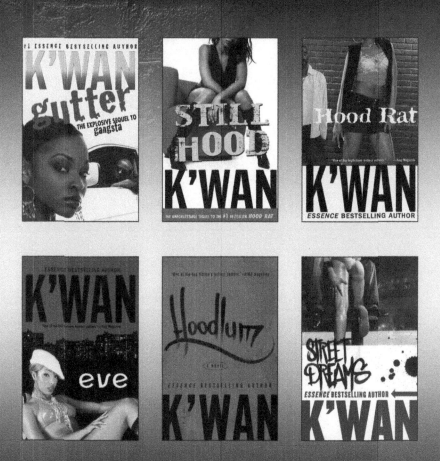

Visit the-blackbox.com and sign up to receive GANGSTA WALK, a never-before-released free short story from K'wan

 St. Martin's Griffin

ACKNOWLEDGMENTS

You would think that with as many years as I've been doing this and for as many books deep as I am that I would've run out of people to thank by now, right? Wrong. One of the most beautiful things about this profession that has chosen me is that I meet new and interesting people just about every day. Most come wearing smiles but have larceny in their hearts, but there are the few who are genuine and for this I thank you for adding on to my life and making it richer by the day.

I first have to acknowledge my wife and children because more than anyone they sacrificed while I was writing this book. It's a hard thing to live in a house with someone who is there in body but their mind is a million miles away, which is always the case with me. To truly create a great character you have to become that character. Thanks, guys, for giving of your time while I knocked out one of the greatest stories ever told.

My mother, who is my constant guardian and strength. There is not a day that goes by when I don't think of you and that my heart does not weep over the fact that you were not here to see in the flesh what you made possible. You birthed me, you raised me, and you empowered me. They praise me for being one of the greatest writers of our time, but I can't take credit for something that isn't mine. This was your gift, and in passing you gave me something that maybe you felt like you hadn't had in life, a way out. No matter what they say or write about who they think I am only you know who I really am . . . your son.

To my grandmother Ethel and my aunt Quintella. I love the both of you more than I can express for making sure that I didn't end up one of the kids that the world forgot about. You may not agree with some of my methods, but I assure you that they are necessary evils. I know that God has and always will take care of me, but sometimes the lamb has to become the wolf to make sure we don't lose the entire flock.

Special shout to Monique Patterson, who I constantly give gray hairs by twisting her publication schedule. I have no sense of time and more often than not I'm rushing to get things done, but one thing I want you to always remember is that I would never leave you hanging. I might jam you timewise, but I'd never stiff you on a project that I agreed to turn in. That's not how I'm built.

Can't forget my agent, Marc Gerald, from the Agency Group. From making sure that my business was finally handled correctly, to helping me birth something I've wanted to do for years, to flying in for my surprise birthday party, you've gone above and beyond. Had I met you a few years ago things may have gone differently for my career, but I don't believe in regrets. It is what it is and will be what it will be. And what it will be is huge!

And I didn't forget you Sarah Stephens, aka Agent Stephens. You've quietly been the driving force and buffer for a lot of the stuff that's gone on. Thank you for helping to make the transition as painless as possible.

Thank you to all my peers in this industry who have always encouraged me to go harder and reach for the stars. It takes a lot to praise your competition in private and public. I ride for you like you ride for me. Let's get it!

A very, very special thanks goes to these jealous mofos who keep throwing jabs. No matter what you say you'll never get me to feed into the bullshit. I would never do yo the honor of speaking your names, at least not on paper. God has given me a blessing and thus I will always remain humble. Instead of trying to bring me out of my character you need to sit with me and try to figure out why you can't seem to get it right. If that doesn't work I'm having a special on mouth-shots. You can get two for the price of one!

And my readers, new and old. I would need about a hundred more pages to thank you for all that you have done in helping to create the monster that my career is becoming! There are some of you who bought *Gangsta* before Barnes and Noble would even think of having us on their shelves and you still support me now. Without you none of this would be possible and without you I would not have found the courage within myself to keep sharing pieces of me with the world. There is no amount of thanks that I could offer you that would equal the love you have shown.

Now on with the show . . .

PROLOGUE

The rising sun had just crawled over the grassy hills and was shining through the four-foot-high picture window on the east wall of the master bedroom. The yellow-orange rays kissed Tionna softly on her cheek, making her flawless dark skin shine like polished onyx. She tried to ignore it, but the rays continued to needle her eyelids. When she tried to roll over, strands of her midback-length black hair got tangled in her bracelets, making her wonder again why she didn't just go ahead and cut it.

"Too early," she grumbled, trying to duck farther under the thick comforter. It helped only until the identical window on the northeast wall got in on the act. She had loved the storybooklike windows when she'd picked out the nearly quarter-million-dollar house on the outskirts of Westchester, but now she wasn't so sure. Maybe she'd have Duhan trick off on some shutters.

Just thinking of her baby daddy/fiancé made her cat jump.

Duhan was short and thick, but hung like a plow horse, and he knew just how to touch her secret places with his tool. The night before, he'd had her speaking in tongues as they experimented with a position they'd seen in a porno. Grinning wickedly, she began fumbling behind her for the precious meat that he always rested against her back when they slept. There was nothing more exciting to her than that "he ain't peed yet" wood.

To her surprise, his side of the bed was cold and empty. It wasn't like Duhan to be up this early when he wasn't on the block, but it had been a while since he had to play the role of corner boy. He was probably downstairs making her breakfast to thank her for the steamy night. She had been in rare form, if she did say so herself. Tionna snuggled into the thick folds of her comforter and decided to rest her eyes until breakfast was ready. The moment of peace was short-lived when she heard a banging on the front door.

"Who the fuck . . ." The words died in her throat as the realization set in. *Police!* Very few people knew where Duhan and Tionna had moved, and even the few that did know wouldn't be banging on the door at the crack of dawn. Though they didn't have any drugs in the house, there were several guns, and those would be enough to violate Duhan's probation and send him back to the joint.

Tionna tried to hop from the bed and do what they'd practiced for months on end, her part as the hustler's wife, but her legs were tangled in the sheets. "Mommy," she heard her older son, Little Duhan, calling. She ignored him and kept trying to free herself from the blanket. "Mommy," he continued. The more Tionna struggled, the more entangled her legs seemed to become.

"Mommy, somebody is at the door!" Little Duhan was now shaking her.

Using all her strength, Tionna broke free of the blanket and rolled onto the floor. When she hit the rug, she didn't smell the Carpet Fresh that she vacuumed it with every morning, but stale cigarette smoke and faint traces of mildew. Little Duhan was standing against the faded and cracking yellow wall, his mouth twisted in disgust, while Duran hugged his knees to his chest on the love seat with a terrified expression on his face.

Looking from the dingy tan shade, which covered an even dingier window, to the tiny kitchen sink and the two roaches sharing a cake crumb, reality crashed back down on Tionna. The plush home she'd grown to love so much was gone, snatched like everything else the dirty money had bought, and now there was only the efficiency she shared with her two children in the battered-women's facility.

The insistent banging on her front door kept Tionna from breaking into a fit of tears. She managed to pick herself up and find her bathrobe, which was hiding in one of several piles of clothes that were strewn throughout the small space. It was a gold kimono crafted of genuine silk, with beautiful dragons embroidered about the back and sleeves. The robe looked out of place in the shabby room, but then again, so did Tionna.

"I'm coming!" Tionna shouted, tripping over a loose sneaker on her way to the door. "What!" She snatched the door open, only to have the anger drain from her face when she saw who was on the other side.

She was five seven and weighed about one forty, but carried it mostly in her hips and ass. The black Nike sweat suit seemed to fit her perfectly, accenting her firm breasts and hugging her curvaceous hips just right. Her signature black Gucci frames slipped down slightly over her button nose, giving you a glimpse of her honey-colored eyes. Had it been anyone else, Tionna would've gone *up-top*, but Gucci was the exception to the rule. They had been friends since grade school and had stuck together through thick and thin. True friends were rare to come by, and Gucci was about as true as they got.

Without waiting for an invitation, Gucci stepped into the efficiency apartment. Though there was more than enough room, she still managed to bump Tionna when she crossed the threshold. Gucci was a project chick who moved with an air of nobility. No matter how you felt about her, you always knew when she entered a room. The look on her face said that she was less than pleased with the accommodations, but she'd never offend her friend by saying so, at least when she was sober. After kissing Little Duhan and Duran on their foreheads, she turned to her friend and asked, "So what's up, bitch, you ready to get up outta this shit hole or what?"

PART 1

WELCOME TO THE BLOCK

CHAPTER 1

The new school year was a week old, so the block was absent of the normal noises of children running around, causing all types of hell. This suited the four gentlemen sitting around their makeshift card table just fine. It had seemed like forever since they were able to enjoy a nice breeze in front of their building without the bullshit young people tended to bring with them. The four old heads were referred to as "the Senate" by the locals because of their constant presence and meddling on the block. More often than not they enjoyed drama-free afternoons, unless of course they were at the center of the foolishness.

"Man, you gonna play or what?" Harley asked in a gruff voice. His ever-present Newport 100 was pinched between his thick lips, bobbing when he spoke. Harley had been a career criminal before old age and lead poisoning had slowed him down. Getting shot repeatedly can do that to you.

"Quiet, fool; don't be in such a rush to get this ass whipping!" Rayfield replied, still examining his cards. The fisherman's cap he always wore was tilted back slightly, showing the top of his balding head. He had been among the first to move into the block back when white folks had started abandoning Harlem. Rayfield wasn't a wealthy man, but his eyes had seen some truly amazing things. From the rise of fall of the last street kings to Harlem's resurrection, Rayfield had been there.

"Man, it ain't rocket science; hearts led, so play a damn heart." This was Cords, the so-called lover of their crew. Though Cords was getting on in age, he still carried himself like a gentleman. That morning he sported a white polo shirt and a houndstooth sports coat. As always, his thinning, processed hair was laid to the side. He'd worn it like that for nearly half a century. Back in the days, Cords had been the bass player for a teen band, but his star had since dwindled. It had been more than forty years since his group had cut their first album, but let him tell it, he could give Chris Brown a run for his money.

"What I tell y'all 'bout that cross-board shit?" Sonny said in his deep southern drawl. He shifted on his crate so that his back was to the street when he poured a snort of Five O'clock vodka into his Pepsi bottle. Dressed in overalls and dirty work boots, with a stained bandanna tied around his neck, Sonny's appearance screamed *country nigga*, but he wore it proudly. Sonny had once been a sporting man who frequented the gambling holes and juke joints of Georgia, trimming suckers of their money and their women. Life was good until he slept with the wrong man's wife and ended up getting his throat cut. Now Sonny was just an old man, humbled by the weight of knowing that he was going to die with nothing.

So it would go with most, if not all, of the men at the card table. They were men of a bygone era with nothing to hold on to except the broken promises the streets had made, only to throw them to the dogs when their numbers came. The game was different and there was no room for old men, or rules. Though the Senate may not have had much, a cold beer and the good company of one another made the days easier to deal with.

"Somebody play a damn card this century!" Harley demanded, dropping ash on the table.

"See, that's the problem with you country niggaz," Rayfield began, slapping a queen of hearts on the table, which to everyone's surprise ended up being *boss* in the suit. "You be too busy running ya damn mouths to focus on the game." He snatched up the four cards and slammed a king of spades on the table and looked to his left, where Harley was sitting. "Jump if you got it, chump!"

"Watch out now, me and mine came to play!" Cords danced in his seat.

"Fuck you, Cords, wit'ya washed-up ass." Harley threw down the only spade he had left, which happened to be a nine.

"I'd rather be washed up than set," Cords shot back, dropping his five of spades onto the pile.

"Say, who the hell that is?" Sonny asked, his eyes fixed on a forest-green Ford Explorer that had just pulled up next to where they were sitting.

"I don't know the two chicks in the front, but them muthafuckas they toting in the back surely had *trouble* stamped on their birth certificates," Rayfield said, fingering the switchblade that sat on his lap under the table.

Everybody in the neighborhood knew Rock Head and they all felt pretty much the same way: that his mother should've let the state have him years ago. Every hood had a kid that couldn't manage to keep himself out of trouble, but Rock was the personification of that. Rock was a snake to his heart, and the moment you turned your back on him he was bound to drive a knife into it. From robbery to drugs to extortion, Rock was with all that . . . at least when he could manage to stay out of jail. Rock believed that if you were weaker than he was, then he could take what you had, but this didn't hold true for the second young man to slide from the truck.

Though he had grown some and now wore his hair in long box braids, Tech still had the face of a teenaged boy. At one point Tech had been one of the wildest young wolves in Harlem, a kid that would put in work just to say that he had. From his first lick he had attacked the streets with vigor, which stacked the odds against him that he'd make it to see eighteen. He was lawless and ready to die senselessly in search of a name, but a tragedy several years prior had caused a change in him.

Jah had been not only Tech's best friend and mentor but one of the greatest tragedies to touch Harlem in a long time. The wily gunslinger had built a name for himself in the streets and was whispered about like the boogeyman because of his antics. It had been like a great sigh of relief when he'd found someone other than the streets to give his heart to, but his newfound happiness had been short-lived. Jah had been murdered over a beef that had nothing to do with him, all because he couldn't let go of a debt. To mourn him he'd left a shell of a girlfriend and the battle-hardened soldier that Tech had grown into. When his friend had died, so had the innocent little boy that Tech had been. All that remained now was the monster his hardships had created.

Rock Head had been trying to get in with Tech for a while and it looked like he was finally staring to make progress.

"I'm telling you, son, these big-head niggaz is getting it down there, but they ain't got a shooter amongst them," Rock was telling Tech, who was busy watching the block. A habit that came from seeing one too many cats get laid out for not paying attention, a good amount of them having been laid down by him and Jah.

"And where'd you say these niggaz was from again?" Tech asked, jiggling his keys in the pocket of his loose gray sweatpants.

"Amsterdam projects, my G. On some real shit, them niggaz be trying to make movies, but they ain't built like that. Duke lucked up and got a mean play on some work and some guns from a nigga that's about to go up and needs some quick bread. There could be anywhere from one to three keys, including the paper if you move during the drop."

"That's quite a piece of change," Tech did the math in his head, "but I gotta ask you something, Rock. Me and you ain't ever done big business together, so why throw me the lookout?"

"I'm trying to bring something to the table, my dude; you know I been trying to hook up wit'y'all for a skinnet," Rock Head told him.

The look Tech gave him clearly said he wasn't buying the story. "So you just gonna let us move on this deal on some goodwill shit?"

"I'm saying I wanna eat, too, but I'm too connected to the situation to avoid the headache that's gonna come from it. My angle is the fact that it's gonna be turf and work to go around once y'all clean house, and I'm trying to get in on the ground floor. You know how it goes, Tech."

"Yeah, I know how it goes, and that's just why I smell more to the story. How you know so much about this kid's business?" Tech asked, still not sure how to feel about Rock Head. He had heard some stories about the kid being a greaseball, but Tech gave everybody enough rope to hang themselves, so that way there was no doubt in his mind when he came to feed you your head.

Rock Head paused for a minute, trying to decide whether to lie or just be straight up with Tech. "Look," he lowered his tone, "the main nigga got a kid wit' my little sister, so I know his MO."

"That's some cold shit, Rock. You ain't gonna feel no way if we put the lean on your little sister's baby daddy?"

"Man, fuck that shit. It ain't like me and Duke got history. The only thing we got in common is my crying ass nephew that he don't do enough for anyhow. My sister is just too fucking stupid to take the nigga to court. We can pluck this nigga's stash and call it back child support!" Rock Head laughed, but Tech didn't.

Tech stood there for a minute, staring at the spade's game that had come to a halt on the curb. "A'ight." Tech turned back to Rock Head. "I'll have some of my peoples look into it. If everything pans out, then maybe we work something out. I'll get with you." Tech turned to leave, but Rock Head grabbed his arm. It wasn't an aggressive gesture, but Tech still stared at his hand as if it were a tumor he'd just noticed.

"Yo, Tech, I think we should move on them niggaz sooner than later," Rock Head urged him.

Tech's facial expression didn't change, but there was something dangerous dancing behind his eyes. He glanced over at the truck and saw that Silk was now standing outside it, smoking a Newport. Her alert brown eyes bored into Rock Head's, but Tech recognized the question behind them. Life or death? Tech turned back to Rock Head and spoke. "I said I'll have my people look into it and get back."

Realizing his mistake, Rock Head quickly removed his hand. "Right, right. Well, you know where to find me when you're ready, T."

"Indeed I do," Tech said before stepping off the curb and back to the truck.

"Fuck is up wit' that greasy-ass nigga?" Silk asked when they were back in the whip and off 140th Street. She wore her Yankee fitted cap broken ace-deuce, with her dreads spilling freely from beneath it. The ends were so fine that no matter how much beeswax she treated them with, they kept curling up on her. Silk was a gorgeous young mix of Jamaican and Puerto Rican, giving her skin a color that resembled rich milk chocolate. Her bowed lips were slightly pouted, exposing the gold across her bottom row of teeth. For as hard as Silk tried to be, there was only so much you could do to hide natural beauty.

"You know that muthafucka, always about a dollar," Tech said, pulling a Dutch from his pocket and splitting it down the middle with his pinky nail. "Got some niggaz that need to be relieved of their burdens and possibly relocated."

"What we talking, chump change or a score?" Silk asked. Tech could tell by the look in her eyes that the girl's wheels were already turning.

Tech leaned over and dumped the blunt guts out the window. "All depends on who you ask. Ol' boy says they'll be a few keys and maybe some cake, but I can't say for sure. The mark is from Amsterdam projects, and I only know of a few cats coming outta there that even played remotely heavy. It should be a good lick either way, but I only give it a fifty-fifty shot at being a great one."

Silk turned around to face the backseat. "We could rush them niggaz and end up only getting a few dollars, if anything. I don't know, Tech, running up on these fuck-boys sounds like greed more than anything else. Sounds like a waste of time to me."

"Then you're still stuck on chapter one of the hustler's handbook." Tech flicked the brim of her hat playfully. "Too much is never enough, lil' sis. You bleed a muthafucka till don't nothing else come out, then you move on to the next vic. Besides, this is about monopoly, not so much the cash."

"Whatever, yo." Silk turned back around in her seat.

"Yeah, I wouldn't mind a few extra dollars, but is this cat's word worth anything?" This was China White, the minority of the group. With bleached blond hair and ocean-blue eyes, China looked every bit of a Nordic princess. Though she was just shy of twenty, she carried herself as if she'd been here far longer. China could best be described as a curvaceous white girl with a brilliant mind and the swag of a hood chick.

Tech pondered it for a minute. "Nah, the boy is scandalous, but I don't think he'd be stupid enough to walk us into a setup. He lay one of us and the Animal is gonna come for his ass, everybody know that."

"I'm sure Caesar said the same thing about Brutus," China grumbled.

"Girl, quit being so damn paranoid, you always think a muthafucka is out to get you," Silk teased.

"Yeah, and it's my damn paranoid thinking that's kept us alive when we were living on the streets," China reminded her, stirring up old memories.

Physically, China White and Silk were polar opposites, but they shared similar passions, and hard-luck stories. Silk's mother was an old-school dope fiend whose only break from the high in a ten-year span was when she was pregnant with her only child and so-called worst mistake. Silk had always been the bane of her mother's existence, proverbial ball to her chain, even, and she made no attempt to hide this. It was never clear why her mother hated her, but Silk was always made to feel like the outsider in her house, and the fact that she was different didn't help.

When dope gets hold of you, the grip is never a gentle one, and Silk's mother was a testament to that. Sometimes she would get so high that young Silk would have to scour different dope to locate her. Silk became her mother's unofficial guardian and a permanent fixture in all the shooting galleries. It got to a point where the blow had Silk's mother so gone that she would even include her baby girl in her *get-high* schemes. Silk was pickpocketing and jacking since she was old enough to understand the hustle, all under her mother's tutelage. To the little girl it didn't seem wrong when her mother asked her to do something, because she was her mother. So, when she asked her to make love to a white woman for money, the girl complied.

Silk had always known she was different, but she had never actually had sex with a woman. She had an idea of what it would be like, but what her first time held was breathtaking. The woman was older and more experienced with the art. She brought life to places in Silk's body that she would look up on the Internet after the experience. Silk never told her mother, but she continued to see the woman for a while after.

The life of hustling and doping came to a crashing halt when Silk found her mother overdosed in her bedroom. It seemed that she had finally found that rainbow she had been chasing. With no family to take the fourteen-year-old in, she became a ward of the state, and that's where she met Sara Lucas, aka China White.

Back then, China was your typical Kelly Bundy—a bleach-blond chick with a nice body and not a whole lot of sense about the way things worked—or so Silk initially thought. She had grown up in small town just outside Rochester, New York, with her parents and three siblings on a small patch of land that had been in their family for a spell. Though the modest farm house didn't seem out of the ordinary, within the recesses of the property the Lucas family harbored a secret. China's father operated a crystal-meth lab that supplied almost 33 percent of the dealers in the Tri-State area. He took everything he'd learned working for twenty-something years in pharmaceuticals and got rich off it. Unfortunately, little China was right there to soak it all up. By the time she was thirteen she was able to competently cook or cut most street drugs.

When the feds finally rushed old man Lucas's barn, he was convicted before he even had a court date. He copped out to fifty years in exchange for his wife getting a reduced sentence. China's siblings were rounded up and placed in the system, but she managed to elude capture and make her way to New York City. Unfortunately, she was arrested for trying to lift a chain off Canal Street. Being naïve about bootleg jewelry, she thought she had a come up, but ended up with a case instead. She was placed in the New York City juvenile-care system. China knew that as soon as her name was run through their runaway system they'd know she was a fugitive from the drug raid. It was her first and last night in the facility.

From the moment China stepped into the cramped dorm, with its rows of cast-iron beds, there was a bull's-eye painted on her back. Being the only white girl there was no way she could blend in. Silk could've predicted how this was going to go down even if it hadn't unfolded before her. Ariel, who had been the resident gooch at the facility, rolled on China with three of her flunkies, demanding that the white girl hand over her earrings. Silk hated Ariel because she was a bully, but this wasn't her beef. She sat on her bunk and watched it play out.

Silk was a little too far from the action to hear clearly what was being said, but Ariel was waving her arms. She saw the white girl try to walk away, only to have her path blocked by one of Ariel's people. Silk expected China to make a break for it or scream for one of the counselors, who wouldn't have done anything anyhow, but to her and their surprise she lashed out and caught the girl with a solid right cross. They worked China's ass something awful, but she just kept coming. It wasn't until Ariel pulled a razor from her bra that Silk decided to intervene.

Ariel raised her arm to cut China, who was already down, but a left hook to the side of her head changed the plan. Wrapping her belt around her fist like a brass knuckle, Silk hit Ariel with a flurry of punches that backed her into a corner. She tried to bring the razor into play, but the strike was untrained and awkward. She waxed Ariel's ass while China kept the other girls occupied. Eventually the staff was able to break it up, but Silk and China knew that wouldn't be the end of it. Ariel's authority had been challenged and she wasn't going to let the ass whipping ride. Later that night, just after lights out, Silk and China fled the place and never looked back.

"Y'all are like an old married couple," Tech joked, fishing in his pocket for a light.

"Bullshit. If we was married, I wouldn't have to argue wit' this bitch about everything," Silk said, lighting the blunt for him.

China turned toward Silk, who grinned at her. "Look, you already know how I feel about that word, Silk; I ain't one of these little girls that you got eating your pussy for Boost phones. Either we're gonna respect each other, or I'm gonna pull this ride over and we're gonna scrap."

"My fault, Ma," Silk said, trying to stifle the laughter that was building up. She loved the way China's blue eyes turned to ice when she was in the heat of the moment.

Tech exhaled the smoke and handed the blunt to Silk. "Y'all can tear each other's eyes out later. We still got business to handle before the sun goes down. C, you do that thing for me?" He leaned forward so she could hear him.

"I put the word out that you wanted to sit down, but he never got back," China told him.

"I can't believe them pussy niggaz down there is trying to stunt, wit' they snitching asses," Silk said venomously. "You want me to go put something hot to one of these whores, big bro?"

He considered it. "Nah, baby girl, I don't think this shit is even gonna go that far. Sometimes a few words can be more effective than shells."

CHAPTER 2

"What up, fellas?" Rock Head greeted the Senate after Tech had gone.

"Ain't much, just catchin' a breeze," Sonny said, not bothering to look up from his cards.

"Let me hold something, moneybags." Harley patted Rock Head's pockets playfully.

"Shit, y'all the ones getting all the money." Rock Head nodded toward the card table. "What's in the pot?"

"And nothing but some change," Rayfield answered, staring Rock Head directly in the eyes. "Why, you trying to lose something?" Rayfield shuffled the cards in his hand.

"My pockets don't run as deep as y'all's." Rock Head was speaking to Rayfield, but his eyes were on the minivan pulling up next to the fire hydrant, in front of the church. When you lived your life shitting on people, you never knew where or when you'd get your turn at the bowl.

"Who that is?" Sonny glanced at the SUV.

"Looks like Veronica's van," Rayfield said.

"Shiiit, Veronica ain't looked like that in years!" Cords added, watching Gucci slide from the driver's side and move to let Little Duhan and Duran out of the back. The two boys took off running down the block, leaving Tionna and Gucci to unload the black garbage bags that were stuffed in the back of the van.

"Damn, T, what you got in here?" Gucci asked, struggling with a large plastic bag.

"A few years' worth of bullshit." Tionna offered a tug and the bag popped free of the rear. She had traded her kimono for a sweat suit, but kept the scarf tied around her head. "Thanks again for helping me out, Gucci, even if you did come by early as hell."

Gucci dropped the bag to the ground and snatched off her shades. "Tionna, you can't be serious? You know just as well as I do that you ain't got no sense of time. If I hadn't come by, you probably would've laid up until it was too late to get anything done. Nah, T, you've been up in that joint long enough, I couldn't stand it another day," she said, as if she'd been the one living in the shelter.

"Me neither. It's bad enough when you got bitches hating from a distance, but when you clump a bunch of us together, you know it's gonna be some shit. Yo, I felt like I had to sit a ho on her ass the first and third week of every month," Tionna said.

"What, you had ya fights scheduled or something?" Gucci slung a bag onto the curb.

"As if." Tionna rolled her eyes. "Them broads would steer clear of me between checks, but when that little liquor-and-weed money rolled in it was like Battery City."

"The price of being young and beautiful," Gucci said, sighing.

"Tell me about it. Gucci, you'd be surprised at the gall of some of these girls when under the influence. Shorty, if you're running around in knockoff Air Max and still buying loosies, what in the hell would make you think that I got designs on a nigga you're dealing with? Get a fucking grip. I'm a made bitch and made bitches don't do the help."

"Talk that shit, T, but you know how it goes when you're young and beautiful."

"And I live with the curse every day, thank the Lord," Tionna said with conviction. Her odd mix of Turkish and black set her in a class by herself when it came to physical beauty. She was tall, with skin that resembled unsweetened chocolate, and rich black hair that had never seen a perm. Tionna was thin like her father but had hips and ass like her mother, who was originally from Georgia. From the time Tionna had slipped into her first training bra, her mother had made it clear to her that she was a bad bitch and must always carry herself as such. That jewel was the only thing her mother had ever given her that Tionna actually held on to.

Gucci wrestled one of the bags over her shoulder. "I don't see how you did it, T. I would've killed somebody or went AWOL."

Tionna reflected on the experience. "It was like hell, Gucci. I mean, I was thankful to have a roof over my head and all, but I ain't used to them kinda conditions. One minute my boo had me living like a queen, and the next, I'm scraping together every bit of change I had to try and keep my black ass outta prison as an accessory and my kids outta the system."

"The price of fame," Gucci offered.

"Don't I know it," Tionna agreed, slinging a bag of clothes over her shoulder. She looked up at the building she thought she had finally escaped. "I can't believe I went through hell and back just to find myself moving back on Fortieth."

"Irony can be a muthafucka, T." Gucci shook her head. "You waited all that time to get your certificate, just to have them pull this shit."

When Duhan took his fall, things got real shaky for Tionna. She had managed to avoid becoming a part of his indictment, but still found herself in a bad way. Duhan had not only been her man, he'd been her provider. He was the one who brought it home and made sure the bills were paid. Now it was up to Tionna to get it while Duhan sat waiting for a date. There was no doubt about her willingness to *get it*, but the follow-through was something else altogether. Granted, she had finished high school, but the girl had no life skills to speak of.

Though it made her feel like less than the queen she knew she was, Tionna went and got on public assistance. Part of her lie that kept her from being charged was that Duhan beat her, so she was able to get into a battered-women's shelter and be placed on a priority list for Section 8. She was supposed to be next on the list when she got the word that the program was being shut down *again*. Tionna now had two choices: move into the projects and participate in the WEP program or take a one-bedroom in one of the newly renovated buildings on the same block she'd vowed never to return to.

"Buck up, baby girl. It's some sour shit, but it's better than being in the shelter with the rest of them bum bitches, no offense." Gucci started dragging the bag up the street.

"Let you tell it." Tionna fell in step behind her, hauling a garbage bag of her own. With any luck, she'd be able to slip in quietly and get settled before the gossip network passed the wire that she was back. This thought was dashed all to hell when she saw Rock Head grinning at them.

"Gucci, what it is, ma?" Rock Head greeted her, with his fake cool smirk.

Gucci dropped her bag and exhaled before answering. "What it is heavy. Do ya girl a solid and help me out." She motioned to the bag.

"Always willing to help a beautiful young lady." He hefted the bag and slung it over his shoulder. "Damn, what you got in here?"

"Stuff," she said, striding past him to the card game. "Hey, fellas."

"Lil Ronnie, what's happening?" Rayfield greeted her.

"Mr. Ray, don't play with me. My name is Gucci; I'm my own woman," she told him.

"Indeed you are." Cords looked her up and down. "Say, girl, when you gonna step out with an old sporting nigga, instead of hanging around with these young chumps?"

Gucci gave him a seductive smile. "Cords, I don't think your heart could handle what I got cooking between these thighs," she joked.

"Shiiit, I ain't ever met a pony that I couldn't ride."

"See, that's the problem right there. I ain't no pony, I'm a stallion!" She turned so he could see the profile of her ass.

"She got you there, old-timer!" Harley half coughed, half laughed.

"Man, to hell with you, Harley, wit' yo chain-smoking ass," Cords said.

"Better the smoker than the smoked," Harley shot back.

"Hey, Tionna," Sonny called to the girl who was lagging behind.

"Mr. Sonny." She nodded.

"You all come to visit with ya mama?"

"Not exactly. I'm moving into One Fifty-three," she said, trying to mask the shame in her voice.

"One Fifty-three? I thought y'all was living out in Mount Vernon or something?" Harley asked.

"We were in Westchester County, but it didn't work out," she said, not bothering to go into the details of her coming back to the block.

"Well, I'm sure your mama will be glad to have y'all close to home again." Rayfield said, picking up on her uneasiness and trying to give her an out.

"Yeah," she said, looking at her feet. "Well, I better get this stuff upstairs." She shifted the bag.

"Y'all need some help wit' them bags?" Sonny asked, in his deep drawl.

"Nah, Rock Head got us." Gucci nodded toward the young man, who had begun to perspire a bit.

"Shit, if y'all got that lazy mofo to do something, then he must want something." Rayfield squinted at Rock Head. Unlike most people, who were afraid of him, Rayfield had no problem showing his dislike.

"Knock that off, Ray; you know we fam on this block," Rock Head said. "Come on, y'all," he turned to Tionna and Gucci, "let's get these bags upstairs so I hit the block; you know this bread ain't gonna make itself." Rock Head headed toward the building.

"Okay, we'll see y'all later," Gucci said, following Rock Head into the building.

"I sure hope so," Cords said, slyly.

"Bye, y'all," Tionna said, waving with her elbow.

"Tough break," Rayfield said when Tionna and Gucci had gone.

"Tell me about it," Sonny agreed. "All that money they was sitting on, just to end up back 'round this piss hole. I was kinda cheering for her and the young boy to make it. I kinda liked his style."

"Yeah, there was something about him that reminded me of the eighties. They don't make young boys like him no more. He was a throwback hustler," Rayfield reflected.

Everybody on the block was a little sad when they heard that Duhan had gotten knocked. Unlike people like Rock Head, he had class about the way he did his business and never shed blood unnecessarily. When he got put in pocket, he used love instead of force to solidify his position, making sure that every man who was willing to work could eat. The residents in the community knew that he sold drugs, but he also did quite a bit of good with his money. He would throw bus rides to Bear Mountain and make sure all the little kids had school supplies every year. Duhan had a lot of love on the streets, because he played the game properly. Not even when the deck was stacked against him would he go against the code of the great institution known to some as Hustler's University.

"Shit, I don't feel no sympathy for her," Cords said. "That girl was running 'round like her shit ain't stink when she was on top, thumbing her damn nose at the block like she ain't grew up here. Look at her ass now."

"Quit being such a damn hater," Harley said. "We gonna play cards or what?"

"Yeah, it's my deal." Rayfield reached for the cards, but Cords's wiry fingers beat him to the punch.

"The hell it is." Cords snatched the cards. "It's my deal!"

"See, this is why I don't like to play with you muthafuckas, 'cause it's always some extra shit," Sonny said, swigging his drink.

It would probably be hours before Sonny, Harley, Rayfield, and Cords finished their game, with all their arguing, but with them it wasn't so much about winning or losing the game, it was the shit talking in between that made the days worthwhile.

CHAPTER 3

"I don't see why we couldn't just wait for the elevator," Rock Head huffed, as he reached the landing between the second and third floors.

"Because it's only the third floor, and you know how that elevator is. I know you ain't crying over that light-ass load?" Gucci rocked on her heel, with her arms folded defiantly.

"Gucci, I don't see nothing in ya hand, so don't even try it," he told her.

"Rock Head, you can just drop it at the top of the stairs if you want. I appreciate you helping out," Tionna said, dragging her garbage bag to the freshly painted door to apartment 9.

"Nah, it's all good, Tionna. You my nigga's peoples. It ain't about nothing," Rock Head said to her.

Tionna knew the hearts of men, so she knew from the time Gucci seemed to effortlessly enlist Rock Head that he had an agenda. Hood niggaz tended to be predictable that way. "Well, thanks just the same." She put the shiny key into the yellow-gold lock. Being that it was new, she had to jiggle it a bit before the lock gave. She offered to take the bag from him, but he insisted on carrying it inside.

"These joints is nice." Rock Head walked casually through the apartment, inspecting it as he went. "They need to tear my building down and rebuild that muthafucka."

"Why? So you niggaz can sell crack out the lobby and piss in the staircases like you've been doing?" Gucci asked sarcastically.

"Fuck you, Gucci!"

"Not in this lifetime, ya big-head muthafucka." Gucci perched herself atop Tionna's new wooden counter. "Rock, y'all niggaz got this whole strip on fire and you know it."

Rock Head shook his head. "Man, the police just don't wanna see a nigga rise up out this shit." He motioned at the air. "They keep they foot so far in a nigga's ass that it's a wonder we don't throw up shoe polish. They slap a case on you as a kid to let you taste the system, and once your beak is wet you accept what they feed you through the years. See, these muthafuckas program us to recognize that money is more important than anything. If you ain't got no bread, you's a subclass muthafucka. Ain't but a weak-ass nigga that's gonna stay broke for too long without eventually hitting the panic button and getting it how he gotta get it," Rock Head ended, as if he were a ghetto scholar giving a lecture at Grambling. He actually made a lot of sense, but coming from somebody like Rock Head, the sincerity was suspect at best.

Gucci sucked her teeth. "Rock Head, that's bullshit and you know it. I ain't talking about the fact that y'all hustle, but it's *how* y'all hustle. Rock, y'all sell crack and stick people up on the same blocks you live on . . . your families live on." She pointed her finger. "If you wanna do stupid shit, do it, but why you gotta make everybody else susceptible in the process?"

Rock Head measured her for a minute. In his mind, the way he did things made perfect sense, but he couldn't articulate it properly. "G, we do what we do because it's all we know. Yeah, the block is hot, but niggaz know they can't roll through here like that. This is the jungle, baby, you know what it is."

Gucci shook her head. "The jungle, I hear that hot shit."

"So what's up? Y'all gonna stand around here and argue, or are we gonna go grab the rest of this stuff out of the van?" Tionna was tiring of their antics.

"My fault, T, but you know ya peoples be vexin' me on some other shit." Rock Head raised his hands and let them fall to his sides as if their word *exchange* had exhausted him.

Gucci just shot him a disgusted glare.

"Well, y'all can go through the motions on your own time; I still got shit to do. I gotta finish unpacking and get right for tomorrow. I'm going to see my boo," Tionna said, glancing at her watch.

"Yo, what's good wit' my nigga Du? He need anything?" Rock Head asked. His eyes were compassionate, but you could see faint wisps of larceny lurking behind the pupils.

"Nah, he's chilling. You know a lot of niggaz loved Duhan on the street, plus his rider is always gonna make sure he straight." Tionna patted herself on the chest, making sure that she looked directly into Rock Head's eyes when she spoke.

"I know that's right, ride for ya man," Rock Head said, trying to laugh it off.

"Till death do us." Tionna held up her ring finger, showing off her diamond ring. It was the last thing of value that

Duhan had left her. No matter how bad she needed money, she refused to pawn it.

"I can dig it." He paused. "But I'm saying, though . . . if he need anything, come holla at me." He touched her arm. It was the faintest contact, but she still felt like she'd have to pay special attention to that spot on her arm when she next showered, and her eyes said this when she looked at him.

"How about I give you his info and you can go up and see him? I know he'd be glad to see his *nigga*." The smile she gave him was that of a serpent that'd just convinced a field mouse that he was harmless.

"No doubt, I've been meaning to get out there, but I just ain't had the chance yet, ya know?"

"Yeah, I know," she said, brushing past him and going out into the hall. She stopped just outside the door, waiting for Gucci and Rock Head to follow her out.

Tionna was just locking her door when she heard the sound of footsteps behind her. She turned to the steps leading down from the upper floors and watched as a pair thick legs and thighs oozed up to a slim waist and breasts that were just reaching the peak of what they would be. When the face of the brown-skinned girl came into view, Tionna frowned. The girl looked down at her and returned the expression.

"'Sup, Sharon?" Rock Head called from behind Tionna.

Sharon was a young chick who was way too hot in the pants and didn't have half as much game as she gave herself credit for. She was an eleventh-grade dropout who lived mostly by her wits and her mother and sister's mercies, occasionally getting a check for shaking her ass in videos. Her sister, Reese, and her peoples used to ring off in the streets of Harlem with their off-the-wall antics and track records for tragedy, and Sharon was determined to walk a mile in their shoes.

There had been a few rumors connecting the young girl to Duhan, but Tionna had never been able to catch them red-handed. Sharon made it a habit to try to get under Tionna's skin whenever she saw her, but for the most part Tionna ignored her because she was young. However, the way things had been going for her lately, she might decide to throw her morals out the window and dust Sharon off if she stepped wrong. Luckily for her, she didn't spare Tionna a second look, focusing on Rock Head.

"'Sup, Rock, where it's at?" She was speaking to him but cut her eyes at Gucci.

"You know I always got that, where you about to go?" he asked.

"I gotta shoot uptown right quick and see my peoples, but I might got a minute to spare. You got that Piff?"

"You know I do." He smiled. "Let's go get a Dutch and be about that. I gotta holla at you anyway." He motioned for her to follow him down the stairs.

"Excuse me," Sharon said in a stink tone, making it her business to brush against Tionna as she passed her.

"Watch that shit," Tionna said, extending her arms a bit, almost knocking Sharon off balance.

"Damn, I know you put on a little weight, but you ain't gotta block the whole staircase," Sharon said sarcastically.

"Sharon, you can play with me if you want to and find yourself getting stomped out on these steps. If I were you, I'd keep walking," Tionna said seriously.

"Whatever." Sharon stepped passed Tionna to the landing where Rock Head was looking on. Just to rub salt on it, she turned around and said, "Oh, Duhan told me what happened. Welcome home, your highness!" She laughed and continued down the stairs.

"You disrespectful little bitch!" Tionna roared. Had it not been for Gucci holding her arm, she would've perused Sharon and whipped her ass for talking slick.

"Chill out, T." Gucci tried to tug her back up onto the landing. Tionna was pulling so hard that she thought they both might end up falling down the stairs.

"Gucci, that little ho is gonna let her mouth write a check that her ass can't cash!" she fumed. "And what the fuck does she mean, *'Duhan told me what happened?'* On the real, after all that nigga put me through, he better not be playing me with that little jail-bait whore!"

"Tionna, you bugging right now." Gucci jerked Tionna around to face her. "You know better than to let a bum bitch like that bring you outta your character." The seriousness in her eyes got Tionna to calm down a bit, but she was still tight.

"This is why I got up off Fortieth in the first place, so I wouldn't have to deal with this kinda shit. Bitches are always hating. I ain't have to put up with this in Westchester." Tionna sucked her teeth.

"Well, this ain't the suburbs, baby girl, this is the block, and you know how shit goes. Come on now, T." Gucci's tone softened. "You a *made* bitch, be it here or somewhere else. A chick like Sharon ain't never had and won't ever have, so you know she's gonna try and cause waves whenever she can. Instead of acting a damn fool out here on the block, you need to step to Duhan about even putting you out there like that."

This immediately got Tionna focused. "You're right, girl.

I can't see why he had to stick his dick in that dusty hole anyway, when this pussy is sweeter than honeysuckle."

"Because that's how niggaz do," Gucci told her. "T, you know Du is my peoples and I got love for him, but at the end of the day he's just like any other nigga. For as much as they claim to love us, they still find the need to fuck other bitches. Now, you took a step back, but this is only a temporary arrangement." She motioned toward the apartment door. "You can go out like a weak ho and fall back into this ghetto shit, or you can carry it like a real bitch and get back on your game."

Gucci's words hit her like a glass of cold water thrown in her face. At the high point of her and Duhan's relationship, a chick like Sharon wasn't even fit to speak to her, let alone try to clown her. Tionna was better than that and she knew it.

Just the thought of him with another woman took her back to the last visit she'd had with him. It was pouring rain that day and she couldn't get a ride, but she still took the trip to see him on Riker's Island. After going through the motions with security, she was directed to a small plastic chair where she was to wait for the inmate. Her heart was aflutter when he came from behind the steel door. His rich chocolate skin was clear and smooth from lack of all the fast food he was used to eating, and he looked to be getting his weight up. His hair was freshly shaped up with his signature half-moon part on the left side. Duhan was so old-school. Tionna smiled, because even in the moldy jumpsuit her man still looked like a million dollars.

"Hey, baby." She accepted his tongue when he offered it. The correction officers were oblivious to the balloon stuffed with heroin that she had slipped him. She'd had to practice the trick almost ten times before she'd gotten it down to a science. "I missed you."

"I missed you more." He squeezed her. For the next hour they talked about the kids, the case, and of course the streets, and before they knew it the visit was almost over.

"So listen, I need you to take care of that for me. Go see my man uptown and he's gonna give you that for homegirl," he told her as they said their final goodbyes.

"I got you, daddy, you know your boss bitch is on it," she assured him. Tionna blew Duhan a farewell kiss and watched as he made his way back with the other inmates. Moving down the row, he had to pass a shapely light-skinned girl who had been visiting with another inmate. Tionna probably wouldn't even have noticed her had Duhan not been smiling so widely. When the light-skinned girl mouthed her number to him, Tionna snapped.

"The both of you muthafuckas must be brain dead with a death wish. Duhan, I will finish you and this yellow bitch for trying to play with my heart." Tionna hopped up and was marching toward the girl. The girl tried to hop up so fast that she ended up falling over in the little chair.

"Yo, chill." Duhan tried to move to break it up, but two of the officers wrestled him to the ground. Tionna had almost made it to the girl when she was tackled by a female officer.

"You fucking bum bitch! I will wash you in here!" Tionna continued to claw and kick at the girl. It took the initial female officer and two males to completely pin her. For her little outburst she had a six-month ban from Riker's placed on her, and Duhan went to the box.

Tionna knew in her heart that Duhan fucked other girls, but she tried to tell herself that he would change. She, too, had stepped out a time or three, but it was usually payback for some stupid shit he'd done. Until then they had both had enough respect for each other not to let their dirt intermingle, but Sharon was too young and dumb to understand grown people's etiquette. Sharon was technically a baby, and Tionna would try to keep this in mind when she saw her again. Still, the fact remained that if Sharon broke fly with her mouth again, Tionna was going to throw their age differences aside and step knee-deep off into her ass.

"I can't believe that bitch called herself trying to run up on me," Sharon said, while licking the end of the cigar to seal it. She fidgeted on Rock Head's lumpy twin bed, trying to find a comfortable position.

"Yo, Tionna is off da hook. You might wanna be easy, Sharon; she used to lay bitches down back in the days," Rock Head said.

"Like that shit is supposed to scare me? I got hand skills too, nigga. Besides, Tionna is washed up. Ain't that bitch like forty? She out here arguing with me and she's supposed to be the adult."

"You did start, Sharon."

"How, by walking down the steps? Just because y'all niggaz treat her like royalty don't mean I got to. Tionna ain't the queen of the fucking hood. The only reason bitches even sweated her like that is because Duhan kept her dipped. Let's see the bitch maintain now that her cash cow is locked up," Sharon said scornfully.

"Duhan was getting a little bread when he was out here; you think he left her holding anything?" Rock Head asked. His mind was always on a lick, friend or foe.

"He might've left her whatever scraps he had laying around

the house, but he ain't leave her no real bread because he wasn't fucking wit' her like that when he got locked up."

Rock Head looked at her like she was crazy. "You bugging, that was his wifey, yo."

"Wifey my ass! The only reason he even fucked with her for as long as he did is because they got kids together and he was trying to do the right thing. What y'all don't know is that before Duhan got locked up, he was gonna leave her," Sharon said, more to convince herself than Rock Head. She and her sister had had countless arguments about her being a fool for Duhan, but Sharon knew that Reese was just hating. Just because she ended up getting pregnant by a guy who wanted nothing to do with his daughter didn't mean that the same thing would happen to her; she was smarter than Reese had been at that age. The streets might've recognized Tionna as Duhan's wife, but he had told Sharon that he loved her, which in her foolish heart was enough to seal the deal.

Rock Head let Sharon go on and on about her hate for Tionna and love for Duhan, while he kept rolling weed, stoking the fire. In under an hour Sharon was so high that she could barely keep her eyes open. "That piff got you, huh?" Rock Head nudged her out of her nod.

"Yo, that shit was fire, Rock Head. Where you get that?" she asked, smiling lazily. In all her years of smoking weed she could never recall being that high.

"You know I stay wit' that, ma." He placed his hand on her thigh, just below the pleat of her skirt.

"Cut it out." She giggled and playfully slapped his hand away.

"You know that shit feels good." He ran his hand down

her arm and watched the goose bumps materialize. He could see her supple young nipples pressing against her shirt and it aroused him. "You know I've been checking for you for a while, right?" He moved in closer and started kissing her neck.

"Nigga, please, you just want some pussy." She shoved him, but not enough to really move him. Between the weed and Rock Head's pawing, she was starting to get horny. Unexpectedly her vagina expelled a puff of air, which they both heard.

"Damn, and I ain't even get in it yet." He hiked her skirt up and admired the bush poking out of her panties. Rock Head ran his finger along the imprint of her clit, causing her to hiss. "You know you like that," he said, kissing the inside of her thigh. She smelled slightly of sweat, but he was so thirsty that he didn't care.

"Cut it out, Rock Head." She dragged her nails down the back of his head softly. The more he touched, the wetter she got. "We can't do this."

"Sure we can." He mounted her, trying to guide his thick penis inside her.

She parted her legs for him. "Hold on, we ain't even got no condoms."

Rock Head was so hard that the head of his dick had already started leaking. He was on fire and only Sharon's love nest could put it out. "Don't worry, baby, I ain't got nothing, I got tested before I came home from prison." He slipped the head in with ease. Sharon was surprisingly loose for a girl her age.

"Rock Head, get a condom," she breathed as he stroked in

and out of her. Every time he hit her walls, she felt like she was gonna explode.

Rock Head leaned up and silenced her with a sloppy kiss. "We good; I'll pull out before I come," he lied before he went back to his pounding.

CHAPTER 4

China White eased to a stop halfway through the intersection at the corner of 104th to let a foul-mouthed little boy cross the street. He screamed something to his friends across the street before grabbing his crotch and continuing on his way. You could tell by his body language that he was a bad-ass kid; at that time of day, Columbus Avenue was teeming with them.

"Damn, if it wasn't for these kids, this muthafucka might as well be a ghost town," Silk said, taking a drag of her cigarette. At its height, the Frederick Douglass housing project had been one of the livest, with the corner of 104th and Columbus being a gathering spot for the locals. Now, it was a shell of its former self, with more young boys in tight jeans who were looking for acceptance than original heads who knew the history.

"All the *real* niggaz are in jail, or squared up," Tech said, sitting up enough to see but not to be seen.

Silk flicked the burning cigarette out the window. "It would seem like it'd make more sense to just run these niggaz up out and do us instead of going about it like this."

"Nah." Tech shook his head. "That's going about it the hard way." He took a minute to examine the face of a girl pushing a stroller. Whether he knew her or not, he never said. "Ain't no profit in killing for free, ma. Money without bloodshed is the sweetest and less conspicuous. I got a line on this nigga that's a mile long, so I got an idea of how to work the angle, so *cool* is the operative word, Silk. We're gonna go in here and speak our piece and boogie, simple as that."

"You really think this cat is gonna go for it? I mean, if it was me, ain't no way in the hell I can see letting a nigga muscle me outta mine. It's death before dishonor, all day!"

Tech smiled at the young girl. "Ain't many niggaz left that's built like you, Silky."

"And that's what's wrong with the game," China added.

They ended up circling the block twice before spotting their mark. It was a wonder that they hadn't spotted him on their first pass, being that he stuck out like a sore thumb, with his pale skin among the darkness of his peers. He was posted up in the parking lot, behind 845, speaking to a chick who wore her hair in fuzzy extensions. Flanking them were several local cats, who were trying their best to look hard, but their eyes said that there wasn't a killer among them. Still, Silk placed her hammer on her lap in case anyone felt like overextending themselves trying to prove how hard they were.

"Y'all niggaz be easy, we ain't the police," Silk said out the passenger's window. Though she was smiling, showing off her grills, it did nothing to ease the tension. "'Sup, Bobo," she addressed the pale young man, then turned to the girl. "Do me a favor, ma, take a walk. Bo will get back with you in a few."

"What?" she snaked her neck. "I know you ain't talking to me?"

"Chill," Bobo urged through clenched teeth.

"Fuck all that you ain't gonna have ya little dyke looking jump offs coming though here talking to me all crazy. I ain't no fucking punk; check ya bitch, yo, for real!"

Bobo tried to calm her, but she kept talking. Even before he heard the car door pop open he knew how it would play out, so he just stepped to the side. Silk moved so quickly that she seemed to just appear next to the loudmouthed girl. The girl pulled a box cutter, which Silk simply slapped away, and in the next motion she jammed her gun beneath the girl's chin. All the bravado was gone as she looked down sheepishly at the much shorter Silk.

Silk leaned in so close that the girl could see the sun glinting off the freshly polished gold of her teeth. "Ho, you must be stupid. You're willing to put yo life on the line for a piece of dick?" Silk sounded offended. "Ma, you's a poor excuse for a bitch." Silk pushed her away and kicked the girl in the ass as she jogged off. "Do something with them nappy-ass braids and your ass might look like something!" she called after her. Now Bobo had her undivided attention. "And your little ass is starting to become more trouble than you're worth."

"Go ahead with that shit, Silk, and tuck that hammer before you have the police blowing my spot," Bobo said, trying to sound easy.

Silk raised an eyebrow. "Yo spot? Bobo, you's a funny muthafucka, but I ain't come here to dissect youre sorry-ass character. Real recognize real and I don't see a thorough nigga left in this whole muthafucka." She motioned toward the projects. "Look, you know why I'm here, so let's not beat around the bush."

"Man, tell Tech I'll get with him," Bobo tried to brush her off. He'd already been ducking Tech for the last few days, so it wouldn't be too hard to duck him for a few more.

Silk smiled. "Nah, you can tell him yourself. He's in the whip."

This was something Bobo hadn't counted on and his face showed it. Instinctively he slipped his hand into the pocket of his hoodie, where his gun was, but he knew that even if he could muster up the courage to pull it out, Silk would waste him. She peeped the move and tried to set him at ease. "Don't trip, man; you know we ain't come down here to do you nothing, so be easy."

"I'm good, but tell him to get out of the car if he wanna talk," Bobo bartered.

Silk gave Tech a hand signal. Tech thought on it for a minute before nodding in approval. He reached for the door handle and uncoiled himself onto the pavement to join them, but before he could take a step, China had made her way around to the passenger's side and stood between him and potential danger.

"This is the cat I was telling you about, Tech," Silk said.

"No need for introductions, Silky, Bo knows who I am. Ain't that right, Bo?" Tech eyed him.

Bobo thought on it for a minute before answering. "Yeah, I might've heard ya name a time or two before Silk reached out."

Tech clapped his hands and smiled. "Knock that shit off, fam. If you don't know my name, you damn sure know my work. Let's not start this thing between us with fronting, life is far too short to waste. You know who I am and how I give it up, so that leaves the question of why you never responded to my envoy." Bobo looked confused, so Tech broke it down into simpler terms: "I sent Silk and China to arrange a business meeting, but we ain't heard back from you."

"Yeah, ya broads got at me and I had every intention on getting at you, I just ain't got around to it yet," Bobo said, as if it were that simple.

"You ain't got around to it yet?"

Bobo shrugged. "You know how it is when you're a busy dude. Besides, I don't know how I feel about getting sent for."

"I can respect that, you being such a busy cat and all," Tech said sarcastically. "But check, I need to speak about some things with you, and the sooner we're done, the sooner we can both go about our days."

Bobo shrugged. "So speak."

Tech looked around at the assembled faces, then let his cold gaze go back to Bobo. "I don't think what I got to say is for everybody's ears, feel me?"

"These is my niggaz," Bobo said, motioning toward the group. "Whatever you got to say to me, you can say in front of them."

Tech smirked. "If you like it, I love it. Styles said you were an interesting dude."

Hearing the name Styles sent a chill down Bobo's back. Until a few years ago, Styles had been one of the ruling factors in the projects. He'd had a good run and been fair with most people, but the judicial system didn't care if you were a nice guy when it came to drugs. Styles and his team had been caught slipping and been taken down on some fabricated charges, strengthened by the testimony of the very same cats they were feeding in the hood. Though they were no angels, most of what the witnesses said during the trial was bullshit created out of fear and jealousy. Needless to say, the testimonies sent them away for some very lengthy bids.

"You still wanna talk in front of ya peoples?"

"Let's walk down to the end of the lot," Bobo said, trying to hide the fear in his voice. It was very possible that Tech could've come to kill him, but he doubted it. He had heard enough about Tech to know that if it was a hit, he probably wouldn't have seen him coming until it was too late.

"Give me a sec, ladies," Tech told China and Silk, before following Bobo down the lot.

"Take ya time, T, we got this under control," Silk called after him, but never took her eyes off the young men assembled.

"So what's up, what you want with me?" Bobo asked, once they were out of earshot.

"I don't want shit from you, duke, I actually wanna give you something," Tech said. He saw the fear flash across Bobo's eyes. "Calm down, I ain't here to kill you. Dig this: what I propose is a partnership of sorts. I hit you with my product, and you have your boys move it through the projects, at a fifty-five–forty-five split, in favor of me."

Bobo looked at Tech as if he'd lost his mind. "You came all the way down here to tell me that? Yo, my man, I could've saved you a trip. I got a good thing going on down here, so why would I want to let another nigga in on it, especially for forty-five percent, when I'm already getting a hundred?"

"Because I know your secret, Bo. I think we both know that you wouldn't be getting shit if you ain't put the finger on Styles as your supplier," Tech said. His tone was neutral, but the weight of his words hit Bobo like a slap.

"My dude, I don't know what you're taking about and I don't appreciate you coming down here trying to call me a snitch." Bobo tried to puff up, but Tech was unmoved.

"First of all," Tech began, "I don't too much give a fuck what you appreciate. It's cats like you that got the game rotting from the inside out as it is. And second, you and I both know I ain't telling you nothing but the truth." Tech handed Bobo a folded slip of paper.

Bobo tried to keep his face neutral as he read the paper, but his legs almost gave out on him. It was a page of the grand-jury minutes from Styles's trial. Styles had been making his life miserable around the hood, constantly badmouthing him, and delivering the occasional slap when called for, so when the opportunity to knock him out of the box and save his own ass at the same time came, he jumped on it. When he'd agreed to become a whore for the government he hadn't given much thought to the aftermath. By crossing Styles, a lot of families went hungry, but all Bobo could see was his own freedom. After a short bid in a county facility, Bobo came home and the projects were wide open. Bobo figured that his treachery would never come back on him, but Tech had proven him wrong.

"Don't look so surprised," Tech said, snapping him out of his trance. "There's a little thing called the Public Information Act, which makes the things sneaky muthafuckas like you do when you think nobody is listening available to the public."

"Yo—" Bobo began, but Tech cut him off.

"Bo, don't even say nothing, because you can't get no lower than you are now. I know for a fact that Styles hated yo ass, so I couldn't imagine him giving you a cigarette, let alone some drugs. You did what you did to save your ass. I can't say that I respect it or you, but I'm the executioner, not the judge. Bottom line is I need some of that money that's coming through this hood. You ain't gotta answer me now, Bo. I'll send Silk back tonight with something for you. If you take it, I'll know where we stand. If not, you might wanna think about arming up." Tech walked away from Bobo without waiting for an answer.

"I don't like that l'il muthafucka," Silk said, still staring at Bobo out the rear window, even as China turned out of the parking lot.

"He ain't for you to like, baby, he's to get fat off," Tech informed her.

"I still don't like the nigga."

"You think he's gonna go for the strong-arm tactic, Tech? I know Bobo is a piece of shit, but he got a few goons out here and he fucking with them boys. There's a good chance that when we pay that next visit, he gonna pull a cross," China said.

Tech shrugged. "More than likely, which is why he ain't gonna get the chance. Bobo is a faggot, but them greasy niggaz who hold his guns think the boy is a god, so we're gonna make him mortal. When he closes his eyes tonight, all his goons are gonna know who sang the lullaby, so when we move in with our product they be hesitant to test us, but we ain't gonna gorilla the block, we gonna let them eat. Them young boys are more loyal to this cake than they are to Bobo. Besides, Styles already dropped the bread on that faggot, so he's on borrowed time. That nigga will be gone soon enough, but his block is still gonna be there."

"When did you plan on telling us that we were gonna kill Bobo?" Silk asked.

"Actually, I wasn't, because it was none of your business,"

Tech informed her. He saw the hurt flash in her hard eyes, so he explained himself. "This meal is for the little ones. They been 'bout they shit thus far, but it's time to test their mettle. Our thing is expanding and we're gonna need more soldiers, so I wanna see exactly what these niggaz are made of."

"Damn, I wanted to tear something up," Silk said, pouting.

"Don't trip, li'l ma, I got something lined up for you and China, too. The old heads reached out and said they wanted to sit down." The car suddenly got very quiet.

"What do they want?" China asked what Silk was thinking.

Tech shrugged. "I can't really call it, yo. Duke ain't sound too crazy on the jack, but I don't trust none of these pussies. I'm taking y'all with me as security."

"Why not Animal?" Silk wanted to know. She had no problem holding him down, but everyone knew Animal was normally the eyes in the back of his head.

"For two good reasons: one, if they see me walk in with Animal, it's gonna put everybody on point. For two, if he ain't feeling the way shit is going, he's gonna act without thinking, and I don't need that. Them niggaz don't know y'all, so they ain't gonna think much of me rolling in with two broads. I got it all worked out, ma."

"So where're we off to now?" China headed north on along Central Park.

"Y'all can do what you gotta do for the day and we'll hook up later. Drop me off at the kennel, it's time to feed the pups."

CHAPTER 5

"Do you really have to go?" she asked in a sultry tone. Her nude body was partially wrapped in the bedsheet, with a shapely thigh exposed.

He took a minute to make sure that his stocking cap was laid just right before pulling on his Yankee fitted cap. "Yeah, you know I got business to handle. The label ain't gonna run itself, smell me?"

"Come on with that. As many niggaz as you keep around you, I'm sure one of them could handle it without you for a day or so." She reached for a Newport on the nightstand, letting the sheet fall away so one supple brown breast was exposed. It looked like a caramel apple with a Hershey's Kiss in the center. She lit the cigarette and took a deep drag, waiting for his response.

"You know I don't trust nobody with my paper, but me," he told her, slipping the icy chain over his head. The rottweiler medallion bumped against his broad chest when he let it drop. "But dig it, as soon as I get finished making my moves, I'll come back and check you." He kissed her forehead, and plucked the cigarette from her fingers. "These things will kill you." He took a light toke and put it out in a half-empty soda can.

"You know I'm getting a little tired of you hitting me with the okey-doke." She crossed her arms over her breasts.

"Come on, shorty, don't start tripping off that shit right now." He wiped his black sunglasses with the edge of the bed-sheet before slipping them on. "You know what it is."

"Know what it is?" Her eyes got wide. "You come through here, talk that good shit, eat, get your dick sucked, and flick channels, and at the end of the day all I end up with is a soggy pussy and a couple of dollars, so no, I don't know what it is. Why don't you enlighten me?"

He glared at her from behind his shades, running his tongue along the roof of his mouth, as he often did when he was getting aggravated. "Shorty . . ."

"Uh-uh," she waggled her finger, "we ain't even gonna get into that *shorty* shit, because I'm tired of telling you about it. My mother named me Patricia, Pat if you're pressed for time. You can save that *shorty* shit for the hos at the videos, because I ain't them."

"Pat, Patricia, what the fuck ever, you know what I meant. Baby girl, you know I'm a nigga who's always in the thick, so why you trying to act like all this is new?"

"It ain't that it's new, but it's getting tired," she told him. "I'm a woman, and I have needs outside of some good dick and you helping with my bills. I give you all of me, and I get the after-the-club calls. I need to know where we stand."

He cocked his head, twisting his full lips. "Pat, you know

you my l'il down bitch, so I don't even know why you stressing me wit' this. I do shit for you that I ain't never did for a bitch, and that's not because ya head is supersweet, which it is," he smirked, "but on the real, you know I keep my motions fluid, so don't go raising walls on me now."

Pat swung her legs over the edge of the bed and looked up at her reflection in his shades. " *'I keep my motions fluid.'* Nigga, do you hear yourself? You're a grown-ass man," she all but shouted. "I'm sitting here making a punk-ass attempt at pouring my heart out, and you can't even respect me enough to speak English!"

His cell vibrated on his hip, saving him from having to spazz on Pat. "Yeah," he huffed into the phone. "A'ight, I'll be down in a sec." He flipped the phone closed. "Yo, Pat, I gotta dip," he told the girl, who was still fuming.

"That's right, run when the streets call, fuck what I'm trying to say," she snapped.

"What you want from me?" he said, with his hand on the doorknob.

"Reciprocity," she said, trying to keep her voice from quavering.

He paused for a minute, as if he might go back and smooth things over, but it was an illusion. "We'll talk about this later," he said before slipping out the door. Had he waited a second or so more, he'd be on the way to the emergency room to be treated for the gash the ashtray she hurled at him would've left in the back of his head.

When Don B. left Pat's apartment, it took all his willpower to keep from slamming the door behind him. She was a classic example of why he wouldn't take a wifey: drama. She was a good chick who did what she needed to do, but she couldn't understand the Don. He had come up from being a hopeless shorty, happy to get a package from the next man, to being a power player in the music industry.

Nearly ten years ago, he had gone on a six-month-long hustling spree to get his dream up and running. Don B. had hugged the block for days at a time, sleeping only when his body forced him to. Back then, it had been just him and his man Pop, running through Harlem, wanting to leave their marks out there with legends. Pop and Don B. had clicked so well because they were like two peas in a pod when it came to the streets.

The need for quick money played a role in their selling cocaine, but it was the high more than anything. Not a blunt or a snort could compare to the soft flesh of a woman or the smell of a new car when you drive it off the lot. Like a lot of young men, they got turned out by the life. The flash and shine of the Harlem underworld sucked at them like vampires, increasing their need to feed the monkey. To be a fly nigga in Harlem was like being a respected god on Olympus, to give you a visual. When they caught the music itch, it only made the high sweeter because they didn't have to hide the money. With the way they were grinding, the team of Pop and Don B. was a sure thing, but then karma reared her ugly head.

Don B. had always been more about the paper and women than the drama and bullets, but Pop couldn't let go of what was and embrace what was to be. He was getting a buzz on the rap scene but still needed to be a dictator in the streets. He saw Big Dawg more as a gang than a business, often making his decisions based on that. To him, Big Dawg was a regime that wasn't to be challenged. A knucklehead that Don B. had exchanged words with at a club over a female ended up being the first example of Pop's new rule.

Pop had blasted the kid in a crowded club, in front of hundreds of people. The kid lived, but refused to testify against Pop out of fear. Still, Pop was in possession of the weapon when they caught him, so they were still able to slap his ass with five to fifteen. Don B. found himself with a potential monster of a company on his hands, and no artist. Don B. knew he would have to shit or get off the pot. And so his emcee persona was born.

Don B. took a hard breath when he stepped from the safety of the building's archway. Though Remo and Devil had surely swept the block beforehand, he was still on edge for danger. With success brought jealousy, and Don B. knew all too well what a jealous person was capable of. His former protégé, True, was a testament to that. True had been the ray of sunshine in Don B.'s life since the day he'd met him. True got it how he got it, but the music had always been his first love. In him, Don B. had seen redemption, but the ghetto had stolen True's life, just as it had Don B.'s soul. The money from True's postmortem album put Big Dawg Entertainment in a whole different tax bracket, but he'd have traded it all to have his friend back.

"What it is?" Don B. slapped Devil's yellow palm. The aging but still brolic cat responded with a nod. Remo stayed behind the wheel of the bloodred Hummer, idling. "We out," Don B. announced, moving to climb into the backseat. When he got into the Hummer, there were already two more people back there, but Don B. had been expecting them.

Night and day occupied the butterscotch seats in the rear of the Hummer. The black kid was a John Singleton throwback in his creased Levi's and white running shoes. An oversized New

Jersey Devils' jersey was draped over a black Champion hoodie, which was pulled over his head. All that was visible within the folds of the hood were bloodshot eyes and a freshly rolled blunt dangling between slightly ashen lips. Fully nodded at Don B. when he slid into the vehicle.

The white boy was brighter, but not cleaner. He wore a tattered USC sweatshirt and a baseball cap creased down the bill. His shifty brown eyes didn't linger on one spot in the car for more than two seconds before moving on to something else. They called him No Doze, and all he did was pop pills and make beats. His drugged-out mind connected with the music in a way that no one could really understand. Some people joked that he had undiagnosed ADD, but that was bullshit. The boy was trained in classical piano, acoustic guitar, and bass drum, and was currently teaching himself to play the violin. His brain was like an organic computer and through the group they turned his skills into money—money that Don B. intended to triple, in his favor, of course.

Chip was the computer junkie and currently absent member of the group. The Lebanese transplant handled computer software like it was second nature. No Doze would put together a dope beat and Chip would taint it, twisting the sound to a uniquely morbid pitch. What he did to the beats was never clear, but it gave them a dark and skin-crawlingly delicious edge.

The group was composed of two burnouts who knew music like Don B. knew grams, and a hard-nosed cat that carried the streets with him like commuters carried metro cards. Multicultural young dudes barely out of their teens, hailing from Los Angeles County, they called themselves the Left Coast Theory. They had a sound that was like a blend of the Neptunes with a live-music presence that was vintage Roots. They were the purest thing to come out of rap since the Black Eyed Peas, and had just as much star power. More important, they were the latest Big Dawg acquisition.

"What it is, fellas?" Don B. pounded each of their fists. "Where's Chip?"

"On his bullshit, yet again," Fully said in his raspy pitch.

"You know Chip, he's probably in the lab doing his thing," No Doze said. Chip's disappearing acts got on his nerves, too, but he didn't feel like they should be talking about it in front of Don B. He had made them a part of his label and by extension his crew, but he wasn't family.

"Whatever, as long as he is where he needs to be come game time," Don B. said, twisting the cap off a bottle of water. "Y'all listened to them tracks yet?"

Fully leaned forward so that Don B. could hear him. "Yeah, we checked them and . . ."

"None of them really grabbed us." No Doze finished the sentence. Before Don B. could say anything, he continued. "Don, the tracks were dope, but they weren't Coast. You know we're better when the whole thing is done in-house."

"Doze, I hear you and all that, but this is a business decision," Don B. told him. "Now, y'all produced over eighty percent of the album, and I'm giving you final say when it gets mixed down. That says that I have total faith in you when it comes to this here, but Left Coast ain't the only pups in the litter. This album is not only gonna break y'all, but it's gonna kick the buzz off for a few more niggaz I got waiting in the wings. Y'all do the music and let me worry about the business."

Doze didn't like the fact that they'd have to share space

with some of the other Big Dawg acts. Some of them were good, while others were just reformed drug dealers that Don B. was looking out for. Doze didn't want that kind of energy spilling onto their stuff. Still, Don B. was the man running the show, so he suffered in silence.

"Did my little man get that out to you?" Don B. asked Fully.

"Yeah, yeah, good looking out on that. I'll get it back to you once we knock this show out," Fully assured him.

"It's all good, my nigga. I'll just take it off the back end of your royalties down the line so you won't miss it. Just be a little wiser with ya cake this go-round," Don B. said, breaking up a block of weed on a CD case.

Doze cut his eyes at Fully. When they had signed, Don B. had given them a six-figure advance. Even when the money was split between the three of them it left each member with enough money to hold him down for a minute. Doze spent money only on drugs and studio equipment, so he didn't burn through it as fast, but Fully had to have the *life*. Back when they'd first landed in New York, they'd made their way by slumming around the club circuit begging for gigs. They'd pass around 40s of St. Ides and appreciate it like it was fine wine, but since signing with Big Dawg he felt like he had to pop bottles to look like he belonged with Don B. and his crew. When they were alone he intended to check him about borrowing against their royalties.

Doze watched as Don B. oozed back into the shadowed recesses of the SUV, and handed the blunt to Fully. Doze's partner accepted the blunt as if Don B. were bestowing a blessing upon him. He'd been doing that a lot lately—hanging on Don B.'s every word as if whatever he said was the gospel. Chip often made slick comments about it but Doze was content to watch from a distance and wondered silently how long they'd be able to keep the music pure before the politics came into play.

Don B.'s shaded eyes made it impossible to tell just what he was looking at, but his face was set in Doze's general direction. There was something about their CEO that unnerved Doze, but he couldn't put his finger on exactly what it was. Don B. had been looking out for them since that night they'd met at The Doll House in Newark. Once they got the word that he was at the spot, they put a Harlem cab on hold and rode all the way out to The Bricks. Don B. and his crew had the place so packed that Fully ended up having to knock one of the bouncers out to get Don B.'s attention. They ended up spending three days in the Essex County Jail, but when they got back to New York they got the word that Don B. wanted to see them. They laid out their package and it had been on ever since. As far as CEOs went, the Don seemed to be on the up and up, but Doze knew business, so therefore there had to be an ulterior motive. There was always a hidden agenda when paper was involved.

"Everything is gonna be good, Doze." Don B. dispelled some of the tension when he laid a mitt on the slim white boy's shoulder. "See, what y'all don't quite grasp is that this here is a double-edged sword. You ain't regular niggaz no more, and at the same time you are, feel me?" Fully looked dumbstruck, as he often did, while Doze's face clearly said that he was lost. "Look," Don B. leaned forward, raining flakes of ash onto his jeans, "being in this business can be a beautiful thing, as long as you see the ugliness before it gets a firm hold on that ass." He clasped his hands together for emphasis. "When you a hot nigga, it's always gonna be shit that people dangle in front of you, making you think that you need it, so naturally you're gonna do everything in your power to get it just to prove that you have the means to do so. The hot nigga is always gonna be the life of the party, but when your star fizzles, that's the end of the road.

"See, muthafuckas on the outside looking in look at the rapper with the big chain and think he's the dude calling the shots, but they got it twisted. The talent advertises the product, but it's the ideas behind the talent that truly control this rap shit. A few years ago I took a bunch of knucklehead-ass niggaz and turned them into made men, but they were hustlers and not entertainers . . . shit, they weren't even rappers, to keep it one hundred wit' you, but I was able to sell them because I'm smart about this shit. Not only are y'all some dope-ass rappers, but y'all are actually musicians!" he said excitedly. "In a hot minute you're gonna have a classic album out under the hottest label in the game and the whole fucking world is gonna know you. Now, y'all are gonna be stars with or without the Don, but with him, you'll be rich. Trust in ya boy and enjoy the ride."

CHAPTER 6

Tionna breathed a sigh of relief when her two rambunctious children disappeared around the corner of Seventh Avenue. From the minute they'd hit 140th they'd been running around like they'd lost their last minds. Tionna was on the verge of laying the smack down right before a neighborhood girl named Pumpkin offered to take them around the corner to grab a two-dollar special at the Cat Kitchen. Hopefully the short ribs and scoop of fried rice would keep them out of her hair long enough for her to breathe.

"Damn, you look stressed." Gucci dropped a milk crate next to the tattered chair Tionna was sitting on and took a load off.

"Them damn kids was driving me crazy." Tionna massaged her scalp. "I swear it seems like there's something about this block that makes them act like they ain't got no sense."

"The kids got more sense than some of the grown people." Gucci watched Rock Head on the other side of the street making a sale. He didn't have the common decency to wait until after Ms. Jordan had passed with her granddaughter before serving the fiend. "But you know I got that stress reliever, right?" Gucci dug into her bra and pulled out a bag of pretty green buds. "It ain't the best, but it's piff."

"My nerves are so bad that I'd smoke some dirt right now and love it. Give me the Dutch so I can spin, because you know your ass can't roll, Gucci."

"Please, Tionna," Gucci tossed her the Dutch Master, "we can't all be fucking addicts."

"Say what you want, but the chronic ain't never did nothing to me." Tionna proceeded to split the Dutch and empty the guts into a plastic bag, spinning the blunt in less than a minute. She had just lit it when Gucci tapped her leg.

"Hold that down." Gucci nodded in the direction of the Senate. The four old men were trying their best to garner the attention of a well-built brown-skinned woman. She wore her hair in a high black weave, trimmed in blue to match her blue nail polish and eye shadow. A pair of tight capri pants hugged her large but shapely thighs. She must've felt Gucci and Tionna staring at her because she cast her blue contact lenses in their direction.

"Damn." Gucci rolled her eyes.

"Don't try to hide it, bitches, because I smell it." The woman snapped her fingers, jiggling her icy bangles. Her clear-heeled pumps clicked against the broken concrete as she made her way over to them. "For as much food as y'all asses done devoured in my house, I know you ain't gonna act stink over a punk-ass blunt!" Her voice was way louder than it needed to be.

"Don't cause a scene, ma," Gucci said through clenched teeth.

"Cause a scene? Gucci, your mother *is* the scene!" She spun around so that her daughter could see she still had it, as if the belly shirt didn't show enough.

"Hey, Ms. Ronnie." Tionna smiled.

"What's up, T.T. baby." Ronnie leaned in and hugged her. "Girl, you know I've been praying for you, right? It's a terrible thing that happened to you, but the devil is a lie, and as sure as my ass is black, the truth shall be revealed." She stomped her foot for emphasis. "Me and ya mama raised y'all to be warriors, Tionna, so I know you're gonna be alright." Ronnie waggled her right hand in the air. "As long as you keep him first, you'll always be alright."

Gucci rolled her eyes at her mother. "Listen to you talking 'bout praise him and you over here trying to hit the weed. That ain't very Christian, Mama."

Ronnie cut her eyes at her youngest child. "And?" She placed her hands on her hips. "I believe that we all have a right to receive the Lord's blessing, and he sure blessed the world with cannabis, so pass that so I can receive." Gucci sucked her teeth and handed her mother the blunt. "So," Ronnie addressed Tionna, "what you got lined up for yourself?"

Tionna shrugged. "I don't know. I guess I'll just kick back for a minute to get my head together and then plan my next move."

Ronnie took a deep drag of the blunt and expelled the smoke through her nose. "Kick back? Kicking back ain't gonna pay the bills, Tionna."

"I know, Ms. Ronnie. I just got a lot on my mind right now

and I need to clear my head so I can focus on getting right, ya know?"

"No, I don't know. When Gucci's daddy got knocked, I fell all to pieces. Though he might not have been the most upwardly mobile nigga, he kept me laid and paid!" Ronnie declared. "Having leaned on men most of my life, I had no clue how I was gonna do for us." She nodded toward Gucci. "We had a little money, but with the way I was used to spending, it didn't last very long. It wasn't until I damn near hit the bottom of the glass that I finally decided to get off my ass and make something happen for myself."

"Is that when you started working for the post office?" Tionna asked.

Ronnie twisted her lips. "Hell nah. That's when I went and got me another baller! You better get back in the saddle, T."

The girls damn near fell over laughing. Ronnie was a trip and a half, but one thing you could always count on her for was some hard truth. Tionna knew that her back was against the wall, but she didn't want to face it. Her mother had always tried to drill independence and education into her, but Tionna couldn't see it. She saw the power her aunts and cousins held over men with what they had between their legs and figured that would be a greater asset to her than a diploma. Seeing her man carted off to prison and all their possessions seized had snatched the wool from her eyes and showed her what it really was. She'd spent countless nights since Duhan's arrest crying and stressing over what she was going to do. The only thing that kept her standing straight was the fact that she wouldn't allow the haters from her old neighborhood to see her broken.

Still, it didn't change the fact that she was on her last legs and would have to shit or get off the pot.

"You ain't gotta worry about me, Ms. Ronnie. I might've slipped, but I haven't fallen just yet," Tionna assured her.

"I know that's right." Ronnie gave her a high five. A blue Saturn with two girls riding in the front coasted by and beeped the horn. "Who the hell was that?" Ronnie asked, trying to get a look at the duo.

"It looked like Billy." Gucci craned her neck to get a last look.

"You mean William," Ronnie snickered.

"Ma, you need to stop."

"Gucci, you know that chick is rougher than most."

Gucci sucked her teeth. "Billy ain't gay; she got a man, and a fine one at that."

"That don't mean shit. You ain't never heard the phrase *down low*?" Ronnie asked.

Seeing Reese made Tionna think of Sharon, and that put her in a sour mood. "If you ask me, there's something wrong with that whole shot-out-ass crew. From that stinking ass Reese to that crazy bitch Yoshi."

"Now that ain't right." Ronnie pointed her finger at Tionna accusingly.

"I ain't the one who put it out there, I'm just repeating what I heard," Tionna defended.

"Yo, I heard that before Jah got killed, he told Yoshi that he was fucking Reese, too, and that's what made her wig out," Gucci said.

"It wouldn't surprise me, because all the bitches in that family are nasty as hell." Tionna folded her arms.

"I can't cosign that because they mama is good peoples," Ronnie said. "Little Sharon need her ass beat, and Reese just can't get right. If them rich-ass rappers would've run a train on me, my ass would be paid."

"Don't no rappers want that worn-ass coochie," Gucci teased her.

"Don't underestimate ya mama, Gucci: this old pussy still got the snap of a bitch half your age!"

"Ma, you need to quit." Gucci laughed. "Yo, speaking of Jah, you seen Tech lately?"

"Who, little purse-snatching-ass Tech?" Tionna cocked her head.

"He ain't little no more, T. That nigga done grew in paper and status," Gucci said.

"If you know like I know, ya little hot ass will stay away from him. That boy is rotten, inside and out. Tionna, you better talk to ya girl," Ronnie warned. Ronnie might've been out of the loop, but she knew what the streets said about Tech and the young crew he ran with. They whispered that he was the hardest young boy on the streets, but not long ago there had been one harder. Like so many, Jah's eyes had been closed way too early, but it was written that way for him, as it was with all the men in his family. Jah's life came to a tragic end, and where his legacy ended, the reign of the Tech had begun.

"Ain't nobody gotta tell me nothing; I'm grown," Gucci said, snatching the blunt from her mother. "Y'all acting like I'm trying to marry the nigga when all I'm saying is that he can get it."

"A hard head makes a soft ass, Gucci," Ronnie told her.

"Then that must be why mine is pillow soft." Gucci ran her hand down her thigh.

"Young tramp," Ronnie capped.

"Old whore," Gucci mumbled.

"Y'all are a hot damn mess," Tionna added.

Gucci rolled her eyes. "If that ain't the pot."

Ronnie pulled Tionna close to her. "Stop being such a hater, Gucci." She stroked Tionna's head. "You gonna be alright, T. We gonna find you another sponsor with deeper pockets."

"Fuck a pocket; he better have a damn good insurance policy. And if you even think about fucking him, you'd better make sure you're the beneficiary, because Duhan is sure gonna cash it in."

"Duhan is sitting on the Island, waiting on a trip to Auburn or wherever the hell they're sending our babies these days," Ronnie said.

"I ain't worried about that. It's a bullshit case and it ain't gonna stick. Duhan has a good chance at coming home," Tionna protested.

Ronnie folded her arms and looked at Tionna very seriously. "Tionna, they offered him ten years on a cop-out, so it's a good guess that they got some kinda case on him. Sweetie, one thing I've learned from being in the streets is how to spot a sour case. They caught him with his hands in the cookie jar, ma; his chances of beating it are slim to none." Though there was no malice in her tone when she said it, Ronnie's statement still stung Tionna deep in her chest.

When they rushed the crib they found guns, money, weed, and a few E pills. That, coupled with the fact that Duhan was on parole, was enough to cramp his style, and maybe sit him for a few short years, but it was a friend of a friend that was threatening to take him completely out of the game.

From the first time Duhan had brought Lee around, Tionna hadn't cared for him. He carried himself like a prison cat and talked way too much to be anybody of importance, but Duhan's connect, Willie Boy, had vouched for him. Willie was a cinnamon snake whose people hailed from some out-of-the-way spot just shy of the Dominican Republic. Willie got birds wholesale from his great-uncle, who was fighting a case and needed to get his weight up. Duhan would in turn cop weight from Lee, who was Willie's liaison, at a way cheaper clip that what the rest of Harlem was getting it at. This was how Duhan and his team were able to come up so fast. "He talks too much, but you can count on him. That's my dude," was how Willie had introduced Lee to Duhan. Lee was a CI that they'd put on Willie during a three-year investigation that caused the arrests of more than thirty people, including Duhan and Tionna.

"I say fuck a snitch," Gucci said, reading her best friend's face. "He better not let me catch him while I'm dirty, or else it's lights the fuck out." She slashed the air as if she were cutting someone up with an imaginary knife. She knew the whole spiel about Duhan's fall and who had pushed him off the ledge. She'd heard that Lee had been spotted around Harlem and the Bronx, but didn't want to upset her friend with news of his freedom.

Ronnie spit on the floor. "A creepy-ass snitch took my daddy, my man, and two of my brothers. I say fuck him, his mama, and his ugly-ass kids." Snitches were a sore spot for Ronnie.

"I'm not worried about it, he's gonna get what he's got coming," Tionna said. Since Duhan had gotten the Discovery Package, they'd be trying to think of a fitting punishment for

Lee and his disloyalty. Most of Duhan's clique had gone down with him on the indictment, and the few who were left didn't have the nuts or the loyalty to do what needed to be done. Tionna hadn't decided how, but she was dead set on avenging her man.

"Enough of the talk about the rats and their cheese. What you heifers getting into tonight?" Ronnie asked, lighting a Newport 100.

"Probably nothing. I gotta go see Duhan in the morning, so I'm keeping it close to home," Tionna told her.

"No the hell you're not," Gucci said indignantly. "Your ass is coming with me to Mochas."

"Gucci, I got shit to take care of in the morning; I ain't trying to be out clubbing."

"It ain't a club, T, it's a lounge, and don't worry, I won't keep you up all night. Them dyke guards on Rikers Island will still be able to grope you tomorrow."

Tionna's brow furrowed. It had been a while since she'd gone out and had a good time, but with less than a stack in her purse she didn't feel right. "I don't know, Gucci, I ain't got nothing to wear, and who's gonna watch the kids?"

"Mommy will watch them, won't you, Ma?" Gucci gave Ronnie a puppy-dog look.

Ronnie snaked her neck. "Bitch, you must've fell and knocked loose what little bit of sense the weed ain't already robbed you of. You know good and damn well that I ain't watching nobody's kids, especially not on no Friday." She shook her head as if the very thought was dreadful. "Nah, baby, y'all can pop fingers and shake ass another night, this one here belongs to me."

"Not even for a forty of Audubon?" Gucci tempted her.

Ronnie hesitated. She could almost feel the sweet smoke tickling her nose. "A'ight, I'll keep them until two."

"Ma, you know it don't really get going until about one; give us more than an hour," Gucci tried to bargain.

"Gucci, I gave you life and my Friday night, what more you want from me?"

"Ma, give us until at least three."

"I'll give you until two thirty, two forty-five if you bring me a Crave Case from White Castle on your way home."

"Mommy, I'm already getting you the smoke; how you gonna tack that on?"

Ronnie placed her hands on her hips and let the cigarette bob between her lips when she spoke. "Look, if you don't like the way I'm putting it down, stay ya asses in the house instead of hoeing."

"Two thirty is good, thank you," Tionna said, nudging Gucci's leg.

"When they come back from the store I'll take them to McDonald's and run 'em on in." Ronnie held her hand out.

"What?" Gucci looked at her funny.

"You said watch 'em, not feed 'em." She looked back and forth between Gucci and Tionna. Gucci looked at Tionna, who just shrugged her shoulders. Grudgingly, Gucci handed her mother a twenty. Ronnie tucked it in her bra and smiled. "Two thirty, bitches. Don't have me come looking for you." She strutted across the street. Cords said something slick to her, which caused Ronnie to flip him off.

"Your mother is still off da hook." Tionna elbowed Gucci.

"You know ain't nothing changed wit' Mommy. Yo ass into

me for twenty dollars and a favor, so you're gonna ride it to the end, bitch."

"Gucci, I ain't trying to break night wit' ya crazy ass," Tionna warned.

"Ease up, Scary J., we ain't gonna break night, but we're gonna throw it on and have a hella time. Come on." Gucci grabbed Tionna's hand and pulled her off the stoop. "We gonna go catch the Dominicans around the corner to get you right, and then we're gonna dig some of that gangsta shit you got outta them nasty-ass laundry bags. Tonight, Harlem is gonna recognize that a boss bitch is back on the scene!"

CHAPTER 7

"Look at them fucking stoop rats." Reese sneered, looking out the passenger window as the Saturn cruised across 140th Street. All of them got dirty looks, but her eyes lingered on Tionna.

"You're one to talk," Billy said, not bothering to look over at Reese. For as much bullshit as she had going on in her life, she was always trying to pick people apart. It made Billy mad as hell, because that wasn't how she rocked, but they had been down since forever so she tolerated it.

"You can't be serious. I ain't never been nothing like them little whores." Reese brushed a strand of her shoulder-length microbraids from her face. Since she'd had little Alex her face had cleared and was now smooth and healthy-looking. "She so stupid, wanting to fight over a nigga when he's hitting everything in a skirt. That's my word—these little bitches is chicken heads."

"Reese, your ass is too old to be out here indulging in your sister's teenage-ass beef, so knock it off. If anything, that cat Duhan needs to get locked up for sleeping with Sharon's little ass in the first place; fuck beefing about Tionna." Whereas Reese was a brown-sugar tone, Billy's skin was closer to olive leaves. Her hair was braided into two pigtails that dipped just below her shoulders.

"Billy, it ain't even about what's going on between Sharon and that bitch Tionna, it's the fact that she looks down her nose at everybody else. The way she was carrying it you would've thought that Duhan was the second coming of Fritz or some shit. Now look: his ass got knocked and she's back to slumming on this sorry-ass block."

Billy looked at her now. "Reese, you know how it was for us when we were their ages, couldn't nobody tell us shit! Me, you, Yoshi, and even Rhonda's crazy ass, we were living like ghetto divas, but look how it played out for the crew," Billy reminded her.

"Whatever." Reese tried to brush her statement off, but it lingered in the back of her mind. In their prime, the quartet of young hood honeys kicked off a series of events that would be whispered in the same breaths as Larry Davis's famed police battle. Each of the girls was dancing on the edge of a different razor. Rhonda and her head games, Yoshi and her torn heart, and Reese with her need for love . . . it all ended horribly. The murders of Rhonda and Jah had taken a piece of them all into the afterlife with them, but it was Yoshi who would take the longest to heal. No matter how much time had passed, her heart would always bleed for Jah.

"But I ain't really trying to stroll down memory lane," Billy said, voicing what both of them felt, "but you do need to check your little sister about the way she's out here living. There's too much shit going around for her to fuck around and end up burnt or . . ." Billy let her words trail off, but it was already out there.

Reese had made the mistake of letting a pit full of vipers convince her that they were all garter snakes. Since she was a little girl all she'd ever wanted was to be the wife of a star, and in pursuing the infamous Don B., she thought she could taste it. At the end of the day, all she proved to be was light entertainment for him and his crew. The scars to her soul and her womanhood were slowly beginning to heal, but every time she looked at her daughter, Alex, and wondered who her father was, she was reminded of the encounter.

"My sister ain't gonna be me, Billy," Reese said, staring out the window. "I'd kill her before I let her make the mistakes I did."

Billy placed her hand over Reese's. "We ain't gonna let it get that far."

The rest of the ride was spent in silence, each girl's mind clutching at different things. In what seemed like no time they were pulling up on the corner of Ninety-eighth and Madison. Reese looked uncomfortable in the looming shadow of Mount Sinai, but Billy seemed totally at ease as she tapped her fingers on the wheel patiently.

"She ain't out here yet," Reese said with attitude.

"Be easy, she's right over there." Billy pointed to a fair-skinned girl who was speaking with a darker young lady. The dark-skinned young lady was youthful-looking, with the curves of a woman in her prime. The light-skinned girl wore a pair of fitted jeans and a long-sleeved black blouse. Her long, wavy hair was pulled back into a ponytail and she wore no makeup, but there was no hiding her natural beauty.

"Who the hell is she talking to?" Billy peered in the rearview mirror. The girl looked familiar, but she couldn't place her.

Reese turned her body all the way around so that she could see. "I'll be damned, ain't that . . . ?"

"Dena, please stop crying before you have me out here balling with your ass." Yoshi dabbed the moisture from her eyes.

"I still can't believe you did this for me," the brown-skinned girl said to Yoshi. She was smiling from ear to ear, but her face was slick with tears. "All my life nobody has ever tried to help me and here you go screwing up the curve."

Yoshi smiled. "Mommy, we girls gotta look out for each other, because the world sure isn't. Besides, I owe you for the strength you showed when I was going through my little drama."

"It was only a phone call," Dena said modestly.

"Sometimes a little goes a long way. It was big of you to reach out to me to see if I was okay, especially in light of what happened to you," Yoshi told her. While she was recovering from her loss, Dena was recovering from tragedies of her own: the betrayal of her lover and the theft of her body. Black Ice was a slick cat who was sought after by all the fast young girls in Harlem, but he had chosen Dena. The young ghetto super-star promised to take Dena into the stratosphere with him, but where he took her there were no stars, only grief.

As it turned out, Black Ice was recruiting young Dena for his stable of whores. She might've been a chicken head, but she was no whore willing to sell her body for money, and he knew this, which was why he used drugs to break her. One night at a big party he hosted, Ice had laced Dena's drink and left her at the mercy of anyone who had the money to spend on her sweet hole. She was never sure how many men had bedded her that night, but from the way her pussy felt afterward, she figured it to be at least a half dozen. As if being gang-raped wasn't enough, the doctors found traces of the HIV virus in one of the semen samples. It had been almost three years since it had happened, and thankfully Dena had yet to test positive, but it was a fear that she would always carry.

The events after the gang rape only made her life more complicated. In retaliation for what had happened, Dena's older brother Shannon had murdered Black Ice and his right-hand man, Shorty. Ice's evil might've been cleansed from the world, but it came at the price of losing her brother. Shannon had been on the run ever since and could never come back to New York for fear of being prosecuted for the murder.

During her recovery, Dena's therapist suggested that she do some volunteer work at a group home for young girls. She reasoned that what Dena had gone through would be an inspiration to some of the girls and it would also help her to find the strength hiding within her, and she was right, because Dena took to social work like a fish to water, which was what brought her to see Yoshi that day.

In addition to being a registered nurse at Mount Sinai, Yoshi's aunt Vivian worked a second job as the director of a group home in Brooklyn. After Yoshi had told her Dena's story of triumph, she had arranged for Dena to enroll in a program that the Department of Social Services was running. The program was designed to train young men and women in the field of social work and eventually find them employment with the city. As if that weren't enough, Vivian had also hooked it up so that Dena could take on an internship at her facility while she was studying for her certificate.

"Yoshi, I can never repay you or Vivian for what y'all have done," Dena said for the umpteenth time.

"Dena, you don't owe me shit, and if you wanna please Vivian, just have your ass to work on time. Other than that, the only person you owe something to is yourself. Live, little girl, let go of that pain and push on."

"I will if you do." Dena extended her hand.

"You've got yourself a deal." Yoshi shook her hand and gave her a hug. "You call me if you need anything."

"I will, and thanks again, Yoshi," Dena said as she departed. Even after the car Yoshi had gotten into had disappeared, Dena was still rooted to the spot, smiling and thinking how she had been blessed with a second chance.

Yoshi said her goodbyes to Dena and hopped into the Saturn. No sooner had she closed the door than she turned to find Reese giving her an inquisitive look. "What?"

"You tell me," Reese shot back.

"Knock it off, Reese. What's up, ma," Billy greeted Yoshi.

"I'm here, can't ask for much more," Yoshi said with a sigh. The years had been the least kind to Yoshibelle, and it had started to show on her face. Under the dome light in the car you could see the dark circles around her eyes. Her skin hadn't completely regained its luster, but at least she was getting her weight back.

Yoshi had been the rebel of the group, using sex as a deadly weapon, until the day when her heart was allowed to taste true love for the first time. She and Jah were like day and night, but there was no mistaking the chemistry between them. In Jah she had found the strength to come in off the streets and in her he had found a reason to hang up his guns. They had finally found the missing pieces to their souls and wanted nothing more than to explore love and life together, until a hail of bullets shattered their picture-perfect image. He had been gunned down while doing security for a rapper named True, in an attempt to find out who had shot Yoshi while trying to kill the rapper. For a long time Yoshi held on not only to the pain of Jah's death but to the feeling that she had caused it. When her mind snapped, nobody thought that she would ever recover, but with the support of her friends and family she had begun to put the pieces back together.

"Ain't that little what's-her-face?" Reese asked, referring to the girl Yoshi had been talking to.

"Yeah, that was little Dena," Yoshi confirmed.

Billy craned her neck. "Damn, I ain't seen her in like two years. She ain't so little no more."

"Your balls are showing, William," Reese teased her.

"Fuck you, slut," Billy shot back. "What're you doing over here with her, Yoshi?"

"Probably getting a checkup. Doesn't that little bitch have the bug?" Reese asked crudely.

"I brought her over here to see my aunt about getting a job. Why don't you get some fucking class, Reese," Yoshi snapped.

"Yoshi, pay this ignorant heifer no mind. I think she's off her meds today," Billy said, trying to smooth it over. Some of the anger drained from Yoshi's face, but the fire still danced in her eyes. "I didn't know you pumped with ol' girls like that?"

"We didn't at first. She remembered me from the video and somehow tracked down my number and called to check on me after Jah died. It started as just seeing how I was feeling and it grew from there. I guess since we had both been some shit we ended up finding strength in each other."

"That must've been one hell of a makeover you gave her," Reese joked. This got Yoshi to laugh.

Billy shook her head. "You're such an ass, Reese."

"The both of y'all are shot out," Yoshi added. "Besides my job, all I did was lend her a few kind words. It's crazy how sometimes the smallest gesture leaves the most lasting impressions."

"Church," Billy chimed in. "But on the real, I think it's dope that you're trying to help the little homegirl out."

"Somebody gotta give a damn about these kids," Yoshi replied.

"I was just telling this one the same thing." Billy cut her eyes at Reese.

"Sharon still out here acting a fool?"

"An ass is more like it," Billy corrected.

"Look, ain't none of y'all bitches no saints, so stop trying to throw my little sister under the bus." Reese sounded offended.

Yoshi leaned forward so that she could see Reese's profile. "Ma, you know us better than that. Anything me or Billy say to you is said out of love. Hate don't live here." Yoshi placed her hand over her heart. "Everybody in this car knows that Sharon is riding a train that ain't gonna do nothing but wreck, and we need to see that she isn't on it when it reaches its final destination."

"Reese, we all came up hard and we all know what's waiting at the end of that concrete rainbow," Billy said, lending her wisdom. "These fast-ass young girls think they've got it all figured out, same as we did, but they don't know shit. It seems like every day another one of these little chicks ends up pregnant or getting something that the doctor can't get rid of, and I can't help but to wonder when we're gonna stop walking into these bullshit setups, but these fraudulent ass niggaz?"

"That's the gospel," Yoshi added. "Reese, you know that at the end of the day we're here for you, but you're gonna handle it however you're gonna handle it, but before you step to your sister, I want you to remember how it played out for little Dena." And Yoshi left it at that.

CHAPTER 8

Tech had the girls drop him off near the D train just off 145th and St. Nicholas and walked the rest of the way, as he often did. Before they peeled out, he instructed them to keep their phones on, but it was more out of habit than necessity. Silk and China were young, but their game and understanding of the life was deeper than most. It was the glue that bound the four orphans.

The sun hadn't fully set, but the dark things of the city streets had already began to stir. Two addicts who looked like little more than hastily dressed pipe cleaners argued on the corner, while a trio of young boys stood around, trying to insti- gate a fight. Neither one of them looked like they had the strength to do much more than take that final blast before drifting off to meet with death. Coming out of the nondescript walkway two buildings from the corner was a bowlegged chick dressed in a plastic skirt and a fur coat that looked like it been woven together from different pieces of discarded carpet. Her face still held the dim glow of what she'd been, but her glassy eyes told the story of what she'd become. She gave Tech the once-over before hopping into an idling Honda Accord parked along the curb. There was a balding white man behind the wheel, tapping his finger nervously against the steering wheel. Tech shook his head when he saw the faint gold glint on his finger. He wondered if his wife knew that he was down in the ghetto, gambling with both their lives.

As soon as Tech stepped into the lobby he heard the music. It wasn't the typical hip-hop song you were likely to hear blasting from one of the upstairs apartments, but something totally out of place in the hood, something darker. *"Wild child, full of grace . . . savior of the human race."* The words were familiar because Tech was made to suffer them whenever he came by, but he never bothered to learn the title of the song. Tech rapped on the door of apartment 3 with his keys and waited.

"You know it's gonna take more than one of y'all to take me in, don't you?" he said with a sharp edge to his voice. His slim, shirtless body teetered back and forth, causing the large medallion hanging from his chain to pound against his chest. It was a red-and-yellow-diamond bust of his favorite Muppet character, Animal.

"I got this under control just fine by myself." She held her Glock lazily in one manicured hand, like they do in the movies. Her blue police uniform hugged her large breasts and thick hips like a second skin. "I see the Animal ain't so rabid when he's on the other end of the pistol." She took a moment to taunt him, which is when he made his move. With blinding speed, Animal knocked the gun from her hand and put her in a reverse choke hold. She struggled, but he was too strong for her.

"Funny how the tables have turned," he whispered in her ear. "Before you say anything, be mindful of your word, because they're what's gonna be etched on your tombstone, pig."

Before Animal could make good on his death threat, she dropped and sent him sailing over her shoulder and onto the king-size bed. He tried to get back to his feet, but she was on him before he could get up, with her weight pinning him to the bed. She outweighed him, but he was able to flip her over and wind up on top. She struggled, but he had her hands pinned firmly above her head. With his free hand, he used her handcuffs to secure her to the bedposts. "Get the fuck off me!" she snapped.

Animal responded by slapping her viciously across her face. "Muthafucka, you ain't in no position to give me orders. I'm running this fucking show, or hadn't you noticed." He motioned toward her cuffed wrists. "Now that I've got your ass in a sling, the question is what I should do with you." He let his eyes roam over her hungrily. When they landed on her breasts, which were straining against the buttons of her uniform shirt, a light bulb went off in his head. With a wicked smile on his face, Animal tore her shirt off and exposed her D-cup bra.

"You'll never get away with it!" She continued to struggle until she was out of breath.

"Sweet bitch, I already have." With a tug, Animal snatched her bra off, exposing her huge breasts, which he proceeded to suck like a starved child. She screamed and called him everything but a child of God, until her screams turned into moans of pleasure. Next, her belt came off, followed by her pants, which revealed that she hadn't worn any panties that day. Animal shoved his fingers roughly inside her, testing her wetness, which he licked off his fingers like frosting. "Your pussy taste like honey, Mrs. Officer, but I wonder if it feels as good as it taste."

"Please don't," she begged, tears streaming down her face.

"I like it when they beg," he replied, undoing his jeans. Animal couldn't have weighed more than 140 pounds on a good day, but he was hung like a quarter horse. She continued to plead, but he ignored her and shoved his entire length roughly inside her. She gasped as if the air had been sucked from her body from the force of entry, but after a few strokes the pain lessened. The thug known to all the NYPD only as Animal was more than ten years her junior, but he was hitting spots that most of the men she'd dealt with had been ignorant of, even her husband. Twenty-five minutes later, she was howling at the moon as both their juices spilled from her pussy and down her thighs.

"Damn you, you little criminal muthafucka, I didn't even come like that on prom night." Her voice was raspy; and she rubbed her thighs together.

"That's because you weren't being fucked by an Animal." He smiled, revealing a mouthful of diamond and gold teeth that spelled out his name across the top row.

"Um, you say the streets gave you the name Animal, but the way you just dug my back out, I think you got it from one of your old girlfriends."

"I guess that will continue to be one of life's greatest mysteries." Animal rose from the bed and stretched. Grabbing a towel from the recliner, he made his way to the bathroom.

"And where are you going?" she asked, lying on her back and looking over at him.

"To wash my ass, where do you think?"

"Boy, you better get over here and take these handcuffs off. My shift starts in forty-five minutes and I ain't trying to be late." She jiggled the handcuffs for emphasis.

"I don't know, I kinda like you like that. Let me think on it for a minute and get right back with you." He winked and closed the bathroom door behind him.

"You better quit playing, Animal, you hear me? Animal? Animal!"

It didn't take long before Tech's multiple locks were undone and the door came open. Tech found himself staring at a beautiful caramel honey dressed in a blue uniform. Her hair was mussed and her shirt was buttoned wrong, so it was clear that she hadn't come here to address the overpowering smell of weed coming from the apartment, or the blasting music coming from the one next door. Tech smiled, but she didn't.

"Hey, Officer Grady," he greeted her with a toothy smile.

She rolled her eyes. "Fuck you, Tech. See you later, boo," she said over her shoulder, before storming past Tech. She and Tech had never gotten along, but they tolerated each other for the sake of Animal and the benefit of having a cop at their disposal. Grady thought Tech disliked her because she was a married woman sleeping with a kid young enough to be her son, but that wasn't it. Grady was actually cool as hell, but Tech had a natural dislike for her because she was a cop and therefore his sworn enemy.

Tech stepped through the door and was greeted by Animal, who was dressed in baggy jeans and a tank top, with orange slippers on his feet. His hair looked like an explosion at a hair-weave factory, but he didn't seem to mind it too much. His attention was more focused on the plastic cup in his hand, which held only God knew what.

" 'Sup wit' you, Tech-Nine," Animal greeted him in his lazy drawl. He had the face of a boy just reaching manhood, but the voice of a small child, which is why he didn't talk much publicly. Nobody was stupid enough to make fun of him, but he was self-conscious about it.

"Just making the rounds." Tech gave him a pound and then a half hug.

"I hear that." Animal lit the joint that he'd just realized was tangled in his hair, just behind his ear. "So, what brings you to the zoo?" Animal picked up an African mask that was lying on top of the box it had been shipped in and held it in front of his face. "You finally ready to sell your soul to the devil?"

"Nigga, you need to lay off that sip," Tech said, taking the mask from Animal. He flipped it over and examined the price tag. All he could do was sigh and place it as gently as he could back on top of the box. Animal was quick to drop ridiculous amounts of money on things that Tech considered junk, but it was one of the youngster's few joys so Tech didn't ride him about it.

Masks and artifacts from different cultures cluttered most of the living room in apartment 2, and what space they didn't take up held books that you were more likely to see in a history professor's office than a street nigga's crib. The thing most people didn't know about Animal was that he was far more than just a street dude: he was also a very deep thinker. He attacked the streets with the same passion he used attacking his books, always paying attention and never moving on a whim.

When Animal handled business, he did it with tact, but his lifestyle was another story.

"At least you know I'll never catch a cold. Come on, the goons are on the other side." He led Tech through a huge beaded archway that led to apartment 3. The building manager was a fiend, so Animal persuaded him to rent out the two apartments for a few ounces. Once he got the keys, he knocked the walls down and connected them. The manager got pissed, but Animal didn't give a fuck, and most people knew better than to argue with him when his mind was set to something.

When they passed through into the second apartment they were engulfed by weed smoke. Hard faces and red eyes looked up at Tech through the mist. Brasco and the young boy Ashanti were flicking away at PS3 joysticks, manipulating the moves of some of the leagues' all-time greatest players on the wide-screen television. From the look on Brasco's face, he was getting the short end of the stick. The way Ashanti kept laughing, it would only be a matter of time before Brasco lost his temper and wanted to fight; he was a hothead like that. Sitting in the corner was Nefertiti, the joker. His dreads bobbed up and down to the music Animal was playing, while he crushed pretty green buds of sweet sticky on an album cover. They were all crew, but these were Animal's dogs, so Tech let him hold the leash.

"Fuck is you doing?" Animal snatched the album cover from Nefertiti, spilling the weed on the floor. Animal gently brushed off the cover and inspected it for damage.

"Nigga, that was that bomb sticky." Nefertiti sprang to his feet.

Animal sneered at Nefertiti, causing him to step back cautiously. "Do I look like I give a fuck about them crumbs when you're using my autographed copy of *Waiting for the Sun* to break them up on?"

"What kinda gay-ass shit is that?" Ashanti spoke up from the crate he was sitting on. He was an undersized fourteen-year-old who had the voice of an old man.

"Gay, do you know how much pussy Jim Morrison was getting when The Doors were popping?" Animal schooled him.

"You do be listening to some cocksucker shit," Nefertiti snickered. When he saw the fire that had been lit in Animal's eyes, the smirk faded.

"What you call me?" Animal tossed the album cover to the ground.

"Chill, blood—" Ashanti began, but Animal cut him off.

"Mind ya fucking business, Ashanti," Animal snapped, before turning his attention back to Nefertiti. "You trying to call me a faggot, son?"

"Animal, chill, I wasn't calling you nothing." Nefertiti raised his hands in surrender. Even though they were like family, he had a deep fear of Animal, as most people did. When he was off his meds it wasn't unheard of for him to become violent. Nefertiti had been with him when Animal had stabbed a kid with an ink pen for making fun of the way he wore his jeans.

"Animal, cool the fuck out," Tech said, trying to step in, but Animal wasn't trying to hear it.

"Nah, big homey, he wanna be calling muthafuckas out so ima make him back that shit up." Animal pulled a small black gun from the back of his belt. "Talk cocksucker shit now, *blood*."

Nefertiti looked to his crew, who had abandoned their

video game and were watching the scene unfolding in apartment 3. "Dawg, chill out." His voice had dropped to barely a whisper. Animal's face twisted into a horrible mask as he pulled the trigger, squirting Nefertiti in his face with water. When everyone realized that Animal hadn't put Nefertiti's brains on the far wall, they all fell over laughing.

"Nef, you was straight shook." Animal squirted him twice more.

"Check his pants to see if he shit on hisself," Brasco added his two cents.

"Man, fuck all y'all." Nefertiti wiped his face. "That was some bullshit, Animal. What if I had been strapped and popped you by accident?"

"You wasn't gonna shoot shit, because you ain't got ya gun on you, and that's part of the problem." Animal squirted him one last time for good measure. "Yo, Nef, how many times I gotta tell you about leaving ya gat in the crib?"

"Come on with the lecture," Nefertiti said, trying to get out of it, but he should've known better.

"Fuck a lecture. I'm trying to tell your stupid ass of something that could save your life in the future. Son, you can't be running around shooting and doing shit to people and then think you can be a civilian when you feel like it. This army," he motioned toward their collective, "is constantly at war, and as soldiers we carry it as such. You can't give out wrong and then not be prepared when it's your turn for karma to come back, and trust that it will. All of us gotta pay forward tomorrow what we did yesterday: it's the natural law of things."

"I can give a fuck about tomorrow as long as I can eat good today, my nigga. As long as the streets still talk about me after I'm dust, I don't give a fuck about nothing else." Ashanti might've been the smallest and thus the least imposing of the crew, but he was arguably the most bloodthirsty.

"I know that's right." Brasco gave him dap. "They're always gonna remember the legends, and that's what the fuck we gonna be, legends!"

"Spoken like some true riders." Animal put Ashanti in a playful headlock and faked punches at Brasco. "You see this, my nigga?" he addressed Tech. "This that *real* street love right here; fuck what you read in a book or seen in a movie. We several bodies, but we share one heart. We kill and we die as one. These little niggaz will tear the chief of police's head off if he tried to come at me wrong, because they know I'd do the same for them, and that's how family give it up." He walked over and stood directly in front of Tech. Whatever he'd been sipping had his eyes glassy, but his words were solid. "When you family, you untouchable."

"Word," Ashanti, Brasco, and Nefertiti said in unison.

Tech studied his young homey for a long moment. He knew Animal wasn't testing him but searching for approval. He had shaped his little crew into a formidable little team and their names had been ringing in the hood before any of them could legally buy a drink. Animal and his young killers were destined for either greatness or death; anything less was unacceptable. Tech had taught him that, and he'd passed it on to his l'il ones, as Jah had passed it on to him. Thinking on his old mentor took him back to the night Animal had come to his attention.

Tech had never been a heavy drinker, but that night he was trying to go over the top. Jah would've been twenty-three that day. It had been a little over two years since he'd been killed, but the wound on Tech's heart was still fresh.

Tech sat perched on a bar stool in the Lenox Lounge, throwing back shots of 1738 like it was going out of style. It had been Jah's drink of choice just before he died. Tech was never sure exactly who had turned him on to it, but he swore by it. Most of the cats in Harlem knew Tech and what he was about and as a result they gave him a wide berth, but not everyone exercised such caution. Two such cats were Bump and Eddy, who were sitting in the back of the lounge, plotting. They were two pissants who weren't worth their salt, but they were determined to be recognized as heavyweights. When they saw Tech stagger from the bar, they saw it as an opportunity.

Tech was so twisted that he never even saw the two haters following him up the block. He was fumbling in his pocket for a light for the blunt that dangled from his mouth when he heard the familiar click. "Damn," was all he could say, because he knew he had been caught slipping.

"You know what it is, so turn around real slow," Bump ordered.

"Be easy." Tech turned slowly. "Y'all can have this little bit of jewelry, just take it easy with those hammers." He kept his hands in the air and his eyes on his assailants. The fact that they weren't wearing masks would normally have been unnerving, but Tech could tell that the robbers weren't killers. He knew their faces, but not their names. It didn't matter. Harlem was too small for him not to bump into them again, and when he did, it was gonna get ugly.

"Ain't no fun when the rabbit got the gun, huh?" Bump taunted him.

"Come up off ya shit," Eddy barked. He tried to look hard, but Tech could smell the fear rolling off him.

Tech began emptying his pockets onto the curb, but kept his eyes on Bump. He might not have known his name, but he knew his face and would make it his business to see it again on different terms.

"Fuck you looking at." Bump pointed the gun at Tech's face.

"Man, stop talking to this nigga and let's get outta here," Eddy said, picking up the contents of Tech's pockets. He knew they were making a mistake by running up on Tech, and initially wanted no part of it, but Bump wouldn't be swayed, so he had to ride with his homeboy.

"I know you ain't eyeballing me?" Bump cocked the hammer. Outwardly he was trying to act hard, but inside he was scared to death, and it was that that made him angrier than Tech's glare. Without warning, Bump slammed the gun into the side of Tech's head. "Don't be muthafucking looking at me!"

Spots danced before Tech's eyes, but he didn't lose consciousness. He tried to stagger to his feet, only to have Bump kick him back down. "Did I tell you to get up, pussy?" Bump taunted him.

"Man, we got the shit, let's just go." Eddy danced in place.

"Yeah, why don't you take your friend's advice," Tech said, struggling to control the urge to rush the gunman.

Just the sound of his voice made Bump flinch, which sent him over the edge. "You trying to tell me what to do, like I'm some pussy?" Tech ignored him. "Nigga, you hear me talking?"

"Let's go," Eddy tried, futilely.

"Nah, ima do this nigga," Bump declared, surprising the hell out of Eddy.

"Man, I didn't sign on for no murder," Eddy told him.

"Shut the fuck up and stop crying!" Bump shouted. He turned his crazed eyes back to Tech. "Yeah, I'm gonna bust ya head for every cat you ever blasted on in the hood, bitch nigga!" Just as Bump added pressure to the trigger, a bottle shattered against his head. The gun went off, shattering the car window just over Tech's head. Bump tried to right himself but was met by a blur of motion.

A frail little boy dressed in a dirty hoodie rushed Bump, fists striking him like flashes of lightning. When Bump tried to turn the gun on the little boy, he sank his teeth into the shooter's forearm and held on for dear life. Eddy tried to help his partner, but Tech tripped him up. The little boy shook his head violently, trying to tear clean through Bump's arm. The boy fought the good fight, but Bump outweighed him by almost a hundred pounds. He slammed the little boy viciously into the wall, dazing him. Bump's arm was on fire and he couldn't feel his fingers, but they were still able to find the trigger of his pistol.

Most children, and even grown men, would've been terrified staring at their own demise, but not the wild-haired boy. With Bump's blood staining his lips and chin, he stared up defiantly and said, "Go ahead, nigga, set me free. I ain't long for this world nohow." Before Bump could grant the boy's death wish, his head exploded in a mass of crimson.

The little boy stared at Bump's body curiously as his life drained into the gutter just off the curb. A few feet away, his partner lay in a heap. His neck was twisted almost completely around, and his eyes stared lifelessly into space. Standing in the center of the carnage, holding Eddy's still-smoking gun, was Tech. The little boy's face was a look of curiosity; Tech's was one of disappointment. Not only disappointment from allowing himself to get caught up there, but he also wished he could've inflicted more punishment before Eddy and Bump died.

Then the little boy picked himself up off the ground and stepped out into the light, allowing Tech to get a good look at him. His long hair had a nice texture, but it was matted and dirty, much like his clothes. It was obvious that he wasn't doing well. The more Tech stared at him, the more he realized that he knew the boy. He was the little brother of a kid name Justice, whom Tech knew by association through the Harlem underworld. The last he'd heard, Justice had caught life on a murder beef.

"Yo, you Jus little brother, right?" Tech asked. The little boy nodded. "What's ya name again?"

The little boy pondered the question before answering. "These days they call me Animal," he wiped his mouth with the back of his sleeve, "though I can't imagine why," he said sarcastically.

Tech looked over at Bump's body and remembered how the boy had attacked him. "A'ight, Animal, I'm Tech. Son, I know you seen me around ya brother, but you don't know me like that, so why the hell would you rush to save me like that, knowing you could've got blasted?"

Animal shamefully lowered his head when he spoke. "I didn't get that dude to save you: I've been planning on killing these muthafuckas for three weeks."

Tech was confused. "Why?"

Animal stared at Tech quizzically before answering, "Because they kept fucking with me. Bum-ass-nigga this, dirty-muthafucka that."

"So you wanted them dead because they snapped on you?"

"Not just because they were snapping on me, because they needed killing. Fam, to most of y'all, this concrete jungle is a playground, but to me it's home. When you live in the jungle you have to live by its rules; the strong get to make it to tomorrow while the weak become food. I can't be nobody's food, man; you don't know what that shit is like." Animal turned away so that Tech wouldn't see him on the verge of tears.

Tech's mind momentarily took him back to a place he had long tried to forget. "Yes, I do," he said solemnly. In Animal he saw what Jah must've seen in him all those years ago, and even if his mouth had yet to say it, he already knew what had to be done. "Don't worry about it, my nigga," he draped his arm around Animal's frail shoulders, "you ain't never gonna have to worry about being nobody's food again."

"This nigga is high." Ashanti's squeaky voice brought Tech out of his daydream.

"Nah, I was just thinking about some business," Tech lied.

"This dude is always thinking. Fuck calling you Tech, you the Scientist," Nefertiti joked.

"That's why I'm in charge, baby boy," Tech shot back. "But check it, y'all little niggaz ready to earn ya keep," Tech addressed the youngsters.

"All day," Brasco assured him.

"Then put that muthafucking joystick down and pay attention. Y'all remember the white boy I had y'all sitting on downtown."

"Yeah, the nigga wit' the haze," Nefertiti recalled.

"That's the one. His ass is a five-course banquet and y'all are the guests of honor. Y'all gonna get a few stacks apiece and all you find, all you keep when you rush this pussy. I need this to go down ASAP, y'all understand?"

Nefertiti made a funny face.

"What?"

Nefertiti could feel Animal's cold stare on him, but he was too afraid of Tech not to speak. "I'm saying . . . ah, me and fam," he nodded at Animal, "was supposed to crash the listening party tonight."

"What listening party?" Tech wanted to know.

Animal flashed Nefertiti a dirty look before answering Tech. "Ain't about nothing, man. Them niggaz from Big Dawg is supposed to be having a little prelistening party tonight at Mochas and we was good if we wanted to roll through. I know how you feel about the boy Don B., so I didn't bother to drop it on you."

"You're damn right I feel some type of way about that muthafucka, and any nigga up under him ends up living on borrowed time," Tech said venomously. Though Don B. had had nothing to do with Jah's murder, Tech still held him responsible for the events that caused it. Jah had been working as a bodyguard for an up-and-coming rapper named True when those cats were trying to come for his head. At the time, it seemed like the coolest thing in the world to young Tech, but it had all turned out to be bullshit. The dudes who were after True had finally caught him slipping, and Jah had ended up going along for the ride. Tech felt that if Jah hadn't been dealing with Don B. and True, he might still be alive.

"Them niggaz is getting wild paper," Nefertiti said.

Tech turned on Nefertiti. "We getting paper, too, dawg. What you trying to say you ain't eating?"

"Nef, shut the fuck up 'fore I smack you, B," Animal

warned him. "Tech, I respect what you saying, but I don't see the harm in taking this nigga's hospitality if he keeps offering it. Everybody in the hood knows I ain't no fucking rapper, so he's wasting his time chasing me."

"Animal, it ain't even about that. It's about the kinda karma that nigga got on him: you don't want no part of that, little brother."

"Tech, I can handle it. Trust in your brother, man." Animal's mind was apparently made up.

Tech exhaled loudly. "You know what, do what the fuck you wanna do, Animal. You can go party with them shifty-ass niggaz if you want, but make sure these knucklehead mutha-fuckas handle business before you get to partying; feel me?"

Animal paused for a minute and just stared at Tech. He knew that he wasn't trying to play him, but he didn't like to be talked down to in front of Ashanti and the others. In their eyes, he was just as much of a boss as Tech. "Man, you be too up-tight sometimes. Y'all niggaz get ya shit," Animal told his crew.

"Where the fuck y'all going?" Tech asked.

Animal tucked his gun into his pants and slipped a track jacket on to conceal it. "You said you wanted a nigga dead, so we going to kill him, big brother," Animal said sarcastically and slipped out the door. The others sat around exchanging uncomfortable glances for a few minutes before following Animal out of the apartment, leaving Tech alone with his thoughts.

Only when he heard the door click shut did Tech exhale. Though Animal did grown-man things, he was still technically a child, and sometimes the traits showed. Animal was in the streets like the rest of them, but he wasn't like them. He had layer to his character, and untold potential, but Animal was hardheaded. He could give Animal all the warnings in the world, but a man-child was going to do as he pleased. Tech just hoped that he grew out of his fascination with the great and powerful Don before he got a real taste of how the Big Dawgz played. Thinking on it, Tech wasn't sure if he was worried more about what Don B. would end up trying to do to Animal, or what Animal was going to end up doing to him.

PART 2

THE BOSS BITCH IS BACK

CHAPTER 9

The minute Tionna stepped out of her building, she knew her night was going to go sour. At the same time as Gucci pulled up, Sharon was coming out of Rock Head's building. Her hair looked a hot mess and she was walking like she had just been fucked by a mule. When she saw Tionna she tried to straighten herself up as best she could, but it was a poor effort. Sharon walked by, sashaying her hips and glaring at Tionna like she wanted her to keel over and die. Tionna's first thoughts were to grab her by her cheap-ass weave and mop the stoop with her, but she let it go.

"Washed-up ass," Sharon mumbled when Tionna crossed her path to get in the van.

"Keep playing little girl and you're gonna get a spanking," Tionna sang.

"I doubt that, boo. You might've been the shit back in the days, but fresh meat is always the order of the day," Sharon shot back and kept walking down the block.

"I can't stand that little bitch," Tionna said, opening the van door.

"You want me to fuck her up?" The voice coming from the back startled her. She turned around and saw two grinning faces staring back at her. She had thought it was just going to be her and Gucci, but of course Gucci had to bring the peanut gallery.

Tracy sat in the back row, smoking a cigarette and sipping something Tionna couldn't identify because it was wrapped in a paper bag. Knowing her, it was some type of beer. Tracy always needed something to kick-start her engine before they went out. She was older than the rest of the girls by a few years, but they'd known her since forever and she'd always been cool. It was Tracy who would go to the liquor store for them when they were too young to buy alcohol. Her doll-like face was still pretty, but age and hard living was starting to catch up with her. The eighties had come and gone, but Tracy still held fast, enjoying booze, men, and cocaine, not necessarily in that order. She and Boots were the wild cards of their crew. Tracy's life might've been like something out of a Treasure E. Blue novel, but Boots was in a class by herself.

Born Earnestine Johnson, Boots was the definition of a hood rat. She had spent more time bouncing around from project to project than a repeat offender being shuffled through the state prison system. A touch of adult acne and a slight overbite took away from her face, but she had the build of a brick house. She had an ass like Pinky and breasts like Carmen Hayes, with the good sense to learn how to use both from an early age. It was whispered around the hood that she could make a man cum in less than sixty seconds. This probably explained why she had six kids by three different dudes. Boots was what the hood called a breeder: if you so much as sneezed on her, she was pregnant. Most of her baby daddies had been hit-and-run situations, but the last one actually loved her, even though she singlehandedly flushed his life down the toilet.

When she met Bernie he was in his second year at St. Johns and already being scouted by the pros. Back then, Boots already had two kids, but Bernie looked past that and got at her anyway. All his friends tried to warn him about Boots, but he was in love with that sweet hole. The next thing you knew, she turned up pregnant and Catholic, because she suddenly didn't believe in abortions. Instead of being sour about it, Bernie manned up and took care of his new baby as well as the kids Boots already had, while still trying to juggle college and basketball. It was sweet for a minute, but it wasn't long before Boots showed her true colors and was back up to her old tricks. Bernie had heard the rumors about her sneaking around, but it wasn't until he saw her with his own eyes that he snapped. Had it not been for the patch of ice he slipped on while chasing her, he would've surely killed Boots that night. Unfortunately for Bernie, he tore a ligament in his ankle and his basketball career was sidelined. He tried to go back to college and even did a short stint overseas, but it seemed like every time he was about to get a break, Boots would pop out another baby. Bernie's dreams to get out of the hood died with his basketball career and he ended up just another fallen legend who was working odd jobs and selling weed to keep food on his ever-growing family's table.

"Damn, Tionna, I can't think of the last time your ass hung out with us," Tracy commented while taking a swig from her paper bag. Tionna took one whiff and knew for sure that it was beer.

"Me either. I missed y'all bitches," Tionna fronted. She saw Gucci looking at her through the rearview mirror and stuck her middle finger up.

"So you back down here now?" Boots asked from the backseat.

"For the time being," Tionna assured her. "Me living back on Fortieth is a temporary situation, believe that."

"I hear you. With me living right on top of the damn bodega, you know I get it all firsthand. These little muthafuckas keep the block jumping," Tracy added.

"Tracy, for as much time as you spend on the stoop, stop fronting like you don't love this hood," Boots said.

"And all the drama that comes with it," Gucci added.

Tracy looked from Gucci to Boots. "Oh, so I'm the only one who hugs this block? We all came up on this raggedy-ass block and I don't see none of y'all make a speedy exit up off it!"

"You a lie. As soon as we get this shit cleared up with my baby, I'm so fucking outta here," Tionna added. The car was suddenly very quiet. Everybody knew that Duhan had been caught by the balls, but it still hadn't set in with Tionna. "What, y'all looking like you know something I don't?" She looked around at her girls.

"Nothing, T, we're all just concerned," Gucci said, trying to ease some of the tension.

"Concerned about what? They ain't got shit but the word of a snitch and the little bit of shit they caught at the house."

"Sometimes that's all it takes," Tracy said, more to herself than anyone else.

Tionna sucked her teeth. "First Ronnie and now y'all; why does it seem like everybody is wishing prison on my nigga?"

"Tionna, you know better than that. We fight like cats and dogs, but at the end of the day we're still family and we wanna see Duhan get out as bad as you do," Gucci assured her.

"How is Duhan, with his big-head self?" Boots asked.

Tionna sighed. "Stressing hisself, and me. That nigga act like I'm Superwoman or some shit for the way he has me running around all the time. Go see this one; I need you to snatch something from that one; you checked in with my lawyer. Word to mine: this shit is starting to take its toll."

"That's what happens when you're a ride-or-die chick. My baby's father had my ass on that musty-ass bus every weekend for the first three years of his bid, before I finally wised up and stepped off," Tracy said.

"That's you and him. I'm always gonna ride for Duhan," Tionna said with conviction.

"You say that now, but what if they end up hitting him with some time? For as much as you might love a nigga, becoming a prisoner's wife changes the rules of the game. I know you're a rider, so you gonna be on point with the visits, but what about the emotional stress? While time is standing still for him, you're out here becoming an old maid. Baby, that's a hell of a sentence for a young girl like you. In a sense, you're literally doing the time with him, because your life is now dictated by the state, too," Tracy said.

Tionna frowned. "How you figure I ain't the one locked up?"

Tracy looked at her quizzically. "Because when you say, 'Baby, I'm gonna ride with you,' it entails just that, *riding* with him. Riding God knows how many hours to see him, helping with the appeal, staying faithful to a man who you can't touch when and how you want; and let's not even go into the financial side of it. Tionna, even with the blessing of the first African American president, the economy is still so fucked up that you'll be working two jobs and selling weed just to make sure he has cigarettes and toiletries."

"I hear what you saying, Tracy, but even if he catches heavy numbers I can't abandon Duhan like that. He took care of me when he was in the world."

Tracy laughed. "Tionna, I would never disrespect my nigga Duhan like that. You're supposed to hold him down to the best of your ability, but promising him that you're gonna put your life on hold completely is putting a lot of expectation on you, and you know how your ass loves your freedom."

Though Tracy had raised a very good point, Tionna would never admit it publicly. She had often thought about what life might be like if Duhan blew trial. The copout was eight to ten years, and if he blew, those numbers were likely to double upon sentencing, and he'd have to eat a good chunk of it before they could even think about getting his appeal heard. She was already feeling left for dead and he'd only been gone for eighteen months. She was twenty-five with two kids and no skills: her life was already complicated enough, without going through the motions of Duhan being locked down until his kids were in high school. She had to ask herself: if the judge called his number, could she really hold him down like she'd promised?

"Fuck all the dumb shit," Gucci cut in. She tossed Tionna a bag of weed. "Roll that up. We gonna hit the liquor store, blow some trees, and party like rock stars, because this is a special occasion."

"And what's that?" Tionna asked, splitting the philly open with a twenty-five-cent razor.

Gucci looked at her as if she'd lost it. "The baddest bitches in Harlem ride again!"

For the rest of the ride it was just like old times. Tionna smoked, drank, and laughed with her girls as they all boasted about how they were gonna shut the spot down. The looser Tionna got, the less she thought about Duhan and more about having a good time.

By the time they got to the spot, three out of the four of them were on their way to the moon. Gucci only dabbled with the bottle because she had to drive, but she hit every blunt that went around the van. Tracy was just about there and Boots was running a close second, but Tionna was just buzzed.

The few drinks and the blunt had snatched the nervous jitters she'd had while she was getting dressed that night. She'd had hell finding something to wear because everything was either too small or still in trash bags, but she finally decided on a pair of skin-tight black jeans and a wine-colored wool sweater that her mother had given her for her birthday last spring. To cap it off, she threw on a pair of three-quarter black boots with needle-thin chrome heels. The shoes were murdering her pinky toes, but they were fly, so she was willing to endure the discomfort.

Gucci had taken it light, going with a tank top under a thin leather jacket. Resting just above her cleavage were two inverted *G*s fastened to a white-gold necklace. Her weed-slanted eyes surveyed the scene from behind her signature Gucci shades and she wasn't impressed. "This shit is looking suspect," Gucci said, rolling her eyes at a dude wearing a tight green blazer, batting his eyes at her like he was the shit.

"You know Mochas is hit or miss," Boots said.

"They can *miss* me with the dumb shit. I thought a listening party for Big Dawg would've been like a media circus," Gucci said, disappointed.

"It's still early. Let's go inside and see what it's looking like before we write the spot off," Tracy suggested as she made eye contact with a young-looking cat who was going inside with his friends.

"This broad is so dick thirsty." Boots rolled her eyes before following Tracy to the entrance.

"Like your throat has seen many dry days," Tracy said over her shoulder. The girls spent a few more minutes arguing back and forth about whether to go in or not, then a commotion behind them broke up their debate.

A fire-engine-red Aston Martin DB9, topless of course, zipped past the club at a dangerous speed. It went south two blocks before making an illegal U-turn and coming back and pulling to a screeching halt in front of the lounge. The price tag on the car was almost $187,000 but the driver treated it like a hooptie. Decked out in a red and yellow track jacket and the matching skullcap, Don B. climbed from the vehicle.

Seconds later, two SUVs pulled up behind the Aston Martin. From the vehicles spilled a flock of artists, homeys, and chicks they'd picked up along the way. The chicks and some of the guys giggled and whispered like groupies as the Big Dawg collective gathered around their benefactor. Choruses of "The Don" and "Brrrapt" could be heard as the entourage moved collectively toward the entrance of the lounge. The king and his court had arrived.

"Is that who I think it is?" Boots nudged Tionna.

"Looking like new money as usual," Gucci said. "I told y'all this was gonna be the spot."

"Gucci, stop fronting like it wasn't just ready to bounce," Tionna reminded her.

"That was then, baby girl. Let's get up in this piece before these hood rat bitches get all up on them niggaz." With subtle elbows and a few choice words for the haters, Gucci led her crew toward the entrance. Before they could make it, a scuffle broke out just ahead of them.

CHAPTER 10

"And where are you just coming from when school let out hours ago?" Reese scared the daylights out of Sharon when she snuck into the house. She was perched on a folding chair in the corner, smoking a cigarette and staring out the window. The only illumination in the living room was that cast by the streetlights.

"Girl, you scared the hell out of me, sitting here in the dark like that." Sharon flicked on the light. "Where are Mommy and Alex?"

"Out." Reese exhaled a large cloud of smoke. "And you still haven't answered my question. Where've you been, Sharon?" Reese got up from the chair and walked slowly over to her sister.

"Out. Damn, why you sweating me." Sharon brushed passed Reese and went into the kitchen. Rock Head had beaten her guts up all afternoon and well into the night, and when she'd asked him for some money for a cab and food, he'd told her that he didn't have it.

Reese sniffed the air. "I'm sweating you because it smells like your little ass has been out fucking." Reese followed Sharon into the kitchen. "L'il sis, when are you gonna learn?"

Sharon slammed the refrigerator and rolled her eyes. "Look, I don't need you all in my business; I got this."

Reese leaned against the wall and smirked at her sister, who was making a huge bowl of cereal. "You got it, huh? You let a nigga tear down ya walls for free, get high, and you got it? Sharon, if that was the case, I would've given you the ten dollars myself and saved your pussy the unnecessary mileage. I should hope you would've at least gotten a few dollars for yourself, but if he sent you home hungry I'm pretty sure he sent you home broke."

"Fuck you, Reese. You don't know shit." Sharon took her cereal into the living room.

"I know way more than you give me credit for, Sharon." Reese followed her into the living room. Looking at Sharon's face—a face very much like her own at that age—she didn't even have the strength to be mad at her. "Little sister, I know you think I be on your back because I wanna control you, but it ain't about that. I'm just trying to put you up on game."

"I got mad game," Sharon declared, shoveling a spoonful of cereal into her mouth. The way she was attacking it, you'd have thought she hadn't eaten in days.

Reese laughed. "Girl, your game is suspect at best if you're coming in here smelling like funk and eating cereal for dinner. I don't know why you be trying to front like I've never been seventeen."

"Things were a lot different when you were seventeen, Reese."

"They weren't that much different. It's the same game, only the players have changed. I can remember back when I blossomed back in the days, sis. You got a nice body for a girl your age, but I was built like a grown-ass woman when I was seventeen. I had ass, titties, and attitude, and dared for anybody to try to tell me anything."

Sharon laughed, thinking back on how Reese used to be. "I remember guys used to sweat y'all in the hood. Every time I would try to run behind y'all, you would shut me down and make me go back to the park. I used to hate that."

"I used to shut you down because we were doing things that we had no business doing, much like you are now."

"I ain't doing nothing," Sharon said innocently.

"You're smoking weed, cigarettes, fucking, and Lord knows what else," Reese pointed out.

"I smoke a little weed, but I don't do cancer sticks," Sharon lied.

"Sharon, cut it out. I got this out of your top drawer." She held up a cigarette. "That's beside the point, though. Sharon, I know you're at that age when you're feeling yourself, and a lot is gonna come at you real fast. All I'm telling you is to be careful; stop and think about every decision before you make it, because big or small, it's gonna affect your future. By you running around jumping off with these dudes, you ain't doing nothing but building a reputation and running the risk of coming up pregnant or burnt."

"Like you did?" Sharon hadn't meant to say it like that, but the card had already been played.

"Exactly like I did. You can't throw that shit at me, Sharon, because I'm over it. But you need to listen to me because I went through it. I got lucky because I had a mild STD and Alex came out healthy, but I could've fucked around and got something the doctor couldn't get rid of. Look at your friend Dena: I ain't no big fan of hers, but my heart goes out to her for what she went through. Do you wanna end up a walking testament of a knucklehead little bitch who didn't know how to listen?"

Sharon sucked her teeth. "I'm going to bed." She abandoned her bowl and stormed off.

"You do that," Reese called after her. "And I hope you dream about some of the things we talked about so it will finally sink into that thick-ass head of yours."

CHAPTER 11

Bobo kicked back on the project bench, surrounded by his team and telling war stories to some of the local hood rats. The stories weren't that interesting, but they stuck around because Bobo had damn near an unlimited supply of haze and they'd already gone through two bottles of Grey Goose, all on Bobo.

"Yo, B, what was that shit I heard earlier about some nigga coming through here pressing you?" Happy asked. They called him Happy because his overbite and high, chubby cheeks always made him look like he was smiling. He was a jovial-looking man with a large round head and a potbelly that didn't quite fit with his average build. But for as harmless as he looked, he was anything but. Happy was slicker than an oiled pig in a mudslide and played just as dirty. Happy had an uncanny ability to get weaker-minded people to take the risk while he reaped all the benefits. Though he wasn't a power player in the underworld, he was said to be handling.

"Just some nigga talking shit; you know everybody wanna sit next to the king," Bobo boasted. A fiend walking up interrupted their conversation. Bobo nodded to his little man on the next bench and the fiend went to get served.

"Man, you ass stay on fire, Bobo," Happy said, getting off the bench. The sale was his cue to make a move, because he had enough heat on him as it was, without Bobo's recklessness adding to it. "I'm gone from it, daddy. You gonna be sitting here all night trying to catch a case or what?"

"You know the candy store never closes." Bobo fixed himself and the girl closer to him another drink. "But fuck all that, Hap; what up with them AKs you was telling me about?"

Happy snickered, making himself look more rodentlike. "You know my MO." He looked suspiciously at everyone sitting on the bench. One thing Happy didn't do was talk business in front of people he didn't know. "When you get rid of that little candy bag and your company, come on and see me, I got everything you need." Happy spun off.

"That nigga be extra P-noid," the kid who made the sale said, when Happy was out of earshot.

"That muthafucka always acting like somebody is out to get him," one of the girls said, adding her two cents.

"He's just scared that somebody is gonna run up and rob his ass for some of that cake he sitting on." This was another of Bobo's people. He was a Spanish kid who wore his hair in a *Miami Vice* ponytail.

"Y'all fuck with that kid if you want to. Happy might not be the hardest nigga out here, but he will kill you over his paper," Bobo said, laughing.

"I hear that hot shit," Ponytail mumbled, still watching Happy walk down the street.

"Yo, yo," said a squeaky voice, drawing all their attention. A young boy who looked barely out of junior high school was staggering toward the benches with a half-empty bottle of Hennessy dangling from his hand.

"Who that, son?" Bobo squinted his eyes.

"Y'all niggaz got that piff?" The kid continued his shamble.

"Shorty, what the fuck is you talking about? Ain't nobody got no drugs over here." This was the kid who had made the sale. He stood up and met the kid halfway.

"Be easy, my nigga. I just came though to cop some smoke. I got a bitch waiting for me upstairs," the kid said goofily.

"A what? Little nigga, you better take your ass on somewhere; you don't know shit about no pussy." The dude who had made the sale laughed and turned to his boss. "Bobo, you hear this little dude?" There was suddenly a rush of wind, and the dude who had made the sale felt a light stinging against his face. He didn't even realize that he'd been cut until he turned back and saw Ashanti holding the bloody razor.

When he opened his mouth to scream, Ashanti cracked him in the mouth with the bottle. Before the kid could right himself, the razor caught him once more, this time separating the soft flesh of his neck. The dude with the ponytail went for his gun, but Brasco stepped from the side of the building and hit him in the chest with the bulldog. The blast took him off his feet, over the railing, and into the grass. Brasco turned his hammer on Bobo and fired two quick shots. Bobo threw himself behind the bench, dragging one of the girls with him. He clumsily climbed to his feet, holding the girl in front of him like a shield.

"What you waiting for?" Ashanti shouted at Brasco.

"I ain't trying to hit the bitch," Brasco said, moving to try to get a better angle on Bobo.

Ashanti sucked his teeth and unexpectedly snatched the gun from Brasco. "Fuck all this shit," he said before pulling the trigger. It had to be the adrenaline, because the frail girl shook Bobo off her and got out of the way before the bullet could make contact. Unbalanced and uncovered, Bobo was a sitting duck for Ashanti. Ashanti was so excited that his next shot went wild and struck Bobo in the hip, instead of the heart, where he'd been aiming. Bobo spun and made an awkward dash for the building, with Ashanti and Brasco hot on his heels.

Bobo rounded the short fence so quickly that he slammed into the heavy metal door. He tried to jerk the door and found that housing had picked that day of any to finally fix the lock. Frantically Bobo banged on the door and shouted for help. God was merciful: a young man was just coming out. With a concerned look on his face, he quickly opened the door for Bobo and pulled it closed behind him.

"Oh God, thank you so much," Bobo gasped, while leaning on the man for support.

"You're bleeding. Are you okay?" the kid asked Bobo, noticing his bloody leg.

"They're trying to kill me! You've gotta call the police!" Bobo pleaded.

"A'ight, let me get my cell phone." The kid reached into his pocket, but instead of pulling out a phone, he pulled out a gun. Bobo's eyes grew as he looked into the face of the wild-haired young man. Though he'd never met him personally, he knew just who he was. When Animal saw the light of recognition in Bobo's eyes, he pulled the trigger and put his brains on the mailboxes.

"Let's go, let's go!" Nefertiti hopped around nervously behind the wheel of the Dodge. Ashanti was in a full sprint, while Brasco jogged behind him. Animal brought up the rear at a brisk walk. The car doors weren't even closed completely before Nefertiti peeled into the street like a wild man.

"Nigga, slow down before you get us knocked with these hammers!" Brasco warned from the backseat. He was trying to be cool, but couldn't help giving occasional nervous glances out the back window.

"You think anybody seen us?" Nefertiti asked.

"Us? Fool, they might've seen me or Brasco, but how the fuck you gonna get spotted when your scary ass wouldn't even get out of the car?" Ashanti clowned Nefertiti.

"Man, fuck your little midget ass. Somebody had to be the getaway driver."

"Well, see if you can *get* your ass *away* from here without getting us knocked," Animal said. "What happened out there?" he addressed Ashanti and Brasco.

"Mother Teresa over here caught a case of good conscience." Ashanti thumbed at Brasco.

"You're damn right. I wasn't about to shoot that broad!" Brasco shot back.

"And you did right," Animal told him. "Ashanti, you can't be getting at no civilians like that, little one. We play this game so we accept the rules, but this," he raised his gun, "ain't for them; the worlds are never to cross. Think about how you would feel if somebody did it to your mother or maybe one of your sisters?"

Ashanti looked at Animal seriously. "Man, my mama gave

me away when I was a kid and I ain't seen my sister in eight years. I ain't got nobody but my gang and my gun."

"That's gangsta," Nefertiti said.

"And how the fuck would you know?" Animal turned his cold eyes on him. "Nef, you been on some real flaky shit lately, and I don't know how I'm feeling about it."

"You have been carrying yaself kinda bitchlike," Brasco half joked.

"Real talk, all you niggaz know that ain't no weak links in this pack; we live and move as one. Now, if one of us ain't moving with the wave, how is that gonna affect everybody else?" Animal questioned.

"It ain't like that," Nefertiti said just above a whisper.

"So I see," Animal replied. "Drop me off at the spot so I can clean up. I'm trying to see what that listening party is like now that the business is out of the way."

"What time you want me to come back and scoop you?" Nefertiti asked.

"Don't even bother. I'm flying solo."

"Hold up, blood. I thought we was in there together?" Nefertiti was almost pleading. He had been looking forward to the party all week.

"I thought we were in a lot of shit together, but I'm beginning to see otherwise."

"But, Animal . . ."

"Nigga, fuck all that shit," Animal snapped. "Like I said, your actions have been suspect, so you can officially consider your ass on notice."

CHAPTER 12

When they finally reached the Broad Street exit off 21-north in Newark, New Jersey, the passengers in the car breathed a sigh of relief. Letting Silk drive on the highway was like staying on the Medusa ride at Six Flags for a half hour. Whenever she got behind the wheel she acted like she was racing the devil, and if you complained about it, she only drove more erratically. Granted, she had yet to get them into an accident, but neither Tech nor China wanted to be in the car when the speedster finally did hit something.

The girls had thrown it on that night. China wore a tight-fitting black dress that looked poured on, with needle-point heels that made her a good three inches taller. The red shrug not only kept the chill off her shoulders, but the lining concealed the Gemstar razors she had taken the time to glue in. She reasoned that if she couldn't get to the .380, which was firmly taped to her inner thigh, she'd need a backup plan. L'il Silk had on a black gangster suit and red fedora. Tech hadn't missed the fact that they'd chosen to fly his colors, which only made him appreciate them more. They would live and die with whatever he believed in, which is why he was glad he'd bought them along.

The ride down Broad Street was a quiet one, unless you counted Plies, who was trying his best to push Silk over the edge. She bumped him when she was about to ride on something and he'd been in rotation for the entire ride. China sat in the passenger seat, staring dreamily at the approaching lights of Market Street. The diamond necklace slung around her neck matched her cold blue eyes—eyes that were filled with worry. The girls were on edge, and with good reason, considering they were about to walk into a room full of the most dangerous men in the Tri-State area.

"Y'all good?" Tech broke the silence.

"Yeah, man, I'm ready to do this," Silk said. She tried to appear cool, but Tech knew her well enough to know when she was on edge. "I could go for a shot of something. I hope they serve Hennessy in this muthafucka."

"Not tonight, Silky. I need your mind sharp. You can get as faded as you want when the business is concluded."

"That some bullshit, man. You know I shoot just as straight when I'm drunk as when I'm sober," Silk boasted.

"Yeah, that's just what we need—your drunk ass shooting up the place," China chimed in.

"Fuck the both of y'all." Silk gave them the finger.

Silk made an illegal right at the corner of Broad and Market and blew through a red light on Mulberry, where they'd built the new Devils stadium. It, like most of Market Street, was lit up like an early Christmas. The tourists frequented the shopping area like it was Thirty-fourth Street, marveling at the gentrification process that the city had undergone. In between trying to throw their mayor under the bus, they'd managed to reconstruct a good portion of the city. They'd done a wonderful job with downtown Newark, but on the other side of town, the war between minorities and the establishment continued.

By the time the cleared the underpass at Penn Station, the scenery had changed and so had the language. They'd crossed into the Ironbound district, which was predominately Latino and slightly quieter, which was why Tech had suggested it. Along that section of Ferry Street, people kept to their own business, and it was outside the red zones in the city.

"Why the fuck we gotta meet these niggaz all the way out here?" Silk asked, busting a sharp left into the parking lot of Iberia.

Tech paid the parking attendant before even acknowledging her. "Because this is the one spot where everybody feels comfortable. It's neutral turf, so nobody has the up."

Silk sucked her teeth. "Man, we thousandaires and them niggaz is millionaires; it ain't about nothing for them to get some killers to off us. For all we know, this Secret Squirrel shit could be a setup."

"Silky." He leaned up so that he could see her. "You know I'd never lead you into the fire without making the necessary preparations. If they get funny, then I got jokes, too."

"So you *do* think it's funny business?" China rekindled an old argument. She'd been against meeting them like this from the start.

"It's always funny business when you're dealing with niggaz of a bygone era," Tech told her. "No worries, ma. We're gonna go in there so they can speak their piece and be done with it."

"What you think they gonna say?"

"I'd be lying if I told you I knew for sure, but whatever they say, they're gonna say it respectfully," Tech assured her. What he neglected to tell China and Silk was that he had called in a favor from a friend of a friend who had a little clout in the town. The fix was already in, so if the old heads decided to flex their muscle, Tech would flex his cunning.

Tech and his ladies stepped inside the restaurant to be greeted by a short Hispanic host wearing a tuxedo. He smiled pleasantly when he received them, but the nervousness in his eyes was apparent to anyone who knew what to look for. The short man led them into an adjoining room that was usually reserved for private gatherings, only to find their party already seated and waiting, as Tech had expected. He had purposely arrived late to the meeting as a show of defiance to the respected men. They might've controlled the movement of the streets, but Tech was his own man. This was the new Commission, as they'd taken to calling themselves. Separately, they were all heavyweights, but together they were the most powerful organization on the East Coast. They all stared, but nobody said a word until after Tech and his ladies took their respective seats at the far end of the table.

"Glad you could make it." This was Bear, a hulk of a man in his early forties who oversaw the drug trade in Mount Vernon and the majority of Westchester County. To his right was his brother, Little Bear, who was at least thirty pounds lighter, but twice as mean. He was an upstart cat who was making a strong push for the Bronx.

Tech greeted him with an easy smile. "Traffic was a little heavy getting out here, you know how it is."

A tall, thin waiter, also wearing a tuxedo, came around and refilled all the water glasses on the table. Even if you didn't notice his hands were trembling so badly he almost dropped the water pitcher, you could smell the fear coming off him. He filled the glasses and made a beeline out of the room, never once making eye contact with any member of the party.

"Well, I don't know how it is, poppy. I no appreciate you wasting my time like this," said the man sitting to the right of Silk in a heavy accent. His beady black eyes bore holes into Tech and his ladies. Rico was a hotheaded Spanish kid who rocked Broadway from 116th Street to 225th. He had little to no patience, and was quick to violence, which is why he was called to group meetings only when absolutely necessary. Rico was unpredictable, which made him a very dangerous foe.

"Nice to see you again, too, Rico," Tech said easily. He knew Rico was trying to bait him, as he always did, but he wouldn't bite.

"Fuck you, muthafucka. Don't act like we friends. It's only because of my respect for these men here that I haven't put you in the ground already."

He and Tech had been at odds since Tech and Jah had robbed and murdered one of Rico's cousins back in the days. Rico had tried to get at them several times for the killing, but none of his shooters ever came back. It had been a joint decision made by the Commission to call a truce for the betterment of their businesses when Tech was made an associate of their group. Neither of them liked it, but neither of them was stupid enough to outright defy the governing body of the streets.

"Okay, okay, we can measure dicks when the business is concluded." This came from the man sitting at the head of the table. He had soft brown skin and didn't appear to be much older than Tech, save for the thin goatee that he was trying to grow. But, for as young as he was, he was the single most powerful man in the city. He was Shai Clark, the boss of bosses and the head of the Commission. Sitting on either side of him were his best friends and most trusted advisers, Swann and Angelo. During Shai's transition it had been Angelo and Swann who kept the streets in a choke hold and dispatched any- and everyone who spoke out against the former boss's youngest son.

"Shai is right, I'm trying to get this shit over with and get back to the hood," Danny Boy said. Unlike everyone else, who was either dressed in a suit or a button-up, he was sporting a pair of jeans and a white thermal shirt. Tied around his neck was the flag of his army, Harlem Crip. When his mentor, Gutter, was murdered, the set was thrown into a civil war, with everyone vying for his vacated position. It was Danny Boy who rallied those who were still loyal to the fallen Crips general and his cause and ended the infighting. Though he had rescinded the death sentence, Gutter had passed on the Bloods in New York; the two groups were still at odds, which is what got him the occasional dirty look from the Bloods representative at the table, Apple, who was a five-star general who held a good amount of influence in Brooklyn.

"Agreed." Angelo nodded. "So, what's new, Tech?"

Tech shrugged. "Same shit, different toilet. I can't call it. I was hoping that you guys could tell me what all this was about?"

"That's bullshit and you fucking know it. We're here about

all the fucking heat you're brining down with these little bastards you got killing recklessly in the streets!" Rico exploded.

"Rico, calm down," Shai said in a low tone. He didn't have to raise his voice for Rico to know he was being given an order, and it showed on his face. "Tech, what Rico says is accurate. I've been getting a lot of calls about how you're conducting yourselves in the streets. You know that we of the Commission have established a certain code of conduct that binds us and our soldiers."

"Yeah, I know the rules, but the last time I checked, I wasn't a member of the Commission, and I damn sure ain't anybody's soldier," Tech corrected him.

"You ain't a part of the Commission because you got a problem with following rules," Bear spoke up. "We made you an associate as a reward for your services in the streets and to allow you to eat from this table."

"A table that you keep spilling shit on," Rico added.

Tech looked at Bear and Rico quizzically, then turned his cold eyes to Shai. "With all do respect, gentlemen, y'all didn't make me an associate as a reward for shit I've done for you or anybody else in this room. You put me down with the team so that I'd stop robbing and killing the niggaz you got working the streets. If we're gonna have real talk, then let's keep it real."

This got a muffled chuckle from Swann. Shai gave him a look, and he regained his composure.

"True indeed," Shai agreed. You were becoming quite the headache on the streets, which caused some of my associates to call for your execution, but Swann spoke up on your behalf, so you were given a pass." Swann had known Tech since he was a little kid trying to sneak into bars and had always dug his ambition. Tech was wild as hell, but for the most part he played by the rules of the street, if not of the Commission.

"And I'm thankful for that," Tech nodded at Swann, "but just because y'all threw me a bone don't make me your dog. Shai, I ain't trying to ruffle nobody's feathers, but I'm out here getting it like I live. When the dogs are hungry, I gotta feed them."

"So you feed them blood—the blood of men who line our pockets?" Rico pressed him.

"Rico, miss me with that bullshit. Y'all asked me to lay off of y'all people and so I have. Everything else is up for grabs— at least that was my understanding of the arrangement."

"You're a fucking liar and a piece of shit." Rico shot to his feet. "You say that you're lying off our people, but I got the word before I left to come out here that your so-called dogs murdered one of my business associates a few hours ago. Bobo spent a lot of money with me."

Tech's face twisted into a mask of hate. "Is that what this is about? Bobo? Let me tell you something . . . as a matter of fact, let me tell you all something." He made eye contact with everyone in the room. "Bobo was a lying, snitching, piece of shit that sent a lot of good niggaz to prison. There was a bounty on his head and I cashed in on it, but to be honest with you, I'd have killed him for free if I ever got a mind to. Him and every muthafucka who thinks like him needs to be lined up in front of the Apollo Theater and shot." He looked directly at Rico when he said this.

"You reacted off a rumor that was never proven," Rico tried to defend Bobo. Tech just looked at him and shook his head.

"Rico, you ain't lying to nobody but yourself and you know

it. You make your rounds through the New York State prison system and speak to some of them niggaz that's looking at the long walk because of him, and then come back and let's revisit this argument. Furthermore, I'm getting just a little tired of you coming at me like you're some kinda boss nigga. Might I remind you all that it was Darius Santana who opened the streets up by whacking the old bosses and Poppa Clark who opened the money line back up in Harlem. Other than Shai and his peoples, ain't nobody in here sat with no real made niggaz. So, if you wanna keep popping that shit, you're welcomed to do so, but ya bitch ass ain't gonna talk it to me."

"Nigga, what . . ." Rico moved toward Tech, but Silk was already on her feet and standing between them. He tried to give her an intimidating stare, but she was unfazed. "Now, this is funny." Rico smiled. "You're supposed to be this bad-ass killer, but you're hiding behind your bitch." He was speaking to Tech but staring at Silk. There was a hard edge to her eyes that made him cautious.

"Why does it seem like I keep running into that word to-day." Silk flexed her fist, anticipating a battle.

"Everybody calm down." Angelo was standing now. "You two shit birds can blast at each other once we get straight. For right now, shut the fuck up and let Shai speak." Angelo wasn't the most imposing figure physically, but he was a cold-blooded killer.

Shai placed a calming hand on Angelo's arm. "Good look-ing, my nigga. I got it from here." Angelo continued standing until everyone was reseated. He gave both Tech and Rico warning looks before returning to his seat next to Shai. "Lis-ten, I didn't call any of you here to air old grievances; I asked you here to address the complaints I've been receiving. Tech," he looked at the youngster, "I like you and I think you're a stand-up kid, but you need to cool the fuck out. If it was up to me, I wouldn't give a fuck who you jacked as long as they weren't a part of my family, but I have to put the concerns of this Commission before my personal feelings. You gotta slow down, my nigga."

"So you trying to tell me that I can't eat?" Tech asked. He was getting heated, but had the good sense to keep his poker face on.

Shai laughed because he saw right through the mask. "Tech, if I ran around telling niggaz that they couldn't eat, I'd be dead instead of the boss of this city. Nah, little brother, I ain't telling you that you can't eat; I just want you to play it a little closer to the rules. I could care less about the low-level cats you bring it to, but before you tackle the big fish, clear it to make sure you're not stepping on anybody's toes."

"Fair enough, Shai," Tech agreed. Everyone breathed a sigh of relief when the young gunslinger agreed with Shai. Most of them expected and wanted him to show his ass so they could finally have him killed, but he didn't walk into the setup, which upset some of them, but Rico was animate about it.

"You hear this . . . this bullshit. Fair enough, Shai, give me a fucking break."

"Be easy, Rico," Danny Boy said, trying to calm him, but Rico was livid.

"I can't believe y'all are going for this shit," Rico continued. "He's gonna shuck and grin like it's all good while sitting in front of you, Shai, but as soon as he hits the streets he's gonna be back at it. I demand that we come to a more long-term resolution to this common problem."

"Rico, you don't demand shit for as long as Shai is at the head of this table," Angelo reminded him.

"Shai ain't gonna be the boss forever," Rico shot back.

"He will be for as long as I'm holding this here." Swann laid his .45 on the table. "If anybody cares to challenge what I said, I ain't got nothing to do for the rest of the night." Swann's eyes went around the room. Everyone in the hood knew that it was almost unheard of for Swann to draw his weapon unless he planned on laying something down. The situation was getting very ugly very quickly.

Rico wisely backed down. "Shai, I mean no disrespect, but please understand my position. I get money uptown, which is where Tech is causing the most grief. He's cramping my style."

"Tech raises just as much hell in Brooklyn as he does uptown and it ain't stopped my show one bit. As a matter of fact, he was actually a big help with the crab infestation I was having. We're itch-free now," Apple said sarcastically, cutting his eyes at Danny Boy.

"Don't play cute with me, cuz. You know I do all my talking with iron," Danny Boy shot back.

"And I don't talk at all, I just react," Shai warned them both. "Frankly, all of this bullshit is giving me a headache. The bottom line is, both of you muthafuckas heard what I said." He looked at Tech and then at Rico. "If there's gonna be any more unsanctioned hits, then I'll be the one sending the shooters, and unlike some of these loudmouthed niggaz, you'll never hear my people coming." Shai rose. "I'm getting the fuck outta here. Either y'all can play the game correctly or you won't play at all." Shai moved for the door, followed by Angelo and Swann.

"I can't believe this shit. We gotta sit idle while this monkey and his bitches run through the streets like rabid dogs," Rico muttered.

"What'd you just say?" Silk sat up.

"I ain't repeating myself, shorty."

"Nah, because if I didn't know better, I'd think you just called me and my girl bitches?"

"If it walks like a duck and quacks—" Rico's words were cut off when Silk grabbed his hand and drove her salad fork through it, pinning Rico's hand to the table. He was in so much pain that he couldn't even find his voice to scream. Everyone watched in horror as Rico's blood sprayed all over the white tablecloth. The bodyguard who had been with Rico grabbed a fist full of Silk's hair, but he froze in place when China placed her gun to the back of his head.

"If you're wondering if I'll really shoot you, you just keep holding on to her hair," China breathed in his ear.

"Y'all must've lost ya fucking minds in here." Shai stormed over to them. Angelo tried to stop him, but Shai shrugged him off. "Shorty, put that fucking gun down," he barked at China. China looked at Tech, who was still sitting there watching it all. "What the fuck are you looking at him for when I'm the one talking to you?"

"Tech?" China called nervously, wondering what she should do.

Tech looked up at Swann, who had his gun dangling from his hand. "Baby brother, you're about to ask a question you already know the answer to. You're my kin, but this is my brother," Swann said seriously.

"It's cool, baby," Tech said, as if he were the coolest cat in the world.

China lowered the gun and backed away from the body-guard. She could see the murder in his eyes, just beneath the embarrassment, but he would save his vengeance for another day. Once China had reholstered her gun, Shai surprised everyone by swinging Tech's chair around so that he was facing him.

"You smug little muthafucka, I should let Rico's boys kill your whole fucking family for the bullshit you and these crazy-ass broads just pulled," Shai snarled. He looked like he was ready to explode, but Tech remained calm. "I don't know if it's because y'all are in the same gang, or because he thinks there's hope for your stupid ass, but it's because of Swann that I still let you breathe my air, kid. My patience only stretches so far and you've already overextended yourself. You don't get any more passes, you understand me?"

Tech hesitated for a moment before answering, "Yeah, man, I hear you."

"Now get the fuck outta here before I forget how much love I got for Swann and blast your ass myself," Shai spat.

Tech stood up and regarded Shai for a moment. For a minute it looked like he was going to make a move, but he didn't. "Let's go, y'all." He motioned for China and Silk to follow him to the door. They did, but they never turned their backs on the Commission.

"This ain't over," Rico threatened, once he was able to free his hand from the table. "You're gonna answer for this shit, Tech."

Tech stopped in his tracks and turned around. "Anytime you're ready, you know where to find me." With that they left the restaurant.

———

"What the fuck was that shit about, Tech?" China started right in as soon as they were back inside the whip. Her hands were trembling so bad that she couldn't even light her cigarette. Silk, who was a bit calmer, did the honors for her.

"Just some old niggaz hating," Tech said, as if it were nothing.

"My G, you just went in there and pissed off Shai Clark. He's made bigger niggaz than us disappear," Silk said. She remembered how, when she was a little girl, her mother and the rest of the fiends had spoken about the Clarks as if they were the black Gambino family.

"I had the situation under control the whole time," he told them.

"Muthafucka, are you high? They could've killed us in there for that shit you and this crazy-ass heifer just pulled!"

"I said I had it under control," Tech snapped and turned to stare out the window. He watched patiently as the bosses and their entourages pilled into their respective vehicles and headed back toward the turnpike. Not long after they had gone, the waiter who had filled their water glasses came out, followed by the host, who was carrying a bottle. He rolled down the window and beamed at them.

"Everything cool?" the waiter asked, giving Tech dap. He had replaced his nervous guise with a street swagger.

"Right as rain, my man. Good looking out on that, Tino."

"Man, you know we got back to grade school, dawg. If anything, I owe you for as many ass whippings as you saved me from."

"You know family looks out for family, blood. It's like I told you the day the big homeys put you down," Tech recalled. Tino's family had been the only Salvadorians on the block back in the days. The Puerto Ricans didn't want him and the blacks abused him, but it all changed when Tech had gotten him *quoted*. From day one to present day, Tino had been willing to go above and beyond for his set.

"Please, I get paid now?" the host asked in a shaky voice.

"Cool out, unc," Tino told his nervous uncle. His uncle had good reason to be nervous, because not only was he putting his job in jeopardy by helping his nephew's friends, but he ran the risk of being an accessory to whatever would've gone down inside the restaurant.

"Nah," he's earned it." Tech handed them two thick envelopes. The uncle took an envelope and stuffed it inside his jacket pocket before handing Tech the bottle. "Yo, I'm about to get outta here, T." Tech shook his hand again. "Yo, if you ever find yourself getting back in the game, we could use an extra man."

"Nah, man, I kinda like being a busboy; it's safer and I ain't gonna get locked up for it. See you later, my man." Tino saluted Tech and walked back to the restaurant with his uncle in tow.

"What the hell was that shit about?" Silk asked, clearly dumbfounded by the whole exchange.

"It's like I said—Tino and me go way back, so I called him to help me out on this." Tech hoisted the bottle of Rémy XO. Silk snatched the bottle and started fumbling with the seal.

"And what were you gonna do with that, club them to death?" China asked sarcastically.

"Actually I was gonna poison them," Tech said, freezing Silk just as she'd gotten the bottle open. "I laced that muthafucka and had Tino slip it into the restaurant in case things got funny. I knew we couldn't win in a shoot-out without taking a loss or two," he looked at the ladies respectively, "so I was gonna down all of them with one shot, literally. That's why I didn't want y'all drinking tonight."

"Man, and I almost downed this muthafucka." Silk tossed the bottle out the window, shattering it in the parking lot. The attendant looked their way but declined to come over and complain.

"How did you know they would drink it?" China wanted to know.

Tech gave her a blank stare. "With the exception of Shai, all of them old heads is closet drunks, and the more expensive the liquor, the greedier they are for it. If things had started to go to the left, I was gonna curl my tail between my legs and offered to buy a round of drinks as a show of my willingness to be accepted."

"That would've been a goodbye toast for their asses," Silk joked.

"Now you get me." He winked at her.

China sucked her teeth because she still didn't find the situation as funny as her partners did. "So now what?"

"What you mean? We get back to business," Tech told her, as if it should've been obvious. "Harlem is a little hot right now so we might wanna look into getting at them folks in the Amsterdam projects."

"Don't you gotta clear it with ol' boy and them? For the kinda weight we're about to move on, dude might be connected to somebody."

"We'll cross that bridge when we come to it," Tech said.

"T, I'm about my paper and all that, but don't you think we're asking for trouble by doing exactly what Shai told us not to?" China was forever the cautious one.

"Fuck all that shit, China; I ain't trying to run a credit check on every nigga I plan to take off. Besides, I don't know this nigga from a can of paint, so the chances are he ain't connected directly to none of them. We might slap him around a little bit, but we ain't gonna kill him, but I'm taking that nigga's shit. Don't flake on me now, C, we done pulled a million licks; this shit will be just another day at the office. It'll be smooth, baby."

"Don't trip, ma, we got it faded," Silk added.

China would've liked to be as confident as her crime partners, but something in the pit of her gut didn't feel right. She thought about pressing her argument to try to get him to see logic, but she didn't. Tech took care of all of them at one point or another, so if he was in, then so was she. The *in* part was easy, but she hoped that she would be able to make it *out* just as smooth.

CHAPTER 13

A chubby bouncer was arguing with one the boys Tracy had been sizing up. He was a hair over five feet, with a boxed-shaped head, but from the way he kept puffing his chest out, you'd have thought he was seven feet tall.

"Come on, fam, I don't even know why y'all are acting like that." The kid adjusted the brim of his Yankee fitted.

The bouncer sighed deeply, as if he was tiring of talking to the kid. "Listen, y'all niggaz know the rules: no sneaker and no fitted caps."

"Forget about it, let's just go," another kid said. He was thin and wore his hair in short dreads.

"Nah, fuck all that, Bobby. These dudes is gonna stop acting like they don't know Hollywood from Harlem. This is Starving/Big Dawg Entertainment over here." Hollywood pounded his chest. He was creating an unnecessary scene and the bouncer was losing his patience.

"So you're with Big Dawg, huh?" the bouncer asked sarcastically.

"Muthafucking right. You know Harlem roll as a unit."

The bouncer just looked at him. "Get the fuck outta here. Look, I wouldn't give a fuck who you was, shorty, ain't nothing popping. Rules are rules, so either come back when you're dressed properly or take your ass to one of them hole-in-the-wall bars to get a drink."

Hollywood looked the bouncer up and down. "Do I look like the kind of muthafucka that party at hole-in-the-walls?"

The bouncer raised an eyebrow. "You don't wanna know what you look like."

Hollywood was about to respond when a voice cut through the night: "Big Dawgz coming through."

Led by Remo and Devil, the Big Dawg entourage made their way to the entrance of the spot. "Pardon me, l'il nigga." The bouncer pushed through Hollywood and Bobby and greeted Don B. "What it is, my man." He shook the CEO's hand.

"Ain't nothing. How we looking up in there?" Don B. tried to peer through the tinted windows of the spot.

"It's light right this minute, but now that y'all are here is gonna pick up."

"Let's hope so. I promised the little homeys a good time." he motioned toward the Left Coast Theory, who were looking around in awe, "and you know the Don is a man of his word."

"Don't worry about it, Don, you know we treat all of ours right in this spot. We gonna make sure ya boys have a good-ass time," the bouncer assured him, moving to open the door for Don B. and his people.

"This is some real bullshit," Hollywood commented,

watching dudes dressed in hoodies and sneakers being allowed inside because they were with Don B. "I guess you gotta know a muthafucka to be treated right, huh?"

"Looks like you've got half a brain after all." The bouncer moved Hollywood to the side so the others could enter.

"Don't put ya fucking hands on me, duke," Hollywood flexed.

The bouncer glared at him. "Fam, if you don't get the fuck outta here, I'm gonna put hands *and* feet on you."

People were crowding around now and all Hollywood needed to show his ass was an audience. "Muthafucka, is you stupid? You better save that tough talk for ya bitches, 'cause I'm a G on these streets!"

"Wood, be easy," Bobby tried to urge him, but it only made Hollywood go harder.

"Fuck that; niggaz get they wigs pushed for less!" By the time Hollywood finished his sentence, the bouncer had a fist full of his sweater. The only thing that saved him from getting his face knocked sideways was Don B.

"Fuck is you doing, buzz'n; you know we don't need that kinda heat out here tonight," Don B. scolded the bouncer as if he were speaking to a child.

"My fault, Don, but this nigga's mouth been going all night. You know this cat?" He gave Hollywood a shake for good measure.

"Yo, Don, tell this muthafucka something. He acting like you don't know big Hollywood!" Hollywood was now sweating like a runaway slave.

"Who?" Don B. scratched his bearded chin.

"Hollywood, man; Starving Entertainment—True's man!" Hearing his former protégé's name made Don B. look closer at Hollywood. He couldn't place him at first, but hearing his annoying voice took him back to the day of the video shoot that had caused the death of his closest friend. "Man, every time I see your little ass, somebody has got you hemmed up. Ain't you ever gonna learn about that mouth?"

"Come on, D, all I was trying to do was come out and show love for Left Coast. I heard the mix tape, so you know I'm thirsty to sample that album." Hollywood was almost pleading.

"Damn, the nigga was gonna take an ass whipping just to hear our album. I'm flattered," Fully said.

"Mind your business, Full," Doze whispered.

Don B. had a good mind to tell the bouncer to take Hollywood around back and punish him just for being a bird, but the questioning look in his new protégé's eyes gave him an idea. "Hollywood, you're a pain in the ass, but your Don is a merciful one so I'm gonna give you a play." Don B. looked at the bouncer. "Let him in."

"Don . . ." the bouncer began, but Remo cut him off.

"Something wrong with ya ears, fam?" Remo's dead glare sent chills down the bouncer's back. He was a tough guy, but he wasn't a killer, and that's what he would've had to do to dance with Remo.

"You got that." The bouncer released Hollywood and opened the door for Don B. and his team. The entourage was ushered inside, leaving only Hollywood and the spectators.

"See, Bobby, I told you niggaz to respect Starving Entertainment. Let's go in there and buy out the bar, son," Hollywood said, loud enough for everyone to hear, while leading Bobby inside.

"Hold up." The bouncer blocked their path.

"Son, what the fuck is ya problem? You heard what Don B. said," Hollywood barked.

"Yeah, he said to let *you* in. Ya man is assed out. Now either come inside or get the fuck outta here; you're blocking the entrance, you midget muthafucka."

"Fuck this shit, Wood, we out." Bobby turned to leave. He got halfway to the back of the line and realized that Hollywood hadn't moved. "Wood, what up?"

Hollywood looked from the increasingly growing crowd inside the club back to his friend. "I'm saying, B, you know I came all the way out from Jersey to come to this joint; there's gonna be mad people from the industry up in there."

"Word, kid?" Bobby frowned.

"Nah, you know it ain't even like that." Hollywood approached Bobby. "Check it, take my car keys and wait for me in the whip while I try to work my hand with this clown-ass nigga."

Bobby looked at Hollywood as if he were the shit on the bottom of his shoe. He had seen Hollywood stunt on other members of their team, so it shouldn't have been a surprise when he did it to him. "Man, fuck you and this club. I'm out." Bobby stormed off.

Hollywood felt eyes on him so he had to make a good show of it. "Word, then fuck you, too! As a matter of fact, you're fired, and that's on the hood. Don't come around the studio trying to eat when it's popping, sucka-ass nigga." Hollywood popped his collar and made his way back to the door. From the way the bouncer was staring at him, he expected him to say something slick, but he just shook his head.

Hollywood spread his arms. "What?"

"If dudes like you are the future of hip-hop, I'm gonna

start bumping country music." The bouncer laughed mock-ingly as Hollywood flipped him off and went inside the club.

"Did you see that sucka shit?" Boots lit her cigarette and tossed the match on the ground.

"Hmph, that's some sad shit," Tracy added.

"I don't see how a grown man can allow hisself to be treated like that. If it had been Duhan, he'd have let one of these nig-gaz have it," Tionna said.

"Shit, Duhan wouldn't have been trying to get in on the strength of another nigga; he had his own swag," Gucci said.

"The way the little dude came through, I thought he was handling a few dollars; I didn't know he was an imposter," Tracy said.

"Most of these muthafuckas are," Gucci said, stepping to the door.

"Good evening, ladies, welcome to Mochas." The bouncer smiled, but Gucci didn't. "Y'all must be actresses?" he said, trying a different approach.

"Nah, we *stunt* bitches." Gucci stepped passed him.

"We do love to stunt." Tionna followed.

"You see it, daddy." Tracy winked. Boots didn't need to speak; her ass did all the talking as she sashayed inside the spot.

The moment Tionna crossed the threshold of the dark-ened room, she felt it. It started in the pit of her stomach and spread to her fingers and toes. The sights and sounds of the Harlem nightlife thrilled her senses to the point where she was almost dizzy. It seemed like every face turned her way and ev-ery light in the joint was pointed her way. It was the stage and she was back on it.

"I gotta go to the bathroom." Tracy spun off on them before they had even made it all the way inside.

"That girl's bladder is weaker than a muthafucka," Gucci said.

"It's either that or her sinuses." Boots held one nostril and inhaled.

"She's still fucking around?" Tionna asked surprise.

"Off and on," Gucci admitted. "She thinks it's a secret, but we been peeped what time it is with Tracy."

"I hope she don't start geeking out this bitch," Tionna said disgustedly.

"Tionna, knock it off. Tracy has been bumping for years and we ain't never seen her selling her ass or her furniture for no drugs, so don't even act like that. Your stiff ass needs to be worrying about having a good time."

"I second that emotion!" Gucci spoke up.

"Whatever." Tionna waved them off and kept walking.

Moving through the crowd, Tionna saw old faces and new ones. Some she acknowledged and some she snubbed, but she took it all in. Gucci parted the crowd like the Red Sea as she and Tionna moved through the room. In the corner, Tionna spotted a dude she knew from the hood who was getting a little change back in the days. From the size of the chain around his neck, it was a safe guess that he had since stepped his game up. Tionna was about to go over and say hello when Gucci yanked her roughly by the arm, causing her to stumble.

"Damn, Gucci, slow ya ass down before I kill myself in these shoes," Tionna said, making her slow up.

Gucci stopped and looked at her. "Tionna, I know you've been out of the loop for a while, but you don't be shouting no nigga out in the club, that's bird shit."

"Gucci, knock it off. I know we know him," Tionna said, as if it was that simple, which got her a puzzled look from Gucci.

"So what if we know him? You don't know his ass like that tonight. T, we're predators, and stunting-ass niggaz like him are the prey. If you wanna get at him, then that's cool, but do it on your own time and make him come to *you*."

"That's my girl, with her mind on game." Tionna high-fived her.

"Constantly, ma. Watch me and you might learn something," Gucci teased, continuing to the bar.

As usual, the bar was a clusterfuck of people. All the stools were filled with people either drinking or shooting the shit, while almost a double ring of people took up whatever standing space there was. Boots spotted a group vacating the stools at the end of the bar and moved to secure them for her friends, but as she was moving in, so was another girl who had the same agenda. They ended up reaching the stools at the same time.

"Excuse you." The girl snaked her neck and looked Boots up and down. She was tall and thin with wormlike toes that hung over the front of her plastic sandals. As if the lime-green spandex dress didn't make her look stupid enough, she had her lavender weave styled in a beehive.

"What, you trying to order?" Boots asked, as if she were ignorant to what the girl was talking about.

"I was about to sit there," the girl told her.

"Yeah, but I *am* sitting here. I'm sure there's another spot down there somewhere." Boots gave the girl her back and waved to get the bartender's attention.

The girl sucked her teeth and tapped Boots roughly on the shoulder. "I know you don't call yourself being funny?"

Boots turned around slowly on the stool and looked the

girl up and down. "Nah, it looks like you got the market cornered on funny, ma."

"What, I know you ain't popping shit?" The girl took a defensive stance. It was just then that Tracy walked up on her. Her eyes were wild and glassy and her lips looked like they didn't want to move when she talked.

"Little girl, please act like you want it, because I sure wanna give it to you just for wearing that ugly-ass dress," Tracy told her. The girl took one look at her and had second thoughts about the seats.

"I ain't got no time for hating-ass bitches." The girl flung her weave and stormed off.

"Tracy, your ass is too much." Tionna slid onto one of the vacated seats.

"You were standing up a few seconds ago, so don't get cute, Ms. T," Tracy said. She snorted like she had something stuck in her throat and kept dabbing her nose with a napkin. Tionna, Boots, and Gucci exchanged knowing glances, but nobody said anything. It was a discussion that they would save for a later date.

No sooner had Tionna turned to the bar to place her order than the bartender was sitting a shot of Patrón in front of her. "I didn't order this." She looked at the glass suspiciously.

"Compliments of the gentlemen down there," the leather-clad barmaid told her, motioning toward a group of guys sitting at the other end of the bar. Tionna's eyes widened as she recognized the man raising his glass.

"Gucci," Tionna nudged her with her knee, "look who sent this shit over." Tionna slid the glass to Gucci but kept her eyes on the sender. Tracy intercepted the glass and threw it back.

"Ain't that ya old boo, T?" Tracy fought back the tingling at the base of her throat. You didn't taste Patrón right off, but you felt it when it got there.

"Bitch, you got jokes," Tionna hissed at Tracy.

Gucci adjusted her shades and zeroed in. "I ain't seen that paranoid-ass nigga at nothing but strip clubs in I don't know how long. Let me find out that the word done got around that you're back on the block. You gonna go talk to him?"

Tionna rolled her eyes at the sender. "Fuck him. Let that nigga come to me." She turned her back and crossed her legs while she waited for the inevitable.

CHAPTER 14

Happy was feeling himself when he stepped out that night. He was dressed in a black suede shirt and dark blue True Religion jeans. He rocked both his white and yellow gold chains, with a rocky gold bracelet and his biggest pinky ring. Yesterday he had come up on a shipment of hammers from Wisconsin and had successfully unloaded all of them by that afternoon. He was a few stacks heavier and a whole lot happier. It was a night for celebration.

Happy was a man who didn't believe in going out to public venues alone, which was why he had snatched three wayward souls from the projects to accompany him to Big Dawg's listening party. They were knuckleheads and had no direction to speak of, but Happy realized that they would do just fine if something popped off and he needed someone to take a bullet for him.

"Yo, it's mad joints in here," little Ron-Ron said. He was

actually thirty-one years old, but they called him "little" because he was just a shade over five feet tall.

"I don't know what you getting all excited for when you know you ain't gonna jump off in nothing," Wise teased him. He was a brown-skinned jokester who wore coke bottle glasses that always seemed to slide down off his nose.

"Why don't you niggaz act like you got some class?" Happy scolded them while filling their glasses with champagne. They downed the bubbly like it was water and held their glasses out for seconds. With a sigh, Happy refilled their glasses and silently wished that he'd chosen another group of youngsters to roll with.

"Hap, ain't that the bitch from uptown you was fucking?" Lou tapped Happy's leg. He was the quietest of the group, but that'd last only until he got enough liquor in his system.

"I fucked a lot of bitches, Lou; you gotta be a little more specific," Happy boasted.

"Not many that looked like this one." Lou raised his arm and pointed to the opposite end of the bar. It was an awkward gesture because his arm was wrapped from fist to elbow in a cast. It seemed like every year he broke a bone.

Happy's weed-slanted eyes traveled the length of the bar and when they landed where Lou was pointing, he suddenly became very alert. It had been a while since last he'd seen her, but her face would be forever buried in his mind. Happy had met Tionna through his friend Bernie and his girl Boots at one of their card parties. From the moment he'd laid eyes on her he had been smitten. He knew Tionna had a man, but at the time they were on the outs, and Happy thought that he could sway her by showering her with gifts and trips, but it had proved easier said than done. It seemed like the harder

Happy went, the colder she treated him, and something about the abuse turned him on. Happy had tried everything from giving her the down payment for a new car, which she and Gucci had spent on Fifth Avenue, to proposing in an attempt to make Tionna his alone, but her heart would always belong to Duhan.

"Shorty looks good as hell," Ron-Ron said, not even realizing that his hand had strayed to his crotch.

"Don't be looking too hard at what belong to me, ya hear?" Happy told his minions while he counted his money out in the open. He wasn't worried about somebody robbing him because it was mostly singles and twenties that he liked to flash for the sake of stunting. He kept his real money in a pouch that was safety-pinned to the inside of his boxers, and there weren't many people willing to go there.

"Last I heard, she belonged to that nigga Duhan," Wise said, rubbing it in.

"What the fuck he gonna do with that when he looking at about twenty years. Shiiit, the way I hear it, that nigga is looking at about twenty years, and that's if he's lucky. That jailbird-ass nigga can't do nothing for that sweet piece of candy, so it's up to a nigga like me to get in where I fit in. To be honest with you, he need to be thanking a boss nigga like me for trying to keep his bitch draped." Happy thumbed his nose like a boxer going into a fight.

"Here he go on his mack shit." Lou slapped the bar, laughing.

Happy whispered something to the bartender and slipped her a twenty-dollar bill. "See, that's where you're wrong." He turned to Lou and Wise. "All that fake mack shit you kicking is for the movies, G; what I'm doing is real. A queen," he cut his eyes at Tionna, "is only gonna respect a king. You little niggaz bust out ya notepads and watch how a real player lays it out." He motioned to the scene unfolding.

Happy watched in anticipation as the barmaid placed the shot in front of Tionna. They exchanged a few words and his heart soared when she pointed in his direction. He raised his glass in salute, to which she responded by frowning and sliding the drink away from her. His soaring heart went down faster than the drink her friend finished for her when Tionna turned her back to him.

"Yeah, man, we sure learned a lot, Hap," Lou said slyly.

"See, that's why your muthafucking arm is broken now, because you always got your mouth in some shit that don't concern you," Happy snapped.

"Hap, I know you ain't gonna let shorty style on you like you ain't that nigga?" Wise tried to hype him.

Happy knew how Tionna could get, so he wanted to leave it alone, but he had to save face in front of his l'il homeys. "You know better than that." Happy slid off the bar stool. "Y'all niggaz give me a second." He bounced in Tionna's direction. Knowing that the threat of drama loomed, the three stooges followed Happy.

"Bird sighting at three o'clock," Boots said when she saw Happy coming their way.

"Oh Lord, I hope this pear-shaped muthafucka don't think he gonna be in here cock-blocking all night, because I will tell him about hisself. You better check that cat, Tionna," Gucci said. She had been right there during Happy and Tionna's twisted-ass courtship, so she knew firsthand how extra he could be.

"I got this," Tionna assured her, with her back still turned to the approaching Happy. Even when he was standing right next to her she still acted like she didn't know he was there.

"So it's like that now?" Happy said to her.

Tionna slowly turned around and gave him a fake surprised look. "Oh, what's good, my dude?" Happy tried to lean in for a hug, but she held him at arm's length and opted to give him a pound instead.

"I hear, you, baby girl," he said, not missing the snub. "So where you been hiding?"

"I've been around, just ain't been on the block," she said, not wanting him to be too much in her business; though as many ears as he had on the street, he'd probably heard one thing or another already.

"I can dig it. So, what you doing out and about? You know ol' boy don't let you stay out after midnight."

"I know you ain't coming over here wit' jokes, because you know my mouth is vicious," she warned.

"Indeed I do," he said suggestively, staring at her lips.

"Muthafucka, don't play yaself, because your head stayed in my pussy more than it did in your hat."

Happy didn't know that Ron-Ron was standing directly behind him until he heard him laugh. "Since you wanna be laughing and shit, you can drink water for the rest of the night, l'il nigga," Happy barked on Ron-Ron, before turning his attention back to Tionna. "Damn, baby, I see you're still cold as a muthafucka."

"My heart is on December all year around, boo." She rolled her eyes.

"So what's up, Hap? Tionna the only one you see?" Tracy spoke up.

Happy was glad for the tension breaker. "What's up, Tracy? What y'all drinking?" Happy pulled out his bankroll.

"Whatever you're buying," Boots offered.

"I see y'all got the whole squad in here." Happy looked down the line. When he got to Gucci, she just sucked her teeth and turned her back.

"What's good, my dude, I can't get an introduction?" Wise tried to work his way into the conversation. He moved next to Gucci and extended his hand. "What's up, baby? They call me Wise, and you are . . . ?"

"I'm good," she said.

"Word? Yo, Hap, what's good wit' ya peoples? She think she all that or something?" Wise was clearly offended.

"Don't waste your time with that one, Wise. Gucci is a tough nut to crack," Happy said.

"An impossible nut when it comes to bird-ass niggaz," Gucci shot back.

"Ima let you have that one, because ain't no wins in an argument with you," Happy said.

"So long as you know," she replied.

The bartender placed a bottle of Moët White Star and a bucket of ice on the bar along with some champagne flutes. "Crack this for me, ma." Happy handed Tionna the bottle.

Tionna studied the label and handed it back. "I'm good; you know I don't drink this shit." It wasn't that she didn't like Moët—in fact she loved the rosier—but she'd had a bad experience with White Star. She drank so much of it one New Year's that she'd spent the entire night throwing up, and it had taken days to get the taste out of her mouth. Her girls knew the story, but she didn't care to share it with the rest of the group.

"I ain't never seen a chick that didn't drink Moët," Ron-Ron said.

"There's probably a lot you've never seen, shorty," Tionna said.

"Like a toothbrush." Gucci fanned her nose.

"Fuck you," Ron-Ron mumbled and walked away from the bar, followed shortly by Lou. Wise had struck out with Gucci but seemed to have established a connection with Boots, so he lingered around the girls with Happy.

"This champagne shit is cool, but a bitch like me needs something stronger," Tracy said, not really feeling how she seemed to be left out of the loop.

"Well, order whatever y'all want, I got you faded." Happy laid some bills on the table.

"You ain't gotta tell me twice." Tracy snatched the bills and ordered for all of them. While Tracy waited for the drinks, Happy went to talk to some chicken head who had been giving Tionna the evil eye the whole time he'd been sitting with her. Gucci was thankful for the interruption so she could talk to her friend.

"I don't see how you let that funny-looking nigga run up in it, T," Gucci said, glaring at Happy and the girl.

"Because he's a trick," Tionna said simply.

"That's a good enough reason for me," Boots said.

"Trick or not, that muthafucka is a pain in the ass. No matter how many times you dis him, he keeps coming back. He reminds me of a herpes outbreak," Gucci said in disgust.

"Gucci, why are you always so hard on Happy?"

"Because I can't stand guys like him; he's a fucking parasite," Gucci said. She hated Happy and men like him because of what they represented. He was a dude who played the role of a big willie, always flashing and bragging, but had really not earned any stripes in the streets. True enough, he had paper, but all the money in the world didn't compensate for the psychological baggage he brought with him. To Gucci he was nothing more than a man of low self-esteem who always acted like he was trapped in his second childhood.

"But fuck Happy: we're hunting bigger game tonight." Gucci glanced over at the Big Dawg entourage camped out in the corner.

"Gucci, I ain't hunting nothing, I'm just trying to have a good time with my homegirls," Tionna said.

Gucci slid her shades down her nose and looked at Tionna. "Who do you think you're fooling?"

"What?"

"Tionna, you think I didn't see the look in your eyes when we came up in here? Shit, when Happy sent that drink down here, I saw the diva peaking. It's only gonna be a matter of time before Harlem take hold of ya soul again and bring that glow back to ya skin."

"Gucci, don't take the fact that I'm back in the hood as I'm back to my hood shit. I might lay my head on Fortieth, but that ain't where my heart is right now. I'm trying to hold it down for my man and my kids," Tionna said seriously.

"Tionna, let's have some real talk between us." Gucci took her shades off so Tionna could see that she was serious. "That 'hold you down' shit was cool for when we were smelling our asses, but we grown now, new rules and a whole new game. We gotta get this money, flip this money, and cuff this money. I ain't got no man, because I ain't met a nigga that can please me around the board. I keep running into the same two types of niggaz: the ones who are cute but broke as hell; and the ones who're ugly with a little paper but is too damn possessive because he ain't used to no good pussy, such as ya man Happy. With that being said, I take a little of this and that from each of them and Gucci is a happy camper."

"Gucci, I ain't trying to have my pussy on loan. Those days died when I got with Duhan," Tionna said defensively.

"First off, T, I ain't fucking every nigga I deal with. Some of them just appreciate having a bad bitch on their arm in the street and are willing to compensate for it. And furthermore, me and you go back like two flats, so don't try to hit me with the *I don't fuck around* line; but we ain't gotta take it there this evening. Look, all I'm trying to tell you is that it ain't no shame in living." Gucci raised her hands in surrender.

"No doubt, I'm gonna live a little, but I ain't really trying to lose focus on what I'm out there trying to do," Tionna said

"So, where're these Big Dawg niggaz that you was so thirsty to get all up on?" Tionna asked; changing the subject.

"First of all, stop acting like a chicken head, and second of all, they're in the corner over your right shoulder. Bitch, I made a positive ID before we sat down," Gucci said, laughing.

Tionna casually looked over her shoulder and scoped the Big Dawg entourage. "That muthafucka got more people around him than the president. How you plan to compete with that?"

"Compete?" Gucci looked at her as if she'd lost it. "Gucci don't compete, ma, you know that. Those fake Eurotrash bitches and them dressed-up project hos don't count for much when a real bitch steps in the building; and the last time I checked, we was some real bitches, true?"

"All day," Tionna agreed.

"I say we drink to it." Tracy slid a shot glass of off-color liquid to each of them.

"Tracy, what the hell is that?" Tionna eyed the glass.

"It's called a Slow Fuck."

"Then that's what we'll drink to." Gucci raised her glass.

"To a Slow Fuck." Tracy threw her drink back.

"To a Slow Fuck," Tionna said and awkwardly downed her drink. She had barely gotten to enjoy the slow tingling in her gut before the bartender was setting another shot in front of her. Regardless of what she said, it was obvious that her girls were going to make this her coming-out party. It had been quite some time since she had let her hair down with her girls, and as she downed her third Slow Fuck, she decided that she would leave her troubles on the doorstep of tomorrow and make tonight all about her.

CHAPTER 15

The soft fall breeze played with the loose strands of hair that were visible from beneath his red Ed Hardy hoodie. The lime-green dragon seemed to glow in the dark recesses of the doorway he had chosen to finish his clip. From where he was standing he could see everyone coming in or out of the spot, without having to worry about being spotted himself until you were right on top of him, and by then it would be too late. Fishbowl-like sunglasses covered his eyes, but it didn't stop their almost-restless moving. Some said he was paranoid, but he liked to think of himself as someone who just enjoyed living.

He absently wrung his hands together like he was trying to wipe away something foul that only he could see. He had showered twice and washed his hands raw, but he still felt dirty. He always felt like that after he put in work. It was as if whatever had been animating his victims' bodies stained him when he parted the two. On more than one occasion he'd thought about trying to explain it to somebody, but they already treated him like a Martian, so he stayed quiet about it.

Tossing the clip, he stepped from the shadows and into the light. There were clusters of people around the club, stunting or waiting on line to get in. He took one look at the only thing standing between him and the listening party and knew he wouldn't have to wait. The same hard-faced bouncer still manned the door, but the two drinks he'd snuck off and downed had loosened him up a bit. He made small talk with the guys and slick comments to the girls, occasionally patting someone down before letting them in. He was whispering something in the ear of a thick Spanish chick when he noticed a shadow appear in front of him. He opened his mouth to comment on the red hoodie, but when he saw the face beneath the hood, the comment died and all he could utter was, "Oh, what up, bl—"

Animal raised his finger for silence. "You can finish that sentence at your own risk, but you and I know we don't eat from the same tree no more, Pudgy."

Back when he was still living in California, he wore the name Pudgy with pride, but that was before Gutter had opened the gates of hell and given them all a glimpse of the devil's true face. He was only supposed to be an emissary between his set and theirs, but he'd almost ended up a casualty of the war he was trying to help prevent. Gutter's minions had kidnaped, beaten, and burned his ass before dropping him off ass naked on the 110 freeway. To make matters worse, they had put footage of him spitting on his flag and screaming "fuck the set" all over the hood. After the video, Pudgy's credibility went out the window. Every other day it seemed like someone was taking shots at him. Eventually the hood got too hot and he headed east and re-created himself as P. That ruse only lasted for a second before word of what had really happened made its way to New York. The homeys didn't kill him, but they turned him into somewhat of a mascot for the hood.

"You know I ride by P now," Pudgy said.

Animal gave him what most would assume to be a smirk. "A man can go by a thousand names, but at the end of the day he can only *be* who he *is*. So what's up, *P*? You gonna waste your time patting me down or just let me go on my word that I ain't here to bring ya peoples no grief tonight?"

Pudgy thought on it for a minute. He knew full well that if Animal wanted to cause a problem, there wasn't much that he could do about it. The kid was a certified whack job who would give it to anybody that felt like they wanted it, but, more important, he had the power to make his life more miserable than it already was. "Yo good, fam-o." Pudgy waved him through without being searched or charged.

"I appreciate you." Animal stepped passed him and into the lounge. As soon as he stepped into the throng of people he could feel himself on the verge of an anxiety attack. The music was almost deafening to his sensitive ears. Fighting back the urge to leave, he made his way to the bar and accidentally bumped into a short kid with a big head along the way. The kid made a face like he wanted to say something, but God was on his side when a shapely young Spanish girl grabbed him by the arm. The kid proceeded to exchange words with her and forgot about Animal, which was a good thing, because Animal would've surely let him have it if the kid had continued to clown.

Animal ordered a vodka and pomegranate, which got him

a funny look from the bartender, but she went off to fill his order. While waiting for her to come back with his drink, he
observed the crowd. His eyes finally landed on the man who'd
lured him out to the listening party, Don B. He was holding
court in a small roped-off section that was erected under the
DJ booth. His entourage was so thick that most of them had to
party outside the rope, occasionally reaching in for something
so people would still recognize that they were with the Don.
Animal felt his heart swell with admiration at how the crowd
hung on his every word. He somewhat understood Tech's dislike for him, but there was no mistaking the fact that he was
the man uptown.

Animal slid his drink off the bar and ambled toward the Big
Dawg entourage. As he neared, he locked eyes with a hard-
faced black kid dressed in jeans and a flannel. The black kid
played the edge of the rope, bobbing his head to the music,
but his eyes stayed on Animal. By that time, Animal was with
within six feet of the area, moving to meet him.

"What's popping, blood?" Fully stepped between Animal
and the roped-off area.

Animal slowly raised his eyes from the drink he was sipping. "I don't think we know each other, so why you over here
talking to me, dawg?"

" 'Cause you about to invade my personal space. Who you
know over here?" the kid grilled him.

Animal could almost hear the fuse in the back of his head
ignite. He looked into the kid's eyes and saw the willingness to
go the extra mile, but he wasn't ready to cross the finish line,
which already put him at a disadvantage when going against
the Animal. He was looking to make an action movie, but it

was about to become a horror. Animal could feel the blood superheating his hand as it hovered just above his hammer. The arrogant-ass kid wasn't even going to see it coming. Just before Animal made the news, a respected voice put everything on hold.

"Y'all niggaz be the fuck easy, we all comrades." Don B. stepped from behind the rope. "Animal," he greeted the youngster with a pound. "Why trouble gotta follow you everywhere?" he joked.

"Ain't about nothing. I was just coming to say what up and Billy Strong Boy felt the need to meet me halfway," Animal said to Don B., but he kept his eyes on Fully.

"You gotta forgive my nigga Fully for that; you know how them dudes out west get down," Don B. said.

"West Coast, huh?"

"Killa Cali, nigga," Fully said, throwing up a set that Animal recognized, but didn't acknowledge.

"Fully, knock that shit off; this is the kid Animal I was telling y'all about," Don B. explained.

Fully looked him up and down. "So, this is the big bad Animal, once of the illest young MCs in Harlem?"

"I rap a little bit," Animal said modestly. Truth be told, his eclectic way of thinking gave him a style that set him apart from the rest. His style was a cross between Large Professor and early Nas, with Ghost Face–like punch lines. Don B. had been on Animal for the better part of the year, but he was reluctant to leave the streets totally behind him and take music seriously.

Don B. gave a throaty laugh. "You hear this modest-ass dude? Yo, word to mine, I'd put my money on Animal against any nigga on some battle shit."

Fully frowned. "Anybody?"

Don B. draped his arm around Animal so that his message was received with clarity. "Anybody." Don B. saw the hurt flash across Fully's face and stored the info for later. "But we'll discuss pink slips later. Come on over and meet the rest of the crew." He led Animal to their table, not bothering to see if Fully was coming. "You already know Remo and Devil." He nodded to his guards. Remo just grumbled something under his breath, but Devil actually stuck out his hand.

"You're Justice's little brother, right?" Devil gave him dap. Animal nodded. "How's he doing?"

"As well as can be expected for a man doing life, I gather."

"Right, right. Well, tell him Devil from One Fifty-third said what up."

"I'll pass the word, thanks."

"And this is the new group," Don B. cut in, directing Animal's attention to two dudes wedged between two attractive ladies. "The white boy is No Doze and the muthafucka nodding in the corner is Chip; Fully you've already met."

The dude who'd been introduced as No Doze gave Animal a light handshake and slunk back into the folds of the couch. It was as if he was trying to become the invisible sheep among the pack of wolves. Animal knew by his stiff demeanor and darting eyes that the spot made him uncomfortable. The Middle Eastern cat, Chip, didn't appear uneasy or interested in what was going on around him. He pawed lazily at the thigh of the girl closest to him, while his hooded eyes stared off into space as if he was seeing something beyond the small lounge. Animal knew that look all too well.

"Yo, where ya man Tech at? I know y'all niggaz move like two peas in a pod," Don B. inquired.

"He around somewhere; you know I don't keep tabs on that man, he's grown," Animal said.

"I hope you extended my invite to him, too?"

"Yeah; he had something to do, so he had to pass."

"I'll bet." Don B. snickered disbelievingly. "Yo, every time I extend my hand to that kid he spits in it. Man, if it wasn't on the strength of Jah . . ."

Animal raised his hands to stop Don B. "Don, let me be clear on something before you go any further. Me and you," he motioned to himself, then to Don, "we cool as fuck, but Tech is my brother. Y'all got issues that go back way before me, so I don't put my mouth in that; but at the same time I ain't gonna have nobody kicking his back in, I don't give a fuck who it is."

"I ain't mean it like that, fam," Don B. told him.

"I ain't saying you mean it one way or the other; I'm just letting you know where I stand with the situation."

Don B. studied him for what seemed a lifetime. Animal was well aware of the fact that he was outnumbered, but he didn't give a fuck, and everyone in the room knew it. Don B.'s lips parted into a wide grin. "That's why I fucks wit' you, Animal, because you a real nigga. I ain't got no problems with ya boy, I'm just trying to extend my hand in friendship. If he don't want it, I ain't gonna force him to take it."

"Fair enough." Animal nodded.

"Make yaself at home, my nigga." Don B. handed Animal a bottle of champagne to break the tension. "You're amongst family now." His tone was almost fatherly.

Animal accepted the bottle and found a spot against the wall to post up. Throughout the party Animal watched Don B. slither around the room, whispering in ears and shaking hands. In the back of his mind he heard Tech's warning and wondered if his resentment toward Don B. was because of his character or Jah's death. Animal fully understood the connection between the two and could empathize with how the death had to have hit Tech, but what he tried to convey to his mentor was that the game was about money and power; ghosts had no room in the arena unless it was in the name of revenge, and as far as he knew, bloodshed wasn't on either man's agenda.

"You good, kid?" Don B. startled Animal out of his day-dream.

"Right as rain." Animal took a deep swig from the bottle. "I'm just over here thinking, that's all."

"I hope you ain't uptight about that whole Tech thing?"

"Nah, Don, we understand each other, so I'm cool."

"Well, while you're over here busting ya brain, I hope you're giving some thought to the offer I made you about this music shit."

"Don, I keep telling you that I ain't no rapper, I'm a street nigga," Animal admitted.

"And so were the members of Bad Blood at one time. Lex, Pain, True . . . all of them were street cats, but I helped them to become stars. See, the difference between me and other muthafuckas is that I make stars. Look at True, God bless, he been a hood nigga since before he came out the womb, but he went on to become a fucking legend under me."

"He also became a martyr under you," Animal pointed out.

That one stung, but Don B. kept his game face. "Yo, what happened to True was some tragic shit, but it didn't come from anything we built. That was a case of a crazy muthafuck that didn't know how to let go of a grudge. I can control Big

Dawg's plans for a nigga, but I ain't got no power of God's plans."

Animal thought on it. "True was successful because he was talented and he was kicking shit the streets wanted to hear; that ain't what I'm putting down. Don, the way I paint my picture of the world is different from how everybody else sees it; they ain't gonna get it."

Don B. took off his shades so that Animal could see his eyes. "Dawg, the fact that you're different is just the reason why they will get it. We made a lot of cake with that hardcore shit at Big Dawg, but at the end of the day it ended up painting us into a category, same as the rest of these niggaz. The music is changing, so we have to be able to change with it. People are ready to accept change, which is why you'll fit right in."

"I don't think I'm ready for this. I mean, I wanna blow up and all that, but these streets are keeping food on my table, and I don't know if I'm ready to give that up just yet."

"Yo, kid, that shit you getting is chump change compared to what I'm talking about. Check it." Don B. pulled an envelope from his pocket and handed it to Animal. "This is one of our standard development contracts, not a record deal. This is just saying that you agree to at least work with a nigga in consideration of a record deal down the line. It's pretty standard, but feel free to have somebody look it over if it'll make you feel better."

"Don, listen—"

"No, you listen," Don B. cut him off. "I'm gonna give you fifty thousand as an advance. We'll get you on some mix tapes and doing features for some of the artists we already got on deck. Once we get your beak wet, we'll see if we can get you thirsty enough for the life to join the team. You ain't gotta answer me now. Think on it for a day or two and get back. But I gotta tell you, you keep refusing my hospitality and I might stop offering it. Enjoy the rest of the party, my dude." Don B. walked off and left Animal to ponder his offer.

CHAPTER 16

"Yo, what the fuck is ya problem?" Hollywood roared at the girl who had unknowingly saved his life.

"What the fuck is wrong with *me*, nigga? What the fuck is wrong with *you*?" she barked right back. "You tell me that you were gonna be at work and I find you up in this bitch, running around like you that nigga. What's up with that shit, Oliver?" She called him by his government name just to piss him off. Of all the chicks Hollywood expected to run into that night, his baby's mother wasn't one of them.

"Yo, they called the shit off until Monday, so I decided to shake out with my niggaz. What the fuck is wrong with that, Gloria?"

She whipped her head back and forth as if she were looking for the ghost that had just slapped her across her face. "I don't see nobody up in here with you, sniffing behind them Big Dawg niggaz as usual." A skinny girl who was at Gloria's side snickered.

Hollywood placed his finger against her temple. "Yo, don't play ya fucking self like I'm in here on some groupie shit. You know how the fuck I roll."

Gloria stared him down. "First of all, you better move that fucking finger before you lose it, and second, yes, I know how you roll, and I ain't how them niggaz roll. Hollywood, I keep trying to tell you about fucking with these fair-weather cats from up the hill, but your ass won't listen."

"Wait. Rewind the tape for a minute." Hollywood's eye started to twitch. "You questioning what I'm doing in the spot and your ass is in here, too. Who the fuck is home with the kids?"

"They're with my sister, who the fuck you think they with? You gonna stop treating me like I'm ya other baby's mother."

"Fuck all the dumb shit. You're supposed to have your ass at home with the babies instead of trying to be in here popping off."

"Pop off? Hold on, you got me fucked up. I bust my ass around that house all day with them kids and the dog your ass never walks, so if I wanna get some air I'm entitled to it."

Hollywood moved in closer to whisper. "Gloria, that's my word. You better get your ass in a cab and go back to the crib. I'll meet you there later."

"Boy you must've let that purple haze fry your brain. If I'm leaving, we're leaving together." She folded her arms. The skinny girl at her side glared defiantly at Hollywood to let him know she was riding with her friend.

Hollywood looked around to see if people were seeing his girl's act of defiance. There were two cackling broads in the corner trying to throw shade, but the dispute hadn't been made public yet, which is what he was trying to avoid. "Gloria, just get your ass in a cab, I ain't gonna have this shit outta you tonight."

"The hell you won't. Hollywood, I'm tired of you always trying to tuck me away. Now, if your ass is gonna be in here getting your drink on, then so am I."

Hollywood grabbed her by the arm. "Gloria, don't make me show my ass in here."

"Show me yours and I'll show you mine," she said defiantly.

"Is there a problem over here?" A bouncer stepped over, sensing trouble.

Hollywood poked his chest out. "Nah, I'm just sending my girl home. You good fam," Hollywood said, waving him off.

"Is everything cool?" The bouncer ignored Hollywood and addressed Gloria.

"*Is* everything cool, Hollywood?" She looked Hollywood up and down.

Hollywood sighed. "A'ight." He handed her his keys. "Go wait for me in the car. I'm gonna give this nigga Don B. this music and I'll be right out."

Gloria gave him a disgusted look. "Oh, you must think I'm stupid. Okay, Hollywood. Come on, Magda." She motioned for her friend to follow as she stormed out the door.

Before Gloria was fully out of the club, Hollywood was on his way over to the section that Big Dawg occupied. Gloria could sit her ass in the car until it bled, for all he cared; he finally had Don B.'s ear and he wasn't gonna blow his chance to get down with Big Dawg. When he reached their section, the crowd had gotten so big that there was no way to tell who was with Big Dawg and who wasn't. Hollywood slipped into the inner circle, helped himself to a glass of champagne, and moved closer to Don B., who was telling one of his classic stories.

"That's my word, when them niggaz started popping it was like the Fourth of July out here. Them lame-duck niggaz Lazy and Chiba fumbled when it jumped off, but True and Jah took it to some movie shit, right in front of police. Yo, it was brains, bullets, and bowels all over the place when them two got it in," Don B. recounted for those who didn't already know the legacy. And to those who did, it seemed like Don B. exaggerated True's role a little more whenever he told it. In all actuality, it had been Jah who was the rider that day. When they shot Yoshi he'd shown a streak so brutal that it only ballooned the legend status that he was already on the verge of creating for himself.

"Word, that was a wild-ass day," Hollywood said, trying to include himself in the conversation, which was a bad move. Everyone got quiet and turned their eyes to Hollywood.

"What?" Don B. grilled him.

Hollywood tensed up. "Nah . . . Ah, I was just saying that it was a crazy day. I was out there with y'all earlier, remember?"

"Some niggaz don't ever learn." Devil moved toward him, but Don B. held him back.

"Hollywood, your ass is like a bad rash, you just keep coming back," Don B. told him.

Feeling the tension among the group, Hollywood's heart began to race, but he managed to find his voice. "Yo, I'm trying to get on and ain't nothing gonna stop me. I'm trying to let you get first crack at these beats, but either way, somebody is gonna hear them. I'd just rather be on a championship team rather than somebody that's still fighting for playoff position."

He held the CD timidly out to Don B. He knew he was taking a hell of a gamble, but it was all or nothing.

Don B. glared at the CD for what felt like forever. When he finally reached over to take it, Hollywood flinched as if he were about to get punched. "Be easy, my nigga, I ain't gonna knock ya block off . . . at least not yet. I'll tell you what, we gonna have the DJ spin this, and if it's dope, we gonna fuck wit' you, but if it's whack, we gonna fuck wit' you." He motioned to Remo and Devil. "You cool with that?"

"Don—" Hollywood began, but he was cut off by Devil.

"Sounds like a yes to me." The bruiser cracked his knuckles.

"Ma, tell the DJ I said to spin this." Don B. handed the CD to a hanger-on without even looking to see who it was. He sat back in his chair with his arms folded, staring at Hollywood from behind his sunglasses.

Hollywood suddenly felt very ill. He wanted to run into the bathroom and throw up the Chinese food he'd eaten, but he was too afraid to break the circle of eyes that were on him. What he felt had to be what a rat felt like after being dropped into a snake's tank. The track his little man had produced was getting a buzz in the hood, but it had yet to be tested in front of a real audience, and in a circle of angry wolves wasn't how he'd imagined himself debuting it. Both his reputation and his health depended on the success of the record, because if it tanked, Remo and Devil were surely gonna punish him, and he had already seen what they could do.

When the track suddenly sprang to life through the speakers, he almost fainted. The CD was a poor quality, but you could still hear the track. When he saw one of the girls who was a part of the Big Dawg entourage make a sour face, he just knew his ass was out, but suddenly Don B. started nodding to it. Once he started nodding, everybody grooved to it. Fully even started kicking a rhyme over the track. Slowly the color came back to Hollywood's face and he allowed himself a slight smile.

"You made this?" Don B. asked, still bobbing to the tune. This gave Hollywood pause. His man had made the beat under the pretense of using it for the mixed CD he was supposed to be a part of, but Hollywood had kicked him out of the group and kept the track. He figured he had the rights to it because it had been made using his studio equipment. With this thought in his mind, he nodded. "Good, I wanna buy it. Come to the office tomorrow and I'll have the paperwork and check ready. I'll give you fifteen hundred up front and another twenty-five once we get it laid down on one of the projects we got popping. We might even be able to fit it on a B-side for one of Left Coast's singles."

"Are you serious?" Hollywood was ecstatic.

"Listen, B, the Don don't play games when it come to this paper. I'm gonna cop this l'il track off you, but when you come down bring ya catalog so I can browse. You might not be so fucking useless after all."

"Good looking, my dude." Hollywood went to give him dap, but Don B. moved away.

"Come on with all that shit, you ain't fam—yet. You made a good first impression, but the final cut will depend on your catalog."

"I got you, fam. Ima bring down all my fire shit; I got it for the streets, Don, word to mine. Yo, thanks, thanks a lot!" Hollywood could barely contain himself. He stumbled back through the lounge with an ear-to-ear grin on his face. After all the bullshit he had endured, it was finally about to go down for him. As far as the kid who had made the track, he wasn't worried about him raising a stink. When Don B. cut the check, Hollywood would just give the kid five hundred for the beat as if he were purchasing it for his own purposes. He was a slow-witted pot head who would more than likely jump at the chance to get some smoke money in his pocket.

Hollywood stepped out into the night air feeling like the king of the world and there was nothing that could knock him off his high horse. He was standing on the corner thinking about what he was going to spend his money on when he saw a familiar flash of white. He looked up in time to see his girl hit a streetlight as she tried to drive off in his whip.

CHAPTER 17

By the time the clock struck midnight, Tionna wasn't feeling much pain. Between the three Slow Fucks and the music, she was on a planet all by herself. Happy had disappeared somewhere with the girl he he'd been talking to, which suited her just fine because she really wasn't trying to waste her night on him. He had his useful moments, but this night wasn't one of them.

Boots and Wise were on the dance floor, grinding so hard that it looked like he would cum at any time. Tracy was hunched over the bar going shot for shot with a dude she'd met, leaving Tionna and Gucci to themselves.

"Huh, drink this." Gucci slid over a bottle of water and a glass of Baileys.

"You must be crazy if you think I'm gonna be in here mixing liquors with your crazy ass." Tionna took a long drink from the water bottle.

"The water is to flush the old shit, and the Baileys is to

settle our stomachs for the new shit; the night is still young."
Gucci winked.

"If you like it, then I love it." Tionna sipped the cool Baileys. "So what up, we gonna keep our asses glued to the bar all night?"

"Listen to you. An hour or go you was on some fake stuck-up shit and now you ready to swerve?"

"I'm ready to sweat some of this liquor out." She pulled Gucci to her feet and onto the dance floor just as the DJ took it back with Bell Biv Devoe's "I thought It Was Me."

Tionna and Gucci were tearing up the dance floor with their old-school steps, drawing a crowd, when a handsome young man who had the build of an NBA player invaded Tionna's space, trying to bounce with her. She tried to play it cool and move away, but he moved with her, and to her surprise he was very light on his feet. With the liquor playing devil's advocate, she decided to let the kid have it. She pulled out her best *House Party* moves, jerking and twisting in front of him. She was swift with it, but he managed to keep up. When Mob Style's Gangsta Shit came over the speakers, the entire place went crazy, including Tionna. By the end of the song, she was sweaty and the kid looked exhausted. When he tried to crack for the number, Gucci stepped up.

"Okay, you've had your fun. Now break it up." She looped her arm around Tionna's.

"It's all good, ma; I just wanna talk to your friend for a minute," he said, licking his full lips seductively. He had the look, with his diamond chain and chunky bracelet, but his swagger screamed *square*.

"That sounds like a personal problem," Gucci shot back.

He laughed. "Damn, that's some cold shit."

"Then get yaself a heavier coat," Gucci replied, before pulling Tionna back to the bar.

"Damn, Gucci, why you always hating? He was actually kinda cute," Tionna said.

"Please, that nigga ain't holding. Did you peep them tired-ass shoes?" Gucci joked.

"Your ass is so foul."

"Somebody's gotta be. Tionna, your ass attracts more pigeons than week-old bread."

"Your ass is one to talk." Tionna motioned toward a dude in a pair of suede pants who was giving Gucci the eye. He winked at Gucci and was rewarded by her turning her back on him. "Where the hell did Boots' ass go?" Gucci looked around.

"She probably took homeboy to the bathroom to suck him off." Tionna laughed.

"It wouldn't surprise me. That girl is like school on a Saturday."

"No class," they said in unison.

When the liquor and weed finally kicked into full gear, Animal managed to mellow out. Don B. passed out blunts and drinks while telling war stories of how great he was. Animal ignored him, opting to enjoy the music and watch the crowd from his perch on the armrest of the sofa. Next to him, Chip seemed to be in his own little world, which consisted of him and the iPod he was bumping. Animal had ignored him for most of the night, other than to pass or take one of the many blunts that were floating, but when he caught snatches of the song he was mumbling, it made him take notice.

I lit up from Reno, I was trailed by twenty hounds/Didn't

get to sleep that night till the morning came around, the song went. Chip must've felt Animal staring, because he turned and looked at him. "What's up?" Chip nodded.

"Pardon me for staring, I just didn't know anyone besides me knew what the hell Jerry was saying at the beginning of that verse," Animal explained.

"You know the Grateful Dead?" Chip asked, removing one of the earphones so he could hear Animal better. He was pleasantly surprised to hear that one of Don B.'s minions actually had an ear for good music.

"I've got 'Friend of the Devil' on wax, but it's all scratched to hell," Animal told him.

"I'll burn you a copy and pass it off the next time I see you." Chip raised his iPod. Then he picked up a blunt off the table and lit it. He took two deep drags and passed it off to Animal. "So, you're about to sign with Don B., too?"

Animal absently touched the contract that was folded in his pocket. "I'm thinking about it. How's it working out for you?"

Chip shrugged. "I don't have to sleep in whore motels anymore, so I guess it's cool. Don B. seems to think we're gonna be the next big thing, but I'm not really tripping; I'm just happy that our music is finally gonna get out there."

"I can dig that." Animal hit the weed. "It's funny, man, because looking at y'all, I wouldn't expect you to be a rap group."

"Yeah, I left my chain and gold teeth at home," Chip shot back.

"I didn't mean no disrespect, my dude, I just meant that you don't fit the normal criteria of what Big Dawg is usually looking for."

"I ain't haven't been around too long, but I get the feeling that as long as you can make a dollar for Big Dawg, you fit the criteria. I don't let it bother me, though. Fully and Doze are the front men; I mainly work with the beats."

"Word, what kinda tracks you do?" Animal was curious now.

"Check it out." Chip handed him one of the earphone extensions and skipped to the correct track on his iPod. When the beat came on, Animal felt it in the center of his chest. It sounded like a distorted version of Jimmy Hendrix's "Purple Haze," but it was being played by a violin.

"This shit is dope. Where'd you get the violin sample?" Animal asked.

Chip looked at him like he was stupid. "Dude, we don't fuck with samples. Everything you hear is us, including the instruments."

"You muthafuckas play, too? Now, that's something you don't see every day. I know you gonna have this joint as one of the singles off the album?" Animal inquired. Chip suddenly became very serious. "I ain't mean to get up in your business."

"Nah, it ain't that." Chip looked around to make sure no one was listening, then leaned in to whisper to Animal. "We got a million more like this one that we wanted to use, but Don B. vetoed them."

"That's ignorant as shit. Why wouldn't he use something as beautiful as this?" Animal knew that even if he never heard it again it would be a beat that would live in his head forever.

"He said they weren't radio friendly enough, that the public wouldn't get what we're trying to say. You know how the business is: if it don't make dollars, then it don't get played.

We might be able to get it on a B-side, though, if I can get Doze and Fully to side with me to fight for it."

"See, this is the kinda shit that's got me hesitant about taking this rap shit seriously. Music is too much about being marketable then being good," Animal said.

"I can dig it: music is supposed to make you feel good. Yeah, it's lucrative as hell, but it's supposed to make you feel something, anything. When I do this, I feel it in my toes, my heart, and my eyes. When I hear a track that I know is the shit, it's like . . . like . . ."

"Seeing in color?" Animal finished the sentence for him.

"Yeah, just like seeing in color." Chip smiled. Casting a quick glance over his shoulder to make sure No Doze wasn't watching, he produced what looked like a birth-control carrying case and asked, "You ever been to Fantasy Island?"

Animal's face lit up as both of them recognized the bond they shared. "It's one of my favorite vacation spots."

Over at the Big Dawg table, the party was in full swing, with bottles, blunts, and broads being passed around. The smoke was thick; the security ignored the smoking ban placed over the entire city because membership had its privileges. Chicks were throwing themselves at any- and everything that they thought was a part of the squad in hopes of getting their fifteen minutes.

"Yo, you would think that this was a strip club, the way those broads are giving it up for Don B," Tionna said when she noticed Gucci staring at the circus.

"And his arrogant ass is eating it all up. The sad part is that most of them ain't gonna end up with more than a hangover and a wet pussy," Gucci said.

"They think they game is so tight."

"Game?" Gucci looked at her. "Them niggaz ain't got no game, it's the flash of it all. Them niggaz is rappers; most of them still got that same hood-ass mentality, that's why they getting all open off them bum bitches sweating them. They wouldn't know how to handle a certified bitch."

"Talk about it," Tionna ad-libbed.

"As a matter of fact, I feel like getting on my bullshit tonight, just because my best fucking friend is out with me."

"Oh no! What you plotting on, Gucci?" Tionna was leery.

"Let's make our presence felt." Gucci pulled out her hand mirror and made sure her makeup was tight.

"We're just gonna barge up into their shit?"

"Hell no," Gucci straightened her shades, "we're gonna get invited." She strutted off toward the Big Dawg entourage. Tionna just shook her head and followed.

Twenty minutes after getting cool with Chip, Animal found himself riding a monster wave. The room swam in traces of brilliant colors and shades, behind his sunglasses, while the music wrapped him in a blanket of varying sensations. The heavy bass from the speakers pinched his cheeks like a kindly old woman, while the lyrics of the various artists fed his brain and added to his own creativity. All was right with the world.

"Glad to see you're finally loosening up," Don B. said, invading his space. Animal looked at him and couldn't help but think how much his glasses and beard made Don B. resemble the devil Tech had always made him out to be.

"All is well. Me and the boy Chip was just vibing and shit," Animal replied, keeping his thoughts to himself.

"Yeah, Animal is cool as hell," Chip half slurred. His eyes

were almost completely closed and the joint between his fingers was threatening to burn him.

"I'm glad y'all hit it off. I was thinking about paring y'all for some upcoming projects anyhow," Don B. lied.

"I'm down for whatever," Chip replied, before drifting off into a nod.

"This muthafucka here." Don B. shook his head. "So what up? You ain't fucking wit' none of these broads up in here? You know when you're a Dawg the world is your oyster." He pinched the ass of a young girl who had wandered too close to the rope.

Animal laughed good-naturedly. "I'm gonna be a dawg for life whether I sign this piece of paper or not, blood."

"Which makes it only more fitting that I have you on my team, little bro. But we can talk about business another day. You having a good time?"

"Yeah, the scene is fly." Animal looked around causally. Just beyond Don B., a woman caught his eye. Much like his, her eyes were covered by sunglasses in the dark lounge, meaning she had something to hide. He watched her cross the room like she owned it and found that he had a hard time looking away from her. It was like her body was radiating some magnificent light show that only he could see.

"Yeah, them two broads could definitely get it," Don B. said, picking up on where Animal was staring. "What up, you trying to snatch that?"

"Nah, I'm straight," Animal said modestly. He turned away, but found that his eyes kept wandering back.

"Stop acting like that, my nigga: I told you this is all about us," Don B. told him. He looked around until he found one of his underlings and waved him over. He whispered something into the young man's ear and sent him off. Don B. turned back to Animal. "Trust in the Don, I got everything covered."

It didn't take long for Tionna and Gucci to receive the full-court press. They exerted so much power and sexiness that they attracted the opposite and the same sex like flies on shit. Gucci stalked across that spot like she was on the biggest runway of her entire life, while Tionna got her money's worth out of the tight-fitting heels. Their whole aura screamed *bad bitches* and the whole spot knew it, including Big Dawg.

"Pardon me." A dude who they recognized as part of Don B.'s crew approached them. He was wearing a Fendi track suit and a gold chain that looked like it weighed more than he did. "Miss, can I speak to you for a minute?" Gucci thought he was talking to her, so it surprised her when he approached Tionna. "My man was wondering if he could speak to you for a minute?" He pointed at Don B., who raised his glass in salute.

Gucci twisted her face. "Tell your man that only chicken heads get sent for." The dude looked like he was shocked by her refusal of his Don, but he went off to relay the message.

Tionna whispered to Gucci, "I thought the whole point of coming over here was to get invited in. Don't you think you're pushing your luck?"

"When you gamble, you play all or nothing, T," Gucci replied. She watched the kid repeat what she had said to Don B., which made him laugh. Don B. said a few words to the kid in the hoodie sitting next to him. The kid looked like he was protesting, but Don B. eventually got him to his feet. Together they broke the protective circle and approached Tionna and Gucci.

"What's up, ladies? My hospitality ain't no good?" Don B.

was speaking to both of them but had his eyes on Tionna. Gucci got ready to hit him with a slick response, but Tionna touched her arm, letting her know she had it under control.

"Hospitality is a wonderful and rare thing, but if you wanna get a lady's attention, you don't send one of your lackeys to ask her over, you do it yourself," Tionna schooled him.

"I'm here, ain't I?"

"With one strike against you already, you wanna try for two?" Tionna fired right back.

Don B. raised his hands in surrender. "I conceded, Ms. My name is Don B. and I was wondering if I could get you and your friend to come over and have a drink with us." He executed a mock bow. This made Animal snicker.

"What, it's funny when a dude knows how to talk to a lady?" Gucci pressed him. She could smell the shyness coming off the young boy and decided to fuck with him, but, to her surprise, Animal was quite the quick-witted one.

"Nah, it ain't that at all. You show me a lady, and I'll show you a gentleman. Show me a bitch and I'll show you a G; not saying that you fall into either category, of course."

"You gotta excuse Animal, he doesn't think like everybody else," Don B. joked.

"Your mama named you Animal?" Gucci asked. He was cute, but he looked to be a little on the young side. She sized him up openly, trying to get an idea of what the man called Animal was about. From the brilliant chain around his neck she knew he was getting some type of cash, but he seemed out of place in a room full of street cats.

"Of course my mother didn't name me Animal." He half smiled at the girl's aggressive approach. He knew she was interested and so was he. "The story behind what my mama named me and what the streets recognize is a long one. You got that kind of time, Ms. . . . ?"

"Gucci," she informed him.

"Your mama named you Gucci?" Animal teased her back.

"Actually, she did," she said seriously.

"You got that one." Animal made a motion like he was tipping his hat.

"So, Gucci and company, y'all trying to kick it with us or what?" Don B. motioned toward their area.

Tionna studied his face before answering, "I guess we can chill with y'all for a minute, at least until something better comes along."

Don B. laughed, while leading them back to the velvet rope. "Trust and believe that this is as good as it gets, ma." He lifted the rope and welcomed them into the circle.

As soon as they crossed the plain, Tionna felt it. The stares, whispers, and overall hate coming from the girls who thought they had already sewn up their positions. Tionna helped herself to a glass of champagne, rosier, and soaked it all in. It was just as Gucci had said: they recognized that a real bitch had just come on the scene.

CHAPTER 18

Happy was leaning against the bar, looking like he had lost his best friend. When he'd come back from letting the girl suck him off in the whip, Tionna was nowhere to be found. He told himself time and again that he wasn't gonna deal with her anymore. After all, Tionna was self-centered and only out for his money, but being around her gave him a high like no drug he'd ever indulged in. It wasn't because of the sex, though she fucked like a stallion, but being with her was forbidden. Tionna belonged to Duhan, which only added to Happy's obsession.

Happy and Duhan weren't friends to speak off, but they were associated with some of the same people. They were getting their coke from the same person, a Jamaican kid from the Bronx who had it snowing in New York all year around. Duhan had weight by the boatloads, which is part of the reason that he found himself on the ass end of an indictment and about to take a long trip. Being that Happy and the kid went way back, he expected to succeed him, but, to his surprise, the Jamaican put Duhan in pocket. Happy had never seen Duhan as much more than a little project nigga throwing stones at the penitentiary, but Duhan had ended up surpassing him and forcing Happy to find other ways of supplementing his income. Duhan knew Happy only in passing, but the older man felt like Duhan was purposely stepping on his toes and he resented him for it. Happy had managed to fuck Duhan's girl, but he wasn't satisfied with that. He wanted his lady, and his connect.

"Why you sitting there looking so sad?" Boots invited herself to the seat next to Happy. Her skin was sweat-slick and shiny from dancing and drinking all night. Her eyes were glassy and low.

"Shit, I'm having a good time, what I got to be sad about?" Happy tried to front. Boots saw through it. "You ain't gotta front for me, Hap, I know the look. Tionna got you over here feeling some kind of way. Why do you keep doing it to yourself?"

"Boots, you tripping; ain't nobody stunting Tionna's ass. It's plenty mo' bitches round this bitch. If I don't wanna go home alone, I sure as hell ain't got to."

"I know that's right." Boots moved closer to him. He could smell the mix of musk and liquor coming out of her skin. Her hardening nipples pressed against the thin fabric of her blouse, drawing his eyes to them, as she had expected. "Wow, my mouth is dry as hell."

"We can fix that," Happy told her.

Boots placed her hand on his thigh. She noticed him harden in his jeans. "Happy, ya mind is always in the gutter. I ain't fucking wit' you."

"What, I was just trying to offer you a drink," Happy lied.

"I'll take the drink for now. Anything after that is negotiable."

Happy couldn't repress the smile forming on his face. "That's what I need to hear."

"Party like a rock star!" Tracy sang along with the song. From the way she was spilling her drink left and right, you could tell she was twisted. "Yo, tell ya boy to get his weight up, he ain't ready to fuck with no grown bitch on this drinking shit," she clowned Wise, whose most recent cup looked almost untouched. When her original drinking partner's money ran short, she relieved Boots of Wise's attention.

"Yo, shorty is on her lush life shit for real," Wise told his people. He gave Happy the jump-off look and inquired about Boots. Happy nodded like they were on the same page, but he was secretly wondering if him banging Boots would ruin things between him and Tionna. She was high siding and he needed to get his rocks off with one broad or another.

"Tracy can throw them back with the rest of them," Boots said proudly.

"Muthafucking right," Tracy slurred. She plopped onto the stool next to Boots and tried to find something to focus on to keep her head from spinning. When her eyes went back to the makeshift VIP section, they spotted a familiar emblem. "Check this shit." She tapped Boots's leg. "How them bitches get back there?"

"The better question should be why the fuck they didn't invite us," Boots said. She had completely forgotten about Happy when she saw how much fun Tionna and Gucci were having. "We're over here partying with these extra-medium niggaz and while they back there on they Ron Brownz shit, I like to pop bottles, too."

"I say we go and see about that," Tracy said.

"How we gonna slip away from these niggaz?" Boots wanted to know.

"Leave that to me." Tracy got up off the stool. She took a step in Wise's direction and faked left like she was going to faint. "Damn, a bitch is tipsy as hell," she said, thickening her slur.

Boots caught on quick. "Girl, I told you about throwing that shit back like that. Let me take you outside to get some air."

"Y'all want us to come?" Happy asked.

"Nah, I got her," Boots said almost too quickly. "She just needs some air."

"Don't take too long, baby; we were having an interesting conversation," Happy said.

"I ain't gonna be long, Hap." Boots winked at him and led Tracy shambling through the crowd. When they had gotten far enough for Happy to lose sight of them, the girls got low and banked a hard left in the direction of the Big Dawg party.

"Why do you keep staring at me like that?" Gucci asked Animal.

Animal took his shades off and examined them as if they were defective, before sliding them back over his eyes. "And what makes you think I'm looking at you?"

"Because I can feel the heat coming off ya ass," she joked.

"You got jokes, Gucci-Gucci, shorty rocked a dobie, had my shades on but she saw right through me," he sang.

"Oh, so you're a rapper?"

"Nah, I ain't no rapper, I'm a street nigga," he said honestly.

"So then what the hell are you doing with Don B.? Everybody knows he doesn't hang with goons in public."

"I didn't say I was a goon, I said I was a street nigga," he corrected her.

"I didn't know that there was a difference."

"Baby girl," he leaned forward so she could hear him without shouting, "let me school you on a little bit of Animal philosophy. See, a goon is a beast, somebody who when you see them coming you go the other way because you know it's about to be some shit. Now, niggaz know me on the streets for having beastly qualities, but the beast doesn't define my character. I call myself a street nigga because I'm a child of the streets. She birthed me, raised me, and fed me. I am for her as she is for me." When he finished his explanation, he noticed she was giving him a funny look. "Now you're the one staring."

"You got that one," she said, laughing it off. "Look, don't take this the wrong way . . ."

"Then don't say it."

"Nah, it's nothing bad, it's just that you're different."

"God made us all different."

"Not like that." She tried to find the right words. "What I mean is, I know you're a street dude—hell, you gotta be with a name like Animal—but you don't talk or act like the rest of these dudes." She motioned toward a guy who was slapping some girl on the ass like they were at a strip club.

Animal studied the guy for a minute before responding. "Some niggaz," he nodded at the spectacle, "gotta show out to make theirselves feel like somebody. Me," he pounded his chest, causing his chain to rattle, "I know I'm somebody."

Gucci took the medallion delicately in her hand and admired the detail in it. It brought back memories of her and Tionna hurrying to finish their dinner so they could watch the Muppet show. "And who are you?"

He stared at her like she was speaking a foreign language that he was trying to decipher. "I'm the Animal," he said, showing off his gold teeth.

"Man, that's the first time I seen you smile all night," Don B. said, disrupting the moment. He had a bottle in one hand and Tionna in the other. She was so high that her eyes were damn near closed.

"Y'all over here cheesing like two schoolkids," Tionna said. Gucci shot her a dirty look.

"Ain't about nothing, I'm just over here picking your homegirl's brain," Animal said, as if he didn't feel the connection, too.

"Yo, Gucci, what up?" Tracy waved from the other side of the rope, trying to get her friend's attention. "Tionna!"

"Do you see these bitches?" Gucci whispered to Tionna.

"Act like you don't see them," Tionna said, trying to not to make eye contact with the girls. They were making so much of a ruckus that security was looking at them funny.

"Y'all know them chicks?" Don B. asked.

Gucci looked at Tionna, who just turned her head. "Yeah, we came with them," Gucci admitted. They were ghetto as hell, but they were still her girls.

"Let 'em through," Don B. instructed his security. The two girls almost caused a stampede trying to get to the other side of the rope.

"Well, well, this is where y'all disappeared to. Y'all wasn't gonna invite us to the party?" Boots said slyly.

"Y'all had ya hands full," Gucci said, sipping from her glass. "Whatever happened to Mutt and Jeff anyhow?"

"Please, we left them right where we found them. They were lightweights anyway," Tracy said.

"So, Tionna, are you gonna introduce me to your friend?" Boots asked sarcastically.

Tionna slit her eyes at Boots to let her know that she hadn't changed that much. "Well, the last time I checked, I saw a television in your house, so I'm sure you know who he is, and furthermore he ain't my friend to introduce; I'm just sitting here having a conversation."

"T, you know I was just playing, so stop acting like that." Boots gave her a fake laugh. "How you doing, Don? I'm Boots and this is my girl Tracy."

"Charmed." Don B. gave her hand a light shake.

"I know that ain't Tracy Stewart." Remo looked closer.

"We know each other?" Tracy made a stink face. The alcohol had her nearly seeing double.

"Come on, stop acting like that. It's Kareem." He spread his arms and smiled. When she saw that missing tooth, a light of recognition went off in her head.

"Oh shit. What up, Reem?" She hugged him. "Nigga, when you came home?"

"I've been home for a minute, sis. I'm working for my nephew doing security." He pointed to Don B.

"Blow-up kid." Tracy nodded in approval.

"Damn, is there anybody your ass don't know, unc?" Don B. teased Remo.

"Man, me and shorty go back to Kurtis Blow."

"Literally, the eighties was a muthafucka," Tracy added, thinking back to some of the wild coke parties she'd attended in her day. "What's that y'all sipping on?" She eyed the variety of bottles on the tables.

"Help yaselves, ladies," Don B. invited them. Tracy picked up a bottle of vodka and poured herself a healthy drink. Boots opted for a Corona, which she brought with her when she squeezed in next to Tionna and Don B.

"You got an opener?" Boots leaned across Gucci to speak to Don B. She made sure that he got a healthy view of her cleavage in the process.

"If you don't get them big-ass jugs off me." Tionna pushed her away.

"Sorry, T, you know these shits be all over the place." Boots smiled innocently.

"Tell me about it," Gucci mumbled.

"And who is this with all the pretty hair?" Boots reached to touch Animal's hair, but he pulled back.

"No disrespect, shorty, but I don't really take to being touched uninvited." He leaned closer to Gucci. When their hands touched, a spark passed between them.

Boots made a face that was somewhere between surprise and scorn. "My bad, Gucci; I didn't know you was claiming shorty."

"Mmm, that little muthafucka is too pretty," Tracy said jokingly. Animal squirmed under her predatory gaze, but he kept his cool. He was used to being the one putting people under pressure, but the two chicks made him feel like he was a mouse trapped between two cats.

"It's getting too crowded over here for me. I'm gonna hit the bar right quick." Animal got up from the sofa.

"Hold on, I'll come with you." Gucci got up.

"Hold on, handsome. With all this liquor y'all got on the table, what you going to the bar for?" Boots called after him.

Animal stopped short and fixed his eyes on her. "Shorty, ain't nothing at this table that I want. You coming?" He extended his hand to Gucci, which she readily took. Before allowing Animal to lead her away, she gave Boots one last glare. Though Boots couldn't see Gucci's eyes, she knew from the set of her face that she was tight.

"See, that's why I don't be fucking wit' these project bitches—they ain't got no class. Let that have been my cake and a bitch played me to the left, I would've zoned out on her monkey ass," Ron-Ron continued his rant.

"Yo, stop being a troublemaker, B, it ain't Hap's fault. If I was a bitch, I'd chose a megastar rapper over him, too." Wise burst out laughing.

"So this shit is funny to you, huh?" Happy turned his murderous glare on Wise. For the past half hour Happy had sat and watched Don B. paw over Tionna and feed her drinks, while she lapped it all up. He could recall a time when he used to feed her drinks, but it seemed as if she had a new sponsor. Happy was an explosion waiting to happen and didn't much care who had lit the fuse.

"Chill, Hap. It's about twenty more broads in here, so you ain't gotta stunt no one. Fuck that bitch; let niggaz toss her up." Lou was trying to defuse the situation, but he had unknowingly added fuel to the fire.

In Happy's mind, he saw Don B. and his minions with Tionna in some fancy hotel treating her like a dime-store whore, and it sent him over the edge. "Fuck that." Happy slid off the bar stool. "These bitch-ass rap niggaz is gonna stop acting like they don't know who the real gangsters are." He started off in the direction of the Big Dawg party.

Lou uselessly tried to talk him out of it, Ron-Ron was at his side, and Wise just couldn't stop laughing.

"I swear, that broad could fuck up a wet dream." Gucci hunkered over the bar angrily.

"Don't trip off that. We all got peoples who act up a little bit from time to time." Animal placed a vodka and palm in front of her. He could tell that she was feeling in a way, because she didn't even ask what it was before she attacked it.

"This shit is a regular thing with Boots. The only reason she was even flirting with you is because she knew I liked you."

"Oh, you like me, huh?" He picked up on the slip.

"Don't flatter yourself. I mean you're good peoples," she lied.

"And how would you know? I could be the boogeyman in disguise."

She frowned. "Boy, knock it off. You look too innocent to be a monster."

"So I've been told," Animal said, remembering how many others had made the same mistake about him. "Don't let them gals ruin the rest of your evening, Ms. Gucci; one monkey don't stop no show. Besides, I don't go for ghetto broads."

"Excuse you, I'm from Forty-first and Eighth, nigga, so watch that." Gucci snaked her neck.

"Easy, ma, you misunderstand me. Gucci, you're hood, but you ain't ghetto; you got swag about you that a lot of these chicks lack."

"Should I take that as a compliment?"

He shrugged. "Take it how you want it, I'm just clarifying myself. Why are you so defensive, Gucci?"

"You bugging." She waved him off.

"Nah, I don't think I am. Everything I say, you try to find a flaw or some hidden message in it, when all I'm trying to do is compliment your style. What's the matter, ain't you used to nobody complimenting you?"

She blushed at the fact that either she was so transparent or he was so in tune with her. "My mother always taught me to be leery of men with silver tongues: nine times outta ten they want more than what they're saying."

"Your mother was right to warn you against men, but I ain't a man, I'm an animal, and I don't want any more from you than what you're willing to give."

"Who says I'm gonna give you anything?" Gucci frowned.

"And who says I'm gonna ask you for anything?" he shot back. This turned her frown around a bit.

"Animal, do you always talk in circles?"

"Only when I'm walking in them." He walked around her slowly, not close enough to touch her, but enough that she could feel the heat radiating from his body. Between the pills and the heady scent of her, he felt like his skin was on fire.

"You're weird."

Animal stopped his circling. "Nah, just misunderstood." She opened her mouth to say something, but her eyes darted just over Animal's shoulder. Instinctively he whirled around, ready to draw his hammer at the first sign of danger. He was a little puzzled when he saw a kid bulldozing his way through the crowd, but he wasn't coming in their direction.

"Here this nigga go with this dumb shit." Gucci sucked her teeth.

"That your man or something?" Animal asked, starting to feel different about Gucci.

"Lord, no, that ain't my headache." Gucci laughed. She watched in amusement as Happy tried to puff his chest out and exchanged words with Tionna. It was all funny until Don B. reached into his pouch and the shit hit the fan.

"That bitch always gotta be the center of attention," Boots said once Gucci was out of earshot.

"And you always feel the need to play yourself," Tionna said, making it clear that she wasn't going to have anyone talking about her friend.

"I forgot y'all were the dynamic duo." Boots sucked her teeth.

"Hate is a color that doesn't suit you well, ma," Tionna shot back.

"Y'all bitches knock it off; in here arguing over a piece of dick like you don't know better," Tracy interjected.

"True story, ma, it's more than enough of us to go around," the kid who had approached Gucci and Tionna on behalf of Don B. added, draping his arm around Tracy.

"Little nigga, you better stay in a child's place," Remo warned him.

"My bad." The kid backed up.

"I should've known that coming out with y'all heifers was gonna go to the left," Tionna said, sipping from her glass.

Tracy fixed her eyes on something across the room. "Don't look now, but it's about to get way more interesting."

Tionna looked up to see what the drunk girl was babbling about and spotted Happy coming in their direction, and from the look on his face she could tell he was pissed.

Devil intercepted Happy before he reached the rope, but Happy acted as if he didn't even notice him. "Can I talk to you for a second," Happy addressed Tionna.

"Fam, ain't nobody over here for you. Keep it moving," Devil told him.

"That's how it is, T?" Happy asked her, still ignoring Devil.

"Hap, I'm kinda in the middle of something." She raised her glass. "I'll call you."

"So you just take my money, drink my drink, fuck me, then act like you don't know a nigga when you get around your new friends?" Happy was breathing heavy now and it sounded like he had to concentrate to compose his words.

"Hold on, B, ya mouth is wild reckless." Don B. was on his feet. Several more men surged behind him. "Tionna," he looked down at her, "I thought you said ya man was locked up. This nigga looks free as a bird to me." He thumbed at Happy.

"This is not my man. Happy, why are you over here trying to clown?" Tionna was now standing, too. With the argument forgotten in the face of a potential threat, Boots and Tracy were at her side.

"Bitch, you over here putting on a show and you're asking me about clowning?" Happy barked.

"A'ight, playboy. You outta order, so now you gotta bounce," Don B. told him.

"Back up wit' all that shit; you ain't the only nigga in the hood with a few dollars, so don't be talking to me like I'm the help. This ain't got nothing to do with you," Happy said, snarling at Don B.

Never being one to be outdone, Don B. went the extra mile.

"Check it." He pulled a huge bankroll from the pouch fastened around his waist and counted off a few bills. "Get yaself a bottle, on me, then go play in traffic, you fucking clown." Don B. tossed the bills in Happy's face. The roar of laughter from everyone who saw it was so loud that Happy couldn't even hear himself think. He knew he had no wins against the entourage, but the smirk Tionna was trying to hide was enough to have him throw logic out the window. Happy's hand had just made it to his pocket when Remo caught him in a reverse choke hold.

"Not tonight, nigga." Remo shook him like a rag doll.

"Come on, man, why y'all tripping," Happy said, gagging. Ron-Ron tried to pull out the small gun that Happy had made him carry, but Devil slapped him halfway across the room before he could draw the weapon. People scrambled to get out of the way as the Big Dawg entourage swarmed on Happy and his crew and turned the party into a battle royal.

Gucci shoved and elbowed her way through the crowd, trying to get to her friend, with Animal hot on her heels. Bottles, chairs, and everything else that wasn't nailed down flew around the room as a full-scale riot broke out. She had almost reached the area where she had left her friends when she heard the first shot; before the second one rang out, she found herself slammed to the floor, with Animal shielding her.

"Get off me. I gotta see if my girls is alright." She struggled under him. Animal was thin but incredibly strong.

"Be easy, Gucci; Remo and Devil got them. We gotta bust a move before them people get here," Animal said. As if he'd spoken them into existence, a swarm of blue uniforms rushed the front door. They didn't even ask questions before they started clubbing and pepper spraying the partygoers. There was no way Animal intended on being caught with his gun, but there were too many of them to even think about shooting his way out. "We gotta go." He snatched her off the floor.

"I'm not leaving without my friends," Gucci said, continuing to try to break away.

"Yes the hell you are." Animal grabbed her around the waist and picked her up. Using the butt of his gun to clear a path, he made a beeline for the steps leading down to the bathrooms.

"Animal, put me down before I cut your ass," she threatened.

Animal ignored her and kept moving. At the end of the hall there was a fire exit marking their path to freedom. Without breaking his stride, Animal kicked the door open, spilling himself and Gucci into the night air.

PART 3
LOYALTY

CHAPTER 19

"I can't believe you did that shit," Gucci fumed as she dialed Tionna's cell phone again. She had been trying to call her friend for the last forty minutes and kept getting the voice mail.

"Gucci, stop worrying: they were with Don B., they're good," Animal said, staring at the Harlem streets out the window of the taxi.

"And how the fuck do you know? They were shooting and the police came—for all we know, Tionna could be hurt!" Gucci was starting to panic again.

"I know because Don B. has police working security for him. They might have to answer some questions, but I doubt if they gotta sit. Don B.'s reach goes a long way. And as far as them getting shot, I seriously doubt that." He laughed.

"I don't see what the fuck is so funny; those were your peoples in there, too!"

"First off, lady, I ain't got no peoples, at least not in there.

Me and Don B. cool, but it's more business than anything. And second, it's a little hard to get hit by a stray when the kid with the gun is shooting into the air. He was trying to get the goons off his peoples, but he wasn't trying to kill nothing."

"And what if he was trying to kill something?" she asked.

Animal smiled. "He wasn't, so ain't no need to discuss what might've happened. What the hell was that dude's problem anyway?"

"That's one of Tionna's old boos who doesn't seem to know when he's been kicked to the curb," Gucci admitted.

"I hope you ain't got no crazy niggaz waiting in the wings for me when I'm trying to spend time with you."

"Oh, so you're trying to spend time with me, huh?"

Animal shrugged. "I'd given it some thought, but I don't know."

"What do you mean, you don't know?"

"I say I don't know because it seems like the prettiest girls always need rescuing from some nut-ass nigga." He laughed.

"You got that one, Animal. Speaking of which, if you're trying to spend time with me, then you might wanna tell me what your government name is. I can't introduce you to my moms as Animal."

This one caught him off guard. It had been a while since anyone had inquired as to his government name and longer still since he'd spoken it aloud. He started to feed Gucci another line, but something in her big brown eyes made him want to open up to her. "It's Tayshawn."

"That's it?" She made a face.

"Is there something wrong with my name?" He sounded offended.

"No, it's actually pretty normal. The way you were being

all secretive about it, I thought it was something all fucked up. How come you'd rather be called Animal instead of Tayshawn?" Animal got quiet. "I'm sorry, I didn't mean to be all in your business."

"Its cool, Gucci. My father named me Tayshawn, after him, but I don't know my dad and he didn't stick around to get to know me, so I don't feel right carrying any part of him with me. The streets were my parents and they named me Animal, so that's what I go by."

"Which building?" the taxi driver asked.

"Up here on the right." Gucci pointed at a brown brick building. She reached into her purse to pay him, but Animal stopped her.

"I got it; it's the least I can do after getting your outfit all dirty." He motioned to the stains on her knees from when he'd tackled her.

"Thanks for that, Animal. You probably saved my life in there," she said seriously.

"It ain't nothing you wouldn't have done for me, right?"

"Boy, you're as fine as you wanna be, but not fine enough for me to jump in front of no bullet," she joked. "But I do appreciate it. I owe you."

"I know, and you'll make it up to me when we go to dinner," he said.

"Oh, so now this is the part where you cracked for my number, huh?"

"Nah, I was actually gonna give you mine and put the ball in your court. I don't like pressure, so I'll leave it up to you to call me." He wrote his number down, then got out and went around to the other side to open her door.

"I told you earlier, if you show me a lady, I'll show you a

gentleman; show me a bitch, and I'll show you a G," he re-peated.

Gucci smiled. "The gentleman side of you is lovable, but the G side is sexy. With so many choices, what's a girl to do?"

Animal stepped closer. "Make your next move your best move." He kissed her. It was a quick and gentle kiss, but it stirred a wealth of emotions in Gucci. "Don't take too long to use that, Gucci." Animal got back into the cab and told the driver to pull off, leaving Gucci standing on the curb, watch-ing the taillights fade. She didn't know if she believed in love at first sight, but she was feeling Animal deeply.

When she turned to her building she noticed two people: Rock Head, who was sitting on the stoop, and her mother, who was glaring down at her from the window. She waved up to her mother to let her know she was coming and headed for the building entrance, where Rock Head started right in with the questions.

"Yo, you just coming from the Big Dawg joint? I heard nig-gaz was shooting up in there," Rock Head pressed her. Gucci hadn't noticed it at first, but he was with a girl she knew couldn't have been in any higher than the tenth grade. His fe-tish for young girls was one more reason that she didn't like to be around him.

"I heard something popped off, but I was gone before it did," Gucci lied.

Rock Head's face said he didn't believe her, but he knew better than to press it. "Gucci, let me ask you something."

"What, nigga?" She was tired and still needed to check on Tionna. She didn't have the energy or the patience to deal with Rock Head's shit.

"Was that who I think it was?" he asked.

"Depends on who you think it was."

"Gucci, you might wanna be easy with that boy there, he's bad news," he told her.

"Rock Head, you got some nerve with all the shit you stay in. That boy there is more of a gentleman that you'll ever be," she defended Animal.

"Gentleman? Gucci, you gotta be human to be considered a gentleman and he ain't human—that little muthafucka is an Animal."

"So I hear." She kept stepping into the building.

"A'ight, Gucci, but when the devil finally shows his horns, you can't say I didn't try to warn you," he called after her.

"Where the hell have you been?" Ronnie was on Gucci as soon as she walked in the door.

"Ma, I'm tired, so please don't start," Gucci said, tossing her purse onto the couch and going into the kitchen.

"You've got some damn nerve telling me not to start when it's almost four in the morning and I told you heifers to be back here by two thirty," Ronnie snapped. Then it dawned on her that Gucci was alone. "Where is Tionna?"

"She, ah—"

"Gucci," Ronnie cut her off, "I ain't flew here, I grew here, so before you even finish that statement you need to know that one, I'm bullshit-proof and two, I'll slap the black off both of you bitches if you try to play me with some funky-ass story when that girl's kids is in my bed instead of their own."

Gucci knew that her mother was in no mood to play, so she came clean. "Okay, Ma, this is what happened." She went on to give Ronnie the short version of the story, leaving out the part about them being in the company of notorious gangsters.

"I knew it, I knew it. The minute I dreamt about your father, I knew something had gone wrong," Ronnie said.

"What's Daddy got to do with it?" Gucci asked, puzzled.

"Whenever I dream about your father, it means you're going to do something to piss me off, just like he used to. How do you think I knew it was really you who spilled Neet all over my damn rabbit-fur coat in eighty-nine? Now, what precinct did they take Tionna to?"

"I don't know, Mommy. Everything happened so fast that we got separated," Gucci admitted.

"What the hell do you mean, y'all got separated? Gucci, I know you didn't leave that club without making sure Tionna was good?"

"But, Mommy, the police—"

"Don't give me that shit, Gucci. I understand you getting up outta the spot so you didn't go to jail, but you wasn't supposed to bring your ass back in this house without finding out exactly where Tionna was and if she was okay. If that's your friend, then that's how you carry it."

"Yes, Mommy," Gucci said. As if she didn't feel guilty enough, Ronnie was making her feel worse. "I'll call around and see if anybody has heard from her. If not, I'll go check some of the local precincts."

"Unless you plan on doing it on the bus, it'll have to wait for tomorrow. If they do have her locked up somewhere, she ain't getting out until sometime tomorrow, and I gotta go to work in the morning. Let her ass sit and stew on it for a while, she'll be okay."

"That's foul, Mommy."

"Don't throw stones, honey. Y'all gonna lean one day. And Tionna better hope the police keep her ass, because when I see her it's on and cracking, leaving me in here with them bad-ass kids, knowing they ain't got no home training. Little Du-han spilled ice cream on my good couch and the stain act like it don't wanna come out."

"I'll take care of it, Ma," Gucci said, fixing herself a healthy bowl of cereal to fight off the munchies that had descended on her.

"You're damn right you will. I'm telling you, y'all lucky I'm saved or else it'd have been some shit in here." Ronnie continued to rant as she went back to bed.

Glad that Ronnie had finally gotten out of her face, Gucci went into the living room and plopped down in front of the television. She tried to call Tionna, Boots, and Tracy, but couldn't reach any of them. It was out of her hands at that point, so she decided to go to bed and deal with it in the morning. As she was emptying her pockets to put her clothes in the laundry, she came across Animal's number. As she admired his remarkably neat handwriting, Rock Head's warning came back to her. She wasn't as naïve as to think that Animal was innocent because anybody associated with Don B. had to have some type of street credibility, but the things Rock Head had said were harsh. With the exception of the time during the shooting, Animal had been polite, funny, and sharp, hardly what she would've expected from the caliber of killer Rock Head had tried to make him out as. But she knew better than anyone how deceiving looks could be. With those thoughts in her mind, Gucci drifted into a peaceful, drunken sleep.

CHAPTER 20

It was going on eleven thirty the next morning when they finally let Tionna go. When the police had rushed the spot, they'd kicked the ass of anything darker than a paper bag left and right. Luckily for them, several members of Don B.'s entourage were on the force, so they were spared the harsh treatment; but they still had to be brought in for questioning about the shooting that had accidentally turned into an attempted homicide.

The police tried to say that it had been a shoot-out between Don B.'s entourage and the local Crips gang that they were said to have been feuding with, but that wasn't what really happened. As it turned out, Ron-Ron had started clapping in the air to try to scare Don B.'s people, but someone had tried to play hero and taken the gun from him. During the struggle, the gun had gone off and hit a girl in the back who had been trying to get out of the way. The girl lived, but she would never walk again.

In the presence of a lawyer provided by Don B., the police asked Tionna the same questions forward backward and sideways, but her story never changed: "I was just having drinks with some friends when these guys started shooting. I don't know who they were shooting at, and no, Don B. did not have a gun." They also asked if she had seen the shooter, which she denied, even though she had been looking right at Ron-Ron when he pulled the gun. The police knew she was lying, but had no way to prove it.

The lawyer was trying to tell her to wait for Boots and Tracy, who would be coming out next, but Tionna wasn't even listening as she made a mad dash for the exit. Her cell phone was dead so she couldn't even call Gucci to tell her that she was out and to check on the kids, but she hoped she'd understand, even though she was sure Ms. Ronnie wouldn't. That was a bridge she would cross when she came to it. She had just over two hours to make it to Rikers to catch Duhan's visit. Tionna was tired and smelled like she'd been partying all night, but she didn't have time to go home. Don B. had offered to give her a ride, but after all she'd been through she didn't feel like being bothered. Promising to give him a call later, she hopped into a taxi and directed him to Rikers Island.

The cabbie was about his business, getting Tionna to the Island in record time. It cost her damn near all the money she'd brought out with her, but it was worth it if it meant she would make the visit. She hopped out of the cab just as the van was loading the last of its passengers to take them across to the Island. Tionna sat next to a girl who smelled like onions and garlic, but she doubted if she smelled much better, so she let it ride.

The whole time she stood on the slow-moving line to the intake building, she kept looking down at her watch. It was bad enough that she wasn't going to get to spend a lot of time with him, but the process was threatening to spoil the visit altogether. She finally made it to the front, only to have a beat-faced hack tell her she couldn't come in because her ID card had expired the day before. Thankfully, she spotted an officer she used to deal with and he persuaded his comrade to let her slide. Next, she went through the motions of the metal detector, which required her to take everything out of her pockets and walk through barefoot. She made it through the arch and filled out the proper paperwork without incident; it wasn't until she was waiting for the bus to take her to Duhan's housing unit that the bullshit started.

Tionna was sitting on one of the hard benches, reading a magazine that someone had abandoned, when she spotted one of the corrections officers coming through with a dog. The dog made his rounds, trash cans and beneath all the benches, searching for God knew what. When he got to the bench where Tionna was sitting, the dog began to bark. Tionna knew for a fact that she didn't have anything on her, but the dog seemed to think she did, and he made it apparent to everyone who was watching.

"Could you come with me, please," the officer said to Tionna.

"Is there a problem?" She crossed her legs to try to hide her nervousness.

"I'll explain it all to you in a minute." He motioned for her to follow.

Tionna nervously did as she was told. Halfway down the

long hall, she noticed that two female officers had joined her, which did nothing to soothe her nerves. One was brutish, almost to the point of looking like a man, while the other was pretty and petite. Both of them wore no-nonsense expressions on their faces. They stopped in front of an office at the end of the hall, where the two female officers escorted her inside and closed the door.

"What's going on?" Tionna asked, looking from one officer to the other.

"It says here that you're here to see Duhan Collins. What is your relationship with Mr. Collins?" the pretty one asked.

"I . . . I'm his wife," Tionna stammered.

"It says here that Mr. Collins isn't married," the pretty one said, double-checking the paperwork.

"She means she's his baby mama," the beefy one said. There was smugness to her voice that made Tionna hate her.

"Yes, we have kids together, but I'm more than his baby mama, thank you. Look, are y'all gonna tell me why y'all pulled me or what?"

"Mrs. Collins," the beefy one began sarcastically, "are you in possession of or have you been in contact with what would be considered a controlled substance?"

"Hell no! Why would I bring drugs on a visit?" Tionna snaked her neck.

"That's what we're trying to find out." The beefy one slipped on a pair of latex gloves. "Take your clothes off, please."

"Are y'all serious?" Tionna tried to appeal to the pretty guard, but the girl ignored her and kept fumbling with a black case that was sitting on her desk. Inside it were round swabs and what looked like a pair of thin tongs. This guard also donned a pair of latex gloves before stepping in front of Tionna.

"Either you can strip willingly, or we can detain you and make you strip. In such a case, you would miss your visit, and we might even be able to see about putting a charge on you."

"A charge? What kinda charge could you possibly put on me for not wanting to give y'all bitches a free show." Tionna was getting indignant.

"Obstruction of an official investigation. You and I both know who your man is, so we know they're paying special attention to him. Make it easy on yourself, boo." The beefy guard slid over a container to drop her clothes in. "Strip."

Tionna wanted to jump on both of them and claw their eyes out, but it wouldn't help Duhan's situation if she caused a scene. Swallowing her pride, she took off her clothes. The pretty guard took the articles of clothing she'd discarded and began to swab them, while the beefy guard watched her like a predator. "I'll need to check your bra and panties, too, to make sure you're not trying to smuggle anything in," the beefy guard said, a little too enthusiastically for Tionna's taste.

"Bitch, you must be crazy." Tionna backed away.

"Chill out," the pretty guard said to the beefy one. "You don't have to take off your panties, miss, just lift your bra and your breasts so that we can make sure there's nothing in there."

Reluctantly, Tionna did as she'd been told. "Are y'all satisfied now?" she snapped.

The beefy guard looked at the other one, who gave her the signal that she was clean. With a saddened look on her face, the beefy guard gave Tionna her clothes back.

"Sorry about that," the pretty guard began, while Tionna

put her clothes back on. "The dog detected drugs on you. We didn't find anything, but you've got residue all in your clothes."

"I tried to tell y'all that I didn't have anything." She wiggled into her pants. "Can I go now?"

"Yeah, you can go," the pretty guard said.

As Tionna was leaving, the beefy guard made a parting remark: "You got a nice-ass body, girl. If you ever decided you do wanna try to bring something in, maybe we can work out an arrangement."

"Eat a dick, you dike bitch!" Tionna snapped before slamming the door behind her.

Tionna had just barely made the bus that would take her to Duhan's building. When the bus reached the Otis Bantum Correctional Center, also known as OBCC, the passengers were herded into another waiting room to wait for their respective inmates to be pulled down. Tionna almost ran through the doors when she heard them call the name Collins. She made to go into the main visiting area with everybody else, but, to her surprise, she was led in another direction. The guard led her into a room lined with two-sided booths separated by Plexiglas.

"Oh, this must be a mistake. I'm not supposed to be on this side," Tionna told the guard.

The guard looked down at his clipboard. "You're here to see Collins, right?"

"Yes, Duhan Collins."

"Then you're in the right place. You were red flagged."

"I was what?"

The guard pinched the bridge of his nose as if she was

working his nerves. "Red flagged, ma'am. You required additional searching, so you're on a noncontact visit."

"No, this can't be right. Please, I haven't seen my husband in almost six weeks," Tionna pleaded.

"I'm sorry, sis, but there's nothing I can do about that rule." His heart went out to the pretty, young girl, but his hands were tied. "Listen, they didn't find anything on you, so this won't be an ongoing thing."

"Thanks," Tionna mumbled and went to the assigned booth. She wanted to cry over all the things that she was going through, but she didn't want to make herself look any more of a mess than she already did. Doing the best she could to make herself presentable, she waited patiently for Duhan.

The moment he came out, she could tell something was wrong. His eyes had bags under them and he hadn't bothered to brush his hair. She greeted him with a loving smile, and though he returned the gesture it was halfhearted at best. "Hey, baby," she greeted him.

" 'Sup, T." He sat down on the other side the glass. "What's the word on the streets?" he asked, getting directly to the business.

"Damn. Well, hello to you, too."

"Sorry, I got a lot on my brain right now," he told her. "I got a visit from the Levine Friday." He said the lawyer's name as if it left a foul taste in his mouth.

"What's he talking about?" she asked.

"More money, of course. I already spent fifty grand with the nigga and he still got his fucking hand out for another five."

"Five thousand dollars, what the hell for?"

"Transcripts, the fee for the private investigator, yada yada.

All this bread and I'm still sitting up, looking at a shaky case." Duhan sounded disgusted.

"Duhan, where are we gonna get that kinda money? I've already pawned everything except my engagement ring." She rubbed her finger.

"I got a few people on the street that owes me bread. Did you reach out to homebody from Fifty-fifth?"

"Yeah; he said he was gonna make arrangements to meet up, but every time I called him after that, he never picked up."

"Then fuck that nigga; I'll try to get the bread up myself. Yo, it seems like I can't depend on nobody but my fucking self to keep it funky," Duhan said. "And what the hell happened to you? It looks like you slept in your fucking clothes or something."

"It's a long story. But what's up with you, babe? Duhan, I know the lawyer got you tight by asking for more money, but you don't have to be so short with me. What's with you today?"

"I'm trying to figure some things out in my head, one of which being this." He pointed at the glass.

"Some bullshit; they tried to say I had drugs on me when I came through," she said, trying to downplay it.

"Did you?"

"Of course not, Duhan. I told you that I wasn't bringing nothing else in here after the last time," she reminded him.

"You told me a lot of shit, but how much you held true to is still in question, T," he said coldly.

"Duhan, what's the hell is wrong with you?"

"I should be asking you the same thing. Where'd you go last night, T?" he asked in an all-too-calm voice.

"I didn't go nowhere, baby," she lied. Tionna had initially been against the noncontact visit, but, seeing the murderous look in Duhan's eyes, she was thankful for the protective glass.

Duhan folded his hands on the table in front of him and looked her in the eyes. "You know, jail is an interesting place. We got all this concrete and steel separating us from the outside world, but it doesn't stop us from getting the word on the streets before anyone else. We get some pretty interesting stuff up here, too. You wanna know what I heard this morning?"

Tionna knew damn well that she didn't want to see where he was going with it, but she asked anyway: "What?"

"I heard that there was a shoot-out last night at that spot uptown, you know that piece-of-shit hole-in-the-wall that you and Gucci love so much—Mochas. Yeah, they said that Don B. and them niggaz got into a big shoot-out with some niggaz from the projects, the boy Happy and them. Ain't Happy the same nigga that I had to check for sniffing around you?"

"I guess," she said.

"Don't guess, baby. Anyhow, they get into this wild-ass shoot-out and the police ended up rushing the spot on some goon shit. They had to shut the place down."

"Word, that's crazy. I wonder what they were shooting about," Tionna said, faking ignorance.

"See, that's the craziest part." He laughed. "I did some digging and come to find out the whole thing was over a bitch. Can you believe that?"

"No," she said, starting to get very uncomfortable.

"Yeah, seems like that bum-ass nigga Happy caught feelings over some broad that Don B. was pushing up on, a pretty, dark-skinned chick from uptown named T. Now let me ask you again, Tionna, and think carefully before you answer. *Where the fuck did you go last night?"*

She thought about lying, but it was obvious that he already knew what time she'd been there, so she decided to tell the truth, or at least as much as was necessary. "A'ight, look, I went out for some drinks last night with Boots, Tracy, and Gucci, and—"

"I fucking knew it," he cut her off. "Every time you get around them whore-ass broads, you act like you ain't got no fucking sense, sniffing around any nigga that looks like he's handling."

"Duhan, it wasn't like that."

"Then what the fuck was it like?" he shouted. He noticed a guard looking in their direction so he lowered his voice. "I'm in here trying to keep from going away until my kids are in college and you're in the street with them fucking cluck-head broads. All I asked of you was to keep it a hundred and be a real bitch, but I guess it was too much to ask. Once a ho—"

"Now hold the fuck on," Tionna said, stopping him. "Since you've been in here I've held you down like a real bitch is supposed to, packages, visits, all that shit. I even put up with these bum-ass bitches you continuously stick your dick in, risking my life and yours, and you got the nerve to question my loyalty because I went out to have a few drinks. Muthafucka, for as much as I've been through, riding for you, I deserve a night out. And the next time you even think about calling me out my name it will be the last time you see me in this bitch. See if you can get your little jailbait whore Sharon to come out here and get felt up every time she wanna see you."

"What the hell does Sharon have to do with any of this?" he asked, a little too defensively.

"Duhan, please don't play with me. Just because I'm not on your back all the time doesn't mean that I'm slow."

"Tionna, I told you I ain't fucking that girl," he insisted.

"Then you might wanna tell her that, since every time I see her she hints otherwise."

Duhan placed his hands on his head. "T, I don't know what that girl's problem is. Ima get at her."

She looked at him as if he was completely missing the point. "Her problem is that you've got her thinking she doesn't have to respect me, and getting at her is what's got your ass in a sling now. You know what, talking to you is like talking to a damn wall. I ain't got time for this shit, Duhan. I'm out." She stood to leave.

"Tionna, wait." He placed his hand on the glass. "Baby, don't leave." She wanted to stay mad at him, but seeing him pleading from behind that glass moved her. With a sigh, she sat back down. "I'm sorry," he continued. "I know you be running like crazy trying to hold me down, T, and I didn't mean to come at you sideways, it's just that this place is starting to get to me."

"Duhan, even though I'm not in here with you, I'm bidding with you. For as long as you're in here, away from us and the kids, my soul can never rest. I'm here for you."

"Always." He pressed his hand to the glass.

"Always and forever, like Heatwave." She pressed her hand over the glass to match his.

"And that's why I love you, Tionna."

"Not as much as I love you, Duhan," she said sincerely.

"Time," the guard called from the end of the room.

"Damn, it seems like we never have enough time together," Duhan said sadly.

"Baby, if a day was forty-eight hours instead of twenty-four, it still wouldn't be enough time. But don't worry, Duhan, this will all be out of the way soon enough."

"One way or another, right." He seemed to deflate after the statement.

"Hey, what did I tell you about that kinda talk? We're gonna beat this, Duhan, you hear me?" she said sternly.

"Yeah, ma, I hear you."

"Collins, I know you hear me, muthafucka!" the guard yelled.

"Hold ya fucking head, son, I'm coming," Duhan yelled back. "Let me get the fuck up outta here before I end up with another charge for fucking this nigga up."

"Don't feed into that, baby, you just hold ya head. You're a boss, and never let nobody take you outta character," she told him as he was walking back the way he'd come. Duhan suddenly stopped short and came back.

"Collins, don't make me come down there!" the guard shouted, making his way toward Duhan.

"Tionna, you know I love my kids more than my own life, right?" he said hurriedly.

"Of course, and they love their dad, too."

"Good. Because if I find out that you're back to fucking around with that nigga Happy, you're gonna have to be the one to explain to them kids why their father is up for murder and they're mother is in a wheelchair. Don't fuck with me, T. You understand?" Tionna was so shaken by the fire in his eyes when he spoke that all she could do was nod. "Good," he said just as the guard reached him.

"You got a problem, convict?" The guard was pissed for having to come get him. He outweighed Duhan by about thirty pounds or so, but he had *bitch* written all over his face.

Duhan looked him directly in the eyes. "Nah, I don't have a problem, but I'm sure I can find you one if you need it that bad."

The guard weighed his options and decided against testing Duhan. "Let's go, Collins," he said with a little less bass in his voice.

"That's what I thought." Duhan strutted passed him. "Remember what I said, Tionna," he called over his shoulder just before he disappeared behind the iron door.

CHAPTER 21

"Hold the fuck on, I'm coming!" Animal shouted from his bedroom at whoever was banging on his front door. His eyes stung too bad to see the hands on the SpongeBob clock mounted on his wall, but his aching body told him it was way too early. After he'd left Gucci he'd gone straight home, but found that he couldn't will the sleep to take him, which was the problem with some designer drugs. They left you wired for most of the night, but when you crashed, it came down on you like a train wreck. Animal slipped on his bathrobe and dropped his .38 in the pocket on his way to the front door. He never had visitors unannounced, especially at that hour. Pushing his hair from his eyes, he looked through the peephole and sighed when he saw who was on the other side.

"What?" Animal asked when he opened the door.

"It's time to wake yo ass, up, son. You know the early bird catches the worm," Silk said, inviting herself inside.

"Silky, the only worms I'm interested in are the ones in the bottom of a tequila bottle. Do y'all know what time it is?"

"We know exactly what time it is, but you don't because you were out partying while business was being conducted," Tech said as he crossed the threshold, followed by China White. "Rise and shine, little brother, we've got some things to talk about."

"Tech, I love you like cooked food, but my head is hurting too damn bad to listen to this shit this morning," Animal grumbled, shuffling into the kitchen. He rummaged through his cabinets, trying to find a can of coffee, but couldn't get his brain and his limbs to cooperate.

"Let me get it," China offered, seeing that he was clearly out of it.

"Thank you, Ms. White." Animal kissed her on the cheek. They were all close, but his and China's relationship was different than the collective. Ever since she'd first come into the clique she'd taken a liking to the little orphan and played the role of surrogate big sister to him. China wasn't that much older than Animal, but she had a wise spirit and he could come to her with anything.

"Animal, what is all this bullshit you got on the walls?" Silk took one of the masks down and started playing with it.

"I wouldn't expect a hood rat like yaself to know the difference between art and bullshit." He took the mask from her and placed it back on the wall. "Somebody twist something up, my head is killing me." Animal took a seat on the couch next to Tech, who was watching the news. An attractive brown-skinned woman was on the screen, recapping two shootings that had happened in Harlem the night before.

"I see y'all took care of that thing," Tech said to Animal.

"Yeah, man, I told you the young boys had it faded," Animal replied.

"How'd they do?"

"Brasco handled his business, but I gotta get at Ashanti about his damn moral system. That boy needs sensitivity coaching." Animal shook his head.

Tech smiled like a proud father. "That boy is gonna make a fine wolf when he comes of age."

"You mean if he comes of age: he ain't got no scruples."

"I can remember a time when they said the same thing about you, and you turned out okay," Tech told him.

"Yeah, because I know the difference between the man and the animal, so I can tell a good situation from a bad situation. Ashanti ain't got that kinda sense."

"Yo, wasn't you there last night?" Silk pointed at the screen, where they were showing the front of Mochas, the location of the second shoot-out.

"Yeah, that shit turned into a hot mess," Animal admitted.

As Tech was watching the screen, a terrible thought materialized in his head. "Animal, I know that wasn't you who shot that fucking club up?"

"Tech, I'm an animal, not an idiot; that ain't had nothing to do with me. Don B. got into it with some niggaz over a broad and muthafuckas started popping," Animal said, as if clubs getting shot up were everyday occurrences.

"That dude stays in some shit." China sat a cup of coffee in front of Animal and went to sit on the recliner with hers. "You'd think with all the money he's got, he'd have something better to do than getting people killed and shot at."

"That's what I keep trying to tell this hardheaded-ass nigga." Tech thumbed at Animal.

"Come on with that." Animal sipped his coffee. "Me and homeboy ain't friends, we're just kicking it about business."

"What kinda business you got with that nigga? You ain't no rapper," Silk joked.

"He seems to think so, because he offered me like fifty stacks to do guest appearances on his artists' tracks," Animal said, shocking them all.

"Damn, Animal, let me find out yo be spitting and ain't tell me," China teased him.

"Nah, what I do ain't really rap, it's just me getting shit off my chest." He went back to his coffee.

"Well, if he got fifty stacks to throw you like that, we might wanna see about snatching his ass. Tech, how much you think his people can come up with to get his trifling ass back?" Silk asked.

Tech could feel Animal's eyes on him so he decided to fuck with him. "I don't know off top, Silk, but for all the records the nigga is selling, I'll bet they can come up with something respectable."

"Man, I know y'all ain't seriously thinking about doing this?" Animal looked from Silk to Tech.

Tech had been joking at first, but seeing the concerned look on Animal's face made the idea seem more appealing. "And what if we were? You trying to tell me that if we wanted to snatch Don B., you'd have a problem with it?"

Animal put his coffee down and looked at his mentor seriously. "Man, I've been banging with you since I was a little nigga running around stealing food. You took me in, Tech, and gave me hope, so I'm with you, but if the question of my loyalty ever comes outta your mouth again, then I'm gonna have to invite you outside."

Tech looked at him for a long while, and for a minute you could feel the threat of violence lingering. "Just checking." Tech smiled and grabbed Animal in a playful headlock. "I thought them Big Dawg niggaz might've brainwashed you." He mussed Animal's hair roughly.

Animal broke the lock and scooted away. "Quit playing, man; I told you I had a headache."

"Yo, but on a more serious note, we met with the Commission last night," Tech told Animal.

"Y'all left me out the loop?" Animal sounded a little hurt that he'd been left out of the big meeting. China and Silk were skilled at what they did, but Tech and Animal were the most lethal of the bunch, which is why they tackled all high-risk situations together; it had always been that way.

"Chill, nobody was trying to snub you, but I needed you to make sure the young boys handled that business. You didn't miss much," Tech said.

"Nothing except Shai about to break Tech's neck," Silk said, laughing.

"That nigga laid his hands on you? Let me get my shit—we gonna ride on that muthafucka!" Animal said heatedly and started pacing the room.

"See, this is part of the reason why I didn't take you, Animal: you're always ready to shoot a muthafucka," Tech scolded him.

"You're damn right I am. Ain't nobody gonna lay hands on my family and not get seen."

"Animal, nobody put their hands on me, and people like Shai Clark don't get seen."

"Tech, for as long as I got eyes and guns, anybody can get seen," Animal assured him. The idea of someone rising up against Tech didn't sit well with him. The big homey had always protected him when he was too weak to look out for himself, and he had been trying to balance the scales ever since he'd gotten his first gun.

"Animal, you better than anybody should know that if I felt like a nigga violated, I would've handled it accordingly. Shit wasn't that serious; they wanted to talk and the conversation got a little heated, that's all."

"Well, what did they want?" Animal scowled.

"The usual shit, trying to put restraints on how we eat. As it turned out, that faggot Bobo was in bed with Rico."

"Didn't he know he was the police?"

Tech shrugged. "I tried to tell him, but he didn't want to take my word for it, like I give a fuck. The money was dropped and Bobo is history, that's how I see it. Shai and them was just tight because we be dropping all these bodies and shit in other niggas' hoods. You know cats with paper are squeamish about bloodshed."

"That's because they done got lazy and lost the killer's edge that put them on top in the first place," Silk chimed in.

"True story," Animal agreed. "Tech, when them old niggaz agreed to break bread, I thought it would be a good thing, but I ain't wit' all these guidelines they're trying to set without even making you a full member. It's bad enough that we kick them five percent, but they wanna oversee how we hustle, too? Shit, I liked it better when we were bandits."

"I'm with Animal on that one," China cosigned. "Them dudes can dance within the rules because they're large organizations and have several sources of incomes, but we're street level and gotta get it wherever it's coming from. All their rules are gonna do is starve us."

"I say we whack that nigga Rico and tell Shai to go fuck hisself. Tommy Gunz was the real power behind the Clarks anyway and he ain't much good to anybody these days," Animal said.

"Nah, Swann is good people, and to get at Shai we'd have to go through him," Tech said, shooting the idea down.

"So what do we do, raise our hands and ask permission every time we wanna go at somebody?" Animal asked sarcastically.

"I didn't say all that, Animal. Shai is pissed now, but it'll blow over in a minute, so until then we just gotta keep off his radar. In the meantime, we're gonna move on that deal Rock Head was telling me about."

"That's what I'm talking about." Animal rubbed his hands together greedily. "So are we gonna hit them before the deal and snatch the money, or after the deal and snatch the coke?"

Tech looked around the room at his team. "We're gonna hit them during the deal and take it all."

CHAPTER 22

Being that Tionna had spent most of what she had taking a taxi to Rikers Island, she had to rely on public transportation to get her back to the hood. She wasn't mad at the long ride because she had a lot on her mind that she needed to sort out before dealing with the kids and the rest of the bullshit in her life.

The fact that Duhan was tight with her failed in comparison to the five thousand dollars she was going to have to get up. Duhan said he had it under control, but Tionna knew without him having to say so that he didn't. When Duhan was home, they made it a habit to live beyond what they should've, and they had never really grasped the concept of saving. Reaching out for the money he had on the streets wasn't working anymore because at this stage of the game, everybody was already betting on Duhan to blow trial. The only lifeline he had left was Tionna.

When she finally made it back uptown it was getting dark

and she knew that Ms. Ronnie was going to be pissed. Her only hope was to find Gucci before Ms. Ronnie found her, which didn't prove to be hard, because when she came up the block she found Gucci sitting on the stoop of her building with Tracy.

"Hey, y'all," Tionna said sheepishly.

Gucci leaned on her knees. "Oh, I know you can do better than that."

"I'm sorry, Gucci."

"Sorry doesn't even scratch the surface, Tionna. Yo, I've been checking precincts and hospitals all morning trying to see if you were okay. The kids were scared, Mommy was scared. The only reason that I even knew that you were still alive is because Boots and Tracy came by the house after they were released, which is what you should've done, too."

"My bad, Gucci. My phone was dead or else I would've called. By the time they let me out I barely had time to make my visit with Duhan."

Gucci looked at Tracy, who just turned her head as if to say she wanted nothing to do with the discussion, before turning back to Tionna. "So, let me see if I follow you: you mean to say that you left your kids with my mother for almost twenty-four hours . . ."

"Without calling," Tracy added.

"Without calling," Gucci continued, "all so you could make a visit? I don't believe I'm hearing this."

"Gucci, I know I fucked up by leaving my kids on y'all like that and not calling to let you know that I was okay, but you can wear of a little of this blame, too," Tionna said, trying to shift it.

"What the hell did I do?"

"I don't recall seeing you at the precinct last night." Tionna folded her arms.

"That's because Animal got me out of there and took me home," Gucci shot back.

"Oh, you was with the pretty little nigga all night? You left that part out of your story, tramp," Tracy teased Gucci.

"I wasn't with him all night, and mind your business," Gucci told her. "Look, Tionna, my main concern is that you're okay, but when my mother catches you she's gonna whip that ass."

"Is she that mad?" Tionna looked around nervously, as if Ronnie were going to spring from the shadows.

"Mad ain't the word. I ain't see her like that since that time she caught us in her bed with those two boys."

"She beat skin off both of our asses," Tionna recalled. "I gotta steer clear of her until I can come up with a way to make it up to her."

"But now that your ass is back from your journey, what's up with Duhan?" Gucci asked.

Tionna lowered her head. "It ain't looking real good. The lawyer needs another five thousand for some shit he gotta do, and you know Duhan ain't got it."

"Damn, T, what you gonna do?" Tracy asked.

"I don't know," she said honestly. "The case is already looking shaky because of all the witnesses they have against Duhan. Any help we can get is a blessing, so I gotta try to get this money up so the lawyer can work his hand."

"I got a few hundred tucked in the bank if you need it, Tionna," Gucci offered.

"And when I get my check on the first, I can hit you with a

little something, too. It won't be much, but it'll be something," Tracy said.

"Thanks, y'all." Tionna hugged them both. "I don't know what I would do without you."

"Wind up becoming the whore of Babylon," Boots said, rolling up on them. She had bags from McDonald's in her hands and Tionna's kids on her heels. "Where the hell did you disappear to?"

"Long story." Tionna crouched down to hug her kids.

"We missed you, Mommy!" Little Duhan hugged her, followed by Duran.

"Mommy, did you have fun in the can?" Duran asked.

"What did you say?" Tionna looked at her son quizzically.

"I wanted to know if you had fun in the can. I asked Auntie Boots where you were and she said that you were in the can, playing with the other girls."

"Oh, she did?" Tionna gave Boots a hateful look, at which Boots just smiled.

"Yeah, she told us that. Mommy, did they have toys in the can?"

"No, baby. I wasn't in the can playing; I had to pick up Boots's mother. They picked her up on a street corner."

"Auntie Boots, is your mother a crossing guard like the lady who stands on the corner by my school?" Duran asked.

"Stop telling these kids that foolishness." Gucci pulled Duhan and Duran close. "Listen, y'all go up the street and sit by Mr. Rayfield and them while you eat your food; we wanna have some girl talk."

"Okay, Aunt Gucci. Come on." Duhan grabbed his little brother by the hand and led him up the block.

"Boots, it's bad enough that you played yourself last night, but don't be telling my kids no bullshit, you hear me?" Tionna let her know.

"T, I was just playing with them; they don't even know what a can is. Glad to see that you're back amongst us. First Gucci disappears from the lounge, then you disappeared from the precinct. I was beginning to think somebody was abducting hood rats," Boots said.

"Ya mama's a hood rat, tramp," Gucci replied.

"Her ass must be in a snippy mood because Animal didn't give her none," Tracy said, slipping into the conversation.

"You slid with Animal?" Boots looked surprised.

"I didn't slide with anybody. It's like I told this motor mouth," Gucci nodded at Tracy, "he got me out of the club and made sure that I got home okay, that's all!"

"I'd have fucked him," Boots said honestly.

"That's because you're a slut," Gucci said.

"I bumped into Rock Head when I was getting out of the cab, and you know he tried to throw salt. He comes to me talking about I shouldn't deal with Animal because I don't know what kinda nigga he is. The ones I know are the ones I usually avoid because I already know how they get down."

"Well, with a name like Animal, you've got to expect something," Tionna said.

"I don't know . . . he must be somebody, from the way Don B. was treating him. I ain't never seen him at a show or in a video, but everybody was acting like he was about something."

"I overheard one of the girls say that they'd seen Don B. give him a bag full of money to sign a contract on the spot," Tracy said, repeating what she'd picked up through the gossip vine.

Gucci twisted her lips disbelievingly. "That's bullshit. You know how chicks gossip. He didn't have no bag with him when he dropped me off."

"So what, you gonna pursue it?" Tionna asked.

"I'd thought about it, T. He seems like cool peoples," Gucci admitted.

"Let me find out you and Tionna are trying to get your own reality television show, *The Real Housewives of Big Dawg Entertainment!*" Tracy slapped her thigh, laughing.

"Tracy, you must've fell and bumped your head. I ain't about to be a housewife to nobody but Duhan," Tionna let her know.

"I know I ain't the only one who saw Don B. all up on you. Bitch, I thought that nigga was gonna propose." Tracy shoved her.

"He was jocking you, T," Gucci agreed.

"Do y'all think about anything other than dick?" Tionna asked.

"Money," they said in unison.

Their conversation was broken up when one of the neighborhood girls walked up on them. She was a pretty brown-skinned little girl that usually kept herself together, but that night she looked worn and her clothes were dirty. When she got close enough, they could tell that she had been crying.

"Y'all seen Rock Head?" she asked, wiping her nose with the back of her sleeve.

"No, thank goodness," Gucci said.

"Well, if you see him, can you tell him I'm looking for him. I have something I need to talk to him about and it's real import."

"We'll pass it along," Gucci said as they watched the girl

shamble up the block. "I don't see how a bitch can let herself go all to pieces over a nigga like Rock Head."

"Gucci, stop acting like you were never young and in love," Boots said.

"Yeah, I've had my share of heartache, but there was only one guy I ever went to pieces of over, and he was a way higher-class of nigga than Rock Head." Gucci was referring to her first *real* boyfriend. The streets had claimed him before his eighteenth birthday.

"I know one thing: if Rock Head don't stop messing with these young girls, somebody's daddy is gonna put a bullet in his trifling ass," Tionna said.

"Church," they all said.

"But back to the subject," Boots picked up, "where'd you disappear to, Tionna?"

"I went to see Duhan."

"You went to see Duhan still dressed in last night's clothes? You're lucky he didn't try to knock your head off on the dance floor."

"He was mad that I went out, but there wasn't much he could do about it with that thick-ass glass separating us. Besides, that nigga ain't crazy; Duhan know what time it is," Tionna boasted, as if she hadn't been shitting bricks about him flipping.

Boots took a seat on the stoop next to Gucci. "Anything new with the case?"

"Nothing but the bastard lawyer asking for more money. I gotta get up five stacks."

"That's a nice hunk of cheese. How you gonna get it?" Boots asked.

"That's what we were just sitting here discussing," Gucci

informed her. "T, you don't have no old slides that you can reach out to?"

Tionna thought on it. All the dudes from her past were either dead, in jail, or just not fucking with her for the things she'd put them through on her way to becoming a boss bitch. Tionna maintained what her mother had always instilled in her—"a man is only as good as what he can give you, or what you can get him to do for you"—and took no prisoners when it came to the opposite sex. She would devour their hearts and their pockets, leaving little more than a shell in her wake. Other than Duhan, she had never felt love for any man.

"None that I can think of that ain't gonna want some pussy in exchange for anything they do for me. Even if I do get in contact with one of my old pieces, I can't just come back after all this time and ask them for five thousand dollars."

"You could get it from Happy," Tracy suggested.

"Did you not see what that clown-ass nigga pulled last night?" Gucci looked at Tracy like she'd lost it.

"Clown or not, I know his trick ass would up that five grand," Boots added.

Gucci ignored Boots and looked at her friend. "Tionna, you'd be a damn fool to ask that piece of shit for anything, the way he tried to show his ass. Nah, we'll find another way to get the money."

"Gucci, you're awful opinionated about this whole thing when it ain't your situation; it's Tionna who needs the money. Are you gonna give her the five thousand dollars?"

"I would if I could."

"But you don't, so she's gotta explore all her options. Tionna, unless you got a job lined up or a hell of a lick, you might have to reach out."

Tionna shook her head. "Happy would be the last nigga I reached out to. All that would be doing is shoving him further up my ass."

"Then you better get yourself a pistol or a package, because that ego you brought back with you to the hood ain't gonna fix your situation or get that five thousand for Duhan," Boots said seriously.

Tionna looked up at the three sets of inquiring eyes and suddenly felt like she was on trial. For most of Duhan's bid she had been true to him, and for his entire bid she had held him down, often going without to do so. She was living hand to mouth, trying to crawl out of a hole that seemed to have no beginning, and she was getting tired of it. There had been a time in her life when it wouldn't have taken much to get up the five thousand and plus some if she really put her mind to it, but here she was getting advice from Boots and Tracy. She was slipping, and it didn't sit well with her. Suddenly an idea formed in her head.

"You know what, I think I got this shit all worked out," Tionna told them.

Gucci's face brightened. "I know that look, T. What's popping?"

"What's popping is that I need to get this money up for my man, by hook or by crook, and I'm 'bout to step to my business."

"Well, don't keep an asshole in suspense," Gucci pressed her.

"A lady never kisses and tells." Tionna winked. "But what I will tell you is that I'm about to show muthafuckas how to really rob an industry nigga."

CHAPTER 23

Boots had never thought she would be so happy to see the brown bricks of her latest project residence. She and the girls had sat up at Tionna's, smoking and plotting, while the queen of the house went on and on about her problems. Boots loved Tionna, but her constant complaining worked her nerves. Boots knew she was wrong for hating on Tionna, but she just couldn't help it. Boots had had to bust her ass for everything she got in life and still couldn't manage to get out of her fucked-up situation, and here was Tionna complaining about everything that had been taken away from her when she hadn't earned it in the first place. She had been on point before Duhan blew up, but when he started getting money, Tionna's shit went to the next level and she wore it like a badge of honor, even after it had been snatched from her.

When she got out of the taxi, she was greeted by an empty courtyard. Even though it was warm outside, the projects were deserted. Two people had been killed there last night and the police had the hood in a choke hold. As she was about to venture deeper into the projects, she heard somebody call her name. When she turned around, she saw Happy grinning at her from behind the wheel of his truck.

"What's up, Boots?" Happy waved to her. His face was a little scratched up, but otherwise he seemed unharmed, considering what had happened in Mochas. She had thought Happy would be locked up with Ron-Ron for starting the situation, but as usual he had slipped through the cracks.

"Boy, you've got some nerve speaking to me after the bullshit you started last night." She folded her arms.

"You know that wasn't none of my doing. Your girl was the one trying to play herself, with her trick ass."

"Fuck what Tionna did; because of you, they had us at the precinct for hours. I'm surprised your simple ass isn't locked up, too, since you put the battery in Ron-Ron to do that stupid shit."

Happy raised his hands in surrender. "How can you detain an innocent man? Ron-Ron did right by keeping his mouth shut; he knows I'll take care of him."

"Happy, you're slicker than a pig in shit," she said, disgusted.

"Call me what you want, but at least I'm out here to hear you say it. And speaking of slick, what up with that slick shit you was kicking last night."

"Hap, go ahead with that," she said playfully. She wasn't at all attracted to Happy, but she secretly wondered what, besides money, could've possibly made Tionna deal with him for as long as she had.

"Nah, I thought sure we had a connection on some grown

people's shit, or was that the liquor talking and you're little girl again?" Happy mocked her.

"For as many kids as I've got, I ain't been a little girl in a long time," Boots shot back.

"And this is what I know, which is why I'm asking you what's good?" Happy asked. Boots looked like she could go either way on it, so he sweetened the pot. "Come on, take a ride with me right quick to pick this bread up. I'll throw something in it for you."

"I can't, Hap. Bernie has been with the kids since last night and his ass is already pissed at me, I should go home," she said, but didn't bother to move.

"I'll tell you what, take this ride with me and before I drop you off I'll get you a few bags of that superweed y'all like to smoke."

That sealed the deal for Boots as she walked around and climbed in on the passenger side. "Happy, you got a half hour to get me back here or I'm getting in a cab."

Happy gave her his signature smile. "Don't worry, Boots, it ain't even gonna take me that long." He laughed and pulled out into traffic.

Ten minutes later, Happy's truck was parked along Morningside Drive, with Boots bent over the backseat while he shoved himself violently inside her. He had heard the stories about how good Boots's pussy was, but feeling it firsthand he knew that the stories didn't do her justice. She made him start with a condom, but for the promise of five hundred dollars she let him take it off so he could feel her walls, and they were as sweet as candy.

"Damn, this pussy is good," Happy hissed, raining saliva on Boots's back.

"That's right, fuck this pussy so you can cum—hurry up and cum," Boots rasped, looking at her watch from time to time. Happy had a wide dick, but it was barely touching her spot. The only pleasure she got in fucking him was the fact of knowing she was intruding on something that belonged to Tionna, Ms. Untouchable.

"Yeah, ima cum; where you want me to put this cum?" His breathing became more jagged.

"Wherever you want, as long as you hurry up and do it," she told him. Boots was taken completely by surprise when he grabbed her roughly by her hair and took himself out of her. Happy turned her so that she was facing him while he stroked his dick. "Happy, you better . . ." As soon as she opened her mouth, he unloaded in it.

"You dirty muthafucka." Boots wiped her mouth with the backs of her hands. Happy's semen tasted like garbage and it was going to take a severe scrubbing to get the taste out.

"Sorry, but you told me to cum where I wanted to." Happy wiped his dick with a paper towel before tucking it back in his pants. He pulled his bankroll from his pocket and counted out six hundred dollars. "The extra hundred is for being such a freaky little bitch."

"Fuck you, Happy. Just take me home," she fumed, looking in her compact mirror to make sure he hadn't cum in her hair.

"Gladly. Your pussy is stinking up my ride," Happy said before pushing the truck back to the hood.

When Boots got into her apartment it was dark and quiet, which was unheard of for her house, so she immediately thought the worst: *Maybe someone saw them?* After all, they didn't live very far from where Happy had screwed her. If that was the case, then death was surely waiting around the corner.

She eased down the hall toward the living room, where she saw the flickering of lights. As she got closer she heard music playing softly. Something was afoot. Boots held her breath and rounded the corner into the living room, expecting the worst, and was surprised by what she saw. Their little coffee table was set with candles and decorative plastic utensils. In the center of the table was a beautifully roasted chicken with all the trimmings. Lying on the carpet, near the foot of the table, was Bernie, and he was wrapped in nothing but a towel.

"What is all this?" Boots asked, shocked by the beautiful welcome. After being gone for nearly twenty-four hours, she'd expected a fistfight.

"It's for you, ma." He got up and stood in front of her and took her hands in his. When she saw all the love dancing in his eyes, she felt sick for what she'd done. "I heard what happened at the club, so I figured you could use a warm welcome. I divided the kids up between my sisters for the night, so it's just us." Before Boots could even react, Bernie kissed her. As his tongue danced around hers, she could taste whatever he'd been drinking mixed with the foulness of Happy's semen.

"Baby," Boots broke the embrace before she accidentally threw up in his mouth, "what do you mean you heard what happened at the club; how?"

"Happy told me," he said. Boots wanted to faint, but there was more. "He told me how that drunken-ass Tracy started a fight in the club and all of y'all ended up getting arrested for it. I told you about hanging with her, she can't hold her liquor."

"When did you speak to Happy?" Boots asked, still trying to make heads or tails of everything.

"This morning; he said you asked him to call me just before they took you," he said as if she should've already known this.

"He did, did he?" Boots was numb.

"Yeah, and the fly shit is that we got to talking and he said he's gonna put me down with this lick he got lined up, so we'll be straight in a minute. I was thinking you could give me a little to celebrate." He tried to pull her close but she pulled away.

"Chill. I've been in jail all night, so let me go wash this stink off and then we can get at it, boo." She was making her way to the bathroom.

"When I get this money, ima buy you a fly engagement ring, Boots, courtesy of Happy. Yo, Happy is a good muthafucka!"

"He's a muthafucka alright," Boots said before slamming the bathroom door.

CHAPTER 24

Tracy was just about to turn it in for the night when she got the phone call. It seemed that she had left a more lasting impression on Remo than she'd given herself credit for, and he was requesting an audience with her. After taking down the directions to his apartment, Tracy took a quick shower and hopped into a cab.

Remo lived in a run-down section of the Bronx that had yet to be touched by the gentrification that the rest of the city had undergone. He met her downstairs and paid for the cab before leading her into the ratty walk-up apartment building. From the cracked walls and the stench of urine, Tracy began to wonder if coming to Remo's place had been a good idea after all. Thankfully, Remo's apartment looked nothing like the rest of the building. It was clean and carpeted from wall to wall. The furniture was beautiful and there were all the latest in modern amenities throughout the place. Tracy could see that Remo was doing well for himself.

"I'm glad you came," he said once Tracy was inside the apartment.

"Me, too; I needed to get off the block for a while," she said, admiring his apartment.

"You want something to drink?" he called from his minibar, where he was pouring himself some tequila.

"You know I do; I'll have what you're having," she called back.

"Bet, I got some tequila but it ain't Patrón." He held up the bottle for her to inspect.

"I'm a guest in your crib: I ain't complaining."

Remo came back over holding two shot glasses and the bottle, which he set on the table. "Won't you join me?" he said, getting comfortable on the plush leather couch.

"But of course." Tracy sat next to him. She almost felt like she was going to sink through the soft leather and hit the floor. "I see you're doing well for yourself," she said, accepting her shot.

"I do okay for myself," he said modestly.

"You always did like fly shit, Remo. Seeing you at the club brought back so many memories." She threw her shot back.

"Same old Tracy," he mused.

"You know I ain't changed since the Roof Top days, Remo."

"So I see. You do you remember when that used to be the official baller spot?"

"Do I! I met my baby daddy in there!" Tracy recalled.

"I was supposed to be your baby daddy." Remo moved closer to her.

"Remo, you and I both know that your ass is scared to death of commitment. You loved the streets more than you've ever loved a woman, which is probably why you stayed locked up back in the days."

"I was getting it in on the streets, ma, you know that. But the days of me going up north for petty shit are over. My nephew really set me up with this bodyguard work," Remo said.

"Fucking with Don B., I know your hands stay full, that boy is a hot mess. And speaking off messes, thanks for getting us out of that situation last night."

"It was only right, y'all was with us when it happened. Besides, that cat was talking reckless. If the police hadn't come, I'd have finished him off. Who the fuck was that nigga anyway? I've seen him uptown, but as far as I know he ain't a player in the game."

"His name is Happy and he's one of Tionna's old pieces," Tracy said, as if he were a nobody.

"He didn't look too happy to me when the ol' girl started shitting on him."

"You know some niggaz don't know how to let go when you put it on them real good." She jabbed him with her finger.

"Girl, you tripping; your shot was alright, but hardly worth me holding on to the memory ten years later. Shit, your walls are probably all torn out after all this time," he teased her.

"Nigga, please, I still got that snap-back cat, you better ask somebody!"

"Yo, remember when we used to meet up after the club for our little freak sessions?" Remo reminisced.

"Yeah, back when you used to come scoop me in your little Suzuki jeep," she recalled. "We used to get coked out of our brains and fuck until the sun came up. You used to keep some good-ass blow."

"I still do," he said, producing a cigar box from under the couch. When he flipped the top back, it looked like the sky had opened up and snowed inside. Tracy could feel her mouth getting moist. "Do you still get down?" He rolled a dollar bill into a tube while he watched her for a reaction. The way her eyes stayed glued to the coke said it all.

"I bump a little something every now and again." She smiled nervously. The shit she sniffed was everyday shit you could get in the hood, but she could tell by from the brightness of it, Remo had some fire.

"Then why don't we really kick this party up." Remo scooped out a healthy dose of the coke and started chopping it into lines with a playing card. He cleared two lines before sinking back into the couch like he'd been frozen in the middle of a brilliant idea. With trembling hands she took the dollar bill from him and did a line.

When the coke hit Tracy's sinuses it felt like she had snorted glass and the back of her eyeballs were being shredded. "God damn, what'd you cut this shit with?" she said in between sneezes.

"Cut?" He looked at her glassy-eyed. "Tracy, you know I don't fuck with nothing cut. I gotta feel it when it hits me." He took the dollar back and cleared another line. "Go ahead and treat your nose, ma, I've got plenty of this shit." He handed her the dollar bill back.

Tracy sat on the couch sniffing coke until her whole face was numb. True to his word, Remo had some boss coke and was very generous with it. Her heart was beating at a hundred miles per minute and the sweat running down her back felt like fingers of ice. To say she was wasted would be an understatement. Tracy was a fair-weather sniffer, never copping more than a half to a whole gram at a time, but she had easily snorted three times that in her one sitting with Remo. Remo didn't look like he was feeling much pain either, staring at the ember at the end of his cigarette as if it were the most interesting thing in the world.

"I feel like I just took my head out of the freezer." Tracy ran her hands over her face, trying to generate some type of heat. She ran her fingers through the leftover powder on the glass coffee table and traced the finger over her gums. "Damn, I ain't flew this high in a long time, baby." She stretched.

"Oh, it gets better." Remo snuggled next to her and started kissing her neck. His hand wandered down the front of her blouse and fondled her right breast.

"So, now I see why you called me over here, you just wanted some ass." She ran her hands over his scarred bald head. Remo's hands were rough, but comforting since she hadn't felt the touch of a man in a while.

"You know I'm hot for you." Remo shoveled a pinky nail full of powder into his nostril. He redipped the pinky nail and treated Tracy's nose. "I've been thinking about this pussy since 1998." He fumbled with his pants until he was able to free his penis. It was just as long and thick as she remembered.

"I haven't seen this in a while." She ran her hands along the smooth shaft. "Now, what could you possibly expect me to do with all this?" She stroked him to a stiff erection. In answer to her question, Remo rubbed a healthy amount of coke on his dick.

"Go for what you know," he breathed in her ear. Remo placed his hand gently behind her head and guided it to his lap. When Tracy's mouth made contact with his dick, it took

Remo back to hot summer days of playing in the fire hydrant on the avenue. Her nimble tongue played around the rim of his dick, before taking the length of him into her throat, causing the big man to gasp and pull her away.

"What's the matter, you can't take it?" She stroked him more aggressively, looking into his eyes the whole time. With the trail of saliva leading from her bottom lip to his glistening penis, she reminded him of a porn star.

"I almost forgot how good you were, girl," he said, panting.

"It's only gonna get better." She stood up and began peeling her clothes off. The years and gravity had touched Tracy's body, but she was still nice to look at, with her full breasts and nice hips. Her stomach bore stretch marks, but didn't sag as much as he'd expected it to. Pushing Remo back against the couch, she straddled his lap and slipped him inside her dripping pussy. She had barely gotten into her rhythm when she saw his bottom lip began to quiver. "You better not." She slapped him across the face. "You can cum when I tell you to."

"Damn, you always were into some rough shit." He rubbed his cheek.

"You know how I play." She ground harder on his lap, while running her fingernails down the length of his body. Remo stood up while still inside her and cupped her ass cheeks.

"Yeah, I know how you play, so I'm gonna make sure you think twice about keeping this pussy away for so long, bitch." Remo began to long stroke her, still holding her ass cheeks apart.

Every time he went inside her it felt like he was spearing her small intestines, but she was a glutton for punishment. "Is that all you've got? Remo, let me find out your ass is getting too old to handle all this good pussy." She reached down and played with the exposed shaft of his dick until her hand was slick with both their juices and then licked her fingers clean. "Fuck me like you used to do in the back of that jeep, you big-dick muthafucka!" she demanded.

Remo pulled out and threw Tracy onto the couch. She opened her legs so he could get all the way inside her, but he flipped her over and smacked her on the ass. "You know what I want." He spit on his hand and stroked his dick.

"Not yet; it's been a minute and I don't think I can take it." She tried to flip back over, but he held her in place with one massive hand.

"Don't worry, ma, it's like riding a bike." He lowered himself and began forcing the head into her ass. Tracy felt like she was giving birth as the massive penis penetrated her. Spots danced in front of her eyes and a time or two she felt like she was going to pass out, but Remo kept going. Blood and shit covered his dick, making it slicker and a little smoother on the entry, if messier. The farther in he was able to force himself, the more excited he became. Ignoring Tracy's sobs, he crammed the entire length of his dick into her ass. After a few minutes of grunting like an animal, Remo finally exploded inside her ass, dripping blood and semen down the back of Tracy's legs. Remo went into the bathroom and came back holding two soapy cloths, one of which he handed to Tracy.

"Remo, I should kill you for ripping me open like that," she said, blotting her ass with the cloth. It came away such a mess that he would surely have to throw it in the trash.

"You used to like it like that," he said, wiping his dick.

"That was ten years ago, Remo, and we always used a lubricant," she said with attitude. Tracy started gathering her clothes to leave.

"Come on, baby, don't cut out so soon when we're just getting reacquainted." He grabbed her arm.

Tracy scowled at him, like she was angrier than she really was. "And why should I stay, booty bandit?"

"You got jokes." He laughed. "I was thinking that maybe we can lay around here for a couple of days and reminisce." He played with his dick.

"Remo, you just wanna fuck and I ain't got time to lay up in here getting my pussy and my asshole pounded to high hell. I got bills to pay, so I gotta be on the street getting that up, feel me?"

"Of course I do," he said, catching what she was getting at. Remo grabbed his pants and retrieved a knot of money. "If it's bread you're worried about, I got you faded, so you ain't gotta run no story on me about cash. Now, I'm gonna go in the bathroom and wash up so we can go out and put something on our stomachs. Then we're gonna come back here and go at it until the sun comes up, like we used to. Let me make love to you."

"Remo, making love and fucking are two different things and I don't think you know the difference," she told him.

"Then why don't you teach me?"

She looked at his face to see if he was serious, and he was. Tracy weighed her options. All she had waiting for her at home were a cold bed and an empty refrigerator and more problems than she knew what to do with. "Hurry up in the bathroom so I can take a shower. And don't think you're gonna have me hostage in here, either; you're taking me out," she demanded.

"Whatever you need, baby." Remo smiled. "Why don't you twist us up some weed while I'm cleaning up. Everything you need is right on the table." He disappeared into the bathroom.

"Indeed it is." Tracy eyed the box of cocaine. She cleared two more lines and pinched her nostrils so she could get the full effect of the cold drip in the back of her throat. She had been polluting her nose with trash for so long that she'd almost forgotten how good a coke high could really be. Remo thought that by having Tracy over and inviting her to his stash, he was rekindling an old love affair, but all he'd really done was open Pandora's box.

CHAPTER 25

Animal was in a pretty place where all was right with the world, as he stared out the picture window overlooking Times Square. Chip sat next to him on the love seat, exhaling a cloud of smoke that smelled like something out of Bath & Body Works. They'd dropped some groovy pills that morning before Animal was given the grand tour of one of Big Dawg's recording studios. It was situated in a very unassuming building just off Broadway.

He'd been surprised to get Chip's call, asking him if he wanted to sit in on a session with Left Coast to get a firsthand look at what they were capable of. He didn't really feel like kicking it with Tech or the pups that day, so he decided the session would be a good change of pace. Don B. was thrilled to see him and immediately insisted that Animal hit the booth. Animal was reluctant at first, but after bit of prodding and a few Ls, he agreed.

The recording booth was the most magnificent thing that

Animal had ever seen. He looked around at the padded room with its overhanging microphone and committed every detail to memory. Just beyond the glass divider, Don B. watched intently while Chip, No Doze, and an engineer named Joker played with the massive board that controlled everything in the room. It reminded him of the old episodes of *Star Trek* when Captain Kirk would be on his cool shit while Sulu and the guy who always gets killed steered the ship.

There wasn't much that rattled Animal, but being in that booth did. There were only a few people in the room, but he felt like it was the halftime show at the Super Bowl. "Just let it flow natural," Don B. said over the intercom. *Natural*, Animal thought, as if it were just that easy. He tensed when the first hints of static came through the headphones, but when one of Chip's tracks came on, everything became crystal clear.

At first he was just playing around, putting together words that rhymed, but as the beat picked up, it got a firmer grip on his mind. Animal closed his eyes and envisioned himself riding the track like the Silver Surfer riding the tail of a comet. He could see every snare, and every change in its tempo before it occurred. The story he told was of a lady, street but sexy in her own unforgiving way. He went on to tell how this lady fed him when he was hungry and gave him shelter when he was cold. He was so emotionally caught up in the rapture of the song that everyone assumed he was talking about his mother or some other instrumental woman in his life, but by the end of the song they realized that he was speaking about the streets.

"That shit was amazing." Don B. wiped a fake tear from his eye.

"You killed that track, bro." Chip gave Animal dap when

he came out of the booth. "You brought to life the exact emotions that we wanted to convey on this track."

"It was pretty fucking intense." No Doze gave him dap.

"It was a'ight," Fully said with a crooked smile. He and Animal were still leery of each other, but even he knew that the boy had talent; it was just hard giving props to someone he thought could potentially be better than him.

"Joker, did you get all that?" Don B. asked the engineer, who was fumbling with the mouse on one of the computers.

"Yeah, Don. He killed that shit in one take. We don't even need to do anything to it other than mix it down and add a hook."

"I didn't know y'all were recording me?" Animal looked from Don B. to the engineer. Joker moved back, but Don B. placed an arm reassuringly around Animal.

"Chill, son, ain't nobody on no funny shit. I just wanted to see what you sounded like on an album. Yo, Joker, play it back one time," he told the engineer. When Animal heard his voice coming through the speakers, over Chip's track, he wanted to break down and cry. He knew they were his words, but it didn't sound like him speaking. What he heard wasn't some street thug, but an artist telling the most beautiful story about his special lady.

"You hear that shit, man?" Chip asked excitedly.

"Yeah, I hear it, but it don't sound like me," Animal said, mouthing along with the song . . . his song.

"It never does when you get that deep into the music." Chip placed his hand on Animal's shoulder.

Don B. took a CD out of the computer and handed it to Animal. "Just listen to it a few times. You got a gift kid, and I can bring the best outta you if you fuck with my team, son, but

I can't force it on you. I got somebody else coming in here to use this studio, but you're more than welcome to sit in on it," Don B. offered.

Animal stared at the CD in astonishment for a few seconds more before answering. "I think I will," he said proudly.

Don B. went back to the board with Joker and cued up the session for the next artist who was coming, while the Left Coast busied themselves rolling blunts or pouring drinks. Animal was about to load the CD into one of the portable players when his cell phone went off. He stared at the caller ID quizzically because he didn't recognize the number. "Who this?" he barked.

"Well, hello to you, too," a familiar voice said on the other end.

"Is that you, Ms. Gucci?" He smiled.

"Ah, you caught my voice pretty quick, considering that we've never spoken on the phone."

"I burned it in my brain the last time I saw you, in case it was the last time I saw you," he told her.

"Flattery will get you everywhere, Animal."

"This is what I'm hoping. So what took you so long to call? I thought you forgot about me."

"Boy, it's only been a few days," she reminded him.

"A few days can feel like a lifetime when you're carrying around this kind of heartache," he teased.

"Animal, I haven't been around you enough to cause your heart anything."

"This is what I'm trying to remedy, ma. When can a nigga see you?"

The line went silent for a minute. "What're you doing tonight?" she asked.

"Picking you up, just give me a time," he said, already thinking on what they would do tonight.

"About nine should be good," she told him. "Oh, there's just one problem."

"Then call me the problem solver," he said.

"I'm gonna be with my friend Tionna, the one Don B. was all up on. I don't really wanna ditch her, because she's going through the motions right now about something and she kinda needs a friend," Gucci said sadly.

"I'd never have you abandon a friend in need, Gucci. I don't mind going out as a threesome." He honestly wouldn't have cared if she brought the whole crew as long as he got to see Gucci again.

"I don't wanna do it like that, because then my attention would be divided, and I'm really trying to get into you," she said honestly. "I got an idea: why don't you see if ya man Don B. wants to roll; they seemed to hit it off pretty good."

"I'm sure she got his number, why don't you have her call him?" he asked.

"I would, but Tionna's ass is bullheaded. If I try to get her to call Don B. because we're hooking up, she's gonna look at it like a mercy date and flake out. I know it's asking for a lot, Animal, but I really don't wanna dis my friend."

Animal weighed it for a minute. "A'ight, let me see what's up. I'll call you in a few."

"Thanks, baby," Gucci said, ending the call.

Animal suddenly felt very warm inside. He had been thinking about Gucci since the night they'd met and it made him uncomfortable. Animal had been with his fair share of women, but that had mostly been out of physical need or loneliness. Next to Officer Grady, he didn't share a connection with any of them, and then in comes Ms. Gucci. There had been no mistaking the fact that she was a hood chick, but there was something more to her that was lurking just beneath the surface that he needed to uncover.

"You know you owe me for this, right?" Gucci glared at her friend.

"Gucci, stop acting like you didn't wanna see Animal, too," Tionna reminded her.

"Yeah, I wanna see him because I wanna get to know him. You wanna see Don B. because you're looking for a come up!"

"And why shouldn't I be, when niggaz do it all the time? You think a guy is gonna look at you and be like, 'Damn, she got a nice-ass brain'? Hell no. They're gonna look at you like, 'She got a phat ass and I wanna hit it!' Don't get me wrong, I think Don B. is sexy-ass as hell, but Duhan is my man, so it ain't gonna go but so far."

"Tionna, any dude giving up cash is gonna want ass, especially a nigga like Don B., who has pussy being thrown at him left and right."

"Gucci, you could put all them bum bitches together and they wouldn't equal me. I got class, ass, and a shot of pussy that needs to be bottled and sold!" Tionna boasted.

"Oh, so you're planning on fucking Don B.?" Gucci asked.

"I never said that, Gucci, but I plan on getting real close to him. Who knows, if his game is tight and he comes correct, I might let him smell it."

"And what about Duhan?"

Tionna thought on it. She had factored Duhan into the whole equation, but it all amounted to something very simple. "Gucci, I love Duhan and I plan on being with him until we're old and gray, but he ain't out here trying to raise two kids and maintain an apartment with nothing coming in but them bullshit food stamps they give me every month. I'm gonna go out there and do me, but I'm doing it for Duhan," Tionna reasoned.

Gucci laughed, seeing the old spark back in her friend's eyes. "T, if you like it, then I love it. Now, let's get our shit right because they'll be here to get us around nine."

CHAPTER 26

Animal was quite surprised when he saw the kid he was going to slap inside the club walk into the Big Dawg studio. Don B. had wasted no time in opening his studio doors to Hollywood in an attempt to fleece him out of some more tracks. The aspiring rapper had managed to sell Don B. several beats in the week since he'd seen him and Don B. was looking to buy more, which brought Hollywood untold joy. He finally saw his dream of going to the top coming true.

Don B. was content to have Hollywood stick to making tracks, but the youngster was determined to get in the booth so he could spit something for him. Hollywood was in the booth, screaming into the microphone, while Don B., Animal, and the Left Coast sat behind the boards, watching him in amusement.

"This nigga can't rap worth shit," Fully said, lighting the blunt dangling between his lips.

"We don't agree on much, but we can agree on that. This

muthafucka sounds like MC Hammer on steroids," Chip agreed.

"Man, I know I ain't much of a rapper, but this nigga is worse than them cats they use for cannon fodder on the Smack DVDs." Animal laughed, sipping something Chip had concocted for him in a Styrofoam cup. It had the sweet aftertaste of licorice but the punch of a kamikaze.

"He might not be very lyrically talented, but he can lay some tracks," Don B. said, turning down the volume in the booth. Hollywood's offbeat rhymes and whack punch lines were working his nerves.

"And the jury is still out on that," No Doze said, browsing through the list of tracks. "This nigga comes in here with all these tracks he was supposed to have composed, but for the two hours you had him on the boards, he couldn't come up with shit. The engineer had to show that fool how to work the damn volume controls on the board. Something is funny about this kid and his whole pitch."

"Funny or not, I bought five tracks from this nigga over the last two weeks to use for y'all album," Don B. announced.

"Don, I thought that the Coast was gonna get final say on the production?" Doze asked, not really feeling Don B. approving tracks without them.

"It's a small thing, Doze. I just heard some fire that I thought would sound good. I sent it to Tone at the main office to let Mr. Zappa hear the joints to get his take on them," he said, referring to the vice president of Big Dawg's parent company, Dope Beat Records. "Hopefully, when he hears the tracks he'll be willing to shell out more bread for the marketing side of it. This album is guaranteed to make the *Billboard* Top 100."

"Speak of the devil." Fully pointed one of the closed-circuit monitors. Tone had just walked into the lobby, and from the look on his face you could tell something was wrong. The quartet waited in anticipation for Tone to make it upstairs to where they were.

"Yo, we've got a problem," Tone said as soon as he walked into the studio. His bald head was sweating like he had just run the New York marathon.

"What's the matter, didn't Mr. Zappa like the tracks?" Fully asked.

"Oh, he loved them, he just ain't gonna use them," Tone broke the news to the group.

"What the fuck do you mean? He ain't trying to use them when I already paid for them? Tone, you're A and R for Big Dawg, so you need to help me to understand what's going on before I send Remo and Devil to find out," Don B. ranted.

"Don, don't shoot the messenger; I'm just telling you what he told me. Look, I took the tracks to Zappa like you told me, but when I got there he was in a meeting with that German cat from Telescope Records. I was gonna wait until the meeting was over, but Zappa wanted to stunt for the competition, so he told me to play the beats while the dude was still there. Zappa loved what he heard, but the German is sitting there all sour like. The next thing you know, this big muthafucka is going on about how we're a bunch of thieves and how he's gonna sue Big Dawg and Dope Beat."

"Sue us, what the fuck for?" Don B. wanted to know. It was bad enough that he already had the wrongful-death lawsuits pending from the deceased members of Bad Blood's families cutting into his pockets, but the situation with Telescope could put a serious cramp in his style.

"Dude claims that we're trying to use beats that he already purchased from some other kid last week. We thought the nigga was bugging until he had his people FedEx over the contracts and master copies of the tracks. I don't know what kinda games ya little man is playing, but he didn't make these beats, and now we're in a nasty situation with Telescope Records over the use of them. The kid tried to trim us and leave Big Dawg holding the bag," Tone said heatedly.

The blood rushed to Don B.'s face, turning him an off-shade of red. It was one thing when he was the one doing the duping, but someone trying to get over on him was an unforgivable crime. "Yo, step out here for a sec, Hollywood," Don B. said into the intercom that connected to the recording booth. "Tone, go downstairs and get some of the little homeys that's lounging in the green room."

Tone smiled, knowing just what Don B. had in mind. "I got you." He ran off to rally the troops.

"What're you gonna do?" No Doze asked nervously. He had heard stories about what went on behind the locked doors of Big Dawg studios and didn't want any part of it.

"Ima slap this nigga's head off when he comes out here," Fully threatened, as he slipped on a pair of leather gloves.

"Hold ya head, my G. The Don got this under control," Don B. assured him.

"Man, I'm outta here." No Doze made for the door, but Don B. moved to block him.

"Nah, Doze, y'all are a part of the team, so you need to know the inner workings of this organization. Just have seat over there with your boys; this won't take too long," Don B. said. It wasn't an order, but it felt like one, and No Doze reluctantly did as he he'd been told.

Hollywood came out of the booth drenched in sweat and smiling like a kid on Christmas. "Yo, y'all might need to get another mic when I'm done, because I'm about to short-circuit this shit," Hollywood said, as if he'd just laid the best verse ever heard.

"Nigga . . ." Fully started, but Don B. waved him silent.

"Yeah, son, you was killing it. I think we might use you on one of the lead singles," Don B. lied.

"I was thinking the same thing. Me and ya man Fully would be ill on a track together," Hollywood said, pouring himself a glass of Hennessy from a half gallon they had sitting in the studio. "I could set it off and he could come in, on some real back-and-forth shit."

"Back and forth, huh?" Animal asked mockingly. It was almost sad to see Hollywood digging his ditch even deeper.

"Yeah, yeah. See, he got that hard shirt, and I got silky delivery. We can make this shit a classic." The conversation was interrupted when the studio door opened and in came four hard-faced young boys who had been trying to get down with Don B. Tone stood behind them, glaring at Hollywood. Hollywood looked from the kids to Don B. quizzically. "Are they part of the group, too?"

"Yes and no. These little niggaz are my human lie detectors, and you're in the hot seat." He slid a chair over to Hollywood. "Sit down, my dude."

"Don, what's going on? Didn't you like the vocals I laid?" Hollywood asked nervously.

"Nigga, your vocals are trash, but I can live with that because you've got an incredible ear for music; ain't that right, Hollywood?" Don B.'s voice was pleasant, but there was no mirth in his face.

"Yeah, yeah, kid. You know how I do it." Hollywood sounded unsure.

"Dude, if you made them tracks, then I'll dig up Lou-Loc's corpse and kiss him smack in the mouth, and we both know that shit ain't gonna happen. This lying piece of shit is giving Harlem a black eye," Fully said to everyone in the room.

"He ain't from no streets these Timbs have ever touched, so we make no claim to that boy." Animal propped his boots on the coffee table and folded his hands behind his head.

"Yo, I don't think I even like the way y'all niggaz is coming at me like you signed any one of them checks Big Dawg cut me," Hollywood said, trying to shift the focus to the hecklers instead of having to address Don B.

Animal leaned forward, with his medallion making a loud clang when it hit the coffee table. "You're right, because if I'd signed those checks and you tried to shit on me, I wouldn't be trying to figure out how or why you did it, I'd be trying to figure out where to dump your body." There was a chill throughout the room when Animal spoke, and everyone felt it, especially Hollywood.

"Don." Hollywood turned to Don B. with pleading eyes. "What's going on, man? Why these dudes coming at me like that; I thought we was good?"

Don B. lit a blunt and began to slowly pace the studio. He got a rush watching Hollywood squirm under his shaded gaze, still trying to make heads or tails of what was going on. When he felt like he'd toyed with him enough, he got down to business. "I'm good with cats that do good business, but I ain't got no tolerance for snakes. I'm gonna ask you a question and your answer will determine whether you walk outta here or are carried, smell me?"

"Don . . ."

"Nigga, shut the fuck up before I wash you," one of the young thugs said. From the way he was dancing back and forth in the corner, you could tell he was looking forward to the trouble that was brewing.

"Hollywood," Don B. continued in an easy voice, "who made those tracks you sold me?"

"Don B., on my kids, those tracks were made in my home studio," Hollywood said, trembling.

"Do I look stupid to you, Hollywood?" Don B. glared at him. "I asked who made them, not where they were made. And while I'm thinking about it, what's your connection to Telescope Records?"

"I don't know what you're talking about," Hollywood stammered.

"A better question, then," Tone cut in. "Who is Robert Morris?"

Bobby—the name slammed into Hollywood's brain like a jackhammer. It was true that the tracks had been made using Hollywood's equipment, but Bobby had done most of the work. He wasn't the sharpest knife in the drawer, but he knew how to work the boards. He and Bobby had tried to shop the demo to Telescope Records a while back, but they were more interested in the beats than the group. Bobby wanted to go for it, but Hollywood had pulled out of the deal. He was more concerned with becoming a star than making smart business moves. When he'd hastily fired Bobby and stolen his beats, it had never occurred to him that Bobby might've had backups. This slipup was now coming back to take a big wet bite out of his ass.

Smack!

Don B. delivered a powerful backhand that sent Holly-wood sailing across the room and crashing into the far wall of the studio. One of the plaques hanging on the wall fell and broke over Hollywood's head. "Do I look like a pussy to you, because you sure as hell are trying to fuck me." Don B. lifted him to his feet by the front of his football jersey.

"Don, I can explain all this," Hollywood said through bloody lips.

"You can save your defense because the sentence has al-ready been passed." Don B. flung Hollywood over to where the young thugs were standing. "Y'all just make sure nothing gets broken in here, and be mindful of his hands because he's gonna need them."

Animal and the others watched as the thugs proceeded to tear off into Hollywood's ass. They beat him nonstop for a full ten minutes before Don B. ordered them to stop. "That's enough," Don B. said, stepping back into the center of the room, where Hollywood was curled up on the floor. In his hand Don B. held a length of chain.

"Please . . . I'm sorry," Hollywood rasped from his fetal position.

"You sure are." Don B. pulled him up roughly by the back of his shirt. He looped one end of the chain around Holly-wood's neck and fastened the other to one of the legs of the control panel.

"What're you doing?" Hollywood yanked at the chain fu-tilely.

Don B. leaned down so close that Hollywood could smell the staleness of his breath. "You owe me money, and until the debt is paid off, you're property of Big Dawg entertainment."

"Don, you can't leave me like this. What if I gotta use the bathroom?" Hollywood pleaded.

In answer to his question, Don B. hit him in the head with a wastebasket, raining cigar guts and ashes on Hollywood. "Knock yourself out, dick head." Don B. walked through the doors that connected to his office. As soon as he was gone, the thugs started fucking with Hollywood, throwing things at him and threatening to burn the bound man with cigarettes.

Fully laughed, Chip shook his head, and No Doze looked too frightened to move. Animal, however, was just disgusted. He was disappointed in Don B. for how he handled the situation, but he understood that no matter how many records he sold, Don B. would forever be a thug. He was more disappointed by Hollywood for going out like that. He was wrong for trying to play Don B. over the beats, but he should've tried to defend himself against Don B. Regardless of what Hollywood had done, he was still a man—well, at least that's what Animal had thought before the show. Tiring of watching the pitiful specimen, Animal went into the office to confront Don B.

"Yo, I'm sorry you had to see that, but I had to make an example out of that nigga for what he did. I can't just have muthafuckas trying to play the Don out, smell me?" Don B. started explaining as soon as Animal walked in the door.

"Man, I ain't really too bothered by that shit. Unlike some of ya peoples, I ain't no stranger to blood. Besides, a nigga who don't even make an attempt at standing up for hisself ain't worth my sympathy," Animal told him.

"You would've fought back even if you knew you could've died for doing so?" Don B. was curious.

Animal weighed the question carefully before answering. "Be it in life or death, all a man has is his nuts. You take those and he ain't got nothing, so he'd be better off dead anyway. I'll always choose death over cowardice."

Don B. shook his head. "You are one crazy little mutha-fucka, Animal."

"My mental health is a matter of opinion, but that ain't what I came in here to talk to you about. Do you remember shorty from the other night at Mochas?"

"The pretty dark-skinned one? How can I forget when she costs me three thousand dollars in lawyer fees? What about her?"

"Her and her homegirl wanna get up with us tonight," Animal explained.

"Say word you bagged shorty with the phat ass?" Don B. asked proudly.

Animal shrugged. "We're trying to come to an understanding. So, are you with it or what?"

"Yeah, I'm wit' it. We can take them broads back to the spot and see about doubling up on them." Don B.'s mind was already scheming.

"I don't know about all that, Don. How 'bout we just play it by ear and see how the night goes."

Don B. stared up at Animal in amazement. "You stuck on this broad or something?"

"Nah, I ain't stuck, just trying to see where her head is at," Animal said, downplaying it.

"Bullshit, Animal. I know that look. Dig this, my nigga: when you getting paper, everybody wants to get next to you. Chicks that would've never given you any play before will fuck your brains out if they think it can get them closer to the brass ring. Those broads we met at the club is bad as hell, but they're sack chasers. I've seen a million Tionnas and Guccis in my day, and I'm gonna see a million more before it's all said and done, and they all reek of the same shit—larceny."

"I can't speak for Tionna, but from what I get from Gucci, she seems pretty cool," Animal defended her.

"Of course she does. Do you think she's gonna come right out and try to tap your pocket? Shorty gotta gain your trust before she even thinks about reaching, and from the look in your eyes, she's already gotten into your head and you ain't hit the pussy yet, have you?"

"No, but . . ."

"But nothing, blood. Look at Tionna, she got a man that's in prison, probably for trying to take care of her, and she's in the club trying to lick the rapper. I believe that a chick's actions speak louder than anything else, and those bitches are suspect at best. If that was my bitch, I'd have her clipped, but her man ain't built like the Don. If he wants to wife her, that's cool, but I ain't trying to do shit but one-night that ho."

Animal shook his head. "Don, you are one of the most warped individuals that I've ever had the pleasure of coming across."

"Call me what you want, nigga, but you won't call me caught up!" Don B. laughed. "I'm just fucking with you, Animal. Yeah, we gonna go on the little double date so you can feel your boo out, but if you knew like I did, you'd have your mind on fucking, because that's what they're coming to do."

"Whatever, man. I'll meet you here at like eight so we can get uptown to scoop them by nine." Animal headed for the door.

"You do that, my nigga, but if you show up with flowers and candy, you ain't getting in my whip!"

CHAPTER 27

It had been a week since Bobo had been murdered and the projects were still quiet. The police had tapered off, chalking Bobo's death up as a drug-related homicide, therefore not a priority on their list of cases that needed solving. You'd think that with the hood back open it would've been business as usual, but it wasn't. With Styles in prison and Bobo in the ground, nobody had a good connect to speak of, but all that was about to change.

"I don't believe the hood is this dead," Bernie said to Wise, as they sat on a bench, passing a blunt back and forth. They had been out there all morning and couldn't manage to sell ten bags between them. It wasn't for lack of product but lack of quality. The shit they had was so weak that all the fiends opted to walk a few blocks up to buy their drugs.

"Yeah, man, ever since Bobo got killed, this shit has been suspect. If I don't get a line on something soon, I might fuck around and have to get a job," Wise agreed. He and Bernie had always been cool, but he had found himself spending more time with him since Happy had gotten Ron-Ron locked up. He secretly hated Happy for the snake move he'd pulled, but as it stood, Happy's handouts and the little bit of crack he sold were his only means of eating.

"I know what you mean, dawg. I got a lot of hungry mouths to feed, and the little money Boots gets from welfare ain't gonna cut it," Bernie said.

"Man, if I was you, I'd either make that girl get a job or tie her fucking tubes!" Wise joked. His laughter came to an abrupt halt when he saw a group of people walking in their direction. The youngest two he didn't recognize, but the guy and the girl he remembered from the day they'd confronted Bobo in the parking lot. "Bernie, you got your gun, man?"

"It's in the mailbox. Why?" Bernie asked nervously. He didn't know the quartet, but they seemed to have Wise spooked.

"I'll explain it to you on the way." Wise slid off the bench and started walking toward the building.

"Yo, my man!" Brasco called after him, but Wise kept walking like he hadn't heard him.

"Let me try it, son." Ashanti pulled his little pistol. "Nigga, if you take another step, I'm gonna shoot you in the ass!" Ashanti called to Wise. This got him to stop. "I told you." Ashanti smiled at Brasco.

"Now why y'all wanna pull some track-star shit when all I wanna do is talk?" Tech asked when he reached Bernie and Wise.

"Dawg, we don't want no problems; we ain't even fuck with Bobo like that," Wise tried to explain.

Tech looked at him like he was speaking a foreign language.

"What do I know about anybody named Bobo?" he said, faking ignorance. "Nah, y'all got me wrong. I didn't come to bring problems, I came to bring gifts." Tech nodded at Silk, who handed Bernie a brown paper bag.

"What's this?" Bernie asked suspiciously.

"The answer to your problems, dummy." Silk shook her head like she was speaking to an unruly child.

"What my homegirl is saying is that we're here to put y'all back on the map," Tech explained. "These projects have become the Mojave Desert and we're the closest water source."

"There were a few cats moving weight under Bobo; we're just bag men, so why bring the package to us?" Wise asked. He needed the money, but he knew that taking that package would officially put him on Tech's radar.

"Because neither of you look like you've got the balls or the brains to try and run off with my drugs. But character assessments aside, either you can take the package or I can give it to someone else; either way you cut it, these projects are under new management." He motioned to Brasco and Ashanti. "Get the word out to the rest of your homeys, too, that we got food if they're hungry."

"What do you think, man?" Wise asked Bernie.

Bernie tested the weight and placed it at about an ounce or so. With the drought that had hit their hood, they could knock it off in no time, especially if it was anywhere near as potent as what Bobo was putting on the streets. "I say I'm tired of sitting out here starving. Let's set up shop."

"That's what I like to hear," Tech said, beaming. "That's all soft, so you'll be responsible for bagging it and cooking it. Y'all do know how to cook crack, right?" Both boys nodded. "Good to hear. Y'all are from this hood, so however big or small you make the bags is on you, as long as y'all got my bread when one of my people come around for it, understand?"

"Yeah, we got it." Bernie stuffed the bag into his pants. "But how do we contact you when we've got your money or need more coke?"

"You don't. This will probably be the last time you ever see me, unless you do something stupid. From now on you report to either Brasco or Ashanti, cool?"

"Yeah, that's cooler than a muthafucka," Bernie said, sizing the two high-school kids up. The big one had a street-brawler look about him and the little one didn't look old enough to have lost his virginity. He would be able to do what he wanted with them running things, or so he thought.

"That's what it is, then." Tech nodded in approval. "Y'all got it from here?" he asked Brasco and Ashanti.

"Yeah, T, go on and handle yours. We'll get up with you later," Brasco assured him. Tech and Silk headed back to the car, leaving Brasco and Ashanti with their very first workers.

"A'ight, fellas, this is the way this is gonna go—" Bernie began, but Brasco cut him off.

"Hold on, fam. Just because we're letting y'all bag this shit don't mean you're calling no shots," Brasco said, stopping him.

"But me and Wise was gonna get the work off together; we always hustle in pairs," Bernie told him.

Brasco shook his head. "Nah, we ain't got enough cats on the payroll to do it like that yet, so we're gonna rock it how Ashanti and me say. One of y'all will go up one end and the other one will stay down here; we don't wanna miss none of the fiends."

"Fam, being that y'all some outside niggaz who ain't never

got no bread over here, I'm just trying to tell you how it goes. How you gonna make us your street generals and not give us any say-so in how we hustle?" Bernie said with a little too much bass in his voice.

"Street generals?" Ashanti looked at him comically. "Brasco, you hear this guy?" He glanced at his partner. "Let me tell you something, silly muthafucka. Just because the big homey came over here and gave you a little pep talk don't mean shit. To me, you ain't nothing but a muthafucka out here working for me, so you best get to work before you find yourself fired." Ashanti pulled up his shirt so Bernie and Wise could see the butt of his gun.

"Or fired on," Brasco said, exposing his weapon.

Fearing that his dimwitted friend was going to get them both killed, Wise stepped up. "No problem, B. It's like you said, we'll split up." Wise pulled Bernie toward the building. His legs buckled so bad that he had to take measured steps. He thought that working for the two kids was going to be sweet, but one thing Brasco and Ashanti had made crystal clear was that there was nothing sweet about them.

"How long do you think it'll take them to get that off?" Silk asked once they were back in the whip.

"For as hurting as these fiends are for some good shit, it shouldn't take more than a day or so. We'll hit them again tomorrow night," Tech told her.

"And how do you figure that when we've been riding around all day hitting different little hoods with coke, we ain't got nothing left in the stash? By making all these promises, you might've finally bitten off more than you can chew, Tech," Silk said seriously.

He looked at her. "Silk, when have you ever known me to do something without thinking it through?"

"Never," she said honestly.

"Alright, so don't ask silly questions, little girl. I got at the boy Rock Head about that deal and the date has been changed: we're hitting them niggaz tonight," Tech informed her.

"Tonight? We ain't even did a walk-through," Silk reminded him.

"Silk, I've been on that nigga almost every night since Shai called his little meeting."

"Tech, we always been tighter than fam, but you've been on some real funny shit lately with all these secrets," Silk said.

"I know, Silky, but there's been a lot of shit in the mix and I've been trying not to come to y'all unless I had something of note to talk about. I heard through the grapevine that the Commission had another little meeting, except we weren't invited to this one. It seemed that somebody had an urge to have us hit, but the motion was vetoed."

"Son of a bitch! I'll bet it was that faggot Rico who tried to sponsor that little going-away party," Silk said heatedly.

"I never got the chance to find out whose idea it was, but I do know that our lives were spared by one vote, and it don't sit well with me."

"So what're we gonna do, go at the Commission?" Silk asked. She didn't like to feel like she was at a disadvantage, so she liked to meet her problems head-on.

"Oh, we gonna let our dogs bark, but not right now. Going toe-to-toe with them would be suicide, and if we didn't get them all, we'd have to run for the rest of our lives," Tech explained. He didn't fear the Commission, but he respected their power, so he understood that money beat muscle any day. "We're gonna rip old boy off for this coke and flood all the little blocks we've laid the pressure on over the last few months. We're hot right now, so we're gonna kick back and try our hand at drug dealing for a while."

"So now you think you're gonna be the black Scarface," Silk teased him.

"Silky, baby, the only thing I know I'm gonna be is alive tomorrow to see another day and another dollar, and that's what's important to me right now. Let's take this shit one day at a time and let everything else fall into place. On another note, I'm gonna need to get the team together to walk everybody through this shit a few times before we move. Have you spoken to China?"

"Not since this morning. She was acting all funky and shit before she left; you know how white folks are," Silk said, laughing.

"Well, make sure you raise her sooner than later. I'll track Animal down."

Silk was quiet for a minute. "Yo, T, you think Animal is ready for this? I mean, I know he's a rider, but his head has been somewhere else ever since Don B. put this rap shit in his ear."

Tech looked at her like she'd lost it. "Silk, Animal might be a flake, but he's the most qualified street soldier to ever come out of a broad. He's chasing this fake-ass dream right now, but once he hears the call to arms he's gonna be all in; this I'm sure of."

CHAPTER 28

As soon as Animal entered his apartment, he knew something was wrong. From the foyer he could see a cup in the sink, and he knew for a fact that he'd washed all the dishes before he'd left that morning. He drew his hammer and crept silently into the living room, where he heard the television playing. Swinging his shooting arm up as he went, Animal jumped in front of the television and almost shot China White.

China was curled up on his sofa, eating ice cream out of the container and watching *Poetic Justice* on the plasma. She was dressed in nothing but Animal's Jackie Robinson jersey and a head scarf. One creamy thigh was visible from beneath the jersey; her black-painted toenails traced lines in the carpet. Her blue eyes studied him while she slowly took another spoonful of the chocolate mint, letting the spoon linger in her mouth until she had gotten all the ice cream off.

"Either shoot me or move. This is the best part of the

movie," China said, referring to the fight between Joe Torre and Regina King.

"Girl, you know better than to be sneaking into my pad like that." Animal put his gun away. He walked over to the couch where she was sitting and sat down. China stretched her bare legs over him and continued watching the movie. "What're you doing here unannounced?"

"What'd you give me a key for if you were gonna get all uptight about it?" she asked.

"I gave you the key to use in case of emergencies."

"This was an emergency, sort of." She took her legs off him and sat up.

"What's wrong, Ms. White?" he asked, sounding very concerned. "If a nigga's wronged you, I'll make him bleed, and if a nigga's hurt you, I'll make him gone," he said, reciting the old mantra.

"Animal, you still remember that?" She smiled a little.

"I should, seeing how I've been saying it to you since I was thirteen years old. Back then I thought of you as my white girlfriend," he reminded her jokingly.

"Yeah, no matter how many times I smacked your little ass for it, you were always trying to feel up on me. You acted like you'd never seen a woman before." She laughed.

"We had plenty of chicks in the hood, but not white ones. Especially white ones that's built like a sista." Animal pinched her thigh, causing her to giggle. "But don't try to change the subject by taking me down memory lane. What's bothering you?"

She thought on it, wondering if she should share her anxieties with Animal. He had always been dear to her heart and they could trust each other with anything, but what was bothering her hit very close to home with him. Still, they'd promised never to keep secrets from each other, so she wouldn't be the one to break the pact.

"I'm afraid," she said finally.

"Not the great China White, the baddest white chick to ever strut a New York block," he joked.

"I'm serious, Animal. This business with Tech and the Commission has got me spooked."

"Them old cats is always salty with Tech over one thing or another. It'll blow over like it always does."

"Animal, you weren't there, so you didn't see what I saw," she told him. "Yo, it was as if Tech was purposely trying to start a war with them dudes. I'm all for getting a dollar by any means necessary, but you don't spit in the hand of a man like Shai Clark when he extends it in friendship."

"I can agree with you on that, China. I'd go at Shai and his people if I had to, but it's not something I'd wanna do," Animal admitted.

"Animal," China began, "you know I love all y'all, you've been my only family since I got to New York, and never treated me funny because I was white, and I am so thankful for that, but at the same time I have to ask myself where exactly we're following Tech to, heaven or hell? Sometimes he's the dude we all know and love, and others, he's a cold bastard who's still trying to prove to a dead man that he's the hardest thing on the streets. He's getting so far removed from the original goals that he's diving into the fire headfirst and taking us all along for the ride."

"What're you trying to say, China?" Animal was getting emotional. The thought of losing China as a part of their family made him sick to his stomach.

"I'm trying to say that I don't wanna die on the streets over some dumb shit," she cried. Animal could feel the sadness coming off China like body heat when he pulled her close to console her. When she looked up at him, he felt like he was staring into two perfect oceans of blue.

"We're gonna be okay." He wiped the tears from her eyes with his thumb right before she kissed him. It was somewhat expected, but it still surprised him when it happened. His tongue explored China's mouth, tasting the sweetness from the ice cream and the love she had in her heart for him. China grabbed a handful of his hair and pulled him so roughly to her that their teeth scraped. They were so wrapped up in the pent-up lust between them that it was as if they had returned to that faithful night a year prior, when they had enjoyed each other for the first and last time. Animal had been young and inexperienced so he was rough at first, but he proved to be a quick study as she schooled him on how to please a woman. Before the flashback could completely materialize, Animal broke the connection.

"What's the matter, did I do something wrong?" China looked up at him.

Animal slid farther down the couch, putting distance between them. "You know we can't do this, not again."

"No strings attached, right?" She gave him a sad smile.

"You know that, China, we both made the promise," he reminded her. There was no doubt in either of their minds that what had happened last year between them was more than just a *fuck*; they had made love, pure and beautiful love. The feeling of oneness had passed as soon as the deed was done, when they both realized the possible consequences of what they'd done. They both lived the lives of outlaws, always one step ahead of a bullet and the law; thus, emotions could not live in either of their hearts when they were handling business. They both knew that if they allowed their feelings to blossom, it would affect their focus on the streets because they would always be worried about each other.

"Well, since I've shared something with you, you've got to share something with me, you know how we do it," China said, trying to lighten the mood.

"I don't have anything to share," Animal said bashfully.

"I doubt that, Animal. With all the time you've been spending with Don B. lately, I know your life has run into some interesting twists and turns. Did you decide whether or not you were going to sign that contract?"

"I'm thinking about it, but Tech says it's a bad idea to fuck with Don B. like that," he said.

"And what does Tech know? Animal, God has blessed you with a gift, and honestly, I think it would be stupid of you to waste it by doing what we do. For as much as I would love to think that all of us are gonna ride off into the sunset when this is over, I know better. Along the way I know we're gonna lose people, so all I can do is hope I'm there to share the memories with those who made it. You need to be one of those people, Animal."

"But what would I know about being some square-ass entertainer, Ms. White? The streets are all I've ever known."

"Then you'll learn to navigate that world like you did this one," she said seriously. "Animal, take that money and run with it. Whether you're a rapper or a thug, be the best at it."

"I hear you, China. I'm supposed to meet up with Don B. again tonight."

"What, y'all going back into the studio?" she asked with a smile.

"Nah. We kinda going out to dinner with these chicks we met at the club," he confided in her.

"Lord, you're going on a double date with Don B., and with a hood rat no less. What's her name, Alize, Sha-quan-janique, or Coco?"

"It's Gucci, silly ass."

"See what I mean? Who the hell names their child after a handbag. I'll bet she's ghetto as all hell."

"Fuck you, China. Gucci ain't no ghetto broad," he said a little more heatedly than he'd intended to.

China's face suddenly became very serious. "You're feeling this chick, aren't you?" Her voice held a mix of surprise and hurt.

"I think so," he said seriously. "China, from the moment I met her she felt perfect, like the piece I've been missing all my life. Have you ever met somebody that you felt like had the answer to every question you've ever wanted to ask?"

"I've been there a time or two." She looked at him lovingly.

"See, but if you were a guy, you'd be looking at me like I was crazy for talking like this about a chick that I don't even know that well."

"That's because men have one-track thinking; y'all ain't got no dimensions to your shit. For the most part, all women have a touch of larceny in their hearts, birthed and stoked by men, but there are some good ones out there. You're sharp, Animal, so I know you ain't gonna let nobody beat you in the head but so much, but please be careful with your heart. The heart is a fragile thing, and until you've had it broken a time or two you'll have no idea of the extremes that it can make you go through."

"Always the wise one." He leaned over and gave her a peck on the lips. When he did, his hair got all in her face.

"Boy, you need to get a haircut." She ran her hands over her mouth to dislodge any loose strands.

"Never. I'm like Samson, my hair is my strength." Animal ran his fingers through the mess.

"Well, if you insist on going on a date with this hood rat, at least let me tighten you up. You don't want her talking about you to her friends when they're at the welfare office." She dug a comb out of her purse and motioned for Animal to sit between her legs.

"She ain't a hood rat and she's got a job," Animal corrected her, before sliding between her legs.

"Whatever, Animal. Just hold your head back so I can help you to show this broad what a lucky woman she is."

CHAPTER 29

"Tionna, why do you always have to take the longest to get dressed?" Gucci sighed, looking at her watch. It was five after nine and Tionna was still barricaded in the bathroom.

She popped her head out of the bathroom, which was still wrapped in a scarf. "Because it takes a lot to look this good." She shut the door again.

"We were supposed to get picked up at nine o'clock and you're still bullshitting," Gucci said, sucking her teeth.

"And nine has come and gone and they still ain't here. Why don't you relax," Tionna shouted through the bathroom door. Whatever else she said was drowned out by the sound of the blow-dryer.

"Slow ass," Gucci mumbled, getting up to check herself in the full-length mirror. She was wearing a fitted black BCBG dress, which she'd picked up from the outlet on her last Atlantic City trip, that made her already supple body appear more curvaceous. The black Gucci pumps added just enough lift to make her ass poke out enough to make sure she had Animal's undivided attention.

The beeping of a car horn drew Gucci's attention to the window. She looked out and saw the Senate, along with some of the neighborhood kids flocking around the sleek black automobile that had just pulled to a stop in front of Tionna's building. Gucci's lips parted into a wide grin. "T, our ride is here," she called to her friend.

"I'm coming right out." Tionna stepped out of the bathroom, finishing her hair. She had blown and pressed it, so it hung down straight like a China doll. The outfit she and Gucci had picked was a red Michael Kors evening gown that was cut into a vee on both sides, showing off her flat stomach and high ass. Thankfully, the kids hadn't sapped so much of her youth that she had to wear a bra with the dress, because she felt like the threat of her nipples showing through the dress gave her more appeal. "It's about time they got here. What are they pushing?"

"A spaceship."

Tionna felt like a rock star when she walked out of her building. Rayfield and Cords were standing in the center of a bunch of kids, trying to get a look at what had to be the biggest whip they'd ever seen. It was easily the length of two cars and painted such a rich black that it looked like it might fade into the evening. She was glad that she'd worn a dress that showed most of her goodies, because all eyes would definitely be on her tonight. She had seen them in catalogs and in videos, but never in her life had she dreamed she'd be riding in a Maybach.

Devil stood outside the car, holding the back door open and scaring the hell out of the kids. From inside the car came the sounds of an unidentified track that had the unmistakable Big Dawg stamp on it, along with thick clouds of yellowish smoke that smelled quite inviting to those who indulged. The girls beamed at their waiting chariot.

"As I live and breathe, look at these two beautiful sisters. Heaven is surely short two angels tonight!" Cords exclaimed.

"Amen to that." Rayfield fanned himself. "Where're y'all off to this fine evening? The inaugural ball was in January."

"None of your business," Tionna said playfully as she stepped past them. She could feel their eyes locked hungrily on her body, which was the effect she was going for.

"I see big things are popping." Rock Head stepped out from the crowd of onlookers. He had a young girl with him, who was dressed like a grown woman but the starstruck look in her eyes said that she was quite younger than she appeared. "Y'all must've hit the lotto or something, huh?"

"Rock Head, why don't you go find something to do instead of trying to fuck little girls." Gucci cut her eyes at Rock Head's little friend.

"Shit, shorty is growner than you think," he said suggestively.

"I don't even know why I bother with you dumb ass. Get out my face, boy, I ain't got time for your shit." Gucci adjusted her shades.

"Oh, since you hopping in Maybachs and shit, you ain't got no rap for a nigga? A'ight, see about me when you back to taking cabs."

"Everything cool?" Animal appeared by Gucci's side as if by magic. He was decked out in a mint-green V-neck sweater and black jeans, with his ever-present medallion scowling on his chest. His hair was braided in neat swirls that crowned his entire head. With the mane out of his face, you could appreciate how handsome the young man really was.

"Oh, shit. What it is, playboy; I didn't know it was you rolling like that." Rock Head extended his hand to give Animal dap, but Animal just stared at him.

"Do we know each other?" Animal scowled at him.

"Not directly, but we got a friend in common. I know ya boy Tech," Rock Head explained, as if it made a difference to Animal.

"Then you address him. Me and you don't know each other so ain't no need for us to be speaking," Animal said in a not-too-friendly tone.

"It's like that?" Rock Head looked offended.

"Straight like that." Animal didn't give a shit.

"That's what it is, then," Rock Head said, wearing an expression that said it wasn't over. "Tell Tech that Rock Head said what's up."

"Do I look like a carrier pigeon to you? Tell him your fucking self. Y'all about ready?" Animal looked from Tionna to Gucci, whom he almost couldn't take his eyes off.

"I've been ready," Gucci said with her head held high. She extended her hand and like a gentleman he helped her off the curb and into the back of the Maybach.

Don B. had never been much of a dater, so he had let Animal plan the evening and agreed to foot the bill for it. As he'd expected, Animal did something out of the ordinary and roped them into taking in a show. It was a production of *Cat on a Hot Tin Roof*, featuring James Earl Jones, which had come back to

New York for an encore performance. Gucci, who had never been to a Broadway show, thought that she'd fall asleep halfway through, but she ended up enjoying it.

Gucci tried to get Tionna's take on it, but her friend had only caught some of the show, because she spent the majority of their time in the darkened theater making small talk and flirting with Don B. One thing that Gucci had to give her friend was, when she made up her mind to get something, she dove in headfirst. Don B. was eating out of the palm of her hand, and by the end of the night she'd likely be eating out of his pockets. Even though it was for a shady purpose, Gucci was glad to see flashes of the old Tionna peeking out.

As they walked through Times Square, people snatched pictures and asked for all their autographs. Don B. was the celebrity, but they all felt famous that night. Gucci knew Tionna was uncomfortable with the pictures, since she was trying to stay on the low, but how low did she really think she could get walking through Midtown New York with a multi-platinum rapper.

Next they went to the ESPN Zone, where Gucci and Animal ran around playing the different games like two kids. In a battle of free throws, Gucci showed Animal why she had set a record for most consecutive free throws when she played JV basketball in school. Throughout the evening, she and Animal talked about everything from hood politics to world politics and he had an opinion on everything. Animal was more interesting than she had imagined, and she found herself wanting to know more about the so-called scourge of the streets.

"Where did you learn all that stuff?" she finally asked, after an interesting debate on why it would be a bad thing for the government to legalize marijuana. Animal made several financial and economic points to support his argument, but his biggest problem was that it would start to get watered because of the increasing demand.

"Books, mostly." He shrugged. "I read a lot, it's one of life's few joys. Most of my time is spent reading or writing; I don't do much outside of that."

"Yeah, right." Gucci twisted her lips.

"What, I don't strike you as somebody who knows how to read?"

"I don't mean it like that; I just mean that you seem like two people," she admitted.

"And what's that supposed to mean?" He was curious.

"Nothing. You know how the streets paint one picture of a person and when you get to know them they seem like somebody else. You gotta ask yourself which is the real and which is the mask, ya know?"

"Not really, so why don't you tell me what it is that the streets are saying, and we can try to make heads or tails of it."

Gucci felt stupid for following up with Rock Head's bullshit, but the cat was out of the bag, so she decided to get to the bottom of it. "They say that you're a bad man, Animal."

"Of course, I'm bad like Michael." Animal did a little spin.

"You're so silly; you know I don't mean it like that. Look, I'm not really one to follow up on rumors, but if I plan on dealing with somebody, I like to know that neither one of us are going in blind."

"Oh, oh, Gucci plans on dealing with me. I need to find a loudspeaker so I can announce this shit." He looked around.

"Animal, are you gonna play all night or are we gonna talk?" she said seriously. Hearing the change in her tone got her his undivided attention. "Animal, you seem like a really nice guy and I wanna try to get to know you better, but from what I hear, you're on fire in the streets. They talk about you like some monster hiding under a little kid's bed."

"You can't believe everything you hear," he told her.

"I know that, which is why I'm asking you myself. I'm not naïve enough to think that you ain't out there getting it how you live, but before I invest my time in you, I wanna know how deep you're in?" She took her glasses off, and for the first time that he could remember, he looked into her eyes.

Animal studied her face and saw what was beneath the mask. Behind those expensive sunglasses there was a little girl who was trying to find her way in life, same as he was. As it had been with him and China, he decided that there would be no lies between him and Gucci. "I'm in deep, way deep," he said as if a weight had been lifted off his shoulders.

"I knew it." Gucci turned her face away from him. "They told me that you were a killer, and that's how you really got the name Animal."

"Hold on now." He turned her face back to him. "I never said all that. People are afraid of me on the streets because they know I get it in. I do what I gotta do to keep from going back to eating out of garbage cans and I ain't ashamed of that. But if you're gonna judge me, then judge me for my actions and not what they say about me in the hood."

The conviction in his voice moved something deep within her. Looking into his eyes, Gucci knew full well that Animal was a killer, but she also knew that he had a soul. It was the same with him as it was with a lot of little boys in the ghetto, children forced to become men way too early or risk being swallowed by the jungle.

"Let me tell you a story." She took his hands in hers. "A

long time ago I dated this guy, we were young, but you couldn't tell us that he wasn't gonna blow up and we were gonna live happily ever after. The deeper he got, the more hectic things became. When I stared getting bad vibes, I asked him to get out, and he always promised he would, but never got around to it. One day I get the call from his mother telling me that he got murdered. The fucked-up part is that him and the kid that killed him went back to grade school. The kid had stole some work from him and he was afraid that my guy was gonna kill him for it, so he got him first. Now, I can't say that I've never dated a street nigga, but since then I've never given my heart to one. I can't take that kinda hurt anymore."

Animal measured his words carefully. "Gucci, these streets are feeding me right now, but they ain't gonna write the story of how my life plays out. I know the Lord has a plan for me, but I just ain't figured it out yet. Who knows, maybe one day it'll fall in my lap like those people who discover they have hidden talent," Animal said, trying to lighten the mood.

Gucci was about to say something, but Don B. interrupted their conversation. "Yo, kid, I was trying to wait for you to finish ya little lovemaking session, but y'all was taking too long and what I got to say can't really wait."

"Damn, you could fuck up a wet dream," Gucci told Don B.

"I'm gonna forgive that insult, because I'm in a good mood right now. Animal, I know I told you that I wasn't gonna do nothing with that track you laid, but I kinda sent it to my nigga Stacks out in Texas."

"Man, you a shady muthafucka, Don. You said that you just wanted to hear how I sound!" Animal snapped.

"Calm your little ass down, Animal. I knew you were gonna

lunch out, but when you hear what I got to say it's gonna cheer you the fuck up. Gucci, can you excuse us for a minute?"

"It's cool." Animal motioned for her to stay seated. "With the big-ass production you've made of it, you might as well say it in front of her."

"Check it, the nigga Stacks had a deal on the table for like five million to put out a group album with my little nigga Soda and his partner Sip. Sip got killed, so they can't do the album, but the nigga Stacks ain't trying to give the bread back, smell me?"

"What the fuck does that have to do with me?" Animal asked, still uptight with Don B. for letting the track get out.

"What it has to do with you is, he wants you to replace Sip and help Soda finish this album. Yo, when he heard the track, he jumped on your dick so hard that he might try to give you some pussy when he flies you out to Texas in two weeks to meet with him. Stacks says you can bring whoever you want and he's footing the bill, first class all the way, baby!"

"Don, you know I ain't wit' no rap shit, especially with a nigga I don't know," Animal said as if it were final.

"Not even for one-point-two million?"

"What did you just say?" Animal and Gucci asked in unison.

Don B. smiled, knowing he now had Animal's attention. "Stacks is gonna give you two hundred thousand, plus points on the album if you help him out. And I'm gonna do him one better and hit you with a million as an advance against the solo deal you'll sign with Big Dawg. That's if you're with it?" Don B. waited for him to respond.

Animal felt like he'd just been spun around a hundred

times and was trying to figure out which end was up. People were always telling him how nice he was on the mic, but they were local. Even when Don B. had begun pursuing him he'd thought it was just hype because Don B. liked to associate himself with dangerous men; but with $1.2 million dangling in front of him, he knew there had to be some truth to it. He looked at Gucci with a question lingering in his eyes.

"What're you looking at me for; he didn't just offer me a million dollars," Gucci said.

"Animal, I don't mean to pressure you, but Stacks is not only impatient, he's stingy as hell. That man don't shell out nothing unless he thinks he can make triple back, so you might wanna get on this before he comes back to his senses. What do you say, my nigga?" Don B. extended his hand.

"Yeah, what do you say, because I'm gonna bust you in the head if you say no," Gucci teased him.

Animal gave her his jeweled smile. "What I say is, how do you feel about taking some time off from work to fly with me out to Texas?"

The happy quartet spent the rest of the night riding around in the Maybach, popping bottles and celebrating Animal's new-found success. Gucci was genuinely thrilled for Animal, not because she had expected anything from him but because she knew that he wasn't going to let his blessing go to waste.

"It's like I told you, my nigga: the Don knows how to make stars," Don B. boasted, hoisting his champagne glass.

"So, Animal, are you excited about all this?" Gucci asked.

"It ain't really set in yet," Animal said as if it were nothing.

"See, this is why I love this nigga." Don B. draped his arm

around Animal. "I just made him a fucking millionaire and he's acting like it's nothing."

"Now that you got all that money, you know niggaz is gonna superhate, so you better be careful before someone snatches you up," Tionna said playfully. Gucci hadn't missed the fact that Tionna was being extra friendly to Animal since Don B. had let her in on their little venture. She didn't think that her best friend would cross her, but she kept her eyes on Tionna anyway.

"And that's just why his ass is officially off the streets," Don B. declared.

"Don, I ain't never had a daddy and I don't think I want one now," Animal told him.

"Dawg, I ain't trying to be your father or your boss, I'm just telling you what it is. Once you sign that contract, you become an investment. There's gonna be a lot of money riding on you to win, and you don't need that petty hood shit you and Tech are into fucking it up, you smell me?"

"Yeah, Don," Animal said as if it were no big deal.

"I'm serious, Animal. I gotta know that if I put this money behind you, you're not gonna fuck it up for either of us."

"I said I heard you, man."

"That ain't good enough. I need your word that you're gonna come in off the block and really see this thing through. If it's money you're worried about, don't sweat it, I'll have a check for a hundred thousand waiting for you tomorrow morning when you sign the contract, and the rest will be paid out to you when the paperwork is properly processed. But I need your word on this one, homey."

The eyes of everyone in the Maybach, including Devil,

who was driving, were on Animal to see what he would say, but he was focused on one person, Gucci. Although she hadn't voiced much of an opinion about the whole thing, he knew what she wanted and he knew what he wanted to give her. "You've got my word," he said to Don B., but he was looking at Gucci, who smiled proudly at his response.

"Now that we've settled that, let's shoot uptown. I know an after-hours spot that should be off the chain about this time." Don B. looked at his diamond-flooded watch and saw that it was just after three in the morning.

"I'm wit' it. You down to roll, Gucci?" Tionna looked at her friend.

Gucci shrugged. "I'm with it; I ain't got nowhere to be. Besides," she looped her arm around Animal's, "I'm in no rush to end this night."

"Let me find out that million dollars got you ready to give Animal some," Tionna teased.

"Knock it off, T. Even if Animal wasn't about to be rich, I planned to give him some," she said seriously. This brought a big grin to his face. "Once he's earned it," she added.

Animal's cell phone cut off the snappy comeback he had for her. When he looked at the caller ID, his spirits picked up even more. "I'm glad you called, family, I got some good news I wanna share with you. I'm with the nigga Don B. and—"

"Later," Tech said, cutting him off. "I need you to meet us at the spot."

"A'ight, I'll see y'all in the morning, then."

"Not the morning. Now," Tech insisted.

"Big homey, you kinda caught me in the middle of something." He looked over to see if Gucci was watching and of course she was. She didn't say a word, but the look on her face said that she knew what kind of call it was.

"Look, Animal, you can go back to chasing that lame-ass dream tomorrow; tonight we got real business to attend to. We're handling that score tonight and I need you to be the eyes in back of my head. I know you ain't gonna bail on your family for your new friends, are you?" Tech said, playing on his sense of loyalty.

"A'ight, I'll be there as soon as I can," he told Tech and ended the call. When he tried to reposition himself next to Gucci, she slid away.

"Is everything alright?" Tionna asked.

"Yeah, just a family emergency," he half lied. Don B. read something in the exchange between Animal and Gucci and spoke on it.

"Animal, I know you didn't forget the conversation we just had that fast?" Don B. sized him up.

"It ain't nothing like that, I just gotta make a quick run." Animal averted his eyes when he spoke.

"Drop me off so I can hop in a cab," Gucci said.

"Girl, where're you going? The night is still young." Tionna snapped her fingers to an imaginary beat.

"I'm good, I just need to go home." Gucci folded her arms and looked out the window.

"Gucci." Animal reached to touch her, but she moved away.

"Don't worry, Animal, she's just mad that her time with you was cut short. She'll be okay—ain't that right, Gucci?" Tionna nudged her friend, but Gucci remained silent. Tionna acted like she was really concerned with Gucci and Animal, but she was really worried that her friend's snubbing of Animal would complicate things between her and Don B. If he had a million dollars to give Animal for an album that didn't exist, then she definitely needed to keep him around for a while.

For the rest of the ride Gucci stared silently out the window. Several times Animal tried to make small talk, but she wouldn't even look at him. Of course, Don B. and Tionna were too busy petting each other and drinking to notice the emotional rift that had so quickly sprung up between the two lovers. When the Maybach reached the block, Gucci hopped out without even saying goodbye, and of course Animal was on her heels.

"So, what, you're never gonna talk to me again because I cut our date short?" he called after her.

"It ain't about cutting the date short and you know it." She continued walking toward the building. "You're a liar, Animal!" she called over her shoulder.

"I didn't lie to you," he said.

Gucci stopped and faced him. The tears hadn't come yet, but he could see the moisture in the corners of her eyes. "Yes, you did. You lied to me and you lied to Don B. when you promised you were done with the streets."

"I am done with the streets," he assured her.

"Then where are you going?" She folded her arms. He couldn't meet her gaze. "Look, Animal, I like you, but it's not like we're seriously involved, so you don't have to make up excuses or feed me lies to pacify me. All I want you to do is be real with me, but I guess it's too much to ask."

Animal lowered his head and sighed. "Gucci, you don't understand. A friend of mine needs me to help him out with something and I couldn't tell him no. Come on now, the big homey has been looking out for me for years; I can't shit on him now. I gotta keep it real for my nigga."

"Animal, keeping it real would be you making sure I get home all right and going home to figure out what you're gonna do with that money when it comes in, not running off to do God knows what with ya man Tech. Why risk fucking everything up just to say you kept it real with a nigga?"

"Because he looked out for me, I owe him, ma."

"Animal, you don't owe anybody shit, but yourself. You owe it not only yourself but to every little ghetto kid who never made it out of the ghetto, to take this opportunity and do something better. It's not every day someone offers you a million dollars!"

"Gucci, you don't understand . . ." he tried to explain.

"No, you're the one who doesn't understand. You're about to risk throwing a promising future out the window because of some bullshit street code that's got all you dumb little muthafuckas brainwashed." She walked up the last few steps to the entrance of her building. "I swear, Animal, you're just like those kids I work with at the center. None of you believe that the stove is hot until you're actually on fire. If you go out there and let Tech get you into some shit, lose my number." She went in and slammed the lobby door behind her.

For a while Animal was frozen with emotion. He knew the car was waiting, but he couldn't bring himself to leave Gucci's doorstep. Gucci was right about him jeopardizing his blessing, but she didn't understand the position he was in. Tech had looked out for him when he was nothing and had nothing. He wanted so badly to tell Tech that he was out and wanted no parts of the heist, but he couldn't bring himself to abandon his friend. He would meet Tech and help him with the robbery, but when it was done he was out, and he didn't care how anybody felt about it.

Tionna was good and twisted when she crossed the threshold of Don B.'s Harlem brownstone. After dropping Gucci and Animal off, they had continued partying until the sky was almost pink. For once, she didn't have to worry about getting back to her kids, because Boots had them for the night, so she was going to milk her freedom for all it was worth.

Don B's crib was laid, but she hardly noticed because her head was spinning so intensely, but not so intensely that she'd lost her focus on the task at hand, which was getting that money up for Duhan.

"You've got a nice place," Tionna said, slipping her heels off and getting comfortable on Don B.'s couch.

"You know I don't do nothing but the best of everything, and if you didn't know, then you'll find out in a hot minute, smell me?" He was behind the bar, fixing them two more drinks, as if either of them needed any more alcohol. Don B. walked over to the couch, holding the two drinks and smiling like he had just hit the lotto. "I fixed us these to take the edge off. You know, a night out with the Don can be a bit much."

"I hear you talking, daddy." Tionna took the drink and took a healthy gulp. Tionna put the drink on the coffee table and stretched out seductively, so he could get a good look at what she was working with.

"That's a blessing in itself, because I don't do a lot of talking." He got onto the couch and stretched out on top of her. Don B. started kissing Tionna's neck and breasts, but when he went for her panties, she stopped him. "What's good?" he asked.

"Hold on, I think you've got me twisted." She sat up and retrieved her drink. "You think I'm some groupie bitch that you can just take to dinner and fuck because you're a rapper?" She took another gulp of the drink. "It ain't that kinda party."

"Yo, I thought we had a connection?" Don B. sat up so that she could see the tent in his jeans.

"We do have a connection, but we don't have an understanding." She looked him up and down.

Don B. smiled because he knew it wouldn't be long before Tionna showed her true colors. "So it's about the paper with you, huh?"

"It's always about the paper with me, but that don't mean that I came back here with you just to get paid. Tionna don't fuck for money, boo, but I'm a high-maintenance chick, real talk." The alcohol had her feeling herself. She tried to get up and ended up flopping back down to the couch.

"See what you get for trying to drink with the Big Dawgz?" he said mockingly. His voice sounded distorted to her ringing ears.

"Nigga, I can hold mine—and don't try to change the subject." She slapped him on the arm a little harder than she'd meant to. "Hold on. What I was talking about?" She had to think about it.

"You was telling me how it's always been your dream to fuck a millionaire." Don B. traced the line of her clit through her panties, sending her body into spasms of pleasure.

"No, I wasn't, you nasty muthafucka," Tionna slurred. "I was saying that you gotta pay to play in this pussy, because I'm a bitch that needs things." The liquor and what Don B. had slipped into her drink had a firm hold on her now.

"You know money ain't no thing to the Don," he said, low-ering himself on top of her with his penis out. Tionna reached down and tested the girth of him in her hand. She was pleased.

"You plan on sticking all this inside me?" she asked, while rubbing the head of his dick against her clit.

"All that and then some." He tried to force himself inside, but Tionna stopped him.

She reached inside her purse and pulled out a condom, which she handed to him. "No glove, no love, baby."

"Never a problem," he said happily, taking the condom from the wrapper and slipping it on. When she was satisfied that he had strapped up, she let him enter her. Don B. fucked her like a wild dog, making sure to christen every flat surface in the living room. The drug had Tionna on him like a mad woman licking, biting, and sucking him at several different angles. When Don B. felt himself about to cum, he pulled out and sprayed her chest, face, and hair, before collapsing on the carpet beside her.

Tionna was wasted, but not so much to where she didn't know that she had rocked Don B.'s world. She had done and said things to him that she wouldn't have dared discuss with Duhan and loved every minute of it. She was pleased with herself not only for getting one of the best fuckings of her life, but for successfully cutting into Don B. She curled up beside her new sponsor and drifted to sleep with visions of the gifts he would shower her with in her head. In all her plotting, she never once suspected that her freak show wasn't as private as she'd thought.

CHAPTER 30

The truck was deathly silent as it coasted down the West Side Highway. Tech stared absently out the window, with his mind on God knows what, more than likely the score. Silk was trying to look hard, but her eyes looked worried, as she tried to focus on the road ahead of her instead of the blind lick they were about to embark on. China just looked afraid, and truth be told, she had good reason to be.

The bulk of their information had come from Rock Head, who was suspect at best, and whatever intelligence Tech had been able to collect on his own. He explained it like he had it all mapped out, but Animal knew Tech well enough to know when he was unsure about something. The fact that he wasn't 100 percent with his information was more than enough reason to call the score off, but Tech insisted. Animal didn't like it, but he was outvoted on the issue, so he was gonna ride it out.

"Everybody knows what they're supposed to be doing,

right?" Tech looked to each of them. China nodded, while Animal said nothing. "You with us, little brother?" As an answer, Animal cocked his gun. "Good to know."

"So how many muthafuckas did you say it was supposed to be?" Silk asked, as if they hadn't been over it a dozen times.

"The cat bringing the work, and his bodyguards, plus the kid, his lieutenant, and Rock Head," Tech told her again.

"He's about a thirsty muthafucka to put himself in harm's way just to make sure he doesn't get shorted." Animal shook his head. In the original plan, Rock Head was to have met them back uptown to get his cut, but at the last minute he had arranged to be in the house by convincing the kid that he needed one more shooter with him in case something went wrong.

"Well, if he happens to get in the way, I might clap his ass and cut him out of the picture altogether," Silk threatened.

"No killing." Animal surprised them all with the statement.

"What the fuck is you going on about, son?" Silk asked.

"No killing. The police ain't gonna be too worried about us robbing a drug dealer, but if we leave a body in there, that's something different. If we was riding on some niggaz in the hood, I'd be a little more reckless with it, but you gotta think about where we about to roll to."

"Nigga, it's a project!" Silk shouted.

"It's a project in Midtown, dumb ass! As soon as we go in there busting off, the police are gonna be all over our asses."

"Alright already," Tech interrupted. "Okay, if it'll make you feel better, we'll only give 'em flesh wounds." Tech grabbed Animal playfully. "Blood, you know us, so you know we know how to handle business. What's with you lately?"

"Ain't shit got into me, man; I'm just saying we should be

extra careful because we ain't got a lot to go on about this shit," Animal lied. Inside, his heart was racing, and a warning kept flashing in his head, telling him to turn back.

"If Animal is spooked, then maybe we should call it off; we don't really know a lot about these vics anyway," China said.

"I can't believe what I'm hearing." Tech looked from Animal to China. "China, you were the main one talking about maybe we should cool out for a minute; that's what this lick is all about. Look, it's a lot of coke and a lot of money gonna be in that apartment, and we need that shit to further our own gains. I promise y'all that once we snatch what these niggaz got, we'll focus on moving this weight shit. We all agreed?"

"Whatever, man," Animal said, pulling his ski mask out of his pocket.

"I'm wit' you all day, Tech," Silk assured him as they pulled up near the projects and parked by a fire hydrant. She slipped her ski mask halfway on her head and got out of the car, leaving it running.

"A'ight then, let's go get this money," Tech said and slid out of the car. They stealthily moved up the path to their designated building and slipped into the lobby one by one. It was a short hike to the fourth floor, with them rotating for the lead at every landing like in the old army movies. Tech approached the apartment door and placed his ear against it. When he was sure that all the pieces were in place, he motioned for his team to get ready.

"How we gonna get in?" Animal whispered.

Tech smiled and showed him a can of WD-40 and a key. After thoroughly soaking the interior of the lock with the WD-40, Tech inserted the key. It barely made a sound when he turned it. The four of them all got down on one knee and said their silent prayers, as was their custom before they embarked on dangerous jobs. Tech raised three fingers and began to count down. When the last finger had dropped, they rushed the apartment.

The meet spot was at the apartment of a crackhead named Shakes. She was a throwback smoker who had been hooked to the drug since it first came out and showed no signs of slowing down. It had been Rock Head's idea to meet at the fiend's house, because they could have privacy in addition to being able to see three and a quarter sides of the building from her window.

Rock Head sat in a rickety wooden chair, chain-smoking Newports. Every so often he would look at his phone to check the time. He'd told him four forty-five; earlier or later could potentially ruin everything. Rock Head knew that the kid with the coke was supposed to be there at four in the morning, so he figured that by the time the pleasantries were exchanged and the drop had been made, everyone would be more re-laxed. Of course, the kid was going to want to count his money, and for the amount of coke he was bringing it wouldn't be a quick job. If it went as he had planned it, Rock Head's little surprise would come just about halfway through the count. But, as it stood, it was four thirty-five and Shakes was still dry-ing the little bit of coke she'd cooked to test. Rock Head started to get a very bad feeling.

"Let's get this over with so I can go," the tall Latino said, pacing the apartment impatiently. It was clear that he felt un-comfortable in the crack den.

"I got you; fam, just let my peoples tell me if it's butter or not," Fred said. He had a big Afro that was partially stuffed under a Yankee cap. Fred was Rock Head's sister's baby daddy, and sponsor of the little party. He wasn't the toughest cat to speak of, but he had done a fine job of turning nothing into something. "Shakes, hurry up so these gentlemen can be on their way." He motioned toward the two Latinos.

"Give me a minute, damn! What, y'all wanted me to smoke it wet?" she said indignantly as she loaded the stones into her pipe. When Shakes lit the rock, she immediately started choking and slobbering.

"Satisfied," the tall Latino said, pointing at the gagging crackhead.

"Yeah, man." Fred tossed him the bag of money. "Tell your boss I said mucho gracias."

The tall Latino opened the bag and gave the bills a quick thumbing before rezipping the bag. "Whatever. Adiós." He saluted them.

Seeing his money walking out the door, Rock Head panicked and blurted out, "Don't you want to count it?" Everyone in the room looked at Rock Head.

The tall Latino paused and tested the weight of the bag. "Why should I have to count it? Should I be worried about y'all ripping off my uncle?"

"Man, you know I'd never do that; I spend mad money with y'all cats," Fred said, trying to defuse the situation.

"Yeah, I know, but ya man is talking real funny." The tall Latino parted his jacket so that you could see the butt of his gun. The short bald man who had been with him jammed his hand into his pocket.

"Everybody be cool." Fred raised his hands in surrender. "My brother-in-law didn't mean any disrespect, but sometimes he doesn't know what to say out of his mouth. Y'all just take money and split."

"How you gonna tell these niggaz they can leave with my money?" Tech rounded the corner. His face was covered by the ski mask, but you could still see his mocking grin, and the .45 he was holding.

"What the fuck is this?" The tall Latino backed up. He looked from the masked robbers to Fred in bewilderment.

"Word to my mother, I don't know what's going on, but we're gonna find out." Fred came from behind the table.

"If you take another step you gonna find out shit, but what it feels like to sit with your lord." Silk gripped the .357 tightly. She had been dying to break it in since she'd gotten it. Animal covered Rock Head and everyone in the room with two 9s, while China brought up the rear with the HK.

"Set out the money and the coke and we'll be on our way," Tech told them.

"Money? What money?" The tall Latino said sarcastically.

Silk walked over to him and looked in his eyes. "You think you're a comedian, don't you?" She smiled like she could actually find him attractive.

The tall Latino matched her smile. "I've been called worse." His grin was quickly wiped off his face when she slapped him across the bridge of his nose with the barrel of her gun.

"Nigga, this ain't no game. Run your shit or get dealt with." Silk snatched the bag containing the money. China made her way over to the table and began dumping the packages of cocaine into a shopping bag, while Fred stared at her with unmasked hatred.

"You ain't gonna get away with this, you black mutha-fuckas. Do you know who you're robbing?" the bald Latino said, speaking up for the first time.

"No." Tech put the gun to his head. "So why don't you tell us who we're robbing." When Tech got a good look at the bald man, he recognized him. "You're one of Rico's boys, ain't you?" he asked gleefully.

"You're muthafucking right, and he's gonna hand you your fucking heart for this shit." The bald Latino spit in Tech's face.

The whole room got quiet after the deed. Tech stood there, frozen in place, as the spit rolled slowly down the side of his ski mask. The bald Latino looked at Tech with defiance, and it was a look that would be forever frozen in on his face, be-cause Tech blew the top of his head off. Everything got crazy after that.

Shakes screamed and made a mad dash for Fred's gun, which had been sitting on the table. Before she could reach it, China fired the HK, only to find that the gun was more power-ful than she'd expected. Not only did she cut Shakes almost in half, but she managed to knock Rock Head into the kitchen with a few strays. The tall Latino managed to clear his gun and tried to shoot Silk, but she knocked his arm away as he pulled the trigger, sending two strays flying through the room. She jammed the barrel of her .357 into his mouth and closed her eyes so she wouldn't get blood in them when she put his brains on the carpet. Fred tried to run into the bedroom and Animal hit him twice in the back. He hadn't even meant to fire on him, but he was in a firefight and moving off instincts. When it was all said and done, the robbery had turned into a multiple ho-micide and China lay bleeding in the corner.

"Shit." Animal rushed to her side. China had a hole in the center of her stomach where one of the tall Latino's strays had found a home. "Hold on, baby, you're gonna be alright." He placed his hand over the wound to try to stop the bleeding. Blood squirted through his fingers, staining his clothes.

"I don't wanna die like this," China cried, watching her blood pool in her lap.

"You're not gonna die, just be still," Animal said, trying to calm her.

"I didn't mean it," Silk said, watching in shock as her best friend and lover bled out onto the dirty carpet.

"Silk, stop watching and get some help!" Animal shouted.

"I swear I didn't mean it," Silk sobbed over and over.

"We gotta get up outta here before somebody reports them gunshots." Tech picked up the bloody bag of coke. "Let's go." He shoved Silk toward the door. Animal continued to kneel over China. "Animal, let's boogie," Tech called to him.

"I can't leave her here like this, Tech." Animal cradled China's head in his lap.

"Please don't let me die by myself," China pleaded through bloody lips.

"I won't leave you and you ain't gonna die, China, just hold on." He rocked her.

"Animal, ain't nothing we can do for China. The police will be here soon and we ain't gonna be here when they arrive." He reached for Animal, but recoiled when his protégé aimed his gun at him.

"Tech, we've known each other for a long time, so you know I don't bluff when I've got a gun in my hand, but if you try to move me from here you're gonna be as dead as them two Spanish niggaz."

Tech looked in his eyes to see if he was serious and found that he was. "Fuck it. Be a dumb-ass little nigga if you want to, but I ain't going to jail with you," Tech said and ran out of the apartment, leaving Animal and China.

"Animal, I'm scared," China told him. Her skin was getting cold and her words were starting to slur.

"There's nothing to be afraid of, Ms. White; Animal got you." He rubbed her cheek, trying to keep her warm.

"Animal," China wheezed.

"Yes, China?"

"How come you never loved me?" Her eyelids began to flutter.

"China, stop talking crazy, you know I love you."

"No . . . not like you love Silk . . . like you love Gucci." Her breathing was becoming more labored.

"China, my love for you is more special than the love I have for Silk, Gucci, and everybody else. You will always be my number-one girl, but because of the game we play we both knew it couldn't happen."

"The game." China sighed deeply, as if it caused her great pain do so. "For all the riches that this funny-ass game promises us, we all end up dying young and broke." And with that last statement, China White's chapter came to a close. Animal stayed with her for a while longer, letting his tears wash the blood from her face. It wasn't until he heard the sirens that he made an attempt to escape. He looked at the carnage around him and thought how ironic it was that the scene reflected his own life, a hot mess. When Animal left that apartment, he said goodbye not only to his friend and onetime lover, China, he said goodbye to the game. He had had enough.

———————

Five minutes after Animal had made his great escape, Shakes's apartment was filled with people in uniforms. The two lead detectives were a black-and-Spanish combo who were notorious for their police work in Harlem. The local precinct wasn't too thrilled about them being called down to assist with the investigation, but the call had come from downtown because one of the victims was currently being investigated by the two detectives.

"What've we got here?" Alvarez asked the medical examiner, lighting his cigarette. He was a handsome Puerto Rican officer with a slick wit and a nose for the streets.

"From what we've been able to piece together, it was a drug deal that went wrong, and judging by the number of shell casings, I'd say it went really wrong," the wiry redhead said. Alvarez had spoken with her on a number of occasions, but could never remember her name.

"Any witnesses?" Brown asked. He was a dark-skinned dude with a boxed Afro and a no-nonsense attitude when it came to tackling a crime.

The medical examiner shrugged. "So far we haven't come up with much. Our best bet is the lone survivor they were able to pull out of this mess."

"A survivor—who?" Alvarez asked.

"Your boy." The medical examiner passed him a folder. "Raheem Levy."

"No shit." Alvarez flipped the envelope open and looked at the picture inside.

"You know him, J?" Brown asked his partner.

"Sure do, and so do you." Alvarez handed him the picture.

"Rock Head?" Brown was surprised.

"Yep," Alvarez confirmed. "Here we are looking all over

the city for him and he ends up coming to us. What do ya know about that!"

"I kinda wish that bullet would've killed his sick ass," Brown said seriously.

"Now, now, partner. We're public servants and that's no way to speak," Alvarez said sarcastically, cutting his eyes at the stunned medical examiner. "What hospital did they take him to?" he asked the medical examiner.

"I think they took him to Roosevelt," the examiner said.

"Let's go, partner," Alvarez said, handing the folder back to the medical examiner. "Hopefully, Rock Head will be conscious so I can see the expression on his face when he finds what we're charging him with."

CHAPTER 31

Animal had spent most of the night sitting by the window, staring at the grim streets of Harlem. Tech had been calling him nonstop for the last few hours, but he ignored the calls. A time or two he'd tried to drift off, but whenever he closed his eyes he saw China's face.

From day one Animal knew that the out-of-town white girl wasn't cut out for the things they were into, but she had tried harder than anyone else to do her part and had never once left them hanging. In the face of danger, she had shown that she had bigger nuts than most dudes he knew, and he respected her for it. To know that he would never again be able to sit and talk to her about the things going on in his life broke him down. When China White died, she took a piece of him with her.

With a heavy heart he made his way to the bathroom and looked at his reflection. His face was ashy and his eyes were swollen and red from crying all night. "How much more do

you have to lose before you wake up?" he asked the mess staring back at him. He didn't need to hear a response to know the
answer. Dressing in a black sweat suit and sunglasses, he went
to find Tech.

It didn't take him long to track his mentor down. Tech was
hunched over on a park bench like he had the weight of the
world on his shoulders. His eyes were fixed on the rising sun,
which was starting to surface in the eastern sky. Tech always
came and watched the sun rise when he had something on his
mind, and after what had happened in the apartment, there
was a lot eating at him.

"What, you come to kill me over what happened?" Tech
asked without bothering to turn around.

Animal walked around and sat on the bench beside him.
"You're my brother, I would never bring harm to you."

"I couldn't tell with that gun jammed in my face a few
hours ago," Tech said. Animal hadn't noticed at first, but Tech
was holding a weapon. Tech noticed Animal staring at the
gun and placed it on the bench between them. "Is this what
we've come to?"

"I'd hate to think so." Animal placed his gun next to Tech's
and folded his hands on his lap.

"I'm sorry about what happened to China," Tech said. His
voice sounded hoarse, letting Animal know he wasn't the only
one haunted by China's death.

"It wasn't your fault, Tech," Animal said.

"Yeah it was. She tried to tell me that we should back out of
the job, but I wouldn't listen. I had to have that score and it cost
us all something more precious than any amount of money. My
greed fucked us." Tech sounded emotional.

Animal had set out in search of Tech to get at him, but seeing his mentor in such a broken state, he no longer had the heart to. Tech was already in more pain than Animal could've possibly inflicted on him.

"We all knew the risks," Animal conceded. "China knew like the rest of us that ain't no guarantees about coming home off a lick. She gone, man, and ain't no changing that, but we're still here. We gotta make sure her memory lives on."

"Yeah, we gotta tighten up our little ship. It's just me, you, and Silk now, right?" Tech asked, but Animal didn't respond. Tech looked at him. "So you're leaving the family too, huh?"

Animal thought on the question. "You can never leave your family, but sometimes life can dictate that you go in different directions."

"It's that nigga Don B., ain't it," Tech accused.

"He provided the ticket, but he didn't make me get on the train. I'm just getting tired, Tech. I've spent all of my life trying to keep from dying, but I've never made an attempt at living. I wanna live, big homey," Animal said emotionally.

Tech nodded in understanding. "I can dig that, little brother, but you know just as well as I do that your heart belong to the concrete. If you ain't in the street, then where are you?"

"Free," Animal said with a smile.

Tech laughed. "You always were the dreamer. So, what're your plans now; you got any bread saved up?"

"I got a few dollars, but that ain't nothing compared to what I got coming," Animal said, beaming.

"What?" Tech asked suspiciously.

"I was trying to tell your ass last night, but you were too stuck on the lick to hear me out. I got a million-dollar contract waiting on me, big homey!" Animal said excitedly.

Tech's face went blank. "That nigga is giving you a million dollars? Shit, we should've kidnaped his ass after all," Tech joked.

"Oh no, big homey, that cat is protected from on high until I get all of my bread. If he so much as catches the sniffles, I'm gonna shoot the germ that brought them on."

"I can't front, I'm proud of you." Tech hugged him. "Don B. is a bitch-ass nigga, but he looked out for my little man, so he gets a pass, at least until you get the rest of your money. But I gotta ask you: if you knew last night that you were gonna wake up a millionaire, then what the hell were you doing with us pulling that robbery?"

"Because you asked me to," Animal said seriously. "Tech, no matter what's going on with me, I'm always gonna be there when you call, because that's what brothers do, they look out for each other; you taught me that."

"I did, didn't I? Man, I'm glad you're gonna be able to do something with yourself, but it ain't gonna be the same without you at my side when I'm running up in a nigga's shit."

"Then stop doing it," Animal suggested. "Tech, we all sitting on enough bread to take a breather, and with me doing this rap shit we can wash that money up and live good. Why don't you and Silk come in off the streets and get down with me?"

Tech looked at Animal. "Man, that's love, that you would even think to spread your newfound wealth around like that, but you know I can't accept that."

"Why the hell not? We've shared everything else, so why not this?" Animal wanted to know.

"Because that's your blessing, Animal. Me and Silk gotta find our own way out here in the world."

"But does that mean you have to risk death or prison to make it?"

"That's all I know, my nigga," Tech said seriously. "You were always different than us, so I know you can adjust to that life." Tech's eyes took on a far-off look. "We're both kids of the street, Animal, but the difference between me and you is that you don't have to die in them. My destiny has already been written, and the day that my blood stains the sidewalks that I have loved all my life, every hustler in the world is gonna celebrate my passing; that's how I'm gonna go out."

Animal took in his words. He knew that even if he sat and argued with Tech until the next sunrise it still wouldn't help to change his mind. "You know we're always gonna be family, right?"

"Of course I do, Animal. Every time you take that stage, just know that big brother will be watching." Tech hugged Animal. They embraced for a while, but Animal felt himself about to break down, so he stood to leave.

"Let's go get Silk and go out for breakfast, it's on me," Animal suggested.

"Silk is still broken up over what happened to China, and I don't think I'm ready to go back out into the world just yet. I'm gonna sit here and watch the sky for a while, but you go ahead and get your celebrate on." Tech went back to staring at the sky.

Animal started to walk away, but stopped short. "Big brother, you know I love you and I'm thankful for everything you've done, right?"

"Of course I do." Tech still didn't face him. "But I also know that this is the end of the road for us."

"No it ain't, this is only the beginning," Animal assured him before he left the park.

Gucci hadn't been able to get a wink of sleep that night. There was nothing good on television, so she decided to do something she hadn't done in quite some time, read a book. She selected a thick book with a simple black cover called *Gangsta* which Boots had loaned her a while back.

She curled up on the couch with a blunt and a cup of coffee and dove into the book, which she ended up enjoying a great deal. By the time she'd gotten to the end of the book it was ten o'clock in the morning and she was an emotional mess. Lou-Loc and Satin's story reminded her of the lover she'd lost, but more so of the one she'd found in Animal.

She knew she had been too hard on him the night before, but she needed him to understand where she was coming from. He had a God-given talent that could open so many doors for him, but he couldn't put the street nigga to bed. She was getting bad vibes all night, but she refused to call him, not only because she was teaching him a lesson but because she was afraid of what she'd hear on the other end of the phone. God had robbed her of one special person and she was afraid of it happening again with Animal.

"Girl, what you doing out here in all this fog?" Ronnie came out waving away the cloud of smoke. She had traded her spandex and crazy hair for a postal uniform and a simple ponytail.

"Just reading." Gucci wiped away the tears before Ronnie could see them.

"Reading? Lord, are ya sick?" Ronnie placed her hand against Gucci's forehead dramatically.

"No, I'm not sick." Gucci pushed her mother's hand away. "I got a lot on my mind, so I was out here thinking."

Ronnie took Gucci's face in her hands and looked her in the eyes. The hurt was written all over her face. "What's wrong?" Ronnie asked compassionately. "It's that pretty little nigga I saw you kissing the other night, ain't it? You know what, I don't even wanna know what he did; just give me his address and we're gonna ride out on that little muthafucka." Ronnie went to the closet and started rummaging around for the lockbox where she kept her pistol. "See, ya daddy was a nigga with good hair and he wasn't shit, so I knew it was something about that little boy."

"Mommy, sit down. I'm crying over the book." She raised the copy of *Gangsta*, "but I was thinking about Animal."

"Animal? What kinda God-fearing people name their child Animal?" Ronnie sat on the couch and folded her arms.

"His name is Tayshawn; Animal is his nickname, silly." Gucci laughed.

"So what makes this Mr. Tayshawn so special that my little girl has picked up a book to chase her blues?" Ronnie lit the clip Gucci had in the ashtray.

"I'd be lying if I said I could tell you," Gucci said honestly. "Animal is different, Mom. I mean, he's hood and all that, but there's such a glow about him, like he was anointed or something. Whenever I'm around him I feel like I'm the only chick in the room."

"Well then, what's the problem? Is he gay, married, broke, or all three?" Ronnie asked, exhaling a cloud of smoke. "I know it's not a situation of him not thinking you're pretty enough, because ever' nigga with a pulse knows my daughter is fine-ass hell, like her mama!" Ronnie declared.

"None of the above. Animal is actually about to sign a recording contract with Big Dawg Entertainment. Animal is a good guy, he's crazy about me, and I feel superloved when I'm around him. He treats me with nothing but respect and has never even brought up the subject of us having sex. I just can't be with him."

Ronnie scratched her head. "Let me see if I follow you: he's fine, has money, and treats you like a lady, but you can't be with him? Gucci, what am I missing?"

"He's in the streets, Ma," Gucci said as if she should understand. When she saw that Ronnie wasn't following, she elaborated: "Ma, the night he agreed to sign his contract, he promised that he was gonna get out of the streets, but as soon as his phone rings he's gone. When I got at him about it, he's telling me how I don't understand and how he gotta keep it real with his man. I ain't trying to hear that shit."

"Watch your mouth," Ronnie warned her.

"Sorry," Gucci said.

"So how long as he been in the streets?"

"Since he was a little boy." Gucci recalled the brief story of his life that Animal had given her. "But that doesn't justify it. Ma, I don't understand why our men are so loyal to these streets and their codes that even when a way out falls in their laps, they have to second-guess it."

"Because it's all some of us know," Ronnie said seriously. "Gucci, we live in the hood but I've always made sure you were taken care of, so you weren't a street kid. When you grow up out there, like I did, it's gotta be all in or nothing; that's how you make it through to tomorrow without becoming somebody else's food. Baby, just because a dude is placed into a situation where he has to do bad things doesn't necessarily make him a bad person. I know my fair share of knuckleheads that's out there getting it, but a few of them are actually good brothers just trying to make it to tomorrow. Gucci, you probably have no idea of some of the things that that boy has gone through. If this Animal is as good as guy as you say, then he'll do the right thing with that record deal, but it's gonna be tough for him to fully break the grip the streets have on him. He's gonna need some help along the way." Ronnie looked at her daughter.

"I don't know if I can do it." Gucci curled her knees to her chest. "What if he never leaves the streets?"

Ronnie picked up Gucci's cell phone and handed it to her. "There's only one way to find out."

Animal had just gotten back into his apartment when his cell phone went off. He figured that it was Tech calling him to say that he had finally come to his senses, so he answered it without looking at the caller ID, and was pleasantly surprised by who was on the other end.

"How're you doing?" Gucci asked sheepishly.

"I've been better, but I'm managing. I thought you were done with me?" Animal reminded her.

"I thought so, too."

"Then what are we doing exchanging uncomfortable silences over the phone?" Animal was fronting like he was still salty, but he was actually glad she had called.

"I don't know, I guess I just needed to hear your voice to know that you're okay," she said.

"Yeah, I'm okay, just going through the motions. I lost a dear friend last night," he told her.

"Oh my God, I'm so sorry," she said sincerely. She knew enough not to ask what had happened over the phone.

"Not as sorry as I am, but at least she ain't gotta endure this madness no more. The streets can't touch her where she's at."

"And what about you, Animal?" she asked.

"Like I told you last night, I'm done, but you didn't seem to believe me," he shot at her.

"Animal, I wanna believe that you're gonna do the right thing, but I'm afraid."

"And I'm not? Gucci, I ain't never wanted to get to know a girl for much more than the purpose getting in her pants, but I convinced myself that you were worth it, only to find out that you ain't really down to ride for a nigga."

"I never said that," she corrected him.

"You didn't have to; your actions spoke for you when you bailed without even bothering to get the whole story. Gucci, I don't know where you come from, but where I come from you don't turn your back on your friends, even at the risk of your own life. This morning I discovered the flaw in that thinking, but it doesn't change the fact that if I had it to do all over again, I would've answered that call. So if you called to lecture me again about it, save your minutes."

Had it been a few hours prior, she would've hung up on him, but after speaking with her mother she felt that she better understood him. "Animal, I didn't call to argue with you, or lecture you about right and wrong; I called to tell you that I was sorry." The word sounded funny coming out of her mouth because Gucci was not a woman who made apologies. "I understand where you're coming from, but please try to look at it through my eyes. I'm feeling you on a way deep level, and I don't want to have to worry about being cheated out of a chance to get to know you because you got killed or locked up."

Animal chuckled. "Only God can say whether any of us

will wake up in the morning, but what I can tell you is that I ain't never gonna be caged. I'd rather hold court in the streets before I let these niggaz chain me."

"See, that's just the kind of bullheaded thinking I'm talking about," she said, about to rant.

"Gucci, calm your ass down. I ain't saying that I'm gonna run up in the precinct or no shit like that, I'm just saying that being caged ain't for me. I've done a lot of shit in life that I'm not proud of, Gucci, but I'm on some other shit. Signing with Big Dawg could potentially take me to places that I've only imagined, and I ain't trying to fuck it up; I plan on going to the top with it, and I could use some company."

"You still wanna see me?" she asked, surprised.

"Silly girl, I can control my actions, but I can't do a damn thing about this foolish heart of mine. From this day on, let's say that we wipe the slate clean and start fresh."

"That sounds good to me, Mr. Million-dollar Man. And don't think that because you're rich that I'm gonna give you some pussy," she joked.

"I hear you talking, Gucci, but I wouldn't want you to give it to me because I'm caked up; I want it because you love me," he told her.

"Well, I don't know about love just yet, but I'm in deep-ass like," she admitted.

"I'll take that and work my way up."

"So are you gonna take me shopping before we leave for Texas?" she joked.

PART 4
WHAT'S DONE IN THE DARK

CHAPTER 32

Rock Head was in a world of pain when he finally came out of his morphine-induced nod. He was disoriented and couldn't quite figure out where he was at first, but as he became more aware, he noticed the sterile room and the tubes running in and out of his body. He was in a hospital.

Bits and pieces came back to him as the fog lifted from his mind. The last thing he remembered was Tech and his crew busting into the apartment and then the shooting started. Rock Head couldn't remember exactly who or what had started the shooting, but he remembered getting hit up. One minute he was lying on the kitchen floor bleeding to death, and the next he was in the hospital.

When he took a breath, fire immediately shot through his stomach and hip. Sitting up as best he could in his weakened condition, he took stock of his injuries. He was wrapped from pelvis to chest in a white bandage that was stained with dried blood. He couldn't see his hip through the blanket, but the fact that he couldn't move his right leg told him he was in bad shape. When he tried to move his arm and discovered that he was handcuffed to the bed, he knew his situation had gotten considerably worse.

"What's up, Rock Head?" a familiar voice said, startling him. Rock Head turned around and found that he wasn't alone. The man sitting in the chair was a well-dressed Puerto Rican with a youthful face. He smiled at Rock Head as if he held some great secret that he couldn't wait to share with the world. The one in the corner was shorter and dark, wearing a plain brown suit. Even if their badges hadn't been visible, Rock Head would've known they were detectives. Everyone in the hood knew Alvarez and Brown, and when they called on you it usually meant that you were going to prison.

"Looks like somebody fucked you up, G." Brown walked over to Rock Head's bed and stared at him as if he were a zoo animal. He lifted the bedsheet and frowned when he saw Rock Head's heavily taped thigh and hip.

"What y'all want with me, man?" Rock Head asked nervously.

"We don't want shit from you, poppy. The paperwork is already in and your ass is going to jail," Alvarez told him with a smile.

"How the fuck am I going to jail for getting shot?" Rock Head asked indignantly.

"Oh, this shit ain't got nothing to do with the lead in your ass." Brown jabbed his finger into Rock Head's bandage, causing him to yelp. "You were going to jail before you got shot; this is just a little bonus."

"I ain't did shit. Y'all ain't got nothing on me." Rock Head turned his head, as if the conversation were over. Pain shot through his neck as Brown wrenched his head back in his direction.

"You call statutory rape nothing?" Brown rained spittle in his face. Detective Brown drew his Glock from its holster and placed it in Rock Head's mouth. "I got a daughter that's around those girls' ages, and as God as my witness, if this was a dark street instead of a hospital I would put your tiny-ass brains all over the street!"

Rock Head was trying to say something, but he was having trouble with the gun pressing against his tongue.

"Is our little songbird trying to speak?" Alvarez asked mockingly. Rock Head nodded as much as he dared with the gun in his mouth. "Ease up, partner." Brown reluctantly took the gun from Rock Head's mouth. "Listen," Alvarez continued, "before you spew whatever lie is in that cocksucking mouth of yours, don't bother. We've got proof and witnesses."

"Man, y'all got me wrong. That chick told me that she was eighteen," Rock Head lied.

"Which one, being that three of them have come forward so far?" Alvarez questioned. "Okay," he got up and went to stand over Rock Head, "lets' say you are telling the truth; you stand a snowball's chance in hell at beating the rape, but you're up a creek on the attempted murder."

"What the fuck are you talking about?" Rock Head's mind whirled. He'd robbed a few cats since he'd been home, but he hadn't gotten into any beefs. The shoot-out the night before was the closest he had come to violence, and even in that situation he'd been the victim. Out of nowhere, Detective Brown open-hand slapped him. Blood flew from Rock Head's mouth and stained the white hospital pillow.

"You think we wouldn't find out what you were doing to

them girls, you diseased fuck!" Brown raged. Detective Alvarez had to physically remove him from the room before he could finish his conversation with Rock Head.

"Enough with the bullshit," Alvarez began, slightly out of breath from the tussle. "You're a piece of shit, Rock Head, and I can't stand niggaz like you. The only solace I get from all this is that you're a walking dead man, but even that can't undo what you did to those little girls. If they ask for my recommendation, and they probably will, you're going to jail for a long time, and I have it on good authority from some of my CO friends that your stay will be a most unpleasant one."

"Alvarez . . ." Rock Head began in a pleading voice.

"Save it, because I don't wanna hear it, pussy. You're gonna do some time, that's just a fact, but how much you do depends on you."

"What do you mean?" Rock Head asked. He knew what Alvarez was getting at, but he wanted to hear him say it before he jumped out the window.

"I need names," Alvarez said, confirming what Rock Head had already expected. "I've got five dead bodies at a coke deal that went to shit, but no drugs or money. Why don't you fill in the blanks for me?"

Rock Head thought on it for a long while. All his life he had considered himself a stand-up guy, one who would never rat on his friends, but the men Detective Alvarez was asking about weren't his friends; one of them had even shot him. Most men say that they would eat the time and never tell, but when the pressure is on them, things can start to look different.

"And what you gonna give me?" Rock Head asked.

Alvarez smiled knowingly. "The rape is gonna stick, but I can see about getting the attempted murder knocked down to a lesser charge." Alvarez scratched his chin. "It's gonna take some doing, but I can call in some favors, depending on how good the shit you give me is. Who were the trigger men, Rock?"

Rock Head took a minute to carefully reflect on what he was about to do. China White was dead, but the other three and their little ones were still dangerous as hell. Silk and Tech were always together, so he knew he could get a two-for-one with them, but what about the Animal? He was a part of their inner circle, but his moves weren't as routine. If the police swooped down and Animal managed to slip through the cracks, there would be no place for Rock Head to hide, so it made sense to get him out of the way first and longest.

"A'ight, the main nigga—" Rock Head began, but Alvarez cut him off.

"Hold on, I gotta record this." Alvarez pulled the recorder from his pocket. He was so excited about the news that he was about to receive. What Rock Head didn't know was that the information he was about to divulge could possibly lead to a career bust for Alvarez and Brown. They had managed to connect the dead white girl to a gang of young killers who were said to be on Shai Clark's payroll. When they took them down, they would be one step closer to the king. "Okay." Alvarez clicked the Record button.

Rock Head cleared his throat like he was about to begin an *American Idol* audition. "There are seven of them altogether—well, six, since the white girl is clipped—but the main one you want is a nigga named Animal . . ." Rock Head said, beginning his tale.

Shai sat in the barber chair, listening, while Rico ranted about Justice. He was no stranger to Rico's emotional rants, but he had never seen the man reduced to tears. The night before, his nephew had been murdered while making an unauthorized drug transaction. Rico hadn't authorized the young man to make the deal; the kid had gone behind his back and done it anyway. He'd only been trying to show that he could help out, but it had ended up costing him his life. It hadn't taken long for Rico to get the name of the man behind it, and he demanded justice.

"Rico, try to calm down, man," Angelo said.

"How the fuck am I supposed to calm down when my sister's boy is laying on a slab in the morgue, all over some fucking pennies," Rico fumed. "This little shit has gone too far and he's gonna die for it."

"Rico, are you sure he was behind it?" Swann asked. He had a feeling that Tech's hands were in it somewhere, but he hoped that they weren't. If Tech was responsible for the death of Rico's nephew, then there would be nothing Swann could do to save his life.

"Of course I'm sure!" Rico said, as if the question were stupid. "My contact with the department told me as soon as he got the word."

"And if everyone is dead, how sure can your source be?" Swann was reaching and he knew it.

"One of them lived and he gave up Tech and his whole fucking crew to save his own ass, that's how," Rico informed him. "Shai, I've played by your rules long enough and now it's time to take the gloves off. You can agree to it or not, but Tech is going to die. Him, his crew, their families, I'm putting them all in the ground!"

"Just give me a minute to think on, Rico." Shai rubbed his temples. When he'd first met Tech and Jah, he'd thought they had so much potential, but since Jah had died, Tech was proving to be more trouble than he was worth. "What do y'all think?" He looked to Angelo and Swann.

Angelo thought on it. "Rico's nephew being dead is one of the primary reasons we told them to check with us before they moved on a big fish—you never know who you're getting at. Shai, I like the l'il nigga, but the rules are the rules."

"Shai, this is a decision that I can't help you on because of my relationship with Tech, but whatever you decide, I'm gonna ride with you," Swann said.

It was one thing to order the death of a grown man who knew full well what he was getting into, but Tech and his crew were barely out of their teens. He wanted to find another way to handle the situation, but he knew that if he didn't flex his muscle on this, his leadership would come into question. With a deep sigh Shai finally said, "I'll see that it's taken care of, Rico."

"Thank you," Rico said sarcastically. He barked something in Spanish to his men and they all fled the shop, leaving only Shai and his advisers.

Shai looked at his men to gauge their reactions to his decision. As usual, Angelo was neutral, but he could see that Swann didn't like it. He understood Swann's bond with Tech, but he had to understand that emotional attachments didn't build kingdoms, tough decisions did.

CHAPTER 33

Tionna got off the train on 135th feeling drained. It had been a week since she'd seen Duhan and four days since she'd spoken to him on the phone. That was unlike him, especially since his trial was coming to an end. Fearing the worse, she had taken the trip to Rikers Island to see him, only to find out that he'd already had a visit for that day. Tionna knew that he didn't have any immediate family in the area, so she figured it had to be one of his bitches. Normally, she would've been cursing, crying, and doing everything else to stress herself out, but not that day. While Duhan was chasing dusty hood rats, she had snagged the prize.

The morning after her and Don B.'s passionate night, he'd had Devil take her home in the Maybach, with her purse two thousand dollars heavier. "Just a small token of my appreciation for the show you put on," is what he had told her. She had immediately taken fifteen hundred of it to Duhan's lawyer and promised to get him the remaining thirty-five hundred as soon as she could. She felt a little guilty about freaking off with Don B., but she eased her conscience by telling herself that she had fucked him for Duhan.

She had tried to call Don B. over the last couple of days to arrange another meeting with him, but he'd said he was busy getting Animal situated, which was to be expected. When you gave someone a million dollars, you wanted to leave no stone unturned. Tionna was glad when Gucci had told her that she and Animal had worked things out and the trip to Texas was back on. A part of her was a little tight because she hadn't even fucked Animal yet and he was taking her on a trip, whereas Tionna had fucked the shit out of Don B. and they had yet to leave Manhattan. Overall, she was happy for Gucci, though. It had been quite some time since a man had been able to make her friend smile without handing her money.

When Tionna rounded the corner to her block she saw police cars near her building. At first she feared that something had happened to her kids, but she breathed a sigh of relief when she saw them on the stoop with Gucci, watching the spectacle. Two female officers emerged from the building next to hers with a young girl between them, who was visibly shaken up. As Tionna got closer she realized that it was the girl from the other night who had been looking for Rock Head. She wasn't sure what the girl had done, but from the sad faces everyone wore, it must've been something serious. Before she could investigate, a silver Honda pulled up next to her and beeped the horn. The girl behind the wheel looked familiar, but Tionna couldn't place her right off. When the driver got out, Tionna realized that it was Tracy.

Tracy was dressed from head to toe in designer tags and

her hair was done in an expensive-looking weave, but something was off about her. You probably wouldn't have noticed it unless you knew Tracy, but she looked thinner and tired. Her face was flawlessly made up, but you could see the dark circles under her eyes.

"And where the hell have you been for the last week and some change?" Tionna gave Tracy a hug, running her hand affectionately up and down her back. She was startled because she could feel the girl's entire rib cage through her clothes, but she acted normal.

"Girl, wait until I tell you! I've just spent the best week of my life with my new boo, Remo," Tracy said excitedly.

"Don B.'s bodyguard?" Tionna asked, surprised. It seemed like everyone was reaping the benefits of Big Dawg Entertainment.

"Yeah, child. I went to see him that day after Mochas and it was on like popcorn. Girl, when I say that nigga put it on me . . ." Tracy fanned herself. "I ain't even gonna go into details, but the nigga takes care of business and me."

"So I see." Tionna looked over at the Honda proudly. "So what's the word? I see the block is buzzing."

"That's what I'm trying to find out. Let's go ask big mouth." She nodded toward Gucci, whose eyes were still fixed on the little girl in the back of the police car.

"What's going on?" Tionna asked Gucci, who was standing next to the Senate and their card table.

"The chickens have finally come home to roost," Cords said with a laugh, slapping a card on the table.

"Man, ain't you got no couth? I don't see shit funny about what that bastard did to them little girls," Harley snapped. He had a niece about that girl's age who lived in the area.

"I'm sad for the girl, but I don't feel no shame over what's gonna happen to that damn Rock Head. I always knew something wasn't right with that boy," Sonny said, laying his card.

"He better be glad that girl's daddy is in jail or else he would've sure killed him out here," Rayfield added.

"They finally caught up with Rock Head for fucking them little girls, huh?" Tionna asked. She wasn't at all surprised, because he was laying his dirty dick into quite a few young girls in the neighborhood. It was only a matter of time before one of the parents caught wind of it and did something about it.

"It goes way deeper than that. I heard Rock Head is in jail for rape and attempted murder," Gucci informed her.

"Murder? That pussy ain't got the heart to try and kill anybody. What he do, scare them to death with that ugly-ass face?" Tionna laughed.

"Nah, T. Rock Head was HIV-positive and he was purposely giving it to those little girls he was sleeping with." This bit of news wiped the grin right off Tionna's face. It was common knowledge that Rock Head was a general piece of shit, but Tionna had never thought that even he could sink that low.

"How could he do that to all those babies?" Tracy's eyes began to tear.

"Because he's a greasy-ass nigga. Them little bitches is stupid for letting a nigga like Rock Head raw-dick them," Tionna said scornfully.

Gucci didn't like the statement. "It ain't all their faults, Tionna. When we were coming up, how many niggaz did you let talk you into having unprotected sex and you did it because you liked them?"

"Yeah, I slipped up a time or two, but never with no dirty-ass hood niggaz. All the dudes I let run up in me raw were too caked up to be sick."

"You think AIDS discriminates?" Gucci looked at her seriously. "Tionna, the most dangerous thing about AIDS is the fact that it has no symptoms. You could be living with that shit for years and not know it unless you get tested."

"Well, I'm clean. The only nigga I fucked raw over the last year or two was Duhan, so I ain't gotta get tested again."

"And how many bitches do you think he's fucked raw on your watch?" Tracy asked. "Every time you let a nigga in you raw, you've slept with everybody else they've had unprotected sex with."

"I know I'm good," Tionna said firmly, but in the back of her mind she was nervous. Both she and Duhan gambled with each other's lives when they stepped outside their relationship, and although she made sure she was protected, she couldn't be a hundred percent sure about him. She cursed herself for putting all her trust in Duhan and made a note to herself to get tested Monday morning at the free clinic.

"And where is this little tramp coming from?" Gucci scowled at Sharon, who was coming up the block. She was dressed in a short leather miniskirt and a shirt that was so tight that it was a wonder she could breathe. She, too, had been watching the police activity, but when she saw Tionna on the stoop, she found somewhere else to focus her eyes.

"And where are you coming from looking all sassy?" Cords asked, sizing Sharon up.

"I had to go visit my man in jail. You know I had to make sure I looked good for him since he has to look at broke-up bitches for most of the week," she said loud enough for Tionna to hear her.

Tionna took a step off the stoop, but Gucci held her arm. "Be easy, T, your kids are out here," Gucci whispered to her.

"Ima chill, but let her keep that slick shit up," Tionna fumed. She was losing her patience with Sharon and Duhan.

"Lord, I don't know what it is about y'all young girls who get caught up with these niggaz in jail. Sharon, your ass is too young to put your life on hold like that," Rayfield told her.

"Well, I won't have to wait too long for him to come home. His trial will be over soon, and when my baby gets out we can finally start our new life, me him and our stepkids." Sharon smiled down at Little Duhan and Duran. The whole block got quiet. This time when Tionna stepped off the stoop, Gucci didn't stop her.

Sharon didn't even budge when Tionna came to stand in front of her. "What, am I supposed to be scared or something?" Sharon placed her hands on her hips. Tionna slapped Sharon so hard that she flew in the air and crashed through the Senate's card table. Before Sharon could even gather her wits, Tionna was on top of her.

"I done told you little bitches about playing with me, right?" Tionna asked before punching her in the face. "Y'all . . ." she punched her again, "hos . . ." another punch, "are gonna learn to respect me." Tionna pulled Sharon to her feet by her hair and threw her into a pile of trash bags. Sharon tried to charge Tionna with a bottle, but Gucci tripped her, sending her sliding across the concrete and landing at Tionna's feet. Tionna went to work stomping Sharon in her face, chest, stomach, and any other part of her body that was exposed.

Had it not been for the two female officers grabbing her, she would've surely killed Sharon on that stoop.

"Let me go so I can finish this bitch off," Tionna said, struggling against the officers.

"Ma'am, if you keep resisting, I'm gonna have to pepper spray you," the larger of the two officers threatened.

"Tionna, chill the fuck out!" Gucci screamed. The kids were becoming hysterical watching the police manhandle their mother.

"You'd better listen to your friend," the smaller officer said, holding a can of pepper spray at eye level with Tionna.

"A'ight, I'm cool." Tionna stopped struggling. She was mad, but not stupid.

Two more officers who had arrived on the scene were helping Sharon to her feet. She was bloody and could barely stand on her own, but it didn't stop her from struggling against the officers to try to get at Tionna. "You snuck me, you bum bitch!" Sharon spit.

"Miss, try and calm down; you need medical attention," the male officer tried to tell Sharon, but she didn't even hear him.

"You always screaming about how grown you are, but you're out here fighting with a teenager. Duhan doesn't want you, so why don't you step the fuck off already. Get a life, you old bitch!" Sharon yelled.

Tionna just smiled. "Fuck you, little whore. Instead of worrying about me and Duhan, you need to be worrying about how long you've got to live. Or didn't you know Rock Head had the monster." It was such a low blow that everyone paused. Even the officers who had been trying to help Sharon took cautionary steps back.

The statement seemed only to enrage Sharon further. "You're a fucking liar, Tionna!"

Tionna raised her eyebrow. "Am I? I guess we'll know if it's true or not when your ass is sitting in the clinic waiting for those results to come back."

"You are fucking history, Tionna, do you hear me?" Sharon tried to charge her again, but the officers held her back.

"Ma'am, you're hurt and we have to get you some medical attention. Would you like to press charges against this woman?" the officer asked.

"You're muthafucking right," Sharon said proudly.

"What the fuck are you doing?" Tionna asked when they were putting the cuffs on her.

"You're under arrest for assaulting a minor," the female officer informed her.

"But she started it!" Tionna tried to explain.

"It doesn't matter, she's still a little girl," the officer said, as she helped Tionna into the police car.

"This is some bullshit!" Tracy shouted at the officer.

"She didn't even start the fight and you're locking her up; where's the justice in that!" Gucci jumped up and down.

"If you guys don't calm down, I'm sure we could find enough room to fit you in, too" the male officer informed them, which took some of the fight out of the crowd.

"It's all good, Gucci. I'm gonna be alright," Tionna assurred her.

"I'm going to get Mommy and we're coming to get you," Gucci promised.

"No, don't tell Ms. Ronnie. Get in touch with Don B. and tell him what happened."

CHAPTER 34

A full forty-eight hours had passed before the correction officer informed Tionna that her bail had been posted. For her little scrap with Sharon they were charging her with assault and resisting arrest. They had set her bail at ten thousand dollars, which she knew neither she nor her friends had, so she figured it had to have been Don B. who had bailed her out; she was expecting a queen's welcome. But when she stepped out of 100 Centre Street, there was only Gucci and Animal there to greet her.

"It feels so good to be free." Tionna stretched.

"T, it's only been two days," Gucci reminded her.

"Shit, in that place two days can feel like two years. Let me see your phone so I can call and thank Don B. for getting a bitch outta jail. I got something special planned to show my appreciation."

"Don B. didn't bail you out, Animal did," Gucci informed her.

"What?" Tionna looked from Gucci to Animal. "Well, he sent you, right?"

Animal glanced at Gucci before answering. "Nah; Gucci told me that you were in a pinch, so I wanted to help out."

"Thanks." Tionna hugged him. "I'm grateful for you getting me out, but why didn't Don B. post my bail?"

Animal didn't have the heart to piss on her parade. "Ima go get the car and let y'all talk." He walked away.

"Gucci, what's going on?" Tionna wanted to know.

Gucci hesitated, trying to think of a way to break the news to her best friend. "T, I don't know how to tell you this, but Don B. is a fucking snake."

"Gucci, what kinda man-hating shit are you talking about now?"

"It ain't about hating, T, it's about keeping it real," Gucci began. "I got hold of the nigga and told him what happened between you and Sharon and told him you needed some help and he just laughed. The nigga had the nerve to tell me that you ain't his property so therefore not his problem and that you should ask Duhan or Happy to see about springing you. I'm sorry, T."

To say that Tionna was mad wouldn't even have scratched the surface of what she was feeling. She'd been so sure that she had Don B. wrapped up that she hadn't even thought twice about putting herself at his mercy to get out of jail. He might've had jokes, but she would have the last laugh.

"Let me see your phone," Tionna demanded.

"T, what are you gonna do?" Gucci was hesitant.

"I'm gonna let that nigga know just what kinda bitch he's dealing with." Tionna was so angry that her eyes were watering, but she wouldn't give Don B. the satisfaction of crying over him.

"Tionna, leave that shit alone and let's go home," Gucci said, trying to reason with her. Seeing that her friend wouldn't be deterred, she handed her the phone and stepped back so she wouldn't get caught in the fallout.

Don B. barely heard the phone over the roar of laughter coming from his living room. Fully and Tone were watching one of his notorious home movies while he narrated the scenes. "Who this?" Don B. barked into the receiver.

"What up, B.?" Tionna said on the other end.

"Who the fuck is this?" Don B. fronted like he hadn't caught her voice.

"You know who it is, so don't play with me, Don B."

"Tionna? What up, ma, long time no hear from." He snickered. He placed his hand over the phone and motioned for his boys to be quiet. "Where you been?" he asked sarcastically.

"Don, you know exactly where I've been because Gucci told you, so I don't know why you're trying to front. On the real, that was some foul shit that you did by leaving me sitting up like it was a joke or something."

Don B. looked at the phone. "Yo, who the fuck do you think you're talking to, shorty?"

"I'm talking to a punk-ass nigga who thinks it's okay to fuck me and then toss me to the side," she shot back.

"Ma, I fuck a lot of bitches and toss them to the side. What makes you so different?" he asked. "No, let me guess: you think because you give some of the meanest head I've ever had, that should make you different? Yo, that's a good one. I'll tell you what, why don't you come by the crib and suck the whole team off? If you can make everybody cum in under an hour, I'll give you the ten thousand." Don B. doubled over laughing, which poured salt on the wound.

"So, you think I'm some chicken-head bitch that's just gonna go for anything?" Her face was slick with tears, but her expression was hard.

"It ain't like that, ma. You good peoples, but hardly wifey material. You got a man that loves you who's waiting on a date, but you're in here making movies with me; I can't accept that kinda bitch as mine, even if she is pretty as hell."

"What did you say?" She had heard him but couldn't believe it.

"You don't believe me? Yo, turn that up," he told Tone while he put Tionna on speakerphone. Tone turned up the volume on the television and Tionna heard a voice that was unmistakably hers coming through the surround sound. She was so embarrassed by some of the things she heard that she couldn't even speak.

"Shorty, I got an album coming out, too!" Fully shouted in the background

"You're a foul nigga, Don B., straight foul. We'll see how funny this is when I go to the press and tell them how you got me drunk and took advantage of me," she warned.

"Bitch, is that a threat?" Don B. was serious now.

"That ain't no threat, bitch nigga, that's a promise," she assured him.

Don B. wanted to wild out, but he had to keep his cool in front of his crew. "Oh, I get it. You see the cars and the videos and you think I'm just some nigga popping bottles for the camera? Bitch, you play with fire and you're gonna get burnt."

346 | **SECTION 8**

"I hear that hot shit. I guess I'll see you on the news," Tionna told him and hung up the phone.

Sharon was a nervous wreck, sitting in the little plastic chair in the free clinic. All around her were boys and girls who were all about her age, and they all wore the same worried expression on their faces. Her stomach was turning so badly that she almost didn't make it to the bathroom to relieve herself. Sharon blamed Tionna, Duhan, Rock Head, and everybody else for her situation, but she knew that if she wanted to point fingers, she'd have to start with herself.

She had replayed the scene over and over in her head and still couldn't come up with a good reason to have let Rock Head sleep with her, let alone without a condom. She had always thought the threat of AIDS was restricted to homosexuals and drug addicts, but she was neither, and still found herself at the clinic waiting for the nurse to come back with the results from her rapid-response HIV test. Had it not been for her family being there with her, she would've surely fled and never bothered to find out if she was positive or not.

"Sharon, would you please stop fidgeting." Reese placed her hand on Sharon's knees to stop them from knocking.

"I can't. I'm nervous," she said.

"And you should be," Yoshi told her. "Sharon, me, Reese, and Billy always make sure you have condoms, so I can't think for the life of me why you're not using them. Sexually transmitted diseases aren't a game, little girl."

"I know, Yoshi; I was slipping," Sharon said.

"Slipping ain't the word, ma. You young girls are too fucking reckless with your bodies for your own damn good," Billy said. She hadn't meant to be so short with Sharon, but she was afraid for her. She was a young girl who hadn't even made it out of her teens and had to wait for a doctor to tell her whether she was going to live or die, all over something that could have been avoided if she'd used protection.

"Number four eighty-eight," the nurse called, looking over her clipboard. Sharon stood and with Reese's help made her way to where the nurse was standing. "You can wait here for her, ma'am, she'll be right out," the nurse told Reese and led Sharon to the back.

Patiently, the three girls waited while Sharon spoke with the nurse. Yoshi and Billy tried to be calm, but Reese paced the waiting room. When they heard the back door open, three sets of eyes locked in on it. Sharon came out, followed by the nurse, who was rubbing her back and whispering something to her. Reese took one look at her little sister's face and collapsed.

Tionna felt like the world had just cocked over and taken a shit in her lap. Not only had she played herself by fucking Don B., she had allowed herself to be fucked on camera. She ended up with two thousand dollars, but she still felt like a two-dollar whore.

"Everything okay?" Gucci asked her friend.

Tionna looked at Gucci and tried to say something, but all that came out were sobs. Feeling like she could no longer stand up on her own, she collapsed into Gucci's arms. "He ain't gonna get away with this," was all Tionna could manage to say over and over until Gucci placed her in the backseat of the car.

CHAPTER 35

Silk sat on her grandmother's couch, watching *Law & Order*, as she had been doing for the last week and change. Since China's death she hadn't wanted to see anyone, not even Tech. He had been calling her nonstop since the fatal night, but she'd just let her phone die and hadn't bothered to recharge it. Her grandmother was in Atlantic City for the weekend, so she had the place to herself. She planned to sit on the couch and smoke until she was numb, or passed out.

A funny noise outside her door caught her attention. When she got up to see what it was, the front door came crashing in and the house was suddenly filled with blue uniforms. Silk didn't even think, just reacted, when she grabbed her gun off the table. "You want me, pussies, then here I am!" Silk barked before opening fire. The first two officers into the apartment caught it the worse. They were dead before they hit the ground. Their partners returned fire, but Silk had already made it to her grandmother's bedroom and locked the door.

With sweaty palms she grabbed the cordless phone off the base and dialed Tech's number. While the phone rang, she curled up in the corner and trained her gun on the door. "Come on, man, pick up," Silk said nervously.

"Yo," Tech answered after the first ring. All he heard was heavy breathing and banging in the background. "Who is this?"

"Big brother," Silk said, sobbing.

"Silky, what's wrong?" he asked nervously. In the background he heard what sounded like a door being broken down. "Silky, talk to me."

Tears welled in Silk's eyes but she could still see the blue of their uniforms. "Game over, big brother," she said and placed the phone on the bed.

"Silk, what's going on? *Silk?*" Tech shouted frantically into the phone, but Silk was already gone. Before the phone went dead he heard a bloodcurdling scream and gunshots.

Animal and Gucci navigated his new BMW through the hectic morning traffic on their way to the airport. In a few hours they would be landing in Texas, where Don B. and Stacks would be waiting for him. He had never been to Texas, but it was where he would be making his residence until things cooled off in New York.

He had gotten word of the downfall of his once-great team and it hurt him to no end. China and Silk were dead, Brasco and Ashanti were locked up, and Tech had vanished. Animal smiled, knowing that they would never catch the elusive Tech; and even if they did, he would take at least three pigs with him on his way out. This just left him. All the police knew was that he was called Animal, but other than that they didn't have any information on him. He had never been arrested, didn't have a driver's license, and, aside from his brother Justice, there were only two other people who actually knew his real name, and one of them was sitting right next to him.

"So how do you think you're gonna like Texas?" Gucci asked.

Animal shrugged. "I can't really say, but I'm gonna learn to like it, seeing how things done got all complicated out here. I just wish you would stay for more than a couple of days." He took her hand in his.

"I can't believe that bitch nigga Rock Head is not only a creep but a snitch, too," Gucci said heatedly. She didn't know how Animal had been able to find out, but he had gotten the wire that Rock Head was the one who had thrown them all under the bus. He had even gone as far as trying to pin everything on Animal.

"The Lord will settle up with him," Animal lied. He had already put the word out that he had twenty stacks on Rock Head.

"Better him than you, right?" Gucci said.

"Right," Animal replied. He happened to look into his rearview mirror and saw that there was a police car following them. Gucci must've felt him tense, because she looked behind them. No sooner than she had done so, they threw their lights on.

"Animal, just be cool." Gucci rubbed his arm.

"Baby, I ain't fit for no cage." He pulled his gun from between the seats.

Gucci's eyes began to water. "Animal, please don't do this with me in the car. I don't wanna die."

Animal pulled over to the side of the road, but left the car running. Over the loudspeaker, the police officer ordered the driver to get out of the car with his hands up. Animal looked from the gun in his hand to the girl sitting next to him. The beast inside him screamed for action, but the eyes of his lady pleaded for calm. "Gucci, do you love me?"

"Yes," she said.

"Enough to be here when I get out?"

"I can't promise tomorrow, Animal, only right now."

"I'll take that and work from there." He smiled. Slowly, Animal got out of the car and placed his hands on the hood.

Gucci watched through the mirror as a female officer got out of the driver's side and approached her man.

"You got any drugs or weapons on you?" the female officer asked while patting Animal down. Animal remained silent. "Oh, you're a tough guy, huh?" She grabbed his nuts.

"What the fuck." Animal spun around and found himself eye to eye with Officer Grady. "That shit wasn't funny." Animal lowered his hands.

"You had to know I was gonna get you back for that shit you pulled with them handcuffs." She smiled. "They're on to you, baby. You've got about twenty minutes to a half to get on that plane, before they think to have the airport checking for you."

"Grady, you know you could lose your job, at the least, if this shit gets out."

She thought on it. Quite unexpectedly, she kissed him on the lips. "For all the fun we've had, I'd say it'd be an even exchange. Now get your ass outta here." She slapped him on the ass and headed back to her car.

"Grady," he called after her, "how did you know I was on my way to the airport?"

Officer Grady smiled. "Young boy, I'm always gonna have my eye on you. Now, you hurry up and get that pretty girl-friend of yours to the airport before you miss that plane." Officer Grady got back into her squad car and pulled off.

When Animal got back in the car, Gucci was staring at him in shock. "What the hell was that all about?"

Animal threw the car into gear. "Just an old friend paying back a favor," he said, downplaying it.

Gucci looked at him funny. "Nigga, you must think I was born yesterday. A female cop pulls up and lets a wanted man go, after kissing him on the lips. You gotta come better than that. See, this is the bullshit I was talking about when I said I didn't want to fuck with no street nigga . . ."

Gucci went on and on, but Animal never reacted. He was too stunned by what had just happened to even feed into what Gucci was saying. Most people would say that Grady's being the cop that stopped him was luck, but he knew better. It was his blessing working overtime.

Tech sat on the small bench watching the sun rise, as he always did when he was stressed. It was strange watching it from the other side of the water, but it was no less soothing, and his mind needed all the soothing it could get.

He was surprised that Rock Head had lived, but he didn't know why, since it always played out like that. The good died young and the worms inherited the earth. Tech had every intention on dealing with Rock Head, but he knew that in this one he shouldered just as much blame as the snitch. His whole team had been taken out of the game in one shot, proving the old adage that nothing comes from the streets but the pen and death; there is no pot of gold at the end of the concrete rainbow. His only joy in all this was that little Animal had made it.

Soft footfalls crunched the leaves behind him, but Tech never took his eyes off the sunrise. He was too tired to turn around and face what he knew was coming. "I'm glad they sent you," he said, then continued his daydreaming.

"I wish I could say that it made two of us." Swann came to stand next to him. Tech knew that if he looked over his shoulder he would see Angelo looming. "You always did have a hard head, Tech."

Tech looked up at Swann. "You know how it is when you're young and chasing paper; you were my age once, Swann."

Swann nodded. "Yeah, but I always knew to play within the rules. When you don't play by the rules, you get benched. I'll be mindful of your face for the sake of your people." Swann raised his gun to let Tech know that it was time.

"You know I ain't gonna go quietly, right?" Tech cocked the slide on his gun.

Swann smiled at the young man he had come to have so much love for. "I wouldn't expect you to die anything less than a soldier's death." Swann took a few steps back to give him some room.

Tech sighed. He'd always known he would go out how he lived; he just wished it hadn't been so soon. "A soldier's death it is, then." Tech rose quickly, but not quickly enough. Swann hit him six times before Tech finally went down. As Tech lay on the ground, bleeding out, his last thoughts were of how big the party was going to be to honor his passing.

EPILOGUE

Tionna almost didn't answer when her phone rang. Since she had put out the rumors about Don B. being a rapist, she had been getting all kinds of weird phone calls. She didn't care, though: her thoughts were on making him suffer for how he had tried to play her. She was glad she did pick up the phone, because it was Duhan's lawyer calling to tell her that the jury was about to come back from its deliberations. She broke a world record getting to the courthouse to support her man. She looked around for Sharon's little ass, but luckily for her, she was nowhere to be found. She'd been MIA since the afternoon of their fight. Tionna couldn't wait to bump heads with her again for being the cause of her having to spend two days in jail.

When the bailiffs brought Duhan out of the back, she waved and tried to get his attention, but he looked over her as if he didn't even see her, which she thought was strange. Paying it no mind, Tionna crossed herself and prayed for the best as the jury was led back to the box. She held her breath as the forewoman stood up to read the verdict.

"Guilty on all counts." The words hit Tionna like physical blows. There was no way he could've been convicted, the lawyer had promised her as much when she'd made the last payment. The room suddenly began to spin and the next thing Tionna knew she had collapsed face-first in the aisle. Two court officers had to help her get back in the seat. When Duhan's eyes landed on her, Tionna mouthed that she would be there for him, to which he smirked. Through tear-streaked eyes she watched her man being led off again for only the judge knew how long.

Tionna was the one of the first people in the visiting room the next morning. She had worn one of her sexiest outfits, and Boots had laced her hair and done her makeup before she left that morning. She sat with her back erect and her chest poked out, letting all who could see know that she was down for her man. When Duhan came strolling over to their table, she stood up and spread her arms to receive him.

The strike was so quick that Tionna didn't even realize she'd been hit until the back of her head slammed against the chair behind her. Through a haze of pain she saw Duhan rushing her and the COs rushing him. Duhan snatched her to her feet and breathed into her face.

"You dirty bitch, do you think I wouldn't find out about you?" He shook her so violently that it was impossible for her to answer him. "And you didn't even have the respect to keep it quiet, you dumb bitch!" Tears had welled up in his eyes. "I knew you wasn't nothing but a high-price whore who I should've left in the gutter where I found her." Duhan spit a green wad of phlegm into her face, drawing an "ooh" from everyone who had seen it. The COs grabbed him up, but not before he was able to kick Tionna in her ass and send her crashing into the next table.

All Tionna could do was lie there and count the aches in her body as she tried to make sense of it all. She knew that the story could've only gotten back to Duhan through Don B., but she couldn't understand their connection. The next day she would find out.

Tionna was at her new job, as a receptionist in a law firm, when she heard the Miss Info recap come over the radio. She loved to hear what the journalist had to say because it was always interesting dish, this day especially. She reported that a superstar rapper had been seen around town with Sweet Tea, one of the newest stars of his adult film company. She went on to say that Ms. Tea's movie would be available for download in the spring and pictures of the two together could be seen on her Web site. The thought that formed in Tionna's mind was too outrageous, but she decided to humor herself. She logged on to the office computer and clicked on Miss Info's site. Her jaw went slack when she saw an enlarged picture of her and Don B. at Times Square. The funny part was, that skimpy red dress looked even more whorish on film.

It didn't take a rocket scientist to figure out how Duhan had found out. This was an offense that he would never be able to forgive, and Tionna knew it. Don B. had cost Tionna her reputation and her man, all for two thousand dollars, hardly an even exchange on her scale. To add insult to injury, she got home to find that a mysterious fire had broken out in her apartment and claimed everything but the clothes on her back. Thankfully, the kids weren't home when it happened. Though Tionna knew that Don B. was behind it, and even told the police as much, it was never proven. Just like he'd said, she found out how the Big Dawgz played.

Ms. Ronnie was nice enough to open her house up to Tionna and her kids until the Section 8 program was able to find her another apartment. It was supposed to be a temporary arrangement, but it ended up lasting six months. Ms. Ronnie was cool about it, especially since Gucci was spending most of her time in Texas with Animal.

It's like Don B. had said: Animal was a star in the making. The mix tape he and Soda put out was killing the South and starting to get a quiet buzz on the East Coast. Several different record labels had become interested in Animal, but he was a Dawg now, and when you became one of Don B.'s, it was until death did you part. Gucci fronted like it was nothing, but Tionna knew she was overwhelmed. It wasn't often that you became the better half of someone who would be leaving a lasting impression on the world. The last Tionna had heard, they'd talked about getting married. Of course, the wedding would have to be out there because the investigation was still pending in New York. Detectives Brown and Alvarez didn't like to be beat, so they put him on their shit list along with Shai.

One day Tionna came in from work and Ms. Ronnie informed her that she had received a letter from Section 8. "I hope they're writing to tell me they've found me an apartment." Tionna fanned the envelope.

"Well, open it up and find out," Ronnie said, lighting a joint. She watched as Tionna read the letter twice. "Well?"

"It says they've got a two-bedroom for me in a building called the Marquis," she told Ronnie.

"What the hell is the Marquis?" Ronnie asked. It didn't sound like any of the buildings in Harlem.

"I guess we'll find out soon enough, because it says I can move in two weeks."